A Margin of Error
Ballots of Straw

Disclaimer: While the risk of an undetected breach to even the most secure computer system is real, this is a work of fiction. All characters, names, places, business entities and events are products of the author's imagination or are used fictitiously. Any similarity to actual persons, living or dead, business entities, and places is coincidental. *The Beacon Bridge, LLC.*

Copyright © 2008.
All rights reserved.
ISBN: 1-4392-0681-3
ISBN-13: 9781439206812
Library of Congress Registration No.: TXu1-338-986

www.BallotsOfStraw.com

LANI MASSEY BROWN

A MARGIN OF ERROR

BALLOTS OF STRAW

A Margin of Error
Ballots of Straw

ACKNOWLEDGEMENT

Thank you, Mary Day. But for the kindness of a stranger. You made a difference.

*To Joe for our world of safe harbors and fair seas,
Our sails forever wing and wing.*

1

I know you, Cady. I know where you are. Leonard leaned closer listening for the sounds of her, the sounds he knew would come. *I'm waiting for you.*

Soon, you'll come to me. You always do…and she was there. He could hear her patio door opening wide, all the way into her bedroom and he could see her now. She switched on the pool light and dimmed it to a hazy glow that hovered atop the misty water. He watched her silhouette dive into the pool and listened to her swim, hands cupped, arms pulling, legs kicking. Then silence while she swam underwater. When she reached the far end of the pool by the rock fountain, her head and shoulders surged high, high enough for him to see her propel herself off the end of the pool on her return lap.

I see you, Cady Palmer. Leonard fumbled in his trousers pocket for his cell phone, latched on to it. Held it close to his face. His fingers knew her buttons and he pressed them, each one. She kept swimming. He couldn't see her in the pool now, not from here, but he heard her body cleave the surface of the water.

Soon, you'll come to me. He dialed again. At last, her splashing ceased. She paused mid stroke and stood chest deep in the water a third of the way down the length of the pool. He could feel her wet skin glisten in the dusky pool light. He watched her reel around from her water dance all sinewy and wet and warm, ascending nymph-like from the dim wet iridescence into the shadows and dab herself with a towel.

She draped the fluffy white towel around her body and tucked the high end over her breast and under her arm. The tail end of the towel dragged along the patio floor as she padded her way barefoot toward the phone, gingerly one tender foot then the other on the bumpy river rock. He savored her timid progress, rushing to catch the phone but cautious lest she bruise her feet, hurrying while smoothing her dripping hair back and twisting it into a tawny loose coil she pulled over her left shoulder. Her towel slipped.

Ahhh. The water nymph answered her phone all wet and shimmering. "Good morning. Cady Palmer here," her voice announced softly to the dark, all business. *Like she wasn't skinny-dipping-naked-wet.*

"Ah-h-h-h," he breathed into the phone and the words strangled in his throat again.

"Hello?" She spoke louder this time into the dark.

"I have a sur-r-pri-ise for *you*," his voice grated, each syllable catching in his throat.

"What? Excuse me?" she asked in the dark. She turned toward him, phone clenched to her ear. "I can't understand you. Can you speak up please?"

"I…have…a…*sur-r-pri-ise*…for…*you*," he whispered, working his fingers as she stood before him all tall and shimmery.

But she was done with him now, she turned away all serene and calm. Her free hand holding the towel to her chest, she leaned over the table to softly lay the phone down on her glistening glass tabletop as she had too many times before.

"Wait!" Leonard lowered his pitch. Her hand hovered midair. "Wait. I…You are Miss Palmer, aren't you?" he drawled out her name across the phone line, affected, artificial. "Susan Cady Palmer?"

"Yes… You know I am," her voice hoarse from holding back anger. She rubbed her throat.

"You manage the election computers, don't you, Miss Palmer?

"I can't hear you. Can you speak up, please? …If there's something important……."

"Important, yes." And there it was. Always before he taunted and whetted and tormented her until…he couldn't stand it. His rules, have a little fun, give a little scare. Get in. Get even. Get out.

But what good is doing her, if she doesn't know she's done? Leonard ached with his newfound might…just 12 yards from touching her, pulling her to him. *What good's slaughterin' the lamb if ya can't gnaw at a piece of mutton, eh?* Already he'd said too much, gone too far. He knew it, but couldn't stop. Give her just a little more, feel a lot more of what he'll do to her today. Sure, she'll be on guard, but the f_____ bitch was always looking for screw ups, always out to get him…and now….

My turn now, missy. He rubbed at his nose with the back of his hand. He'd waited long enough. Too long. Every morning, early, setting up surveillance outside her bedroom waiting for her to meet him, squatting here at his peephole in this thorny jungle on the wrong side of her privacy fence. Every morning grappling his way into this thorny tangle of bougainvillea and working her fence, peeling away at another few splinters, wobbling the same three boards loose from their bolts, aching for her to materialize.

And now, today, his day, she stood there dripping and naked in the misty light, waiting for him to talk.

"Here's a hint for you, Miss Susan Cady Palmer," he whispered louder this time. Not too loud or her whole freakin' neighborhood would be out here on his tail. "Powerful people, they want this bad. So I'll get there early. Will you feel me? I bet Izzy will. Izzy, she'll know. And ya know what else…here's the good part. You see, after it's over? …Then I come for you, Cady. Then I come for *you*."

"Who is this?" she demanded.

And she was boss again. *You don't own me now, bitch.*

Then, "Shit!" He swatted a mosquito and another, snagging his hand on the thorny talons that clawed and scraped his flesh. Blood soaked into the cuff of his jacket. "Shit!" his words echoed from her phone. Leonard froze. But Cady, once more she just leaned forward and set the phone down, gently. Only this time her eyes scanned her backyard in the dark. Leonard held his breath, certain her cat's eyes could see him through the dark, through his fence. She backed up a pace, two. Then forward again before glancing into the dark of the yard. Nothing.

She walked back toward her bedroom, slowly, all straight and tall like he wasn't there, like he hadn't even called her this morning. But then she pivoted at the threshold and faced him directly. And she stared out at him in the dark and reached her arm back through the doorway to the light switch behind her on her bedroom wall. *She knows. She can see me now.* But she didn't move toward him. As the floodlights brightened, the whole patio glowed, radiating light into her backyard, right up to the edge of his wall and his post in the thorny hedge. She walked toward the pool and beyond…to him. And he saw the rise and fall of her breasts and the heave of her belly and he breathed hard with her. But she just kept walking, past the pool steps, past the table where her phone lay dormant. Closer, closer.

Stop her. Stop her now. He flipped his phone open again. His fingers jammed her numbers. Cady didn't stop. He swiped at the buzzing whirring mass swarming and stinging his face and Cady looked his way again. She looked straight at him. She turned a quarter-turn and walked toward the screen door opening into her backyard.

Leonard flushed in hot sweaty tremors. *She's really gonna get me now.* He snapped his phone shut, tucked it into his pocket, stooped forward and backed out of his gnarled cave. The jumble of branches scraped at his neck and scalp, and thorns speared his sleeve, ripping the lightweight jacket as he tugged it free. Unnerved he stepped on another brittle twig cracking it as he hastened his retreat.

"Who's there?" bitch called after him. "Kitty?"

2

"Kitty?" she called, more quietly this time. "Stop sneaking around like that." Cady paused at the dark edge of her patio, dripping wet and shivering. She rapped the screen door handle with the butt of her hand. The door unlatched with a clank and she pushed it open…slowly and stepped into the dark. One hand clutched her towel, the other clasped over her mouth suppressing the gag erupting deep in her chest.

Another snapping twig, a heavy crunch. Cady turned toward the sound. "Who's there?" she demanded with more nerve than she felt.

Her dogs heard it too. They bolted past her in a flurry of fur and tails. "Okay, guys," she whispered, reaching her hand out to trail after the big one's back as she scrambled by. "Quiet, now," she hushed after them as the burly black lab loped across the yard chasing the yippy dachshund. A misfit pair. "Be careful that cat doesn't scratch you." She laughed nervously, but stopped when it sounded like they'd cornered something. No playful yipping or barking, just that low steady rumbling snarl that means business, though she didn't pick up on anything unusual. Her dogs probably just fixated on the cat, long gone or perched on top of a fence post waiting patiently for the perfect moment to pounce.

Cady hugged the towel around her shoulders. Braver now that her dogs made their rounds, she followed them toward the fuss along her fence. They'd sniffed around that spot for weeks now. After the election she'd check it out for varmints.

And the phone? Just words on the other end of a phone line. Cady's fingers slipped her ring back and forth along its delicate gold necklace. *Okay.* She squared her shoulders. The pranks, the calls not unusual during election season. But the grating words played again in her mind and she knew. *He's not through toying with me.*

5

These last calls, not heavy breathing or gibberish like the others. Her mind sifted through a collage of random thoughts. Crank calls. That's all they were...until now. She mulled over her caller's words. "Powerful people want this bad." This morning's threats made up for all his previous jabber. He knows who she is, knows her job. Someone close? Forget it. You cave, he wins. She glared over at the offending phone, so innocent, resting serenely now on the table in a puddle of water where she left it.

Cady stepped farther away from the light and into the dark shadows of her banyans. Somewhere close by, a swoosh of leaves gave up the location of her neighbor's cat, that or any one of a rag-tag menagerie of wild things that had taken refuge or blown in on the winds of this year's storms. Cady snugged up her towel. Down the street from her house the whir-coast, whir-coast of the paperboy's Econovan followed the plop...plop of Miami Heralds hitting the concrete circular driveways. In the distance a jogger clipped along on his way to the park.

Cady clicked for her dogs. "Come on guys," she whispered. But they were too busy worrying at something over by the fence to give up now. They'd follow through their doggie door when they were good and ready. Cady closed the screen door more softly than she had opened it and walked back to her phone. The patio went dark.

In the distance, a refugee peacock shrieked its beseeching woman's scream.

***

Cady grabbed the phone from her rumpled bed where she tossed it on her way in from the patio. Her supersize man-tee clung softly to her thighs and she paused, smoothing down the waves of loose fitting cotton. Outside, her swimming pool glistened liquid midnight, reflecting only a faint iridescence cast off by her desk lamp. Beyond the caged patio, her backyard vanished into black. Only her neighbor's floodlight glimmered like a dim hazy second moon above the north wall of her privacy fence. Decidedly a soft November...outside.

Inside...Cady readied for today's election. Just another ordinary election, only this time, her stomach lurched. *A stupid phone call, Cady.* She pulled out her election schedule and dialed Mario. As Cady's chief guru, he'd called her on and off for a few hours now, filling her in on the string of set-up problems, asking advice. Now it was her turn.

"Mario, have you talked with Izzy this morning? She put in another late night last night. Do you know if she's up and about?"

"No, not yet, Cady. We haven't needed her.... Speaking of Izzy, who was the suit hanging out with Stan yesterday?"

"Haven't talked with Stan. What's it have to do with Izzy?"

"You see the guy, you'll know. Tall, good looking, nice threads. Not like the usuals. Stan showed him around. Cady, the guy asked so many questions. I thought it might have to do with Stan's.... I don't know how he does it. He's gotta be paddling upstream in a leaky skiff."

"You rumormonger," Cady laughed. "Seriously, Mario, look around. This election doesn't sail smooth, we all swim."

"You're the only swimmer here, Cady."

"Not for lack of trying to lure the rest of you in.... Mario, listen, I want you to pick up Izzy on your way to the office."

"Her car acting up again? I told her she needs to get a real car." Mario's timber shifted gently. "Cady? Is she okay? ...It's that pervert again, isn't it?" His temperament not so cool with Izzy, Cady's lead analyst.

"I don't know, Mario. She hasn't called in and I didn't want to wake her..."

"So why..."

"He just cranked it up a notch. That's all."

"She'll raise a stink, you know," his voice softened.

"No. I don't...besides, her little snits are so...Isabella. Kind of fun, isn't it?"

"You don't have to ride with her," he chuckled. "You gonna tell her?"

"No, I leave that to you," she laughed softly.

"Hmm. Cady, you're not swimming this morning, are you?"

"Did it already. But only a couple of laps. Maybe I'll finish up before I head to the office. I've still time. Why?"

"You hound me to fetch Isabella and you go swimming out there alone in the dark? Not today, Cady."

"It was just a phone call, Mario." Though she knew it wasn't.

*****

In the corner by her bed, Cady's dogs already snuggled back in their blankets, once again oblivious to this morning's drama. Still early for their routine. Not so for elections. Reporters were already filtering into the media room, setting up for the big day.

Calmer now, Cady walked over to the oval mirror beside her dresser. Even in the dim light she looked awful. Dark smudges rimmed her eyes, green eyes etched with jagged pink-red streaks. Too much close work, too little sleep. Pale freckles sprinkled her nose on skin grown too milky from being deprived these past weeks of sweet Florida sunshine. Her hair still wet and uncombed corkscrewed around her face and down her back with its usual independent attitude. And her lips…her lips were chapped from long hours spent in the dry chill of the computer room. *Oh, well.*

Enough of the haggard woman in her mirror, Cady headed for the pool again, pulling off her man-tee and tossing it onto her bed as she passed by. Naked but for the thin gold band dangling from the delicate chain fastened around her neck.

As she stepped toward the patio the phone started up again. She hoped it was Mario, but knew it was not. Just as she knew she must answer it. To do otherwise would give into her fear. And here she'd be, little Susan Cady cowering in her bedroom afraid to come out today.

"Good morning. Cady Palmer, Electronic Voting Services."

Again the silence, then the wheezing. Cady leaned over her desk, her ring bobbing on its chain, sparkling in the light as she quietly tucked the phone away in its cradle. *Can't hurt me from the other end of the phone line.*

"Bastard," she mumbled, starting out for her swim again. "You're not going to ruin my perfect day," she announced to the dark. All the same, her fingers brushed at the damp on her cheeks as she stood in front of the open door, looking out at her caged patio. One moment, two, about face. She headed directly for her closet to rummage out a bathing suit. *Bastard.* She yanked the suit off its hanger…poised to tug the wretched thing on, but instead crumpled it up in a tight wad and hurled it to the floor, hard. *Bastard.*

In her bedroom, Cady's radio alarm whisper-soft broke silence, announcing the start of her day. "THIS IS NPR NEWS... ALL EYES ARE ON FLORIDA THIS MORNING... IT'S THE FIRST TUESDAY IN NOVEMBER... MANY VOTERS WILL FEEL A HUGE SENSE OF LOSS TOMORROW IF THEIR CANDIDATE DOES NOT WIN......"

Okay, Cady. Get on with it, Elections don't wait for tantrums. She turned to the clothes she set out the night before: dark tan business suit, straight skirt, matching hip length jacket tapered at the waist, buff-colored silk shirt with pearl buttons, crimson scarf. Cady smoothed a hand over the scarf. *Let's do this thing.*

"**STAN CORBIN**, MIAMI-DADE COUNTY ELECTION SUPERVISOR ... CAREER TROUBLED BY CONTROVERSY ...... FLORIDA **GOVERNOR BUD DANIELS** SAYS TURNOUT CRUCIAL FOR BOTH PARTIES... CAMPAIGNS MAP STRATEGIES ...... ELECTRONIC VOTING MACHINES PRONE TO FAILURE... PUBLIC TRUST ......

"PORT OF MIAMI ...... **ARE WE SAFER TODAY?** MOST PEOPLE WE INTERVIEWED BELIEVE ANOTHER TERROR ATTACK IS IMMINENT... NOT IF, BUT WHEN... CUBA... RUSSIA... IRAN... NUCLEAR WEAPONS..."

3

"Neal. Pick up. Neal!" Brice barked over the speaker-phone, edgy, irritated. "Neal. You there? Neal!" he shouted, rifling through papers he'd strewn across his desk the night before.

Neal groaned several times before finally giving in to the racket. Then he rolled onto his belly and maneuvered across the width of his California-king, leg-tangled sheets trailing behind. Closing in on the source of Brice's pre-dawn thunder, Neal flailed away at the nightstand, first fumbling with the TV remote and tossing it aside before grabbing at the phone. The braying ceased. Neal glanced toward the clock as he yanked the phone to his ear. *Damn.*

"Yeah?" Neal grunted his voice hoarse with sleep. The two of them spent last night pouring over specifics of what, when, where Brice needed attention to layers of detail he couldn't or wouldn't entrust to his staff. Then Neal caught the red-eye home, a quick puddle jumper from Tallahassee, but a late night all the same.

"Nealboy, I've rethought this election thing," Brice's exhale gusted across the phone lines. Neal could almost smell the thick swirling smoke plumes from Brice's ubiquitous Cuban cigar. One of the more recent jags in Brice's complex nature that troubled Neal. Brice Upton "Bud" Daniels had pole vaulted to state political icon and he entertained even higher aspirations. He should be making rules, not flouting them. But here he was thumbing his nose at the law, at his loyal constituency with those damned cigars. He and everyone else knew they were illegal, yet he sucked on them, fingered them, waved them around indiscriminately like flags at a pep rally. And it wasn't just the cigars. There were so many other niggling suggestions, whispers.

Another gusty exhale…inhale… "I've rethought it." Exhale… "Scrap everything. Head over to Stan's. This morning. Now."

"What's wrong?" Neal flipped on the light, sitting upright on the side of the bed. He tugged at the hems of his Polo boxers, twisted and bunched from another restless night.

"Nothing. Not yet. But I don't want any surprises. Make sure he doesn't screw up again," his voice trailed off, fizzling nasal, vapid. Neal picked up on Brice's poor-me tenor, strained from shouldering his badge of many burdens. Still Brice's overall exasperation fluctuated within tolerance levels or he'd lapse into the run-on drawl of his youth.

"Right. Brice, Stan walked me through his whole operation yesterday. Everything checked out. Anything I should know?" Neal wondered what fired Brice up during the scant hours between their meeting last night and now.

"No. Stan'll arrange a press pass for you with Security. You can hang out in the media room, front row seat and all. Keep an eye on the mood, catch up on all the chatter…before it's…uh …news." Brice stubbed out his cigar, hard, scraping the brass ashtray across his polished old-growth heirloom cypress desktop.

"Sure thing. Brice, what's happened to…?"

"No, I said. Nothing. You gotta understand. Can't just let it ride in cruise control. Fanning out all the boys, the whole squad to uh…every hot spot. For sure Stan's got a raging inferno down there. Can't trust him to run a smooth election. Hell, a damn cumquat's more cerebral."

"Specifics?" As for Neal, Stan's gushy kiss-up spewed yellow flags all over the playing field and he was amazed Stan hung on so long, especially given Brice's more vocal disdain of late.

"No. I just don't trust him." The gold lighter flicked across the line. Flicked again. Deep inhale. "Rumors, irregularities, I need to block 'em before the media spin's outta control again."

"Where'll you be?"

"Tethered here. You know duty first and all. Got some things…uh…people…depending on me today."

"That it then? I'll trek on over to Elections."

"Yeah. Just call me when you get there. See Stan straight away."

"Right."

"And, Nealboy, get in with that, ah...that computer gal. See if you can chat 'er up. Stan keeps assurin' me she's on our side."

"That so?" *Our side?* Neal considered a grab bag of implications, but let it ride.

"Yeah. Get me a sneak preview of...how it's really going. Ya know? Spend time with those geeks. You know the gal I'm talkin' about right, Stan's deputy or whatever? Hang out with 'em in their tabulation room. Ya know? If something's not right that computer gal, I hear she'll be on it. Things start goin' bad, get a handle on it. Hell, dump the whole bunch of 'em down there if you have to." Brice hung up the phone.

"Sure thing, Brice. I think her name is Cady... Her name is Cady Palmer...." Neal responded to the dead phone before the dial tone bleeped him.

4

The slate colored BMW 530i whipped into the north lot, headlights swallowed by pre-dawn fog, it's tires squealing as it wedged into a cramped slot hogged on one side by a faded powder-blue van and pinched by a dingy coupe on the other. A security guard taking a smoke observed the speedy entrance of the ultimate driving machine. Then crushing his smoke on the blacktop, registered briefly the apparent carelessness of the owner, squeezing into that sliver of a space with a vacant spot only yards away. "Probly joinin' his crew. Thems newsguys do alright." The guard sauntered off muttering, continuing on with his rounds. "Gotta be the newsboys. Way early for politicals 'n legals…"

The Beemer's engine whispered briefly, then hushed, as the slight figure inside pulled down his visor, flipped the mirror open and studied his now unfamiliar reflection in the bright vanity light. Gone the diamond ear stud, the scraggly goatee. Slinky-nouveau-fashion wire frames swapped out for retro horn rims that overwhelmed his too-narrow face. He smoothed stained bony fingers over his flattened hair left to right. The shaggy platinum spike now ink-black, slicked down and lacquered stiff.

Leonard snapped the visor shut, stuck one mechanical pencil behind his right ear and the other in the left breast pocket of his shirt, still white and crisp and sporting the edgy squares of new-shirt folds. Then he stretched into his navy Hart, Shaffner & Marx sport coat, the press badge securely penned to its lapel. Maybe too pricey for his newsguy disguise, but no time for a switch now.

Ready. Leonard surveyed the parking lot. Too late. Too light. But still early. It should work. Clusters of cars and trucks dotting the lot most likely belonged to cliques of reporters and crew from local stations. Probably congregating according to prearranged meeting times. Leonard squirmed the keys into his right pants pocket then pulled his camcorder over his shoulder and grabbed his briefcase with the rest of his camera gear from the passenger seat. He expected tighter security. So far he'd spotted only the one guard. Considerate of the Elections Department to post schedules and security details on their website. Leonard watched and waited. Silent.

Then, finally a stream of six vehicles filed into the parking lot forming another little cluster not far from where he was pressed between the junker and the clunker. Leonard waited for the thunk-thunk-thunk of car doors slamming shut and the chatter of eager media big names and wannabes. When it came, he opened the BMW door, bumping it against the side of the junker and squeezed out. With his own hushed-thunk, he hurried over to the chattering group, bringing up the rear.

"Hey. Another close one, eh? Think they'll get it right this time?" Leonard asked in a loud whisper as he scurried up, crowding between the last two reporters.

"Yeah. They've worked on it long enough," one answered, too early in the morning to object to the intruder.

"We're about to find out," the second responded, more to his buddy than to the skinny stranger.

"You with one of the *local* networks?" Leonard emphasized the word local, trusting they might then assume he worked for a bigger, national outfit. Wannabes are sure to be more accommodating to a national affiliate.

"Yeah. Who you with?"

"Washington Corr…" Leonard's voice dangled then trailed to a mumble. One thing to label his press badge, nobody read the things anyway. But he sure couldn't voice specifics and be found out a loner once the media hangouts filled up with the little cliques. "Well, we're expecting the unexpected again this year," Leonard teased. He couldn't help himself.

"Like what?" one of the group leaders queried, glancing back over his shoulder as they approached the Elections building.

But Leonard didn't hear the man. He was so gnarled up in the torment of coming here again. The last time he even drove within miles of the place was over a year ago. Not much changed. Two wings of the building reached out on either side of a small cement courtyard area, dotted with planters and benches, a small fountain, and oversized urn ashtrays, not for smoking for extinguishing.

When Leonard worked here, the white faux-stone building glistened in the morning sun and the pink oleanders lining the walkway dripped with a profusion of caterpillars. He edged closer to the center of the walk to avoid the oft offending branches. A damned obstacle course to get from his car to the front door. Not unusual to see creepy crawlies on someone's back. Leonard sniggered. He just watched the squirmy things crawl up and up.

"I say, whataya lookin' for this election?" the man asked again, slowing down to be in step with Leonard as they walked past the front entrance and toward the side media door.

"Well, you probably heard already, but…" The group tightened around him, eyes eager, ears primed for a story, just as one of four security guards opened the south door and light flooded around them. The question, the answer all but forgotten as the troop funneled in single file through the door held open for them by the guard.

A sturdy partition wall blocked the entrance into the lobby. Leonard smirked. The weenies actually put up a barrier, smack dab in front of the entryway. It stretched the full width of the lobby and was so tall it obstructed his view. Huge, pasty-white and no nonsense, it didn't look like a permanent fixture. But the way it was installed with thick yard-long braces, it would take a powerful force to topple it. A walkthrough metal detector bisected the wall and butted up alongside the x-ray conveyor belt.

"Morning folks. Passes and drivers licenses out, please. After inspection, all passes must be pinned to your left lapel." The guard holding the door repeated his greeting to every few reporters who passed by. His holstered gun bump-bumped against the door each time he shifted his weight from one stubby leg to the other.

A second guard pointed to an oversized logbook on the table to the right of the entrance. "Sign here at the register please." She accepted the identification held out to her by the first few reporters, compared documents to each other and pictures to the owners. One by one reporters signed in, emptied their pocket of coins and keys which they placed in plastic trays before loading cameras, notebooks, briefcases onto the conveyor belt.

Leonard in position toward the end of the now clamoring group, signed in, held out his driver's license, but fumbled, dropping it on the floor in front of the table. "Sorry," he smiled sheepishly after retrieving it. His best clearly-embarrassed look smeared across his face. Then fiddling with the press badge too tightly pinned to his lapel. "Ouch!" His hand flew to his mouth and he sucked furiously on the side of his forefinger. "Can you help me with this?" he asked in his soft-sweet-helpless voice, his young-boy smile now plastered on. The guard shook her head a couple of times in feigned dismay, then turning toward the door where the door guard admitted the next gaggle arriving, she waved Leonard on lest a morning newsworthy bottleneck form.

Gotcha! Leonard heaved his gear onto the conveyor belt and walked through the metal detector arch. "This stuff's been through enough x-rays to glow up the room," he joked to the guard inspecting his rolling paraphernalia. Cleared the metal detector without so much as a beep, but once on the other side Leonard froze. Razor-edged panic racked through his legs as he dragged them forward, pulling him to the end of the conveyor belt and to the guard tugging his gear off the belt. The guard. He recognized the guard from before, a little grayer, a little chunkier, but same guy. *Pull it together. You're almost there.* And the guard recognized him too. Leonard saw it. The quick where-do-I-know-you-from flicker, saw him mentally index through employees and politicians and patrons and media and...employees....

"Hey, how's it going?" Leonard pushed up at the bridge of his glasses, smiled brightly and reached for his camcorder. "Should've packed this thing in the briefcase."

"Good. Good. You?" the guard responded.

"Looking forward to the big day," schlepping his briefcase strap over his shoulder. "Well, you've got a truckload of media headin' in." *That oughtta do it.* "Have a good day. See ya."

The guard's eyes left Leonard's to check the growing horde crowding up to the entrance. "You too, Mister, ah..."

Leonard caught up with the others and followed his little troop toward the media watering hole. Earlier conversations forgotten. In! He got in! He broke off from the others pronto and beelined to the media room, claiming the table closest to the door. This he hogged with his collection of cameras and gear scattered strategically along the full length of the table, notepads on each end. Then he commenced making ready for the long hurry up and wait. Maybe he'd call Izzy again. For sure he'd do Cady. He flipped his phone open. It flashed Cady's number. He smiled as he exited the double doors and made way for the handicap men's room down at the end of the corridor. No one would be there now. Hell, these neophytes wouldn't even know about it.

***

Leonard stretched out his legs, edging one cautious foot slide forward then the next. Wouldn't do to waddle back into the media room with a big fat sopping ring around his butt. Jeez. Another stroke of genius to commandeer his little handicap throne room here. He could play around on his phone forever with only the occasional rude tap-tap on the other side of door. But damn it was cramped. And every time he shifted his weight he was afraid he might fall in. He checked his watch again.

C'mon, Cady. I know what you're doing. *Pick up.* But Cady…Cady ignored him. *I'm not through with you, bitch, not through at all. Just wait. This morning…and later on… You'll see.*

Maybe after awhile he'd try again. She expects lots of calls today. Her job, she's gotta answer. No. Now. Must be now. His fingers worked the buttons on his phone. He flushed in hot sweaty tremors. But she was done with him. Nothing for it but the wait. She'll be here soon enough. He snapped his phone shut, tucked it into his pocket. He'll feel better with Izzy. She'll whine and whimper and mewl. She'll do what he wants. Leonard dug the phone out of his pants.

5

Stan splashed a puddle of Aramyst on his left palm. He rubbed his hands together and patted his face and neck. Opening the small white and silver capped jar beside the sink, he dipped his middle finger in and dabbed the thick cream under his eyes. He brushed his hair, left-left-left, right-right-right centering and perfecting the part before spritzing the flawless coiffe to a firm all-day finish. Last his mustache. He leaned closer to the gilded mirror and preened his mustache with his diminutive gold comb, trimming a few wayward hairs with miniature gold scissors, pausing briefly to wipe the smear of chalky pink from the corner of his mouth. Then he reached for his phone and dialed Cady at the office.

"Cady, I'm wrapping up a few last minute items here. Got a couple of early phone calls to get out of the way. I'm on my way if anyone's looking for me."

Stan swigged a jigger of antacid. Pink chalky stuff adhered to the tips of his mustache. Ignoring the pink dribbles spotting the brass sink and black marble counter, he called out to his wife for his newspaper and second cup of coffee.

***

Cady knew better than to start Stan's day off with issues. As long as his office didn't burn down, he wanted to stay obliviously out of the loop. Otherwise the whole department would suffer the brunt of his daylong pyrotechnics. Wiser to let him ease into his day, take in one crisis at a time. Cady leaned against her desk looking out her window at the parking lot below. Just once she'd like to throw a party when nobody came. But judging by the number of cars already, today's election should play to a full house.

When Cady's phone interrupted her thoughts, she ignored the insistent jangling on the far corner of her desk. Whoever it was could leave a message. Then Izzy called out to her.

"C-c-cady?"

"Yes, Izzy, it's me. I'm here," Cady soothed then held the phone away from her ear and waited all the while Izzy wailed. Not the first tears of the season. Young, vibrant, first generation Cuban-American, Esmeralda Isabella Palacio shed her quota of tears, especially during recent months as they geared up for the election. But Izzy's tears usually sprang from frustration, fatigue, anger. These tears, they flowed for a more daunting cause.

Cady let Izzy cry. *Dammit she deserves it.* Under Cady's tutelage, Izzy blossomed from flighty college intern into one of the most astute programmers on Cady's election team, weathering a barrage of pre-election debacles and voting machine fiascos. Only Mario surpassed her in technical savvy.

When Izzy's sobbing reached its crescendo, Cady knew it would only be a few moments before her jagged heaving dwindled softly into muffled sniffles. *Bless Izzy's lively girly-girl heart, these phone creep calls could bring down a world-class blimp-sized sumo wrestler, let alone poor Izzy.*

"C-cady...C-cady...I...he...Cady..."

"Izzy, Izzy, don't let him ruin it for you." Poor Izzy. It's been such a choppy ride.

"C-cady, I'm so scared. At first I thought he was just one of those freaks, you know," Izzy sobbed. "A...a cochino, you know another nutcase getting off on.... So, as soon as I figured he wasn't one of our techs out in the precincts...I...I'd just hang up as soon as he started his breathing bit. And I'd just go back to sleep. No big deal," Izzy sniffled.

"Good. Then what?"

"Then *mierde*, these last calls when he started talking about the election, I thought maybe it was one of the guys playing tricks on me. Cady, do you suppose...?"

"No, Izzy. I don't. Izzy, tell me what he said...exactly."

"He said, Cady, he said there's no way we'll ever know the election's right. Said he can flip the numbers upside down and we'll never know it. We'll never find it. Said *he's* super boss now, Cady."

"Oh? So the creep listens to the local news. For all the world we're voting with matchsticks at a bonfire...ballots of straw."

"*Mierde*! How *will* we know it's right, Cady?" Izzy sobbed.

"Let's not go there, Izzy. We're doing all we can. Come on. Tell me the rest of it."

"It's just I'm scared. I'm so scared, Cady," Izzy whimpered.

"Isabella? ...Isabella!"

Izzy hiccupped her response, high-pitched gut wrenching hiccups.

"Listen, Izzy, the guy's just some freako, a bully, a coward. He's calling you and he's calling me. But he's not calling any of the guys. Why do you suppose that is?"

"I...I don't know."

"It's because he thinks we're weak. But we're not, Izzy. We're strong. Izzy, he can't hurt us from the other end of the phone line."

"But you said..."

"Yeah. Yeah. It's while he's not on the phone, that's when I worry. I know you can't erase the jerk from your mind. But, Izzy, he's a no count, a loser. He...he's a jackal. That's all he is. Pure putrefied jackal scat."

"Jackal scat?" That did it. Izzy chuckled through her tears.

"Yeah. The guy's whacko. And his middle of the night scare calls are terrifying. But the freak's not calling a macho man. He's calling you. He's a coward, a creep and not worth one sniffle, Izzy."

With Cady's sympathy softening the edges of Izzy's pain, her sobs took control once again.

"Izzy... Izzy! Have you talked with Mario?"

"Last night. Is Mario okay? Does he need me this morning?"

"No, Izzy. He's doing okay, but he's picking you up on his way to the office. Does that make you feel better?"

"Oh, Cady. It's not just...the whacko. It's today. It's those rickety voting machines. It's this election. I'm all jittery and anxious that something'll go bonkers, that nothing'll work and our numbers'll get all tangled up. And...and the whacko just..."

"I understand, Izzy. Believe me, I do. So remember what you do about your jitters? Remember?"

"Yes, Cady," Izzy sighed. "We lie."

"And how's that, Izzy?"

"We lie to ourselves about the gnarling in the pit of our stomachs. We just slap some fool-yourself-into-believing-you're-having-fun labels on all those icky feelings. Like exhilaration not apprehension, excitement not dread, animated not frenzied, exuberant not frazzled. Oh, I feel better now, Cady," her words dripped with sarcasm.

"Come on, we can do this, Izzy," Cady dished out all the confidence in the world. But she herself teetered within nanoseconds of hightailing it back home, back to her bedroom where she could dive into the safe soft cocoon of her lonesome bed and curl herself up in a hug-tight sob-all-day ball.

Resolved calm, not panic. It is what it is. Our process is sound, our own software rock solid. Then like a bad head song, the niggling thought rewound and spun itself into replay... *Not necessarily so with the voting machines. Not before, not now, not solid.*

Composed, unruffled, serene even. As for the voting machines...skittish. *There are people...big, powerful people...they want this bad.* Well so do I. And so do a whole lot of other people who've been working their tushies off. You haven't a clue, you miserable miscreant viper-scat.

6

Stan tossed the Sports section on top of the bathroom counter as he grabbed for the phone. "Stan Corbin, Supervisor of Elections."

"Stan. Called your office. Everything okay?" the terse voice boomed on the other end of the line.

"Oh, Brice, uh, good morning. Thought you were one of my guys." Stan strained to keep his voice steady. Brice always sucked the breath out of him.

"Hardly. You forget what day it is? This is a big f_____ deal, you know? And you're not anywhere showing your face."

"My manager's...things don't really get started for a while yet, Brice. My manager's got everything under control." Cady always had everything under control. But today, now...maybe that was Brice's problem.

"I don't give a rat's twanger. Besides, Stan, just who's in charge down there? You or that technocrat programmer?" Brice bellowed. "The polls are *open*, Stan. Networks milling around your turf for hours now with nothing to do but speculate on what you're gonna mess up this time.

"Brice, the whole crew over there...they..."

"Let me tell ya something, Stan. This election better run smooth as a silk butt wipe. If there's a flinch...a spark, you snuff it out. Understand? You stop it flat and you call me pronto."

"Yes, Brice. The truth is, I was on my way out the door when you called."

"You better hope your gal over there.... How's she doing by the way? She gonna play nice?"

"Like Rebecca at Sunnybrook Farm. I told you, she's one of us."

"You just bet *your* farm on it, Stanboy. Those tech types get all intellectual, philosophical. Never know which side of the fence they're on. May jump outta your corral altogether. Can't trust 'em."

"She wants this, Brice. Her credibility's at stake here too, you know. She'll keep it…"

"See to it. Good thing I'm sending Neal over. Should be there any minute. Could be there right now, sittin' at your desk, Stan."

"My…Brice…"

"Your goons…See to it if he wants something, he gets it. He's there sniffin' out the stink you miss. Anything he needs…office, assistants. If he wants the damn vote counting computers, he gets 'em. Handover your keys to the whole f_____ kingdom."

"Bri-i-i-cce, wait. Even the auditors, they can't mess with the computers. It's protocol. Besides, it's Cady and her team too."

"Back to her again. Scared of a little skirt? You just said she'll play nice," Brice taunted.

"She will, Brice. But she does it…right. By the book and you think she's a pushover. But damn, she's got a set of steel ones, when it comes to her team or…their sacred protocol."

"I see. Get rid of her," blunt without skipping a beat. "Then the rest'll follow your lead well enough."

"Brice…?"

"What? No one to run your show? All right then, *you* be there. Take care of my boy. And you get a whiff of trouble, escort that techno-skirt out of the f_____ building."

"Brice, listen, what about…you know my Board, the Florida Commission. What do we say to them? They'll scrub the whole election if they find out."

"Then what? I ax you? You forget somethin', Stan? I am the f_____ Florida Elections Canvassing Commission. Hear?"

"Yes, Brice."

"Shoulda been there, Stan."

"Yes, sir. On my way out the door, sir." Stan held the phone to his ear, bracing for the next command. Instead the line clicked and he slammed his phone down with a firm *clack* onto the marble counter. He grabbed his giant, economy size, 16 ounce, candy-pink antacid, twisted off the cap and swigged straight out of the bottle.

"Good morning to you too, Brice, you…" Stan's words trailed off as he studied his tormented reflection in the bathroom mirror. "You'd just better keep your word, or this stellar rise of yours is gonna burst like helium balloons in a crematory." He swiped the telltale pink coating off his lips and the cracking at the corners of his mouth.

"You're a real bastard, Brice, you know?" Stan said to his own reflection in the mirror. Then he picked up the phone again and dialed Cady.

7

Cady pulled the phone away from her ear and scanned the tabulation room to see if the others could hear Stan's morning shout fest over the phone line. But no one seemed to notice, or if they did, chose to ignore it. She turned to face the whiteboard, away from the others, away from the media room window and waited for his next salvo. *Well, I'm not going to let YOU ruin my perfect day either, Stan. If you're looking for a fight, go find someone else to pound. You won't get it from me.*

Dammit. Cady shut her ears to Stan's background noise on the other end of the phone line. *You chat-pee with your governor friend too?*

"Cady?" Stan's toilet flushed. "You said the precincts are still starting up voting machines?"

"Yes, Stan. A few."

"What's your holdup? We in trouble here, Cady?" Stan grilled in rapid fire, his pitch climbing higher. "A*gain*?"

Cady cleared her throat, smoothing the ragged edges from her tone. "No, Stan. It's a lengthy process." She spoke her words deliberately, soft and slow, refusing to counter Stan's angst with her own. As though they hadn't talked about this every day in their morning status meetings, at least those he attended. "Stan, we're okay. We're close to the timeline we projected. At least the majority of machines are up at every precinct and voters at the polls are voting. Just not to full capacity. We'll get there soon." As if all of this wasn't published in large, bold print on his election schedule.

"Why the hell not?" Stan's voice cracked and rumbled at screaming pitch. "Did you cram in more of your security crap? That why it's taking so long? ......You didn't......... Did you?"

Cady took another deep breath. "No, Stan."

"Well, we should be up 100 percent," he concluded with a petulant exhale.

Yeah, Stan, we should. And the voting machines should work.

"What else?" Stan barked. "The governor chewed me a bloody new one first thing."

Stan's toilet flushed again. *Makes it a little hard to concentrate, Stan.* Surely he stopped paying attention. But she continued on, "Timing issues. Some machines didn't start up correctly and...... Stan, did you get my message?"

A short burst of running water on Stan's end. "Message? No. No messages."

"Stan, Security's on alert...the phone stalker...his calls heated up last night. He's threatening to hijack the election, Stan." Cady paused, giving him time to take it in, ask for detail. Instead she heard his sharp intake of breath...then nothing, no sound at all.

"Stan?"

"You're cinched too tight, Cady. Need to loosen up some. You've gotta stop overreacting to this stuff. Of course you get prank calls. What do you expect? They know they'll get a rise out of you."

"Stan...I don't think you realize," Cady tempered her frustration by lowering her voice.

"Sure I do. You're blowing a few phone calls all out of proportion. Now, calm down. You've really gotta get a hold of yourself, Cady. Oh and, Cady, before I forget, Neal Charles will be dropping by. Arrange security clearance for him. Top security."

And he had stopped listening, switched subjects between flushes. She might as well be talking to the wall about a last year's toe cramp.

"He could show up any minute."

"Neal who? Don't think I know who he is, Stan. What's he want?"

"Not important. Just another snoop."

"And who is he?"

"Some guy from Tallahassee."

"Where? Secretary of State? What do you need from me?"

"You know, red carpet. Show him around. Keep an eye on him. In fact, he goes where you go. Your new best friend."

"Stan…"

"No choice. Total access to anything he needs. Tabulation room. Might need to poke around a bit on your computers, you know, see that things check out. He wants it, he gets it."

"Stan, I'm not sure I understand…"

"What's there to understand?" Stan raised his voice again. "Give him anything he wants."

"Stan…the rules. We break the rules and…"

"Cady, obviously you can't hear," he bellowed. "It's government stuff. They want in. To observe. Look, do what you have to, to keep this guy happy. Thrust your virgin piece at his feet. Screw protocol."

"I…"

"You want your job, Cady? He's your new best friend."

The plastic casing of Cady's mechanical pencil cracked in her hand. "Y-yes, Stan. Of course…" She glared at the blurring whiteboard on the wall in front of her, all the while rolling the broken pencil back and forth in her hand, the cracked plastic making small clacking sounds. *Not this time, Stan. I won't break the law for you and I won't risk this election.* Her pencil snapped. *Enough. Suck it up, Cady.*

"What was it you were saying? Oh, yes, Stan, you need Mr. Charles welcomed and informed for Tallahassee. And you want me to be in charge of his information flow. He's permitted access to everything. That right? You don't really need the aggravation of screening information I feed him, do you?"

"That's the point. You just keep him happy and off my back."

"Sure. Now you don't want me telling him things you don't want him to know, right?"

"Of course not."

"And how do you want that to play out? I mean when I provide him with complete access and full information, he gets it. It's done. How will you know what he knows when he grills you for more, which he probably will? No buffer, Stan."

"You'll tell me, Cady."

"Stan, you know how it is around here. If he's in the tabulation room, he'll find out lots of things that I might not know about. I'm certain he'll balk when I put earmuffs on him."

"You'll just have to control it."

"What do you want me to tell the auditors? And what about the media? You don't think they'll be curious?"

"It's what the gov...government, what Tallahassee wants."

"May be another way, Stan. How about if I brief Mr. Charles on the election processes, set him up close to the media room window so that he can observe away at everything that goes on in here."

"What good will that do?"

"Well, if he understands the processes and pays attention to what we're doing, then he'll know when to seek more information ...from you, Stan. And he'll actually be less confused without all the technical fuss here in the tabulation room."

"And?"

"And he'll go see you. That way, *you've* got control. You manage. You filter what he learns and you won't have to second guess what I or someone else tell him."

Stan grunted.

"Stan, our priority is today's clean election. Maybe we don't want to start off dirty. At the same time we should be able to keep this guy happy...and away from the hodgepodge in here." With that Cady turned toward the media room window to see a tall man in a dark tailored suit standing by the entry door. "Stan, I think he's here now. I think Mr. Charles must have used his own credentials to get through security." Stan slammed down his phone and Cady jerked her own phone from her ear before the line went dead.

How will you know its right? And the phantom-freak-jackal-scat's whispers crept into the fray cozying up beside Stan's rage and her own fears. *How will you know its right?*

8

Oh, shit! He could f_____ reach out and touch her. There he was focusing his fisheye lens on the tabulation room, waiting for her grand entrance and *shit,* her all-business suit assaults his damned camera. Leonard lowered his camera against the gargantuan blur, then snapped it back. *Stupid. She'll recognize you.*

Jamming the camera to his eye, he held it at an angle so he could follow her with his one free eye, hoping the camera followed her as well.

"...And the table in the far corner over there butted up against the media room window really offers you the best vantage," she said to the man. Leonard heard her laugh softly. "That is if we can claim it before someone else does."

"Ah, yes. I can see that Ms...ah, may I call you Cady?" the man asked. Leonard knew the stupid man wanted her already. *Bitch.*

Bitch laughed. "Of course. Everyone else does. You'll find we're all pretty relaxed here..." Her voice trailed off as the two of them started walking away. But then bitch stopped. Leonard braced himself, sure she recognized him. His legs turned to liquid fire, no longer supporting him. He grabbed for the chair. Then in a flash, she was off again, catching up with the man obviously in a rush to seize his precious table.

***

Cady peeled her eyes away from Mr. Charles and peered around him to make sure his table was still empty. She may not have a choice in entertaining the jock from Tallahassee, but she didn't have to study the man's backside either. She glanced over to her tabulation room. The floor-to-ceiling media room window separating the two rooms was made of soundproof, bulletproof glass. Considering the ruckus out here, her team did well to be isolated in their own little number-crunching corner of the universe inside the tabulation room. Where she should be now. Where her teammates worked on without her, busily fielding helpline calls and tapping on keyboards, oblivious to the world outside their window.

Yet here she was, playing tour guide to some hack from Tallahassee. One more quirk in a day that really hasn't gone too well. Cady pasted her best gracious-team-hostess face on before darting after Mr. Charles, dodging reporters and zigzagging around the maze of tables cluttered with cameras, computers, sketchpads, and scrunched-up wads of discarded paper.

Mr. Charles seemed pleasant enough, so far. But just wait until things start cracking. You could always tell a type, the core of a man…or…woman by the way each responded to election pandemonium. She remembered noticing Mr. Charles during the last election, but knew nothing of his affiliation with state government. Interesting. But government or no, what Stan demanded regarding total access? Well, it was troubling. *Virgin piece? Screw protocol?* Stan's not just being Stan this time.

Well, Mr. Charles, let's just see where this twisted trail leads. How about it, best buddy? Cady queried Neal's back, so deep in thought she didn't notice when he stopped abruptly in front of her to yield right-of-way to a flurry of equipment laden reporters. After nearly colliding into his pinstripe suit, she determined to stick to the task at hand, dumping one Mr. Neal Charles. *So, here we are, Mr. Charles, you and me and a cast of thirty or so reporters and whatever else…* Neal started up again with Cady trailing close behind.

What's your purpose here, Mr. Neal Charles? …Neal? She liked the name. Neal. Not one of the regular ol' huff-and-puffs. At least he didn't fit the pushy, give-it-to-me-now-or-else type. Not yet anyway. And judging by his apparent good shape he was no chair-hugger… Neal. She smiled. Neal.

No young stud-puppy either. Flecks of gray staining chestnut in an otherwise perfect head of casual but well-groomed hair suggested the man had a few miles on him. Again she speculated his mission. Heck, he might even be in line for Stan's job. Now, *that* would cause Stan's current bout of histrionics. No telling. Anyway, she wondered if *Neal* really wanted access to her computers. She smiled to his back. And if he did, had he the *cajones* to take her on? Perhaps not...Perhaps. Cady's smile perked up, impish.

Neal slowed down and glanced back over his shoulder flashing a warm, easy smile her way, then moved on. *Dammit, Cady.* Red heat prickled her neck, flushing her cheeks. We've got an election to run, there's a phone stalker claiming the win, I'm squabbling with Stan......and now I'm measuring the pinstripes across the breadth of some jock-in-the-suit's shoulders?

9

When Neal reached the small table, he turned to face Cady, his eyebrows raised in the unspoken question, *Is this it? Is this where you want me?* Then he presented her with a warm eye-crinkling, I'm-here-with-you-we're-in-this-together smile.

Surprised by the unwanted intrusion into her business-only world with this unaccustomed assault on her senses and Cady's keen wits crumpled. Cheeks afire, her eyes shot down to the floor, then over to the media window, the clock above the door and finally back to Neal. Slow-to-judge Cady, she liked him...already?

"Y-yes. It's fortunate...this table...that no one...claimed it yet." Cady regained her footing. "From here, you can observe practically everything going on in the tabulation room," Cady waved her hand toward the media window and the tabulation room beyond. "And you can also observe the reporters observing the tabulation room," she laughed softly. He laughed with her.

"Now, you see the table on the other side of the window?"

Neal's eyes left Cady's and looked into the tabulation room. A long table butted up against the media room window right in front of him. A short supply cabinet lined up to the left of the table, followed by a copier and three printers rounding the corner against the adjacent wall. Next, another small table held a phone, an ample stack of message pads and legal pads in assorted colors, a few scattered pens, pencils and a box of multicolor markers. A whiteboard hung on the wall above the phone table. Neal couldn't make out the words scrawled across it. He looked back to the long table and then found Cady's eyes again.

"That's the communications table, basically the election reporting nerve center." Cady again pointed to the table. "All election protocol, the rules and checklists are organized along the left side, that's your right as you face the table." She pointed to several binders lined up along the back edge of the table. "The remaining documents placed there, include our status reports, communication logs, incident reports, and so on."

"Incident reports? That's for when something doesn't work right. Like your voting machines, when there's a problem?"

"Yes." He's quick, she thought.

"Where are they?"

"There are only a few hardcopies at this time. But once they're logged in, they'll be stacked over there on the right most edge of the table," she smiled, this time directly to him.

"Does that mean it's a perfect election today?"

Cady hoped she masked the disappointment in her eyes as she glanced at her team immersed in perpetual phonedemonium, providing assistance. Most of it mundane but some she considered serious stuff.

"Hardly, Mr. Charles." She laughed softly, making light of his perceptive question. "A lack of reports at this phase of *any* election means only there've been no showstoppers yet." She glanced over at the fax machine, noting the growing stack of reports.

"How do I get a copy of the incident reports?" Neal asked casually.

So it begins, she thought. "Actually, Mr. Charles, you don't. Basically, nothing leaves that room." Cady nodded her head toward the tabulation room.

"I see. You're setting me up with a spot in there?"

"Actually, no. Only the certified team goes there." Cady paused, allowing him time to object. When he didn't, her eyes sought his, waiting, holding level until his eyes joined hers. "When I learn more of your mission, I may be able to help you. Until then, I'll make sure I explain as much about the *process* as I can throughout the day….And, Mr. Charles, an important part of that process is when you see us running around in circles, tugging at our hair you'll know we're having…issues."

"I see," he chuckled softly.

"Okay. Now over there," Cady waved loosely to an area just past the door on the other side of her table. "The auditors congregate in that general vicinity. You'll notice them going through the incident reports and other paperwork to make sure we're following protocol, so they can certify all's right with the election world." Cady hoped the sham of it didn't seep into her words.

Neal looked from Cady to the empty area then found her eyes again. He nodded. "...And your crew, Cady?"

"Yes. See the man sitting at the console in the center of the room? That's Mario Valdes." Cady smiled Mario's way. His crisply starched shirt, so white the lights gleamed off his back. "Mario's our lead operations and tabulation guru. He's unique, a programmer who's brilliant in anything to do with this system."

"Hmm. Mario." Neal chuckled a moment. "Maybe we guys can get together for a couple of drinks or...it's early, I think coffee." Cady watched his eyes sparkle. "Then maybe, I can learn a little about what's actually going on here."

"Yes, Mr. Charles. And I'll ask Mario to bill the outing to his expense report. Sadly, of course then he'll be looking for new employment on his own time."

"Right. I expected something dastardly might come of it." Another chuckle. "I'll tread cautiously, Cady. Promise."

"See that you do, Mr. Charles." She smiled along with him.

"Didn't we agree we're on first name basis?"

"*Nee-aa-l.*" This man set her at ease, too much so. He might be Stan's best friend, but she herself would guard against considering him her friend or work friend or anything other than a...spy.

"Thank you, *Caaa-d-y.*"

Cady couldn't help herself. She laughed out loud, too loud for the setting. "Okay, Neal. This is serious," she straightened her face. "We've a lot of ground to cover. See the woman over by the print station?" Cady turned toward the left and held out her hand in the direction of the printers. "Yes, the one watching us watch her. That's Izzy. Esmeralda Isabella Palacio. You see why we call her Izzy? She's lead analyst and brilliant with statistics and election reporting. Life would go on without Mario and Izzy, but it would never be as easy."

"Mario. Izzy. I'm impressed by your talent pool, Cady."

"Me too. We're very fortunate."

Cady looked over at Neal...Neal assessing Izzy...and back to Izzy...Izzy appraising Neal. *Oh, Izzy.* Long, dark thick, wavy hair, tumbling about her face and shoulders. Large flashing Cuban eyes, flawless olive skin. Exceptionally beautiful. Intelligent. Quick, clever, astute and Izzy happened to be the most overtly feminine and sexual female Cady had ever known.

Cady sighed as she followed Neal's eyes...to cleavage, always eye-popping, gotta look twice to make sure I'm seeing what I think I'm seeing cleavage bursting out of plunging necklines. *Izzy, heaven help all the ogling men of the world. How many will be seared by your flame before you yourself are wed? Will Neal be one of them?* And for the first time in so long, Cady felt a pang akin to envy, so physical she reached up and tugged at her collar loosening the crimson scarf draped about her neck.

"And the others, Cady? ...Cady?"

"Oh. Mario has four programmer-operators reporting to him," she pointed to the opposite side of the tabulation room. "Two programmers report to Izzy. But we try to be interchangeable. Never know what we'll need when it's all hands on deck."

"Looks to be a boring election after all."

"Sure, like always. Neal, we'll try to help you with whatever you need. So don't hesitate to ask. But again, please understand you may have many requests we simply can't respond to."

"I understand, Cady, I do."

Sure. We'll see, Neal. "Okay. Before I desert you," she smiled. He smiled. "That door in back of you," Cady pointed to the door just behind his table on the wall adjacent to the media room window.

Neal turned toward the door.

"Yes, the one with the big bold No Admittance sign. That means everyone but you, Neal. The door opens into the main corridor to our offices. Stan's down the hallway at the front of the building. Use Stan as your up-to-the-minute-information source. Get whatever you can from him. My office is across the hallway."

Neal raised his eyebrows.

"In case you need to find me when I'm away from the tabulation room. There's also a restroom in my office, but the whole team uses it now and then, especially during elections. So beware, it may not be as private as it looks."

"Really."

"Yes, Neal. But trust me our break room's more interesting. It's down the hall to the right. Help yourself to any goodies, coffee, stale pastries, whatever. Do NOT touch the computer or anything else that might look interesting. They're off limits."

"I understand," he smiled.

Cady glanced at the wall clock. "I really do need to get back. Neal, don't forget Stan. We'll help you all we can…legally. But track Stan down. He may provide you with more…guts. Neal, I need to go."

"Thank you, Cady, very much for your time and everything."

"Sure thing, Neal. Mario and Izzy will head to the break room in a while. Give them some time to regroup and you can join them there. Or you can wait 'til later."

Cady held up her hand in a see-yah fleeting wave. But for the second time this morning, Neal held out his hand to hers, his grip firm and dry and confident. Reassuring…and he wouldn't let go.

"Cady," his eyes locked on hers. "It's not enough."

"What?"

"I need to be closer. I expected…I've been assured complete access to all relevant…"

"No, Mr. Charles. Not from me."

His eyes seized hers. "But they said you were one of us. Pledged your full support."

"One of…you got it, Mr. Charles. Everything I can give you and still be in compliance. Stan may tweak the rules for you, but I won't. Now if you'll excuse me…."

Cady smiled politely at the lout, twisted her hand free of his and about faced. As she marched toward the tabulation room, her mind whirred through the bizarre turn of events this morning. Stan. Psycho-phone-stalker. Stan. Neal. Stan. *Stan's just nervous. Doesn't understand the implications. Still, it stinks…… Neal. Spy. He'll be a pack of trouble before the day kicks in gear. Neal. Later, Cady.*

He sure did gander at Esmeralda. Is Neal interested in Esmeralda? And the pang zinged her again. *Hmm. The games begin.*

10

Neal's eyes trailed after Cady as she turned from him and stepped briskly away from his table on her way back to her tabulation room. Hands down she denied him both access and information to Brice's all-important election. Yet, if Neal was annoyed, it was only mildly so. Instead he gave her credit for standing up under pressure. He might've pushed harder, but she wouldn't cave anyway. He respected her for that.

Besides it didn't take long for him to catch on to the secrets she did share. Without breaking rules or bestowing privileged information, she merely outlined the process and suggested, albeit a might obtusely, "Watch me. Watch the incident reports. If I look harried, go talk to Stan. Get what you need from him." *So be it, Cady.* Stan was anything but tight lipped. Too bad he couldn't be relied on for accuracy, especially when his image was threatened.

No, Cady didn't cave. Yet, she couldn't be more professional or accommodating, at least in everyway except for the one that interested him most. Information. Pure, fast, precise information.

I get it, Cady. Your mission, my mission, perhaps they're not so different after all. Maybe we can help each other. Or maybe it will be an eventless day. Let's hope. But, Cady, fringe data isn't good enough for all I need to do. I must push harder, dig deeper. I need more…from you. I've got to pressure Stan for you. And this, Neal regretted knowing that what he must do would cause more trouble for Cady. Still, it couldn't be helped.

One thing's certain. If there's a mess here, it won't be the result of Cady or her teammates breaking rules on this end. A good thing…at least for this election, which is what Brice says he wants most. But definitely not a good career move. Though, I've enough interaction with Stan to know that Cady just might not care all that much about sticking around. Neal considered the strain working for such a man must create for a woman like Cady, or any woman for that matter. *Sorry, Cady.*

***

Cady smiled weakly at Izzy from outside the media room window. She jammed her access card into the cardkey slot, yanking it out when the buzzer sounded and the lock clicked. She shoved the solid door open and walked through, letting it swing closed behind her with a resolute metallic bang.

"Brrr! It's freezing in here." Cady pulled her jacket tighter, buttoning the two middle buttons. Next she fiddled with her scarf, snugging it around her neckline. *One of us?* Neal's comment irked…inappropriate. *Lout.* She slipped the crimson thing off her neck, scrunching it into her pocket. Turning her back to the window, she pulled off her yellow ribbon pin and buried it in her pocket next to the scarf.

"Yummm," Izzy murmured, leaning over the communications table feigning interest in one of the lesser manuals, her filmy blouse straining with the added burden pushing against her bodice. But Izzy fooled no one. For her eyes slanted up under thick dark lashes skipping over the table entirely, locking in on Neal. "Yummm," she said again, this time standing up straight, turning to face Cady.

"I heard that," Mario chimed in from his console.

Cady laughed out loud, then whispered, "Down girl, down. Plenty of opportunity later."

"You don't mind?" Izzy flashed her large brown eyes at Cady, all innocent, a child pleading for a shiny new toy.

"Oh, Izzy. He may look interesting, but he's a spy. He's from Tallahassee. I think he's a spy."

"*Mierde.* I never rejected the government be-fo-o-re! Do you mind?"

Those eyes…Izzy eyes. Cady knew she couldn't resist even if the toy Izzy teased for was the only toy in the box. No matter. Cady harbored no interest in state officials or computer geeks or work associates or blind dates or a host of other complications, at least not yet. "Mind? Oh, Izzy. Like the moth to the butterfly, I ask you, would it really matter? Just please, let's keep our focus here until after there's a decisive win tonight."

"Of course. Besides, he's probably outta my league anyway. Watch, he'll show up tomorrow with Miss Florida or somebody. Or maybe YOU, Cady. Maybe he's more YOUR league. He sure seemed fascinated with whatever you were talking about."

"That's because we were talking *elections*, Izzy. But I think he's fair game. I didn't see a ring."

"Oh…" Izzy paused, surprised Cady noticed. "I hope not. What a waste."

"Izzy, you're incorrigible."

"I know. But it's such fun, isn't it?" She grinned playfully. "So, Cady, what's his fatal flaw?"

"Flaw?"

"Yeah. You know. Like he's beautiful and rich and whatever. But he laughs like a hyena." Izzy's own laugh was soft and melodious.

"I don't know Izzy. His voice is kind of low, kind of gravelly. No. Not gravel, grit. His voice sounds like whiskey and grit." She smiled.

Izzy grabbed her stomach. "Ohhh…" and the button on her filmy iridescent blouse popped open.

Cady laughed along with Izzy, all the while quelling the unaccustomed fluttering in her own belly as well. *Not good. Not good at all. He's the enemy.*

Then she motioned to Izzy's and her miscreant button. *Well, here we are, Izzy. No cute little swirly skirts flipping up to your high thighs today. No one needs to remind you to dress for the media. You're wearing your business suit, to the letter. Albeit, slithery tight and slit up one side to your hips.* Cady smiled to herself. At least every few months, Cady evaluated then tucked away her own uptight middle-class morality judgments before reminding Izzy of her quick mind and career potential. "Dress the part, Izzy. Try to be a tad more conservative. Don't stifle your success by dressing to your feminine side, dress to your business side."

But Izzy, grew up flourishing between two cultures and she was alive and vibrant and colorful. Her high Hispanic upbringing demanded she always be well guarded and chaperoned, if not until marriage, then at least into adulthood. As a result, like many of her contemporaries, Izzy wasn't overburdened with cultural mores insisting she protect herself in the Anglo sense of cross-your-legs-properly-at-the-ankles-knees-together, hands-folded-demurely-on-your-lap, protect-your-reputation, prim and proper demeanor.

No, Izzy was totally carefree to enjoy her beauty, with bold, less modest styles. Unshackled, she reveled, even overtly flaunted her beauty, her sexuality, donning her most colorful, alluring plumage, enticing the most viral testosterone-pumped males to briefly sip of her nectar before fluttering off to sample the next flower. She'd be heartbroken of course, but after a few days she'd jump back in the contest. Asking her to tone down her flamboyant style was akin to ordering flowers not to bloom in the Florida sunshine. *Bless you for your joyous, vibrant, spirited heart. Will Neal's heart soon be yours?*

***

"Hey! Cady! Yo! What? Am I invisible here?" Mario asked in his best Cuban flavored New Yorker accent.

"Sorry, Mario. Girlspeak. Izzy's about to snag another gilded arrow out of her quiver."

"Izzy! I should have known. Such a wonder you are."

"Mario, you're only trying to embarrass me."

"No, Izzy. Sorry. Just glad my hats not in the ring. I'd hate to suffer the fate of all those poor boys trapped in your snare. Izzy shows mercy for no man. Imagine what she'd do to an old widower papi like me."

"Suffer? That's not fair!" Izzy turned back to her window and Cady turned to Mario.

"Mario, things stabilizing now?" Cady rolled a chair over to Mario at his console and sat down facing him, away from Izzy… and Neal.

"Yeah. Mostly tech support is handling the calls now. The fax is pumping out incident reports, nothing you're not aware of though." Once again Mario was all business, prepped by this morning's flurry of incidents. But his eyes focused on Izzy and her fascination with the stranger on the other side of their window. "Cady," he whispered, "That's the guy. He's the one I told you about this morning."

"Oh?" Cady glanced over at Neal to see him watching her. "Interesting." She paused a moment, then turned back to Mario who continued on, all business as before.

"Here's an update of the phone log. I just printed it out." He handed her the report without commenting on its size.

"Good. We'll plane out soon." She looked over the report, then lowered her voice. "Mario…the new program you're working on? The one that traps quirky new viruses our vendor programs miss?"

"You mean the program I tabled to work on election prep?"

"Yes. Do it," Cady said firmly. "Slam it in the mix along with your vendor programs."

"Cady? You know we can't make changes now," his voice so low Cady guessed more than heard his words. "It breaks protocol. Besides, Cady, I didn't send it through quality control yet."

"Just do it. It'll make me feel better. Besides, you know how I like overkill."

Mario shook his head, but his expression was warm as was his smile. "I believe I do, Cady."

"And, Mario, you're right about the protocol. Even if your program stands sentry outside the election boundaries and doesn't go in, I'm still breaking the rules. It's just…I'll set you up with the authorization document. I'll leave it on your console."

"This isn't because of him," Mario nodded toward Neal. "It's the phone creep, isn't it? He *really* got to you?"

"Oh, yeah. I'll tell you all about it once things slow down. But yes. He knew too much about our operation…about me…about Izzy."

"Cady, shouldn't you call the police? Want me to?"

"No, Mario. Thanks. Just a big bad phone call. Besides, you've got enough going on."

"Yeah, more than I had a few minutes ago," he chuckled softly. Then looking from Cady over to Neal, he smiled. "Hey, Izzy, as to your Miss Florida," Mario nodded his head toward Neal. "You mean like her?"

"Ah-h-h…yeah," disappointment clear in Izzy's tone as she appraised the tall beauty leaning over Neal's table. "Hmph."

Cady looked away too quickly.

***

"Right. I'll switch over right away," Neal agreed, accepting the new cell phone, but not rising from his front row seat.

"Later?" she leaned over whispering into his ear, her mouth glossed rubies.

Neal pulled his head away and looked up into blue ice. He shook his head. Still trying, tall, statuesque, perfect in everyway, she might have been chiseled of the finest marble. Her soul was as cold and hard as the beautiful stone. She turned and left, as silently as she appeared. Neal placed the new cell phone atop his yellow pad. Did Brice really want him to start with a new phone already?

Neal turned back to Cady's window and studied Cady-on-display. She paused beside Izzy at the communications table right in front of him. Only the window prevented him from reaching over and touching her hand. And Neal switched gears in spite of himself. *Well, Brice. You did me a favor, old boy, on two counts. I'm here in the middle of election central without a hitch and the whole thing was your own idea. Besides this part is more joy than I've felt in a long, long time.*

Neal looked on as Cady and Izzy chatted briefly. He couldn't hear them through the soundproof glass, but he knew. They talked about him. He watched them laugh, look his way, then felt Izzy's eyes devour him. *Wow.* Flushed with the raw honesty of her unguarded appraisal, Neal thought to check his fly, but was too stunned to move. No novice, Neal experienced his share of encounters or near encounters, especially after his divorce. But the blending of these two women standing side-by-side unabashedly discussing *him*...he tugged at his tie.

Neal studied them back. First Cady, next Izzy, back to Cady, then Izzy again. To call Izzy a knockout was blatantly inadequate. She was glorious. And no fluff, at least not according to Cady. But Neal's interest in playing around was on the wane. And Izzy didn't have quite enough years under her belt, not a rich enough tapestry, yet. Besides, Neal wasn't interested in arm candy. But then Cady... well, Cady was something else. He'd known exactly who Brice talked about during his wake-up call this morning, remembering her so quickly from the election two long years ago. That spoke volumes about Cady. Didn't it?

Cady impressed him in the last election. But then his jet-set marriage had just careened off course in a full-throttle nosedive and he shoved everything aside but his desperate need to survive after the crash.

Neal studied Cady now with a calmer, easier eye. She was no fluff either. Not a beauty, but attractive, very little makeup and no pretenses either. He liked that about her. He suspected that if she wanted to pay her dues by spending the prerequisite hours at the beauty salon and in front of her mirror slathering on face goo and frou-frouing her honeyed hair, she would be very pretty indeed. As it was, she had a casual glow. Her hands weren't all soft and pampered either. He remembered the warmth and energy of her hand in his. Her nails were manicured, but casually, no acrylic talons, no red war paint. He wondered if she enjoyed fishing. Bet she could bait her own hook, too. And she had a presence, an easy self-assuredness that comes with liking oneself. Tall, but not too tall. Not overly slim either.

Neal looked back and forth from one to the other again. Izzy was hot, yes. But Cady...Cady felt all warm and cozy, someone to snuggle up with. It would just feel good to know she was on your side, behind you all the way. Neal didn't think she was married. Would he know? She didn't wear any rings. He wondered if she had children. He wondered if she wanted children.

Maybe after this election stuff wrapped up.... No. Hell no. At least not as long as he worked for Brice and she worked elections. What was Brice's motto? "Never f___ a screw or screw a f___ or screw a skirt you're gonna f___." *Or something like that. Brice could sling it raw. Others were less graphic,* "Never friend or dine or wine a bleep on Brice's radar."

Neal turned back to the high drama playing out behind the display window, studied Cady and her team interact with one another. Brice said to watch out for her, can't trust her. But behind that glass, her people couldn't trust her more. High pressured stuff and here they were easy and calm and enjoying the moment and each other. *Wonder what happens when the going gets rocky.* He hadn't hung around long enough during that part of the last election to know. This time Neal was here for the whole show.

Neal pulled a business card out of his pocket, looked at it briefly then dialed his phone. "Hello, yes. Stan Corbin, please. This is Neal Charles. He's expecting my call." *Sorry, Cady.*

11

"Let's go. I need my coffee. Now." Izzy shoved her book into its slot, pirouetted on one spiked heel and motioned for Mario and Cady to follow as she sashayed off for the break room.

"Izzy, wait. Mario, before I forget. In case you're curious? Our friend out there, he's Neal Charles." Cady looked from Izzy to Mario then to the floor. "I told him he can use the break room."

"No way…" Mario started but was cut off quickly by Izzy.

"Alri-i-i-ght!" she beamed. "Hmm…Neal…."

"Whoa girl."

"You guys. Hold on." Cady raised her hand.

Mario cast a stern look at Izzy as they waited for Cady to speak.

"I know it's an imposition, but…"

"So, why'd you do it then? …You know, Cady, it's not your job to entertain some slick suit on Election Day." Mario did nothing to conceal his annoyance.

***

Neal held the phone to his ear, turning away from the tabulation room so he faced the wall and the No Admittance door. Even with his back to the reporters, the media room offered scarce privacy. He couldn't see Cady now. Odd he felt her watching.

"Stan, I need to go over a few things with you. How about I drop by in a few minutes?"

"Yes, Neal. Anything you need. It's just…I'm afraid right now I'm up to my kneecaps in alligators here. Can we put it off for a bit?"

"Of course, I understand. Stan, I expected to be observing from your tabulation room."

"I gave orders to that effect. You know between you and me, I do have my challenges here."

"Oh?"

"You know I can't always rely on my staff to… Well let it suffice, she does have her ways."

"I see. I'll remember."

"Now the tabulation room?"

"Yes."

"Cady didn't give you what you need, uh? You still want access?"

"Yes."

"You're as good as in. You sure you wanna be on display like that."

"Yes."

"I'll arrange it. I sure will. I'll have another little talk with Cady, set her straight. Actually, you know we'll have a doozey of a time explaining you to our auditors. Not to mention the media."

"Is there a better way for me to understand the processes? Stay in front of the curve?"

"Understand? Listen I told her to explain the whole damned thing to you, all the regulations and all. She do that?"

"Yes and I'm meeting with her team later."

"Oh…? So what else you need? I'll keep you informed on every minuscule detail……you need to know."

"Will you be observing from the tabulation room then, Stan?"

"Too much frenzy. My staff keeps me informed."

"Your staff? In the tabulation room?"

"Well, yes. Cady keeps me informed. It's her job to keep me informed. And if she doesn't, well it's her job. Now, Neal, you understand there are rules about things we can share with an outsider."

"Cady filled me in on that too." So Stan's got scruples after all. "Listen, should Florida be in the thick of it again, particularly Miami-Dade County, I must have reliable information for what I need to do with regards to managing your damage control, as well as that of Tallahassee."

"Absolutely. What I mean to say is I'll keep you informed, but so much information falls under regulated procedures, I just want you to know that discretion is...uh...essential here. Understand?"

"Yes. Information as well as my sources strictly confidential."

"Good. We understand each other then."

"Yes."

"Now as far as Cady's concerned, she's a little upset I altered her plans today. She uh...doesn't like to share her toys. You know? She could...well you can't always believe everything you hear around here. Did I say she's upset with me today? She's apt to tell you things that may not be...accurate...about me."

"Oh? I'll keep that in mind."

***

It took Cady a moment to respond to Mario's not-your-job grump. He was right of course. Stan shouldn't have pulled Cady off task to techie-sit some snoop who had no business horning in this close to elections. She resented it. But when she finally answered Mario it was with the tattered dialogue she repeated to herself often enough. "You know, Mario, that's exactly how I felt. Then I checked the organization chart again. And you know what? I'm NOT in charge. And as long as what Stan asks is not immoral or illegal, it's my job if my boss says so." She looked over to see Neal on the other side of the window, chatting it up on his cell phone, grateful at least he didn't try to plow his way through her.

"Why do you put up with so much crap from him, Cady? From Stan."

"Because everyday in everyway I'm rewarded by you treasures." Cady swept her arm from Izzy to Mario then toward the others around the room. "Besides, just what would you have me do? Stan's run this shop for a lot of years. And apparently no one ever told him his behavior is...unacceptable."

"So why is it again you gave the suit free run of the break room?"

"Wish I knew. He's the enemy. He doesn't belong here. Anywhere. But he's smooth, Mario, really and he just made me feel...I felt obligated. Well, actually he wanted to hang out in here, watch us work our magic."

"No. He can't do that, can he?" Izzy no longer so enthused about the stranger when he might infringe on her tabulation room. Playtime was one thing, running an election quite another.

"No. Of course not, Izzy. It's against protocol," Mario reassured her. "So, why'd you do it, Cady?"

"Actually, it's what Stan wants. Stan insists he should be in here to observe. I think I bartered him out of it…maybe. But now you understand about the break room and my office. Amazing isn't it? I guess I felt like I had to give up something."

"Your office too? Right. It is amazing. You're such a pushover."

"Well, help him out all you can with…generic stuff."

"Swell. I mean, sure thing, Cady," Mario agreed.

"You bet. C'mon, Mario," Izzy said nearly skipping with anticipation at helping the tall stranger so long as he stayed in his place and out of her computer space.

"I'll see you in a few minutes. I've got some reports I want to check out," Cady's voice trailed after them. She heard Mario's beeper sound off as the door closed behind him.

12

Cady studied the phone log propped opened on her communications table. Scores of phone-ins, nothing earth-shattering individually, but steady, annoying. And by now, too familiar. ElecTron failed miserably once more in their feeble attempts to provide reliable voting machines. *I just hope the ones that are working are counting the votes.*

Cady's fingers traced a line down the page, scanning the entries, then flipped to the next page. *Let's see, the ubiquitous startup problems. The polls have been open for hours and we're still booting up and crashing voting machines.* Continuing down the phone log, more machines crashed and burned than should have in a whole month of elections. *I wonder if we're storing them in the right climate conditions.* Good point. Cady stepped over to the whiteboard and scrawled, "Check climate," in red marker along the bottom of the board. Then she walked back to her post at the communications table.

Cady stared blankly out the media room window, pondering the possibilities of storage rooms being too hot or too humid, when a movement off to her right caught her attention. She looked over to see Neal watching her. He smiled. She smiled. She waived a quick waist level half-wave. "Spy," she mumbled as she bowed her head down over the phone log once more.

Neal. When Cady looked up again, Neal leaned forward in her direction but he didn't watch her now. His head bent over the yellow legal pad in front of him, his left forearm rested on the table, while his right hand jotted notes across the pad. Every so often, he'd pause, rub his forehead and look up for a moment as if summoning the next idea. Then his hand would glide over the paper again.

His hands. Cady studied his hand skimming back and forth over the page, large, bronzed. She thought of his handshake, how his hand felt holding hers, warm, kind of...not rough really, but definitely not smooth, not rich-boy-pampered softy, maybe a little calloused. Maybe a tennis player. Maybe... *Neal. Dammit. You're not on my schedule today. Get out of my head.*

Let's see. Cady flipped to the next page, she glanced up to see Neal again, watching her again. She turned away quickly, back to the phone log. No time for this, for you, not now. Still, as she perused the next page, her errant thoughts strayed. Neal. His chestnut hair brushed against the back of his collar. A little long really, but not unkempt, just casual, earthy. And those gray flecks fanning out at his temples reinforced the perception of power, of quiet authority. Maybe that's why she offered him access to her office and the break room. *I don't trust you any more than I can reach through this glass wall to smooth back that wisp of hair from your forehead. Can't give you keys to the kingdom, but here, take this instead. Take my office, our break room. It's your right. You're so powerful. You deserve it. Take...hmmm.*

Tall, lean. Swimmer? His shoulders amply filled the broad tailored jacket, a charred mesquite brown, power color, so dark it was almost black with thin stripes so fine they were barely visible from just a few feet away. The pale muslin hue of his shirt contrasted sharply with the brown-black of his suit. Dusky blue stripes slanting down his tie complemented his eyes, eyes the color of the Gulf Stream just before a summer storm. Nice combination. Tailored. Well made. Obviously well groomed, taken care of...the jab to Cady's gut was palpable. Of course. Cared for. One Mr. Neal Charles happens to be very married after all. *Forget you, Mr. Neal Charles. Forget Izzy. What do I care, you spy.*

Cady didn't hear the phone ringing in the background until its third ring.

***

Pen to paper, Neal completed his thought. Then as was fast becoming habit he lifted his head from his notes to check the wall clock just above and to the right of where Cady stood pouring over those ever so top-secret binders. Invariably his eyes drifted down, down and left, and rested on Cady, Cady working, Cady frowning, Cady... She looked up, looked right at him... *And damn, I did it again. Look away fool. She'll catch you drooling, frat boy.*

Okay. Regroup. I'm here purely as an observer. Well, not exactly. I'm here as a biased observer on a mission. Ward off bad publicity should things snarl up again. Keep Brice informed. Brice doesn't trust Stan. Now there's a surprise. But I'd bet money he can trust Cady. Biased in that as well, eh?

Centered, grounded. Is she committed? She wouldn't go for halfway. For sure she'd expect a committed relationship. Precisely what women like Cady do expect. And deserve. How would it feel to find a life partner like...well like the polar opposite of before? Done with I-I-I, Me-Me-Me, I'm so pretty, so alluring. Joyless, lifeless, lonely. What about we? Common interests, interests in each other's joys? Okay, so I wasn't interested in the social whirlwind la-de-das, the parties, the fundraisers. But at least I supported her in it, all of it.

Neal looked up at the wall clock then back to Cady...again. This time though when their eyes locked, her demeanor was anything but soft and friendly. *She looks...hurt? Actually, she looks really pissed.*

Then, quickly Cady turned on her heel and walked away from him.

***

Cady paused at the white board and scribbled a note before answering the phone.

"Cady, thees is Juan. Meester Stan Corbin wants to see chou. Now. Sorry."

Cady's sigh rushed over the phone line before she could snatch it back. She covered for it with a short embarrassed laugh. "Sorry, Juan. Be right there...in just a minute. Do you know what he needs?"

"No, Cady. But chou know he did say something earlier about resididals. Cady, chou know what resididals is?"

"Residual votes, Juan?"

"Maybe."

"You know when you turn your calculator on, it starts off at zero? ...Well it's supposed to be the same with voting machines. After all, they're just big 'ol calculators, prettied up PCs. And they should start out with zero votes."

"Jes, of course."

"Well, Juan, sometimes the voting machines hiccup and they startup with votes already counted. Those are residual votes, Juan. It's very serious and should never happen."

"But it does, Cady? How many?"

"We don't know, Juan. As soon we found the first residual votes this morning we called all the precincts, cautioned them to be on the lookout. But by then, most machines were already up and running" *Dammit. What if they hadn't caught these? And there could be more. Could be hundreds of voting machines that initialized this morning with votes already counted, before the first voter even sidled up to vote. Dammit.*

"What to do now?"

"There's nothing we can do. After the voting starts, there's no way to go back and re-do it." Dammit. Had she been thinking, she would have brought a few of those machines in for evaluation. Well, if it happened again, that's what she'd do.

"No wonder Stan, he's so angry. But I don't think that's his problem just now."

"No? Well, Juan, there's plenty to go around. He can take his pick today. I'd better get going."

"I've got something for chou, Cady."

"Oo. I'm on my way then!"

13

Cady didn't need eyes to find Stan during elections. The cloying scent of his cologne lingered long after he concluded his more pressing election duties and took off for the Keys. She opened his door and let herself in. There sat Stan, puffed up and ready behind his desk in his grand office chair. Its burgundy leather polished and shiny, complementing the reddened hues of his mahogany office suite.

Stan shifted in his chair, fingering his ample mustache as Cady approached. The lip coiffure a little too bushy, a little too rusty, a little too much atop his slight overbite. His slate-flecked blond hair parted stiffly in the middle of his receding forehead. And the paunch under his maroon club tie swelled just enough to spill over his belt.

Cady gripped Juan's candy bar in her left hand. It felt good, the only thing tasteful in Stan's entirely too-impressive-to-be-impressive office. *Just let me do my job, Stan. You do yours. I'll do mine. Why is this election any different from all the others?* But Cady knew the answer. A record of botched elections and Stan grew antsy. *Give the guy some slack. Just not so much slack they self-destruct for not following the rules.*

Stan glared at Cady now standing before him. She was good at her job. Damned good. He admired her begrudgingly with a matching disdain festering beneath his own inadequacies. Her requests, her directions always presented with clear-cut pros and cons. She never came to him anymore without substantial proof, pure, concise, and complete logic. Her detailed reasoning always made sense even if it took a few tries for him to get it. By then he generally reached bully grade.

So now when his own faulty reasoning failed, when he wanted to go in another direction for his own secret reasons, a direction that wasn't backed up by protocol, logic or facts, he fell back on his time-honed bullying. Brice made it so hard…and Cady, particularly headstrong today.

"He's on our side, Cady, one of us. What's your problem?"

"What do you mean, our side? He works for you now, for the Elections Department?"

"No."

"What then?"

"You know."

"I'm afraid I don't. He's an auditor?"

"No, Cady, of course not."

"Then what is this, twenty questions? How is he one of us? Is he from one of the other counties? Another election team? A Floridian? Black? White?"

"He's Republican, Cady."

"Stan?"

Stan tweaked his mustache. Of course that didn't work. Crap. Cady's overdeveloped follow-the-rule convictions overrode muscle and he knew it. Why bother to reason? There was no reasoning with her.

"Well, this is nice, Cady. Remember who you work for, eh?"

"Yes, Stan."

"Well, then." When the bullying failed, Stan counted on crushing her resolve, her spirit in other, more demeaning, ways. He rather enjoyed these diversions and would today except the ante was too high. Still each time after his bad boy played itself out, when she reached her limit of crap and turned in her notice, he begged forgiveness, bestowed another hefty raise or bonus, promised to be a good boy, and they'd be generally okay until the next election or the next big hurdle.

The snit's too smart for her own good. Brice is right. I should can her. Would too, but she really knows her stuff. Knows my stuff too. Makes this department hum. Besides the last election wasn't her fault. Though Stan often ranted to her and anyone else who'd listen that it was. Deflect the blame. Same with all the other elections, the whole freakin' string of 'em.

"Well, Cady." Stan looked behind her to the open door gaping into his reception area. "Now that we've got that straight…" Just the two of them here in his plush office. He liked it here, it boosted his alpha power.

Stan reached deep into his big-boss magic bag for his most powerful kick-down-Cady charm. And he casually looked her up and down, pausing at the V of her blouse, resting his eyes on each firm breast, individually, her tummy, the secret V of her thighs. Cady's clothes never clung, but Stan knew from the loose creases where to direct focus and he did so until she fidgeted. She always fidgeted. Just as she almost always cowered before conceding to his alpha power. Didn't matter that she was usually on target with her pros and cons and crap. He was in charge, the boss, commander in chief. Miss Muffet's alter ego would do well to assimilate that one important fact into that pointy head of hers. Still no matter, this trinket always boded success. His ace in the hole…exactly where he'd like to be. A leer slithered across his face. He'd show her a thing or two. The smugness of his tilted smirk was only partially hidden beneath his rusty moustache.

But Cady didn't flinch, didn't fidget. She waited him out. And when his eyes ceased their offensive and looked back to her face, they met her calm ones, steady with her damned stubborn resolve. Today of all days, with Brice and his henchman breathing down his neck.

"Put a sock on it, Stan."

"Cady?"

"It's not working. Or hadn't you noticed?"

Stan gaped, bereft of words, intelligible or otherwise.

"As I told you earlier, I'll set him up with what he really needs. Give him the lowdown on the processes. But, Stan, that's as far as it goes. You want to break the rules, fine. I'll even help you do it. I'll squeeze another worktable into the tabulation room for you. You can mosey through election documents until the lights burn out. You can chat it up with your auditors. You can listen to the tech jargon. You can watch. You want to bang away at the computers, the tabulation system. Fine. But it's all on you, Stan. You escort him in. You escort him out. You baby sit the one-of-us guy.

"Now, Stan. I've got an election to run…that is unless you have some better ideas, unless you want to take charge. We done here?" Cady turned her back on him, somehow mustering enough will to pull one leaden foot forward in front of the other lest she collapse in a puddle of tears on his too-plush burgundy carpet. She always felt so tainted, so dirty during his episodes and she despised herself for conceding him that power over her. And she loathed him more for taking it. On her way out of Stan's suite she paused at Juan's reception desk, thanking him again for the candy bar, now mangled and hot beneath its wrapper.

14

Now that's the look she warned me about, Neal thought, watching Cady walk toward him on the other side of her window. She veered over to the printer long enough to snatch a stack of papers from the bin. Then she returned to her post at the table in front of him, flipping through her pages and building several small piles within his reach. He couldn't read the small print upside down, or right side up for that matter. But he could read Cady with her face pale, rigid, expressionless and her eyes steamy. If that didn't broadcast trouble. She didn't look at him. He sensed her pain and suspected he might be the cause, even if indirectly.

No sooner had Cady returned, when something behind her caught her attention. She headed for the table under the whiteboard and picked up the phone. For a moment he imagined her friendly greeting to whoever was on the other end of the line. In a heartbeat her head bowed forward, nodding left then right then left again. Then just as suddenly she jerked to attention, her shoulders squared off, her back ramrod stiff. She turned around and smiled. A few more words were exchanged and she laughed, all the while scanning the room beyond her window. Visibly relieved that the disarray outside her room continued on as before and no one noticed her raw, albeit brief reaction to the apparent bad news. She turned back around, picked up a red marker and scribbled a few numbers on the whiteboard without interrupting her conversation.

She's acting for the camera and media and...me, he thought. *Good recovery, Cady. Now tell me what's really going on here. And what's with the I-could-kill-you* look? It's just business after all.

***

"Cady, Mario here."

"Mario? Now that's good. Afraid to poke your head around the corner? Where are you?" Cady looked away from her window, from Neal and toward the break room.

"Got beeped by the church precinct. Came down here to see for myself."

"Dammit."

"Sorry I didn't let you know, Cady. It's just I wanted to get here before…"

"No. That's not why. You did good. Tell me."

"Cady, it's the weird stuff again. We've got a ballot scanner spitting back half the ballots. I can't tell if it's counting votes or not. We've got a touch screen that hemorrhaged ink and then dried up so it's not printing any ballots at all…" his voice cracked. "And we've got another touch screen printer with paper jammed so tight we can't free it up."

"Mario? Are you okay?"

"Yes, Cady. It's just…that's not the worst. Cady, we've got a voter here…she voted straight down the line Democrat, but when she finished her ballot, it switched to Republican all the way."

"Maybe she just thought she selected Democrat candidates…? Maybe she…" Cady stopped herself. She knew she was wrong. No matter feather or lead, when the reality of it settled on her shoulders along with the fast mounting pile of morning hassles be they election or the two-legged kind, Cady felt the physical weight of it. Her head bowed forward. Her shoulders stooped. Briefly, then it was over. She took a deep breath, even managed a vacuous smile for those reporters on the lookout for a good scoop…and for Neal. She turned facing the window. The chaotic world outside swirled around unabated.

"No, Cady. The lady, she tried to re-enter her ballot five times or more she said before she asked the poll worker for help. And then when I got here, I watched her do it. I watched her chubby little fingers select her candidates, select her issues, submit her ballot…every step of the way. I watched her."

"And you cleared the ballot before she re-entered it?" Cady queried, then laughed, knowing how ridiculous her question sounded as soon as she asked it, and especially when she heard Mario chuckle on the other end of the phone line as well.

"Hello, Cady. This is papi here. You askin' me if I cleared the ballot?"

"Sorry, Mario. No. I'm just talking…taking up time-space while I think with my mouth on Groundhog Day. You feel it?"

"I do now. Forget what I said earlier about smooth elections."

"Jinx. Mario, do you suppose…my phone calls this morning? Do you suppose the creep actually…?"

"No, Cady."

"Had to ask. Okay. Did you send your voter to another machine?"

"Yes."

"Okay. So she submitted her ballot? The way she wanted?"

"Yeah. She got it and she was really nice about it. I got her name, phone and voter registration number. She said she'd be happy to help us out if we need to talk with her again."

"You did good, Mario. You pulled her machine offline?"

"Yeah. I pulled the ballot scanner offline too. The techs are working on the other machines with printer problems. I'm keeping my fingers crossed…. Tell me what to do, Cady."

"You got a baseball bat?'

"No. I forgot my tool kit."

"A good thing. Listen, don't reset your voter's machine just yet and don't power it down. Okay?"

"Yeah. I closed the booth flaps to keep it from being used."

"Listen, just pack it up and put it in your car, okay? Make sure you don't turn it off? The battery's good, right? Grab the other machine from this morning. You know the one with residual votes. Okay?"

"Yes, Cady."

"I'll ask the techs to meet you down at the loading bay, lug the machines into the tech room and plug them in. I want to get answers from ElecTron before we take the next step on this."

"I'll finish up the incident report before I leave."

"Good. Tech support will alert the other precincts. Your poll workers on the lookout for any other voters who seem…"

"Yeah. We're...they know to keep their distance, but we're watching to see if any other voters seem fidgety, take a long time, look anxious. And they're prepared in case the voters ask directly for help like this lady did."

"What about voter wait time? Do I need to send over another voting machine?"

"No. Not yet."

"That's a relief. I'll call Stan as soon as I get your incident report."

"He won't be in for a couple hours yet, will he?"

"Mario..." Cady started gently then dropped it. They all struggled with their Stan-attitude. She more than they, especially after she'd just been slimed. "Yes, he's here, Mario. He's here already. It's just now..." First the pesky Nealspy hovering too close. Then Stan, now this, and little Susan Cady doesn't want to play anymore.

"Later will be soon enough, Cady. He doesn't do anything with all the information you feed him anyway."

"Mario, wait...there's no media around yet, is there?"

"Not that I've seen, but I haven't been outside since I got here."

"How about election observers, exit pollsters?"

"Milling around."

"I'd better try Stan now."

"As if he...Cady, Izzy and I were supposed to meet your Neal in the break room. Can you let them know I'll catch them later?"

Cady looked over at Neal's empty chair. "He...Izzy...maybe they started without you." Cady fumbled with her thin gold neck chain. "Mario, go ahead and fax your incident report. Better you make nice with Neal on your way in. Bad enough to have the snoop poking around. He's already too curious without us revving him up. I'll get started with your voter on this end." Slipping her ring back and forth along its chain, she mumbled her goodbyes.

Cady took a deep breath then dialed all of Stan's numbers, office phones, cells, before calling tech support to give them a heads up. She'd leave Izzy for later when they could walk through the incident report step-by-step together.

15

*I*sabella. *My feisty Isabella. Disarm the poor man with your charm then zing him with another spirited salvo.* Mario knew where to find Izzy the moment he rounded the corner. Her voice met him, filtering gaily down the hallway, softly at first and then with more gusto the closer he got to its source. Frilly little flower that she was, she blossomed on debate offense, presumably with Cady's spy.

Mario paused outside the break room door. No need to rush in. Izzy rendered Cady's spy *ocupado*. Mario leaned his back against the wall. Time to regroup. Before Cady. Before Izzy and Cady's spy. When would it end? The same errors boomeranging election after election was not simply disconcerting, it was appalling, inexcusable. Now these new machines smacked them with a rash of new problems.

Mario took his time, listening for a moment to sounds more than words, relaxing in its normalcy.

"Yes, but what I'm trying to tell you, Neal, is that it matters very much. We asked Iraq to show us proof they didn't have nuclear weapons. And they didn't give us proof, did they?"

"Well, Izzy, prove to me you don't have nuclear weapons."

"That's absurd!"

"So, prove it. Where's your evidence?"

"I...I...There is no evidence because it's preposterous. I have no weapons."

"Prove to me that you don't have secret labs somewhere."

"How can you prove something that isn't?" Izzy demanded incredulous, realizing Neal was winning this round. "So, you're saying the end justifies the means, eh? In Iraq?" Izzy switched sides. "You tell me. Civilians, children, enough collateral damage to populate a city, say the size of...what Miami? They didn't ask for this. We simply got them murdered, Neal. We're supposed to be the good guys, aren't we?"

"Gruesome, Izzy. Horrific. Maybe we should have known. We could have done it better. But still, we are the good guys, Izzy."

"Tell that to all those grieving mothers and orphans."

"Izzy, the tortures, people tossed into prison on a whim…"

"Seems to me we gave as good as we got."

"Okay, Izzy. New subject. Do you have a personal projection for this election? What's your opinion on the Cuban vote? Where's that going?"

"Well, you've got new leadership, the wet-foot-dry-foot thing."

"You think immigration will play into it?"

"Every Cuban-American family has stories. He wouldn't tell you this, Neal, but when Mario was seven years old his father walked him, walked his mother and his brother and sister, he walked them through Mexico to escape Cuba."

"So that means you, Mario…all Cubans? You would be pro immigration then? For…say…Iraqis and Pakistanis? Haitians? Mexicans? Or just Cubans?"

"You mock me and you know it. If Mario's family stayed in Cuba, well they all of them would have been butchered."

"I understand. And this is a big country. But there are limits. There should be, yes?"

Izzy laughed. "Now that I'm here and Mario's here, yes there must be limits." She continued laughing.

Mario nudged the door open and peered around it, only his head and right shoulder visible to the two sparring inside the break room. "Quite a debate here. You going to solve the world's problems on your own? Or can anyone join?"

Neal laughed, "Busted. Come in. We've been expecting you." Neal stood up extending his hand to Mario, "I'm Neal Charles. Cady…" Neal looked down at Mario's hand clasped in his, raised it a few inches and smiled. "You are human. The way Cady talked about you and Izzy, well, I had my doubts."

Mario chuckled. "Cady warned us you were smooth. So you'll be spending some time with us today?" Mario pulled them back to Elections.

"Yes, Mario, for the duration actually."

"We've been asked to provide you with anything you need, that is within…"

"Understood, Mario. I'll be looking forward to it. Thank you."

"A word of caution, Neal…and, Izzy, you know better. Neal, your debate with Izzy?"

Neal shrugged, raising his eyebrows.

"Strict rules, Cady's rules, no talking politics during Election Week," Mario answered.

"Oh, is that what we were doing?" Neal smiled.

"No. No, Mario. Mr. Charles and I, we would never!" Izzy smiled demurely looking over at Neal.

Always with Izzy. Mario's smile was melancholy.

"Got a lot of rules here, I see. You can't talk politics. And you can't tell me the good stuff…."

"No, sir," Mario's tone somber now. "Some of it's Florida law. Some of it's Cady. She takes this very, very seriously, Neal."

"Yes. So I've found. More seriously than Stan Corbin, her boss?"

"Oh, yes."

"Wonder why. See I thought maybe it was just me," Neal teased. "I figured she didn't care for me being from Tallahassee or on the wrong team or something?"

"Who, Cady?" Mario chortled. "Heck no. Like I said, we're not permitted to talk politics here, so this didn't come from me. You're from Tallahassee. So, we can assume you're with the in crowd? And Cady…plays for the red team, a long family line of them."

"How do you explain her adamancy?"

"Well she nurtures some extremely liberal…uh…open views. She's so naïve. She always, always wants to…do the right thing. You know, maintain the sanctity of the Constitution. Save the world, free the oppressed, feed the masses, medicine the masses, educate the masses, save the babies…the unborn…"

"Don't forget pay down the national debt," Izzy chimed in.

"I get it. Full of conflicting views, is she?"

"Oh, yeah. But there's lots more to it. She's got *pedigree* ya know. History, a whole parade of ancestors backing her up and pushing her forward..." Izzy's tone softened, "And then her mother..."

"Izzy!" Mario scolded.

"I just told him what he wants to know."

"No. You were just gossiping, Izzy."

"Not if it's true, Mario. And I found it, all of it on the Internet. So there."

"Now I'm curious. How about a quick rundown."

"That you can do yourself, Neal. Just start with her...think about her name and work backwards and then way before that."

"You mean Cady? It's short for Catherine? Or a trendy spelling for Katie?"

"Oh, no, no, Neal," Izzy toyed with him.

"You're talking riddles here. Give a guy a break."

"Okay, Izzy. Just tell Neal your short version, no embellishments. Hear?" Mario warned.

"Yes, Mario. Okay, Neal. It's Cady. Susan Cady, C-A-D-Y."

"Well, that's nice, but I don't..."

"Oh you man!"

"Elizabeth Cady Stanton? Susan B. Anthony?" Mario looked over at Izzy.

"Yes. Her grandmothers to the fourth and fifth powers both campaigned with Susan and Elizabeth," Izzy beamed.

"Interesting. You mean they were suffragettes?"

"Well...yes...suffragettes. But more, Neal. As a man you obviously don't get it. More to the point you probably want it all back."

"Oh? And what would that be, Izzy?"

"Property. Neal, it wasn't all that long ago that women in this country couldn't vote, but we couldn't even own property. We were chattel, Neal. We were property ourselves! If a woman owned real property, then she turned it over to her husband when she married."

"Logical arrangement, don't you think, Mario?" Neal taunted.

"Hmph. You can smug all you want, Neal. But if you really want to understand Cady...then know this. It's not only what Cady believes, it's a part of who she is. Anthony and Cady-Stanton were the real deal. But neither of them got to vote because it wasn't yet *time* for *women* to vote. It wasn't until 1920, do you hear me, Neal? It wasn't until 1920 that women in *this* country won their right to vote. Women in Soviet Russia voted before we did! You hear that? Russia and Australia and Finland and…and… women in all those countries voted before we did in the United States. And bless their poor patriotic souls, neither Susan nor Elizabeth lived long enough to vote herself."

"Izzy," Mario nudged her arm playfully. "Izzy, you talk like you had something to do with it. You're from Cuba or at least your family is."

"Shame on you, Mario. You know this country's lifeblood, the blood of every woman flows through these veins!" Izzy held her hands out showing the creamy flan soft of her forearms.

"Izzy, I see no veins, nada. You have no blood. You see how it is around here, Neal? These women. Izzy's fanatical about it. Imagine how Cady feels. I mean does a guy have a chance?"

"Joke all you want, Mario. But Anthony and Cady-Stanton were the real deal. And so were Cady's ancestors and they didn't just talk about doing the right thing, they lived it." Izzy's voice softened, "And so did Cady's mother. Cady gets a lot of it from her mother. You know that saying of hers, Mario, 'If not you, then who will do it? Someone must.' That comes from Cady's mother."

"Does Cady's mother live here? In Florida?" Neal asked.

"Cady's mother," Mario looked over to Izzy. "Cady's mother was…murdered…."

The room silenced.

16

"Geez!" Leonard hunched his shoulders to slacken his jacket and peel away the frowsy shirt that fused to his body like a second skin. "A f_____ wiener steamer in here." He staked out this table for its proximity to the exit and relative ...hah...seclusion from the tight cluster-cliques of reporters. But since his arrival early this morning, the incessant chatter, the whang-bang of the door...and the heat. Even with the nonstop A/C blasting out the vent behind him.... *Geez. Might as well be in the exec's sauna. Sweaty. Noisy. Gallons more frou-frou than the execs maybe...no...jugs...more jugs for sure.* He smirked. *But if another one of those little chickies holds coffee klatch by this freakin' revolving door... persistent prattle near drivin' him nuts.* Leonard squeezed his middle finger between his Adam's apple and the itchy collar-tie gismo. The tiny top button choked off his circulation. He rubbed his finger around his neckline where the taut new-shirt fabric chafed his sticky virgin neck. *Last time I play dress up in this monkey suit.*

Leonard glanced up at the round clock over the media room window, synchronizing his watch, again. He'd staked out here looking real busy for hours now, textbook reporter stuff. Attentive, eager, interested, sharp-eyed. He'd observed the action, all of it. Shot pictures, lots and lots of pictures, still shots, live walking-talking shots. He shot wide-angle, fisheye, panoramic views. He'd shoot for a while, play it back and shoot again and again and again. He brought three cameras with him and shot them all near capacity.

Leonard opened and closed his fist, shaking his cramped hand at the wrist. His hand was beginning to seize up on him, his forefinger swelling. The good reporter, he took so many pictures...pictures of Cady. Cady talking. Of course he couldn't hear her behind her glass wall, but he knew what she was saying.

Cady checking reports. Reports he couldn't see, but he knew what they were. Cady chatting it up with auditors. Cady overseeing computer operators. Cady planning with her programmers, heads together all huddled in their secret speak. And when Cady hovered over her long table in front of the media window, he zoomed in until he saw the spark in her eyes, the crease in her forehead, the shimmer of camera floodlights playing on her hair, the swirl of her earrings. He shot the mole at the V of her neckline, at first veiled from view by the stupid red scarf tucked beneath her silky blouse...not now. He could see it now. Leonard touched his chest.

Leonard snapped his last batteries into his camera. *Shit*. He wanted to catch it live, on film, wanted to feel it, smell, taste her anguish, her panic, her failure just as things started heading south. Trap freeze-frame the horror on her face the moment she knew it was going down. Too risky. Besides, he was late reporting in. Although nobody beeped him yet, things probably started pinging at the precincts already. There was a moment there when Cady answered her phone, he thought she got her first...surprise. But the call was so quick and when it was over she was laughing... laughing, still oblivious to all Leonard's plans for her, today...his day.

Leonard sneered. The snow princess and her little suck-ups looked mighty jolly. Their stars gleam bright this morning. *Not for long, chickie. How could I ever have wanted to work with that? More hands-on, more fun, more power at ElecTron. No picky little tartlets like you bossing me around, chickie. Hell, they do everything I say. I'm boss or might as well be for all they know.*

C'mon. You're late. Break time kiddies.

***

Cady checked her scribbles on the whiteboard before grabbing the phone again. She speed-dialed Stan's office. No answer. Cell. No answer. Speed-dialed his receptionist.

"Supervisor of Elections. Thees is Juan. Con I help chou?" His cheery lilt tempered her dark mood.

"Ah, Juan, such a pleasant welcome after..."

"After such a messy blast off…no better, Cady?" he interrupted cheerfully. "What I con do for chou?"

"Is Stan around? He's not picking up in his office."

"I'm so sorry, Cady. Mr. Corbin, he says he's not in, Cady. Give me your message."

"Well, it's not an emergency, yet. We've run into a few glitches in the field. I want him informed. You'll let him know?"

"The minute he says he walks through this door I'll tell him to phone chou."

"Thanks, Juan. Got some more chocolates handy?"

"Ah. I knew I forgot something. Anyway it's too soon after your last one."

"I don't think so, Juan. I don't think so at all. Thanks again."

***

Again. Leonard synchronized his watch against the clock on the wall. First he thought they'd never leave. Now it feels like they'll never come back. Cady's crew had been on break long enough.

Okay, Cady. You got three minutes. You'll file in all happy and primed, ready to go another round. Leonard needed to time his move out for the exact moment they pranced in. While the floodlights burned on their grand entrance, obstructing their view out the window. While they still busied themselves with their little startup tasks, before they settled down enough to peer into the media room.

Okay. Okay. Made it this far. Let's go all the way. Wrap this baby up. Slinging his camera strap about his neck, Leonard set off on his cloak-and-dagger two-step across the media room. Slow down. Speed up. Slow down, step, step. He meandered casually, the essence of the perfect reporter…newsman of the month, pausing here and there, snapping pictures of the nearly empty tabulation room, his most affable quiver-smile plastered across his face, feigning interest in several vantage points as some of the other photographers had done earlier. He skirted the tables of milling, instant-messaging-obsessed reporters.

Slowly, casually, deliberately Leonard snaked his way in and about cluster after annoying cluster of buzzing reporters, studying the eyes of the swarms. As expected, they were all of them wrapped up in their own wonderfulness. He was ignored, absolutely and utterly invisible. Another pause, a few more pictures. Then finally, after passing the small table snugged up to the media room window, he reached his destination, the door into Cady's inner sanctum, the private hub of Elections Department offices. Turning around to face the media room he'd just crossed, he leaned his back against the wall immediately to the left of the door and snapped a few more pictures, melding himself into his surroundings.

The wall clock above the media room window ticked by another minute. He waited. They're late. The website, the schedule, it said live camera feed, fully manned tabulation room... *So, where are they? Whole f_____ team's tardy.* Leonard sniggered to himself. The room knew it too. He could feel it. "Something wrong?" he sensed them all asking, crazed for an early scoop. Cell phones clunked down on tabletops, cameras clicked, notepads and pens and pencils at the ready. The buzzing increased. Floodlights snapped on. The pack grew antsy, all but the solitary man at the small table in front of him. No, he'd sauntered in a few minutes ago through the No Admittance door, Leonard's door. Gave ol' Lennyboy a jolt all right. But now he stayed all heads down, scribbling on his yellow pad, reading and rereading his missive. Leonard studied the man. Tall, lean, not a reporter. Security? Undercover? No. Too at ease, too himself.

***

Neal jotted a few more notes on his legal pad, summarizing his observations and impressions: smooth operation, tight team, focused. Observed two more communications that might identify problem areas. Neal had watched the act unfolding behind the window almost nonstop since he got here this morning. And then he paused only long enough to meet up with Cady's team. *It's my job. Nothing personal going on here.* He lied to himself. Conceding his *job* wasn't nearly so interesting without Cady standing there in front of him.

Neal watched Cady take what appeared to be some fairly serious calls, at least judging by the wilt of her shoulders. Each time, when she first answered the phone, he wanted to rush to her. But no sooner had he derided himself, than she had shaken the disappointment off and put on another winning performance for the media. And for him. Smiling out to her audience, chatting gaily into the phone. Damn she was good.

The auditors hadn't given Cady's communications table more than a cursory perusal since their arrival. They may not be interested in its hoard of secrets, but Neal was. Neal found himself rooting for Cady and Izzy and Mario and the rest of her team. Sure he wanted a crisis free election for Brice. But more, he wanted it for Cady. Next break, Neal decided he would join Cady and crew again in the break room. Perhaps he could glean some of this morning's challenges, just out of curiosity though. Since nothing had occurred to interrupt the operation, nothing needed intervention or spin.

When it neared time for Cady to return, the media room chatter faded to the plastic plink of pens and pencils tossed back onto tables, the scraping of chairs, a shuffling of feet and the clicking of cameras…they're restless, ready for some action.

Point of fact, the fidgeter behind him hovered anxiously, breathing heavy for several minutes now, presumably waiting for just the right moment, the perfect angle for the ideal entrance photo.

Suddenly the click-clack-flash of cameras announced the trio coming back from break. There was Cady, flanked by Izzy and Mario all in step. Cady's expression was serious, all business but not worried. A good thing. They advanced toward their stations, ready to pick up precisely where they left off, no doubt. Cady to resume her post at the communications table, thumb through the more recent reports before joining the auditors at their post just behind the window.

Distracted by the whoosh of the door behind him, Neal looked back over his shoulder just in time to see a gray blur of trousers disappearing behind the closing door. *Guess I'm not the only one she invites to her lair,* he thought, then refocused his attention on the changing of the guard.

17

Ahhh...My turn now, Cady. When all eyes shifted forward and the swarms fixed on the tabulation room, when the solitary man looked up from his scribbles to leer at the tiny parade entering the arena, Leonard advanced to his next step. He turned, grabbed the doorknob, twisted and pulled the heavy door toward him, opening it just enough to slip through sideways.

With a swoosh-thud, the door closed behind him, its solid thump reverberating down the empty corridor. Lucky for him Maintenance still hadn't secured that door. Why bother? Anyone in the media room gets checked by Security, right? Follows the rules, right? A lot of good the stupid No Admittance sign does to keep real people out.

Leonard looked left then right, up and down the wide corridor. The bustling nerve center of the Elections Department was void of personnel today. All nonessentials scattered about the county for the usual election duty hoopla and hysteria. Almost.

Muffled voices filtering down the hallway startled him. He didn't consider the tabulation programmers rotating off shift would hang out in the break room. He needed the room to himself. He checked his watch. The big shots back in the tabulation room, they're the ones who count. Some of the others might remember him, but probably not today, not in his current suit-tie-combed-dyed state.

Just then, the break room door swung open. He heard a laughing male voice, "Byte me, gig boy, eh?"

"I would, but you're not on my Menu," a second man teased.

"Neither's she. Bow out, man, before you lose your cajones," the first man added. Several jovial voices chimed in with muted wolf howls.

"Yeah. Sure thing." More laughs.

Hyenas. Stunned by his first encounter, Leonard vaulted past the doors to his left and bolted into the men's room, tucking himself safely into the far stall. Prickled heat spritzed his upper lip. He yanked a wad of toilet paper free, dabbing at his lips, his forehead, neck.

The men's room door opened followed by a shuffling of feet, a stream of pee, a flush, shuffling feet, a gush of water, shuffling feet and the door swinging open and closed.

Leonard dabbed his face again. *Get a grip, man. You knew you could bump into these guys. Get on with it.* Leonard unpinned his press badge, pricking his finger for real this time. He stuffed the badge into his pocket and dug out his Elections Department visitor label, pealed it and smacked it on his lapel. Then he tugged a latex glove onto his right hand with a quick snap. Last he pulled out the manilla envelope from inside his jacket and unfolded it, making sure to touch it only with his gloved hand. The official ElecTron 3-by-5 label on the front of the envelope was addressed: **Urgent** Supervisor of Elections. *Just stick to the plan. You're in.* Everyone in the department's sure to be tied up in their own private little twirly knots. No one would think to question him now. He already passed through Security. Besides, he, Leonard came on official business, see the envelope?

Leonard splashed icy water on his face and neck, careful not to splatter his clothes, his paper badge. He grabbed a few paper towels and wiped his face dry. A final check in the mirror and he was surprised once more at the stranger staring back at him. Not bad. Okay, on with it.

He wandered past the programming area. His old cubicle devoid of life. Same computer, same printer. The book cabinets above the workstation hung open and empty. A few stray papers littered the desktop. No pictures. No personal desk paraphernalia. Only a dull layer of dust. Leonard sneered. Probably no one wanted his space after the lies she told.

Across the maze of cubicles, Cady's office window beamed yellow swaths of sunshine into the area otherwise devoid of light with the blinds drawn in all the common rooms. No one opened them today.

Leonard walked toward the light, into Cady's office. Generic, mostly, it could have belonged to anyone. Basic office stuff: desk, credenza, bookcase, all 2nd or 3rd generation office furniture. Generic, unisex. That is until you looked more closely at the detail. Original American Indian prints decorated the walls with ancient gods of health, wisdom, mischief, whatever. Brass ivy pots topped her credenza and bookcase. All neat and tidy and understated. The desk coulda been anyone's too. Except for those stupid colors, legal pads, buff, blue, gray with matching file folders stacked in a tidy pile. Before, in the good times when he worked for her, he'd ask for information, she'd pull out a color. How sick is that?

But then there was that little cluster of girly shit, fresh-mind-you daisies in the Waterford vase, sticky notes in an Italian alabaster box, chocolates in a flowery Nippon nut dish. She even stored her paper clips in a friggin' cloisonné bowl. Gauche. Stupid. Insensitive. He figured the friggin' thing cost more than he earned the whole time he worked for her. Yet there it sat, for the world to see and smash.

Other shit was still there too. The pen and pencil set her little suck-ups gave her on Bosses Day. Bitch. Still there in it's velvet box. Probably hasn't moved. She'd gotten all teary eyed, said she'd give every one of them a set when they worked their first trouble-free election, said the stupid things'd be her imperative, her inspiration. Well, not again this year, chickie. Besides, he didn't buy her cheap little act. Probably no one else did either. She just didn't like the friggin' pen set. There it sat, collecting dust – well somebody probably dusted it for her.

Leonard picked up the cutesy picture of her dogs, the big black lab with the soft brown eyes and the scrawny brown wiener curled up in a black and brown cuddle-ball with their squeaky toy monkey flopped under the lab's nose. All smoochy-oochy. What dogs would do that? Even her friggin' pets were odd. They sure had scared him though, a couple of times now when they came scrambling out their door, racing toward him at his hole in the fence. He hoped they stayed penned up, holding their pee until they couldn't hold it anymore. He hoped they'd explode all over Cady's floor. Leonard smirked. Might be good for something besides gator bait after all.

Leonard plopped the freakin' picture back on the desk. Hurry. One more glance around the room. To his right the door into her private bathroom. Bitch. To his left...the chair. *Shit.* How could he miss the chair? It was right there bumped up against the side of the friggin' desk. Leonard mopped his forehead. Prickly heat assaulted his face, his neck, his hair. Nausea gripped his gut and lodged in his throat in leaden unsprung heaves threatening to claim him. The chair. He kicked it, toppling it over. Kicked it again. *Bitch.* She summoned him into her office, held out her hand toward the chair and before he had time to scoot his butt back in the seat the bitch fired him. HIM! She terminated him...for cause! Security waited at her door for him with the lone cardboard box of personal crap they scooped off his desk. Not wasting any time, they escorted him out the building and off the premises. Vomit rammed up his throat. *You f___. You're off task. Get outta here.*

Clenching his gut, Leonard bolted away from the chair and Cady's office, back to the main corridor where he jerked to a stop and hunched over listening for voices. Silence. He raced to the break room. His breath hot, armpits clammy. *Can't get me now, Cady. And the rest of them are so self-important, tied up in their own little tight-trite worlds with their super-stupid-critical election tasks.*

Soldier now, Leonard marched into the empty break room, bee-lined to Izzy's computer along the wall. *Present arms!* He snapped Izzy's computer on, jerked the CD out of his right pocket, rammed it into Izzy's drive. He stood transfixed, glaring at Izzy's computer, waiting and listening to the CD drive grind, click and whirr, past the login screen, skipping the security password, then *ping*...he hooked into the network file server. *Bingo.* Leonard's boss man now. *Good. Good.* Then the black screen...the black screen...the computer seized-up, blank. Only the curser blinked on and off and on again...still alive...still thinking, thinking. *Come on. Come on. Go you mother.* Leonard froze staring at the damned thing for eternity, then just when he'd given up, big bold letters flashed red on solid blue, "****Blitzkrieg** -- COMMENCE FIRE!**" Hah! He blasted clear through their firewall. *Besides, firewalls only keep the honest people out, eh, Cady? Magnificent Cady? Well, right about that, 'cause here I am.*

Bingo. LEONARD ÜBERALL. A simple program, really – a little wormy-worm to chew up space on Cady's file server. It would just keep churning and churning until it shut everything down to a crawl and then Bingo! Death to the server! They'd find it. As soon as the server started choking up they'd poke around until they found it. But the slick little mother would just fire up again, that is until they killed its source, this little baby here. Leonard patted Izzy's computer. And he didn't care how long it took them to find it. Just a diversion really, a decoy. Fun. Leonard powerful Leonard, whole not since Cady dumped him.

So many ways to infest Cady's network with his little plague. But none so touchy-feely, so thrilling. He coulda done it from outside. Hell, he coulda done it from home. Instead, ahhh…he returned to the scene of his demise. He challenged and he, Leonard conquered.

Flushed. Relieved. Elated. Supreme. Eyes fixed to Izzy's computer, his power, Leonard edged backwards, making ready to split. When bang, he bumped hard against Izzy's chair sending a jolt up his backside. *Shit.* He looked down. *Scared the hell outta me…* "Well, hell-o-o," he said to Cady's scarf, scooping it off the back of the chair. He pulled it to his face, held it, breathed in, deep, inhale-exhale-inhale, deeper. Then he squeezed it, stuffing it into his pants pocket.

On winner's high now, Leonard raced out of the break room and down the hall. He ran past the No Admittance door. Past the programming cubicles. He didn't stop until he skidded into the front of Cady's desk. Time paused. He glared at Cady's things. He glared at her alabaster box. He gripped the box tightly with both hands, raised his arms high above his head and crashed the box swiftly and firmly down upon the diminutive cloisonné bowl in a miniature explosion of paperclips and ancient shards of brightly colored enamel and alabaster. *Bingo! I killed it,* he sneered. *I killed it dead.*

He checked his watch. Hurry. He grabbed a red marker and scrawled across her walls. Then in four quick giant steps he stood facing the mirror in Cady's private bathroom. "GOTCHA," he etched in bold scarlet letters across her mirror. Not enough. He swiped at the girly shit in her cabinet, flinging it about the room and out the bathroom door. Quick. He snatched a lipstick and scrawled, "BITCH," in full-bodied, long-lasting 18 hour Fatale. He bolted back to Cady's office, jamming the lipstick and marker into his pocket on his way.

Hurry. He yanked Cady's jacket off her desk chair and lunged at her desk, flailing the jacket back and forth hurling her shit to the floor.

He snatched up the scissors before they fell. *Ahhh*. He fondled them, turning them over again and again in his hands. He pushed his fingers into the holes, hard. *Izzy…. If not for you…Izzy who keeps no secrets…I'd still be here, maybe sitting at this desk….* He worked the scissors in his hands. *Izzy, you raven haired witch. I have a surprise…for…you.*

Leonard checked his watch. *Later, Izzy…later I come for you.*

18

"Izzy! You leave your break-room computer on?" Mario never looked up from his console. "I told you not to launch anymore of your monster programs." He scrolled though his flashing list of jobs running, jobs completed, jobs scheduled to run, computers hooked to the network. "Izzy? I'll find it. And when I do…"

"MARiO-o," Izzy huffed.

"This is serious, Isabella. If your computer's signed on with your high-priority password and somebody wants to get rough, they'll cream my network."

"I'm not about to breach security today," she said credibly.

"You did before."

"Only once, Mario. Never again. Okay, so I let up a little last week. Bad habits and all. But we weren't on absolute election protocol then, at least not exactly on account o' it wasn't Election Day, Mario."

"Well, today is Election Day, Isabella, and I could write you up for security violations."

"Sure. But you won't. Besides if you did you'd be mucho embarrassed, 'cuz you'd be wrong, papi."

"No? Well, whatever you're NOT running is chewing up space like crazy, Izzy."

"Don't be so tetchy. I haven't even touched that computer today."

"Hey. Mario! Quick, vary the backup server offline." Cady tossed her markers onto the table beneath the whiteboard and stood bumping against Mario's chair before her red marker rolled to the floor. "What jobs are running?" her words crisp, concise.

Without a nod to Cady, Mario's hands flew back and forth across his keyboard. His head leaned in so close to the computer screen, flashes of light flicked across his face. "Izzy. Go check the break-room computer," he commanded softly, eyes still drilling his computer screen, hands clicking the page-down page-up buttons. "Yank the plug. Don't do anything else. I don't care what's running. Don't touch the keyboard or switches. Just yank the plug. Yank the network cable." Mario scanned active jobs, files linked to those jobs, the size of the files, the time of day they were created. "Coña," he murmured under his breath. "Cady."

Cady pulled up a chair and edged in beside Mario, so close she could feel his body heat. Izzy returned from the break room and stood behind them where their shoulders joined.

Suddenly, Mario's computer beep-beep-beeped. Bright, neon-chrome tangerine letters flashed bold on black, "Warning. Warning. Illegal operation. Program number 57."

"Here it is." Mario pointed to the program screen. "I don't know how it got in, but here it is. I'm sure of it. Watch…" Mario's fingers tapped the keyboard and pointed to numbers growing exponentially with each tap. The proliferation of files displayed on the screen growing row by row, page by page chomping up valuable disk space, kilobyte, megabyte, gigabyte, gigabyte, gigabyte. "Now if I can just delete the program creating these suckers before the server seizes up. But first…" Mario highlighted several pages of files before clicking delete.

"Okay." Mario grabbed his mouse, moving it deftly around the tabletop, clicking and double clicking at several checkpoints. "This is it. Izzy, you didn't start any jobs this morning? How about the other guys?"

"No. And no. I checked."

Mario clicked on the job. Delete! "Yes, dammit. Burn you sucker. Okay. Let's see what happens."

"Damn. You guys are good," Cady spoke softly. "Now, smile pretty for the camera," she managed a hesitant, painful little laugh. "Mario, it's going to take a while for you to ferret this out and run diagnostics, yes?

"Oh, yeah. I need to make sure this is it and the only one. And I've got to find out its entry point. Cady, the firewall, the virus detectors they're current. I swear."

"I know. Mario, your new program, that's the one that trapped this little heller, isn't it? ...Mario?"

"Yes, Cady."

"Hah!"

"Cady? Mario?" Izzy looked from one to the other. "Somebody tell me what's going on."

"Well, Izzy, Mario's homegrown program here killed a snake. Mario, this is a new virus, yes? Can you tell if it's specific to us? To slither in under our radar here? From where? Do you suppose it slipped in by one of the voting machines? But..."

"I don't think so, Cady," Izzy whispered. "My break-room computer was on. I yanked the plug like you said, Mario, so I don't know what it was doing. But it was on. I didn't turn it on and no one else uses it but me or sometimes you two."

"I know, Izzy. I've got to stay here and dig in on this. Can you go back to the break room? Double-check you unplugged the network cable. Turn your computer back on. If you have to touch the keyboard, use the tip of a pencil. Okay?"

"Right. I'll grab another mouse so I don't get prints on the one there. Right?"

"Yes. Good."

"Be back in a minute."

Mario flipped back and forth through several screens. "Cady, I think we got it. I'll run diagnostics on the backup server as well. But I think we got it."

"Too close, Mario," their eyes fixed on each others with an understanding born of too many years of knowing, striving, fear, pain, relief. Then it was over and Cady looked away. She angled her chair toward the media room. "Which precincts are scheduled next for data uploads?" Her eyes swept across the room, left to right pausing on Neal. Neal and the man standing behind him and that worthless No Admittance door silently slamming shut.

"Call Security! ...No. I'll do it." Cady grabbed Mario's phone from the console. "Mario. Look!" Cady nodded toward the scrawny man with the slicked down hair staring back at her.

***

Shit! F____! She saw me! Looking for boyfriend here, she saw me. And the f_____ door still isn't f_____ shut!

Leonard's legs ignited with spikes of fire piercing his veins. *Steady. Steady.* He fought the urge run. *Okay. Pretend I belong. She just met boyfriend here…no clue who boyfriend knows.* Leonard's chest heaved, his lungs finally emptying the spent air he'd been hoarding too freaked to breathe. *Okay. In-out-in-out-in-out.*

He studied Cady's demeanor, cautious, concerned. Her eyes may even be anxious…*but smooth. She doesn't know. Bitch. She's no clue who I am. She's no clue what I can do!* He gambled, *I could shoot outta here. Shit no. That'd just prove I'm the enemy and her little buddies there'd race out and grab me before I push my way through this jungle of hot freakin' flesh. Or I can hang here. For all she knows, I could be one of boyfriend's buddies.*

Leonard leaned over Neal's shoulder, Cady's jacket clamped under his arm beneath his own jacket. "Hey, got the time?" *Any asshole knows the f_____ clock's on the wall, but boyfriend here didn't even flinch. Asshole.*

"Sure." Neal held up his wrist, verifying the time against the wall clock.

Leonard played along, "Geez. How dumb. I know the clock's right there. Stupid of me, uh? Thanks though, buddy. Better get back to my group. See ya."

Smooth as silk. Leonard's hand plunged into his pants pocket. His fingers clenched Cady's scarf, rubbing the silky thing around and around as he slowly, methodically ambled through the mass of tables and chairs and reporters and tripods, centimeter by excruciating centimeter.

Smoth as silk, Leonard repeated to himself, his fingers swirling the silky thing hard now, faster, harder. He passed the midway, passed the tabulation room door, passed the auditors huddled beside the door. He could no longer see Cady or her geeks in the tabulation room without turning his head, which he would not, could not do.

Leonard ambled on, sweat drenched and trembling, bravado depleted, gears jammed in automatic pilot, his well-practiced young-boy smile freeze-dried across his face. No one rushed out to stop him. *Keep going*, he willed his mutinous legs to tread slowly. *Keep going*, he willed his body to cross the room without bolting.

Smooth as silk. He reached his post by the revolving door, jerked the camera from around his neck, tossing it into his brief case. Next he dragged his right arm across the table, scooping his other cameras and gear into the brief case in a cluttered ill-fitting heap. He looked up. Nothing amiss in the tabulation room...so far. *But it's comin'.* He wasted precious seconds trying to zip up his too jumbled, too fat case before schlepping the strap over his shoulder with the thing gaping open.

Suddenly a gaggle of chickies swung the damn revolving door open almost smacking him in the face. *Shit!* Leonard, smiling freakishly now, grabbed at the door handle and held the f_____ thing open for the bitches. Then slowly, cautiously he slipped around to the exit side of the door and peered out at the lobby.

***

By the time Security answered Cady's call the man was skirting back first around the open media room door, his bulging briefcase flapping against his hip. The case and its contents wobbled back and forth with each step. The camera straps dangling over the top of the case slapped against his leg as the door closed behind him.

"Close down all exits. There's a man leaving the media room. He's on his way out now. Stop him. He just came out of the office area. We've had a breach. He may be the one. Stop him."

"Whaddya mean breach?" the security guard asked.

"Computer breach. It doesn't matter. Just stop him. I'll fill you in on the details later. But right now, we need to stop him. He's wearing a navy sports coat and gray pants. He's carrying a brown leather computer case. It's jammed full."

"What if he doesn't wanna stop and talk? Do I shoot him?"

"No. Just stop him. In fact, for the next few minutes or so, until we get this thing under control don't let anyone out of the building."

Cady set the phone down and turned to Mario. "Did you see him? Mario, did you see him?"

"Sort of, Cady. Mostly his back. Skinny little guy, wasn't he?"

"Yes and the way he slinked out of here, he sure looked the part, didn't he?"

"He did that. If he isn't our guy he must be on the lead of some really hot story."

"Right. Well, for the moment, I'm assuming someone set off the virus from our break-room computer. If that's so, whoever did it should still be in the building. I'd rather inconvenience our reporter friend than take the chance of letting our hacker go."

"I think you're right, Cady."

"I'll go find out if Izzy's made headway."

"I'll keep banging away in here."

"Good. Just think of where we'd be now if you hadn't been at the console, if you hadn't installed your genius program, if you hadn't set up all your quote-quote overkills."

"No. I feel so bad, Cady. With all that, the guy still blasts through."

"Don't, Mario. He didn't. You stopped him. Besides, the only sure cure for a computer virus is to never turn the computer on. Otherwise if someone wants to badly enough, they'll get in."

***

Only two guards were standing by the sign-in register now, both facing away from him toward the building's entrance. One of the guards clutched a phone to his ear with one hand while the other hand rested firmly on his holster. *That could be my call. Look sharp.*

Leonard dodged into the men's room, flinging the ungainly briefcase to the middle of the floor with a resounding thud. Then hoping to change his appearance from the image he knew Cady would have fixed in her brain, he tore off his jacket. Cady's jacket tumbled to the floor in a heap. He wadded the jackets together in a tight ball before jamming them into his briefcase along with the other crap. He pushed and shoved the awkward stuff around inside until at last he could tug the sides of the briefcase close enough for the zipper to work....

Shit. Precious time wasted. He ripped open the zipper, pulled out his jacket and unpinned the press badge. This he pinned to his shirt before cramming the jacket back into the case. He pulled and tugged the jumble closed again before hoisting it up, off the sweat spattered floor. Wait. He plunged his hand into his pants pocket and grabbed Cady's scarf, kneading it between his fingers as he switched pockets and pressed it firmly to the bottom. He yanked off his glasses and crammed them into his pocket next to Cady's scarf.

On his way out the men's room, Leonard wiped his sweat-drenched face with his shirtsleeve. Then he pushed his hand back into his pocket and wrapped it around the handle of Cady's scissors, now warm with body heat. He adjusted the scissors, point down, handle up. Ready, aim…go.

***

Slow. Smile. Slow but with purpose. Slow. Smile pretty at the guard. Leonard walked toward the building exit. He didn't recognize either of the guards. They must have changed shifts sometime after his arrival. As he closed in on them he realized they were both engrossed in the big guard's phone conversation. The shorter guard's pudgy fingers stroked the handle of his pistol.

"Wha'd you say he looked like again? …Yeah…Yeah…How tall? …What's he wearin'? …Yeah…."

Leonard smiled his best good-boy smile at the silent guard, "Tough day, eh?" Then he paused a few agonizing seconds longer than necessary before turning his back on the guards and casually leaning over the visitors log book. He pulled his pen from his pocket, flipped back a few pages before finding his name and signing himself out, "9:30." Then he flipped back to the half-empty page. Let's see 'em figure that one out. They'll be lookin' all the hell over for a 10:30 sign-out. Sucker!

Easy. Easy. Leonard pushed the door open and breezed through letting it bang closed behind him. *Never look back. Stupid assholes. Dumb setup for the f_____ media door to be on the south side of the building and make us all park north of the building at Miami West Park for shit's sake.*

Walking briskly now, Leonard fished the car keys out of his pocket. *Home free,* he opened the unlocked door, flung his briefcase in the backseat and swung behind the wheel. *Home free. Gotcha, bitch!*

19

Neal flipped his phone open and pressed it to his ear. *Damn.* Brice fibrillated between pester and manic. He'll be in rare form tonight.

"Bri...uh," Neal caught himself. Most people didn't think of Bud Daniels when they heard Brice's name, but blurting it out to this crowd could spark a blaze of unwanted curiosity. "I'm in the media room. I can't really talk here."

"Don't talk then. Just listen... Hold on, what do you mean, media room?" Brice drilled in curt syllables. "Why is it you're not in there gettin' the goodies?"

"Aah, for an otherwise bright guy... Let's assume the election crew lets me in. Guaranteed as soon as the reporters out here see a fresh face they know doesn't belong, they'll be on it quicker than you can flick the ash off that giant stogie of yours. Besides, they're your laws." Neal paused for Brice to butt in. When he didn't Neal considered briefly what he himself understood too well. Brice could recite most Florida laws from memory. Yet over the years he'd grown increasingly adept at skirting legalities. All the while Neal grew more disillusioned with his old school chum. Neal continued, "We break your laws, you might as well renege the whole damned election."

"I didn't ask you to f_____ regurgitate all hundred and forty-nine pages of legalese crap," Brice snapped his gold lighter.

"No. Not about to dig my spikes into that cliff again." Neal cringed, still smarting from his marathon debates with Brice when Brice's cronies revised Florida's election laws. Even now Neal didn't understand why Brice persisted in condoning the legal ambiguities. "Look, you've been here. The tabulation room where you want me posted is set up like a damned theatrical production with the whole cast of national networks gathered around, eager for the next act. International observers are due in any minute."

"Yeah, so what?"

"So far no one's recognized me, or at least no one's let on they've recognized me. And if I lie low, they probably won't."

"So?"

"So, I'll learn more by keeping a low friendly profile than I would by shoving up in their faces. Besides, I'm cleared to use their private offices and hang out in the break room. Stan can fill me in on the details if they run into any rough patches."

"Yeah, right. Okay, Neal. It's all cool then? No hotspots?"

"Didn't say that exactly. I've smelled a little smoke, but so far no one's dragged out the fire hoses."

"What's that supposed to mean?"

"Just that there've been a couple of peculiar vibes. I was on my way into their offices to see what I can find out when you buzzed."

"Keep on top of it, right?"

"That's what I'm here for, Brice."

"Don't let 'em sneak anything past you, right? Nealboy… that gal give you any trouble?"

"Who? Stan's Deputy Supervisor?"

"Yeah."

"No. Most accommodating, that is within your election rules. Good team here, they're…."

"Wait……You see that! We're plastered all over the news… Wait… Every channel's got instant replays of a voter who can't figure out how to vote. You gotta see this. They're making a big f_____ deal out of it. Some lady on the tube right in front of me is saying how the machines flipped her f_____ votes. What d'ya know about it?"

"Damn. Nothing yet. But I can't say if anybody here knows anything either. There haven't been any incident reports filed. I can see those from here."

"Yeah? Well there's a f_____ incident goin' on in front of me right now all right! How'd those guys get this so fouled up?"

"Brice, they don't program voting machines here. If there's a problem, ElecTron owns it."

"I don't care who's got the secret decoder rings. Find out from your gal what else is going on and quash it."

"I'll see what I can do, Brice. Wait. Stan's coming into the media room now. I'll get the scoop and call you back."

***

Cady faced her whiteboard, marker in hand. *Okay. Call Stan. Breach. Get update from Security. Check my precincts. Who was that guy? Mario, poor Mario. He takes this stuff hard, though you'd never know it to look at him.* Cady glanced over at Mario, stooped over his console, hands intermittently flitting across the keyboard then spinning his mouse around. *First Stan, then Mario.*

Cady reached for her phone just as Stan sauntered through the media room, smiling nicely to the cameras.

"Oh no. Not here," Cady muttered to herself, surprised Stan hadn't made his appearance before now, cranky that she knew what was coming. She needed to talk to him, just not in his special way in front of the cameras. She turned to let Izzy know, but Izzy'd already deserted her reports spewing topsy-turvy out of the printer.

Stan how-are-ya'd everyone on his grand swagger through the media room. Neal stood up from his table and stepped toward him, but Stan took a sharp right and made for the tabulation door. One of the auditors opened the door for him and he strutted though it without even a glance to Neal. Must not have seen him, Cady thought.

Cady straightened the growing piles on the communications table, all neat and tidy for Stan while he chatted with the auditors. She pulled the log book forward and opened it for his photo-op inspection.

Earlier skirmishes with Stan behind her, Cady made ready for the next round. She squared her shoulders and greeted Stan when he joined her at the communications table. Even the most astute observer would never sense the earlier friction between them.

"Did you recertify the protocol this morning?" he barked. His lips smiled but the stern crease between his brows exaggerated his all-business-I'm-the-man presence. He tilted his head back. "Print the pre-election reports. Secure the auditor sign-offs. Establish communications at the polls..." *Wipe your bottom?*

"Yes, Stan, but..."

"Well then, let me see it."

"Yes, Stan. I've set out the log book for you. It's over here," surprised he recalled so much of the drill, distressed she couldn't get his attention.

"You put that vote-machine monitoring tripe in place yet?"

"Yes, Stan. First thing this morning. Stan, I need to talk with you outside."

"And how's that working for you?"

"It's working well. Stan..."

"Oh...? Well, let me know if you need anything."

"Yes, I'll do that. In fact, I've been trying to reach you. Can we talk outside?"

"No, Cady. I'm already late...I..."

"Stan, there've been a couple incidents. Most important is a security breach here on our network server. The other is one of the voters..."

"One voter. Cady, don't you have more important items on your agenda than to focus on one voter?"

"Stan, we've had a break in here. Someone set off a virus in our server."

"You sure? No. You check it out. You'll find it's one of your mega statistics programs or something. You know, Cady, didn't I warn you this morning about...?"

"Yes, Stan. We did check it out. Someone did set off a virus. And we have been breached."

"Not here, Cady. As for your one lone voter?"

"We're keeping close watch at the precincts. But I don't want you...caught...off guard. Could play out on the news..."

"I'll catch it later." Stan rushed out through the back door.

***

Shit. What now? The phone on Leonard's hip vibrated on and off for an eternity. The bastard used only the finest prepaid cell phones, so Leonard could never be sure who summoned him by screening caller phone numbers. By now he just assumed if he didn't recognize the number, the bastard was on the other end. Cretin. Steering the car with his left hand, Leonard pulled the phone from its leather pouch with his right.

"What the hell's goin' on? I'm paying you to f_____ do a job... For ME!" The last word screeched in Leonard's ear and he jerked the phone back a few inches. "UNDERSTAND? Got that? ME!"

After several moments of finger-strumming smoke gusts in the background, Leonard pulled the phone back to his ear. *Did the bastard hang up?* Could he be so lucky? *Shit no.* The quickened breathing on the other end of the line promised more.

"...And here I am now with my face plastered all over the news again because some voter doesn't know how to vote. Then I think, Leonard. Leonard's gettin' cute on me! Is that right, Leonard? Is it?"

"Shit. Is that what this is about? The vote-crossover shit?"

"You f_____ named it? F___! No more cute stuff, you hear?"

"Sure."

"No. Not 'sure.' Just remember, I'm payin' you ta do a job for me! I'm payin' f_____ generously for you ta do a good, clean job for me. Clean. Not payin' you ta be cute. Not payin' you to show how clever you are. This thing goes down, there'll be... more... than... hot molten HELL...FOR...YOU!"

Leonard waited.

"Just remember that. You're standing alone in this. Remember that too. Your head's popped up real tall and you're the only dog on the prairie. Got it? Goes down...it's you. You f_____ little pipsqueak. Idiot!"

A horn from a car in the next lane blared beside him as Leonard attempted a lane change, then swerved back into his own lane not sure of where the blast came from.

"What's that?"

"That's the moron in the car next to me. I'm on the expressway heading back to the office."

"Whaaa...? Keep it up and you won't have a car. What've you been doin' all morning? I knew you were the one causing...who knows what? Anymore booby traps out there ready to trip off?"

Leonard waited.

"Listen up here. You should've been there hours ago. You're s'posed to be monitoring those f_____ machines. What if somebody else starts lookin' into it...the...situations? ......Your little tricks are gonna work, aren't they? How will I know?"

"You won't...No one will," Leonard droned.

"When will it start?"

"What time is it? How many people voted?"

Cretin.

20

Cady shut the door on her glass house with its media spectators and harsh lights…and the persistent scrutiny of Nealspy. Here in the break room, only Izzy bowed over her errant computer tapping intermittently on her keyboard.

"Reprieve, eh, Cady?"

"Oh yes. Left Mario for wolf bait."

"You'd think. But he really just wants to fix his network."

"I know. He's all heads down in there until he works the kinks out. Just turns his back to the frenzy and zones in on his console…. How goes it with your beastie?" Cady scowled at Izzy's computer.

"This is it. Somebody slithered in and popped in this CD. So my computer starts up, looks to the CD and kicks in the virus?"

"Then what? It brings up your main screen? You can't even tell it's there, can you?"

"Worse than that, Cady. The virus mutates every few minutes as long as the computer's powered on. And if Mario hadn't told me to pull the network cable, it'd be kicking in all day."

"Ouch. For all our work to tighten up voting machine security, here we are with a snake ramming into our server."

"I was about to shut this monster down and get back to work. You want to see it in action before I do?"

"No, it's contained. We're good to go…. Izzy, I'm going to a take a minute, then I'll make my calls, try to update Stan again, follow up with Security, check with the other teams…"

"*Mierde.* Count me out. I'm gonna go help Mario."

"Good. I'll be here or in my office. Mario knows Security can catch me on my cell phone."

"I'll remind him."

"Thanks, Izzy. We'll figure out another way for you to keep a privacy computer in here. It just won't be that one."

"I never wanna touch that computer again. But as long as I can get to the network, I'm good."

"Izzy, I don't tell you and Mario often enough…"

"You do tell us, Cady, all the time. Why do you think we're still around? Sure isn't for that ol' creak walrus lips."

"Walrus what?"

"Uh, just never you mind."

"Hmm…Izzy, we've bumped up against any number of catastrophes and near misses over the last few elections. But this one's toxic. You do well to stay so cool and easy."

"Cady, you know I don't feel so cool on the inside. First this morning. Now this. I'm still all a jitters. But if I let it out just a little in here, I'm afraid I'll slip up with the auditors and cameras out there." Izzy flipped her hand toward the tabulation room.

"And we know about slip-ups. Amazing how speculation explodes warp speed across the internet."

"Yeah. We're all on high alert. We must be good, Cady, 'cause I'm watching the auditors and the reporters and…Neal. None of them seems at all interested in what we're doing, except Neal."

"It's still early. They're not tuned in yet."

"That's probably it. Cady, do you remember how awful it was that time with the crazy lawyer guy banging on the door demanding that we stop everything?"

"Oh, Izzy, I remember…."

"Let me tell you I was sure askeered then. That guy was loco. Still, Stan shouldn't have stopped the recounts no matter what."

"No, Izzy, he shouldn't. But for today, now, we may have dodged another meltdown…I hope."

"Do you have to tell the auditors? You know if you do, they'll be all a hover and it'll take us forever to figure things out."

"We'll take a few minutes, glean the facts and contain the incident before presenting them with a complete rundown… unless they smell blood."

Izzy shut down the computer and stepped quietly back into the tabulation room, holding the door from closing with a loud clank so as not to disturb Cady already deep in thought.

21

Cady ticked through her must do's. Stan. Security. Breach. Call list. Voting machine glitches. Nealspy.... She hunched her shoulders, rolled her head forward and side-to-side working at the kinks in her neck. The assault troubled her more than she let on with Izzy or Mario and she welcomed this lull away from the media entourage and from the spyman's prodding eyes.

"Okay, Cady. Get over it already. Assess, learn, improve, move on," she grumbled, flipping though the first few pages of her thin computer breach protocol. But no sooner had she scanned her to-call-in-the-event-of list than the hallway door swung open.

"Hey, Cady. How's it going?" Neal burst through the doorway with his all too jolly greeting. "Thought I might catch you here," he smiled.

Not n-o-o-w-w-w! Dammit. You, Mr. Nealspy-best-buddy-Charles, should know how it's going. You're the one chatting it up with the hacker who blasted our network. She corrected herself. *Or may have blasted us anyway. Dammit. Am I really that paranoid to suspect Neal...?* Her thoughts unnerved her. And Neal, maybe especially Neal unnerved her. *Here I am teetering on meltdown and you slink in here all fresh and...sane. What the hell was I thinking to let you in? Obviously I wasn't thinking. Shouldn't be so damned accommodating, offering you access to the whole wacky department. But Stan was so adamant. So what else is new?... Now what, Cady? Mustn't let the spy see me rattled. Or does he know already? You can do this, Cady.* Cady inhaled a long, deep breath before tilting her head back a notch and walking past Neal to the cupboards in the kitchen area.

"Hey," she countered with a mouth-only smile she didn't feel. "Well, Neal, finally taking a break?"

"Thought I'd better or my backside might permanently attach to that abominable chair out there. Not very comfortable, you know."

Hah! She chuckled to herself. "Don't want anyone falling asleep on us now, do we? We must have some clean cups around here somewhere." Cady banged one cupboard door closed and reached into another. Stretching on her toes, feeling around the top shelf she observed aloud to herself as much as to Neal, "Supplies get a little sparse around here with the 24-7 non-stop-get-it-done-and-tweaking before an election."

"Aren't there cutoffs spelled out by your election rules?" Neal probed, as much an exercise in learning as curiosity about this election.

"Yes, but those cover only a narrow definition of procedures. Ah, here's one." Cady held the mug out for Neal. "Better rinse it out. Don't know how many years of dust collected on this one."

Neal smiled wryly at the cup's crisply printed logo, *Arthur Andersen Worldwide*. "I see what you mean," he laughed.

Cady laughed along with him when she recognized the black letters etched around the mug's bone-white base. As miffed as she was by Neal's invasion of her sanctuary, she grudgingly admitted standing here with him offered up a surprisingly pleasant diversion of sorts to the day's madness. Their moment was cut short by the beep-beep of the phone. She picked up but held her breath for several seconds before answering.

"Hello, this is Cady," she spoke calmly into the phone.

Neal walked over to the sink and rinsed their mugs. His back toward Cady he stepped sideways to the coffee pot, filled Cady's mug and carried it to her. She tucked the phone under her ear and reached for the mug with both hands, absently wrapping her hands around Neal's as she jostled the mug away from him. Neal lingered, his eyes waiting for hers. She paused, looked up at him, stuttered, then smiled her thanks and returned to her phone.

Neal smiled too and continued smiling as he walked back to the pot and filled his own mug…as he leaned his back against the counter, busying himself looking around the room, reading the bold print of announcements posted on the bulletin board, and observing what he could of Cady's team in the tabulation room through the small square window in tabulation room door while Cady took her call.

"What do you mean he's not in the building?" she asked. "Then how'd he get out? Aren't guards posted at all the exits? Did you check with them?"

Neal heard the muffled male voice drone excuses on the other end of the line.

"Of course he wouldn't look suspicious." Cady was incredulous the man could have strolled though the maze of reporters, exited the media room, jaunted through the lobby, signed himself out and passed through Security at any one of the exits. She should have nabbed him herself. Now that would cause a stir. "Look, he blended in well enough with the reporters to make it through Security this morning. Probably had credentials. He could be a reporter for all we know." *Be careful, Cady. Not all scary looking little weasels are computer-geek hackers. For all she knew he could be an associate of Neal's.*

Neal listened to the voice on the other end of the line.

"Did you check your log to see who signed out?" Cady asked.

More muffled droning.

"No. There could be perfectly reasonable explanations. All we know is that he was in the off-limits area. Maybe he wanted to use the restroom. The point is he was inside a restricted area. We had a problem. He's gone. I want to know if he had anything to do with it. Or is there someone still here ready to pounce again?"

Cady's eyes narrowed, boring into Neal's. *No plausible explanation for Neal to be involved in launching a virus. Didn't the two of them both seek a successful, incident-free election this time around.* Cady pondered a moment more before concluding, *Screw communications protocol. I need information from him. In truth this has nothing to do with protocol. Involved or not, Neal's a witness. Besides he must be discreet. It wouldn't look good otherwise, for any of us.*

The voice on the other end raised an octave.

"Well, how about making the rounds again. This time, ask your people if they saw anyone *normal* leaving the building. And check the logs for recent sign-outs, actually for any sign-outs. He may have logged a wrong time. And if no one checked his ID, he could have intentionally logged out by someone else's name.

Meanwhile, Neal Charles from Tallahassee is here in the break room. Mr. Charles was talking to the man. Can you come up here now and talk with him?"

Cady listened as the voice went on, all the while studying Neal and the apparent effect her last words had on him. He raised his eyebrows briefly. Nothing else.

"Well, yes. Now. You haven't found him yet, but he could still be in the building. Or he could be coming back later. Did you check the offices? How about the restrooms? ...Yes the women's too."

Blah. Blah. Blah. Neal thought. He couldn't tell from the one-sided conversation exactly what set Cady off, but one thing was clear, by the sound of it Security dropped the ball. And he, Neal was involved somehow.

"Hmm-hmm. I want a guard posted by that door for the duration."

Drone. Drone. Neal concluded Cady had lots more stamina, knowledge, backbone than Brice gave her credit for.

"No. Not negotiable. You know the sign only keeps the honest people out. We don't have any time left to handle further proof of that. If you can't do it, I'll pull someone in from the field. We can't take more chances. We're vulnerable and now we know it. Next time it could be the whole election on the line."

Drone. More than he himself had given her credit for as well, Neal concluded. But not a lot more. Except that to his own stranger's eyes, when he thought he caught her with her guard down, she looked...ravaged.

Neal watched her, the anger she felt all but contained within her all-business voice. Hell, he was frustrated with the blockhead from Security. She must be frazzled. Yet even her imperatives were mostly smooth, professional though pointed. Every now and again pain, exasperation would break through her settled expression. *Then she'd pick herself up and paint her business face back on.*

"Hmm-hmm. Okay. Thanks. Keep me posted."

Blah. Blah. Neal didn't know her well, but he found himself impressed with all he'd seen and heard so far today.

Cady glanced at her watch. "Yes. I'll wait here with Mr. Charles," she smiled blandly up at Neal. But she really wanted to smack him down his rat hole for invading her space, encroaching on her election…intruding in her thoughts.

Neal smiled at her. Warmth. Admiration. Concern. And he was rewarded as her smile warmed in return. Then he watched her shield visibly wilt and her stoic mask lift. Her eyes reddened.

Cady turned away from Neal…fast…before…*dammit, Cady. Suck it up. Focus.* And she did. Her attention veered back to the phone, her voice still calm but less decisive than before. "But we've got schedules to meet, so it has to be soon."

Cady hung up the phone while Neal watched and waited, his eyes holding steady for hers. "What's wrong, Cady?"

"The man you were talking to earlier, friend of yours?" Cady's voice faltered.

"Wha…"

The tabulation room door swung open. Mario and Izzy breezed in, beaming. One quick look at their visitor, then at Cady with her eyes steamy red, her face ashen and her upper lip pulled inward absentmindedly nibbling away, and Izzy's smile frosted over.

"Mi madre."

Their good humor doused by Cady in trouble, they moved in to flank her. Never had they seen her so discouraged. Then the two split apart so fast Neal didn't even know he'd been shanghaied by Izzy when she pinned him in at the counter until Mario closed in on Cady, face-to-face, nose-to-nose, blocking Neal's view.

"Cady? Everything okay here?" Mario asked softly.

"Forget about here, Mario. Give me the good news. Okay?"

"You got it, *hermana*…sister." He leaned in, lowering his voice to a whisper. "You rest easy now. We got it…all. Just a simple little bleep of a program."

"I knew you did it. It's just that I…" Cady's hands smacked onto her cheeks and she laughed, hard, a big grateful belly laugh of raw relief and her eyes stung with it.

"I know, Cady. I know. Wish I could take credit, Cady, but to tell the truth, it was a stupid little nothing. Not at all technically complicated. Just a copy files. Nothing tricky, not even with the file names. Had it figured out before you finished your call to

Security. Just wanted to make sure I got it all. Good news, eh, *hermana*."

"That's the understatement of the century. No permanent damage then? What if you hadn't caught it when you did?"

"The network would've ground down to a crawl. Diagnostics would have flashed and beeped warnings. One of us would have checked it out and it'd be gone. Cady, the hacker must have been technically challenged. If he'd been after real damage, he'd have wiped out system files, reformatted drives. Would have taken forever for us to fire up again. But this was just a stupid nothing."

"Nothing, maybe. But they dinged us. Still, why go to all the trouble of sneaking in here if you're not going to do real damage?" Cady paused, shaking off a chill.

"I know, Cady. And what's scary is that we have the firewall, we have the virus protectors, but a little stinker of a program like this…well, they wouldn't stop it. Cady, you don't think this was an inside job, do you?"

"No. Never. Not that it couldn't happen, but we're all so close, we'd know."

"My take on it too. Had to ask…. C'mon, Izzy. We've got work to do."

"Security's on their way to talk with Neal. I'll be in as soon as we untangle a few loose ends. Have we restarted the uploads yet?"

The pair glared at her, then looked at each other and laughed.

Cady laughed too. "I know. I know. You say you've been a little busy? …Okay. I'll see you in a few minutes."

22

"Neal, tell me about the man..." Cady studied Neal's expression. His eyes fixed on hers, his eyebrows pinched etching two straight furrows above his nose. He actually managed to look puzzled. "Neal, you were talking to a man in the media room."

"Cady, I really don't know what you're...the fidgety little guy with the camera?"

"Go on."

"Cady, I don't know really. He was standing behind me for several minutes, so close I could hear him breathe. Then when you returned from break, well he left just when you came back into the tabulation room."

"Left?"

"Yes. I thought he was...like me. You know, someone you let in. He seemed to know his way around...through the door you showed me, the one I used to get in here."

"The No Admittance door?"

"Yes."

"No, Neal. You're the only one. Then what? You were talking with him."

"Then the door banged. I remember because it banged shut the instant you stood up from your huddle with Mario. Your face, you were alabaster white. Are you okay?"

"Neal, this isn't about me. Then what happened?"

"The door banged and the guy was back. He asked me the time. Clocks all over the place, watch on his wrist. And the guy asks me the time."

"That's it?"

"Yes, except that he was slimy with sweat..." Neal's head jerked back like he'd taken a left jab to the chin. Then his eyes found hers again. "Damn, Cady, I wasn't thinking. Just wanted to get the creep away from me so I could watch you, watch you and figure out what was wrong. But clearly, the sweat, the fidgeting, the heavy breathing.... I don't know what happened, Cady, but if it's bad...he's your man. I'm sorry, Cady."

"Sorry?"

"Yes. All that stuff with Security. The little slime's your man and he got right by me. I didn't know." Neal stepped toward her, reaching out for her hand. She let him take it without returning his hold. Instead she stood there not moving, studying his hands cradling hers before she finally pulled away.

"Not your fault, Neal. How could you know? How could any of us...that door...I..." Cady rubbed her hand. It tingled where he touched her.

"Cady, you're team. They really care about you."

"And I care about them too. Too bad the rest of it isn't.... Sorry. Not going there." She picked up a pencil and busied her hands with it, her eyes fixed on the wall clock over Izzy's computer. "Security should have been here a while ago. Wonder what's keeping them."

Neal smiled. But the smile didn't reach his eyes. And Cady thought it more melancholy than humor. She arched her eyebrows a notch and waited.

"Cady, you've all been through so much already. Believe me, I hate to do this..."

"Et tu, Neal?"

"No. I'm on your side. Cady, I am truly on your side." Neal paused for her reaction. Instead her expression was suspended in that professional demeanor of hers, her look whispering, "This is business. I'm listening. You have my undivided impersonal attention." Her perfect features as still as the face of a cameo.

"Cady...I just had a call. Bad news unfolding a few minutes ago. Some voting machine kept kicking back erroneous votes. That what this is about?"

Cady's genuine laughter surprised him.

"Why, Neal, you know I can't comment on this election." She toyed with him, considering anything on the news as fair game.

"But if I were to comment on this election, I'd say that might be old news you've got there."

"Old news?"

"Brand spankin' out of the box first thing this morning news," she said too cheerfully for comfort. "And, well, I'd tell you that Stan might be able to give you a more thorough take on it, but so far I haven't pinned him down long enough to listen." She frowned. "I apologize...caustic, uncalled for."

"Excuse me, Cady. I missed everything you said after news."

Cady rewarded him with a smile so genuine, so warm, Neal felt it pierce through his early morning resolve.

"Cady, I'm not asking you to disclose your privy information," he chuckled, wondering if she'd catch his double meaning until she laughed subtly along with him. "I'll save my battles for one I can win."

"Then what is this if not asking me about this election?"

"Tell me about the voting machines, Cady. Don't talk about today, now. Just fill me in on these machines as a reliable voting method."

Now it was Cady's turn to be surprised. "Why? What do you want to know? And why?"

"Purely personal. I know it sounds lame. Here we are in the middle of a contentious election and I'm asking you about the damned machines."

"Incredulous actually. Sort of late to be..."

"I wasn't in the thick of it until now. But I'm here now and the fracas with the voter this morning...well, I'd like to know more about the machines from the source, from you. You know, functionality, stability of equipment, specifics..."

"From the source?"

"Yeah. Well, they are your babies, aren't they? It's your department, right?"

Cady's skillfully sculpted mask peeled off along with her gloves. Her expression didn't change perceptibly, but Neal felt her sneer.

"Look, give me a few minutes, okay?" she said. "Then I'll tell you a thing or two alright."

"Sure, Cady," Neal reached over to the water cooler. His throat parched from this last encounter. For an *innocent* observer, he seemed to be wading waist deep in the muck of it.

"I mean...leave. I need to call my boss."

"Of course. You want me to wait outside here? Or you think you'll be a while?" Neal reached under his jacket for the phone buzzing on his belt and checked the caller's ID before returning to Cady's gaze.

"You need to make a few calls too? Why don't I meet you in my office? You can use the phone in there. Better reception than your cell. And we can spread out without disturbing Izzy's filing system here," Cady drew an imaginary line above the long worktable cluttered with file folders and a mass of computer reports, mostly scribbled across in varying shades of red and blue and green and purple fine-point fluorescent highlighter. Sticky notes poked out along the side of the table closest to Izzy's computer.

"You sure?" He smiled devilishly. "Nothing in there I shouldn't get into?"

"You do and I'll break your fingers," she countered.

"Hmm. I believe you might."

"Wait. Neal. Better meet back here after all. I forgot about Security." Cady looked at her watch. "I wonder what's keeping them."

23

"Stan, this is important…" Cady's tone suggested a calm she didn't feel. "There is no question, we've been breached. It's contained now. But a man, at least we think it was a man, got through Security and powered up a virus on the break-room computer."

"What the hell! What precinct?" Stan sputtered over the phone line.

"No. No precinct, Stan. Here. Our network server. In this building. Someone apparently slipped in through the media room and launched a worm from right here in our break room. He scored a direct hit."

"I told you, you need better controls. What's next? Tonight's tabulation?"

"No, Stan. No lasting damage. Mario caught it right away."

"Good thing *he's* on top of things. Why the hell didn't you tell me, Cady?"

"Stan…" *Ten, nine, eight, seven…*

"Well?"

"Stan, actually…" *Six, five, four…*

"It's irresponsible. You know how I don't like surprises, Cady."

"Yes, Stan." *No point in whipping this dead donkey again, Stan…… Said it. Memo'd it. E-mailed it. Keep your phone on, Stan. Batteries charged, Stan. Tell Juan where you're off to on Election Day, Stan. What's your itinerary, Stan? I need to keep you in the loop, Stan. Well, step to the back of the line, Stan. You're not going to ruin my perfect day.*

"Cady, you said a man…"

"I saw a man come into the media room through the No Admittance door. You know the door into our offices."

"You saw him? You sure?"

"I can't be sure he's the guy. I called Security, but he left the building before they could nab him."

"You think? You don't know?"

***

Stan phoned Brice as soon as he finished with Cady. "Must tell you, Brice, I'm more than a little concerned," Stan whined.

"Now what, Stan? Just what now?"

"Somebody broke into our computer room. Set off a virus."

"What? The tabulation room?"

"Yeah."

"Let's get this straight. What you're sayin' is you can't finagle my man into your girlie's play box. But she went ahead and let somebody else in to f____ with her computers?"

"Yeah. Well, not exactly. They broke in through a computer station outside the tabulation room. That's how they did it."

Stan pulled the phone away from his ear and glared at it, the dead line growled back at him.

24

"Now, Neal, you were *as*suming..." Cady bristled, standing tall by bracing one hand, fingers extended, arm stiff on the edge of Izzy's cluttered worktable, puffing her shoulders a fraction higher. But for a few...several inches, she'd face the spy nose-to-nose.

"All I said was I want to know more about these voting machines. They're in your cybersphere. I *as*sume you're in charge, you acquired them, manage them...fix them. Yes?"

"Why, Neal," Cady smiled. "You do slice down to the sweetmeat," she drawled softly. If she could spit solder she would. Instead she yanked out Izzy's chair and plopped into it, hard.

Neal walked over to the counter and poured their coffee. He set it on the table in front of Cady where he pushed aside clusters of printouts, careful not to commingle them or alter their relative positioning. "Yeah. Well, they are your babies, aren't they? Your department, right?" He asked, making himself comfortable in a chair across the table.

"My babies? Let me tell you about my babies!"

Neal watched Cady's lip curl in a sneer so fierce he could feel her snarl. "*Touch-y* subject?" Neal chuckled. "Sorry. What'd I say?"

"Well, Neal, comfy up 'cause I'm about to tell you. My department? Yes. My voting machines? Not a chance. Never."

"I don't get it."

"Ah! There you go. Neither do I. None of us does. Neal, these junkers are invariably blamed on me, but no..." She repeated with more emphasis. "I didn't get any of these machines. We looked at several vendors but ElecTron wasn't even on our radar. Didn't solve our problem."

"Problem?" Neal leaned forward, resting his forearms on the table.

"Yes, Neal. You need to define your problem before you can fix it, don't you?" she asked with more sarcasm than intended. "Sorry, I'm so over this whole…. Anyway, we said our problem is to reliably count votes and prove the number of votes we count is correct today, correct tomorrow and tomorrow and tomorrow. One voter --- one vote, one count. Every time."

"Makes sense even to me. And ElecTron?"

"Not even close. Then and now, they're consistently shaky, erratic, quality unconscious. Too unstable. Problems with all their voting machines, including those first touch screens we got stuck with. Problems with their optical ballot scanners. And, Neal, this morning's wake-up call with the voting errors…not the first time."

"At least the error counted for the right side," Neal laughed. "Get it? 'Right' side?"

"How about this, I'm seeing *red!* How can you? Does it really matter who wins if our vote, our voice, our rights are violated?"

"Whoa! Hold on there. I get it. Really."

"Okay, so maybe a little humor's a good thing. Especially right now…. Where were we?"

"ElecTron doesn't solve your problems. But bring it down a couple notches for me to understand. Okay?"

"The irony here, Neal, is that I think you do understand. I think at the purest level, everyone understands. It's just that what I'm saying seems so implausible you can't believe you understand."

"Yogi logic… Cady, you too young for Yogi Berra?"

"Nobody is." The caught-ya smile brushing her lips was not lost on him. "I'll have another go at it. What do you expect from your bank account?"

"My bank? Count my money of course. Keep it safe. Track what I spend…."

"Yes. Count your dollars. Tell me, Neal, what's the first thing you do when you find an error? Look at the check you wrote? In the absence of a check, say when the transaction's a credit card, you look at the original receipt you signed. Right? Or do you simply take the bank's word for it?"

"No. Of course not."

"So how can we figure out the votes are right if we don't have the voters' receipts, their ballots? Tell me, what's more important, your checking account or the fair and honest election of our president, our governor?"

"So, why did you...uh, Miami go with ElecTron?"

"Surely being from Tallahassee you already know the answer."

"Cady, I really haven't a clue and I'm not sure anyone else up there does either."

"Okay, one fine day Stan called us in for a meeting and led off with 'Whaddya think about ElecTron's voting machines?' Said the Florida Representative of County Government recommended ElecTron. Said we were going with ElecTron. Period. Stan rammed it through procurement no questions asked. We hadn't even seen ElecTron's proposal."

"Can he do that?"

"He did it. But clearly, he didn't do it on his own. For one thing he's not that savvy. Stan's watch, Stan's call, Stan's budget. But he took orders from a higher power. Think, Neal. Who protects him now? And while we're at it, who skewed the interpretation of Florida's Election laws to allow broken elections with broken machines to stand?"

"You believe that higher power was the governor?"

"Neal, when something seems irreconcilably illogical, such as Stan's selecting *any* system, especially one that isn't right for the task. It probably is...illogical, that is......So why'd he do it? Who gains? Who has the power? ...Neal, who rules everything election, every county, every precinct?"

"Cady, do you have proof?"

"I've said too much already."

Neal sat silent for a moment, head bent in thought. Cady watched his shoulders stoop forward and his chest cave, like air rushing out of the last life vest on his sinking ship. And she was sad she had been the one to puncture it. Then just as soon as she recognized it for what it was, it was over. His eyes found and held hers.

"I...a day of profundity." His eyes smiled into hers. "Cady, afterward, when this is all over...... Would you...could we..."

"Neal...I...No..." Her own eyes held fast. "Well, they're going to wonder just what it is I do around here if I don't show my face in that monkey cage out there. Can you wait here for Security?"

"Sure." Neal watched her slip her cardkey in and out of the lock beside the tabulation room door. "Cady. How many on your team? I'll buy lunch." He glanced at his watch. "Closer to dinner, isn't it? Will you have time? Cuban or Italian?"

On her way through the door, Cady turned her head back over her shoulder and tossed an eyes-arcing-to-the-ceiling smile his way. The door and its cardkey lock clamped shut behind her.

25

"How'd you wrap it up with your Mr. Charles?" Mario asked casually, his eyes not leaving the computer screen at his console, the innocence in his demeanor doing little to mask his curiosity.

"Brrr, it's cold in here." Cady ignored Mario's question, recognizing his feigned nonchalance for what it was. He already knew something and wanted more. Mario was adept at tossing out a question while holding back on specifics. Generally he succeeded in gleaning a wider range of information than he might otherwise by pursuing explicit details.

She wheeled her chair closer to Mario's before sitting down and rubbing her arms to ward off the chill.

"Izzy left to tell you the latest flash reports were done but hightailed it back here. Said you and spyguy were exchanging blows."

"Close. He just wanted information about the voting machines."

"Poor guy. Your evil twin spring into action?"

"Felt like it." Cady rubbed her arms again. "Did someone turn down the thermostat in here?"

"No. I don't think so. It's all that heat you generated in the break room, must have worn off and left you chilled." He looked over at her, "Where's your jacket?"

"Dunno. Gone. My office maybe."

"Want one of the guys to fetch it for you?"

"No. Thanks. It'll turn up." Cady rubbed her arms again. "Mario, I did let the spinmeister get to me a bit more than I should have. Blabbed more than I should have too. I dredged up all the old muck. He gave me nothing. But, Mario, hmm-hmm it felt good." Cady laughed aloud. "...If he only knew."

A MARGIN OF ERROR

"Knew what? That ElecTron's machines are pieced together with superglue and rubber bands? Or that stinkbugs clutter their program code? Or that we got zapped...in here?"

"I forgot about the rubber bands." Cady looked around the tabulation room. "So where is Izzy?"

"She scooted out the other door. Didn't want to interrupt you and nice guy again by going through the break room." Mario turned toward Neal's corner. "But...he's fair game now."

Cady followed his gaze to see Neal holding the No Admittance door for Izzy. The two of them bent toward each other laughing over some shared secret before leaving the room together. Cady tugged on her ring, pulled it back and forth and back along its chain. "Mario, how long did it take after Natalia, I mean, when did you start dating again?"

***

Dammit, Stan, you can't run an election from your car or whatever. Cady speed-dialed his number again. *Dammit. Okay...*She dialed Juan.

"Have you heard from Stan yet?"

"Jes, Cady. He was here for a few minutes. He got a call and he left."

"Did you tell him I need to talk with him?"

"Jes, Cady. I did! Cady I tell him already to phone chou. He just left. He took his call and he left."

"Juan, I don't want him learning these things over the local news."

"Jes, Cady, I know."

"Juan, do me a favor. Next time you see him, please just call me. I'll either be in the tabulation room or I'll have my cell phone on."

"I'll do it, Cady."

"Okay, Juan...Thank you. I'll keep trying his cell."

***

Cady leaned forward over the communications table, glancing briefly at the upload summary information, before straightening the pages of her most recent report, tapping them lengthwise against the tabletop. Then she stapled the report together, rechecked the date-time stamp, and scribbled her initials beside it.

The sudden blaze of floodlights outside in the media room forewarned the surge of commotion and Cady was again thankful for the glass wall insulating the tabulation room from the brouhaha of the war room outside. *Maybe Stan's in the media room. Maybe the little man is back. Maybe Security apprehended him. Hah!* Cady perused the room beyond her window. *No. Nobody of interest. Neal's back at his post. Izzy nabbed him for a while, but he's back now.* Cady smiled, perplexed, not knowing what to do with that particular Neal-Izzy revelation or her peculiar reaction to the spy.

Cady concluded the scurrying outside had nothing to do with her election system or her team, then went back to her reports. She flipped through several pages, pausing briefly at one page before stacking the report on the growing mound of papers labeled Flash Reports. Then she stepped a couple of paces sideways along the length of the table to the black binder labeled Election Protocol. She thumbed through several pages outlining the election system technical procedures, regulations, and requirements, turning to the section documenting the flash upload reports. She located the precincts printed in the upload report just completed and logged the date, time and total number of records transferred. She browsed through another few pages before closing the binder and resting her hand lightly on the front cover.

First the residual votes, then the voting errors. Now she needed Izzy to work on trapping another problem, one even more menacing if her suspicions played out. Vote counts must go up, not down. Trends plod forward. They don't reverse. It seemed implausible they hadn't flushed this kink out of the voting machines during their pre-election tests.

Cady glared at the big fat black book. She wanted to pick it up and smash it against the wall. All that damned protocol. It could save them from themselves. It could save them from an intruder…as it ultimately had from the virus, of course with Mario at the helm. But could it save them from their vendor's flawed computers? They'd accepted ElecTron's assurances that all systems were upgraded, identical. They had to. But if the errors she suspected hadn't resided in the program during their tests then…it would mean someone breached the voting machines as well as their network server. *How will you know its right?* The words ricocheted back and forth in her mind like a bad CD on a bumpy road.

Cady shook her head.

Back to the damned black book, Cady. Cady looked over at Neal. He was busy talking on his cell phone, his back toward her. She grabbed the book and headed to the worktable in the break room to study her numbers more closely before frazzling Izzy with yet another red flag.

26

Cady slammed the election protocol binder on the breakroom table, wishing she'd chosen another color. Black, so ominous...she cringed...so fitting. Next election, that is if...*if* she stuck around, she'd choose another color.

Cady flipped the hefty book open to the flash upload tab, snapped open the rings and spread several pages of the log on the table in front of her. She located her pet control precincts and tore one page from each of three colored legal pads. One colored worksheet for each precinct: 1. Fire Station-ecru, 2. Church-blue, 3. School-gray. She didn't label her worksheets. Next she copied a column of numbers from the log to each of her corresponding worksheets, her left index finger inching over one digit at a time. When satisfied her worksheets contained enough information, she closed the binder and pushed it to the side of the table. She'd cart it back in a few minutes. Then she went back to her numbers, one page at a time: ecru, blue, gray. As if staring at them would change the results, as if colors could make them better. She slapped her worksheets on the table.

"As for you..." Cady stood up and reached for the binder to return it to the tabulation room, when the hallway door swung open.

"Here. Let me help you with that," Neal offered, holding his hands out to the binder snugged up in Cady's arms, pressed tight against her chest.

"Excuse me?"

"Here. I'll help," he reached for her binder.

"I think not." Cady jerked her arms away from him, as close to being indignant as she had been all day considering the man's nerve. Either he assumed she was naive enough to fall for his charms or he thought she was too stupid to realize the book gave him the full scoop on their entire election. Didn't matter. Didn't work. She jerked again for affect, twisting her body away from him, shifting and tightening her grip. But the cumbersome binder slipped, its sharp plastic edge slicing a tiny nick in her finger.

"Ouch!" The binder slipped again.

"Here, Cady." Neal grabbed for it but was too late. Cady's big fat abominable book toppled to the floor, crashing in a flurry of hen-scratched colored papers comingled with bold black on crisp white. Cady tumbled after it, onto her hands and knees scooting across the floor, scooping up papers. Neal followed her lead, shuffling and stacking. Each consumed with the mission, neither conscious of the other's path as they circled the floor crawling on their knees, spiraling their way toward the center, gathering and scooping and shuffling, closing in on the book and each other…closer…closer…until the two forces collided, bumping heads in the middle of the floor over Cady's big fat black book.

But for Neal's one quick gasp, the room hushed and so did they. Then slowly, imperceptibly, Neal tilted his face into Cady, breathing in her hair, her fragrance, her own quickened breaths. "Cady…"

Cady leaned into to him, her eyes closed and she rubbed her cheek against his lips, closer, closer, tighter, her lips ever closer to his.

"Cady……"

"Neal, I…no," she pulled away from him. But her voice was raw and this time the chill of her words failed to mask the heat in her thoughts.

"I know so, Cady. Not here. Not now. But you know it too, don't you…Cady?"

Dammit. "I know no such thing. What I do know, Mr. Charles, is that your making moves won't work on me…not for this."

"Cady, I'm sorry I…… Wait. Work on you for what?"

She pushed back and plopped on the floor in the middle of her papers. "You know what. This, all of it, it's off limits and you know it. You think you can stroll in here all power and pinstripes and…and you can just mesmerize me with those awful eyes and take what you need."

Neal sat beside her, reaching for her hand, holding it firmly in his own two hands. "What? No, Cady. I...I don't know. I was only thinking how heavy it looks."

"Right. And I'm Archimedes. Now if you don't mind..." She yanked her hand back.

"I do, Cady," he smiled, knowing he wasn't alone in this. She felt it too.

"Tell me, what were you going to do once you got hold of it?"

Neal shook his head. "Cady, if you want to confuse me, well done then. I'm confused."

"Really? You don't know what this is?" She latched on to the open binder trying to keep the remaining pages from spilling to the floor.

"No, Cady, I don't."

"Lesson number one this morning?" Cady lowered her voice. "Wow. Sorry. This is the election protocol binder."

"Here, Cady? Pilfered from your sanctuary?"

"Swell."

Neal laughed. "I won't give way your secrets, Cady. Especially those I share."

"Oh, my sincerest gratitude, kind sir."

"I see. Rougher day on the inside than it appears on the outside, yes?" He reached over and rubbed her arm. His hand rested on hers.

"Aye." She yanked away from him and started sorting through her papers.

"I'm sorry, Cady. I'm doing this badly. Wrong place, wrong time...but..."

"Wrong person, Neal. Now, you need something? Or did you come back here just to..."

He handed her a stack of papers. "Yes, I...but now that we're here and since you've already broken your laws, how about...that is without divulging any privileged information...how about filling me in on more of the detail here?" He reached over and strummed the binder spread open on her lap, but pulled back when her eyes narrowed.

"Neal, I've got...I don't have time for... Swell," she rose to her knees and slammed the book down on the table. "You've got ten minutes. Then you're to march out of here and leave me alone," she looked over at the clock above Izzy's computer. "Until I figure something out."

"What's that?"

"You never mind." Cady turned away from him and toward the table. "You see this? It's all here in this big fat damned black book," Cady slapped the binder, "...all the nauseatingly minute details of each trivial step of every procedure from the inordinately complex to the mundane, Neal. It's all spelled out here in monotonous and laborious detail."

"Got it. At least that much anyway."

"Look at this." Cady flicked the binder. "All this detail, logs and procedures and..." She tugged at a few tabs. "...and planned or unplanned communications with the pecincts or vendors or whatever. It's all logged here. No action or inaction is trusted to memory."

"No action?"

"None. Not if it has to do with the actual election. And see this?" She paged to another section. "Checklists. All checklists. A veritable proliferation of checklists in protracted, intricate specificity down to the most simplistic level:

STEP 1. TURN ON THE COMPUTER.
STEP 2. VERIFY DATE AND TIME.
STEP 3. ENTER YOUR ELECTION DAY PASSWORD.

And so on. And you know what? We still can't guarantee we'll get it right. Look at this. All of it and...and..."

"And you're dealing with a serious case of overkill, aren't you?"

"Yeah and I'll tell you why, Neal. Because we just keep trying to make it work. Besides we all learned that the second we sidestep a checklist, especially when election activity heats up, when we're 24-7-plus dog-tired and mostly when we need to be dead-on precise, that's *The Existential Moment*. We skip a beat, miss a step."

"Then what?"

"Well, it might be nothing. But then again, it might be a bona fide catastrophe, like deleting a series of files...ah...ballots that can't be recreated or forgetting to include a precinct in our votes-to-count upload parameters."

"Or not counting a box of ballots?"

"Exactly, Neal. And that's precisely *The Moment* it all comes crashing down. *The Moment* we can't take back, when an innocent blunder ruins an election."

"Is your whole team paranoid, Cady? Or just you?" Neal hoped to lighten the mood, but she was already picking up speed on the downhill run, in fact had been before his intrusion.

"Paranoid? Neal, every election we discover more kinks with our machines. You already know about the big one, the no paper-proof-count-em-again-Sam ballots. But do you know that when some of these machines hiccup, there's no way to recoup, no way to scoop up the ballots and do it again? The input's gone."

"Back to that again, are we."

Cady sighed. "No. We moved on. We're just trying to make sure its right." *Dammit. How will you know it's right?*

Neal watched the pain cross Cady's eyes, "Cady? You okay?"

"Sorry, Neal. Yes, I'm fine. It's just for the last couple of weeks, I…Izzy and I've deflected a flurry of crank phone calls. And this morning, early, they crossed over…."

"For weeks? Cady? Did you call the police?"

"No. Besides, until this morning the calls were creepy little annoyances, that's all."

"Tell me about this morning. How was it different?"

"I can't now, Neal. Let's just say he got in my election face…and then the hacker…and now…" Cady said softly. Then she picked herself up again. "Okay. Okay. Back to Protocol 101. Talk about head-knocking, cage-rattling near fisticuffs to herd all the players into the same pen, on the same page. We've come a long way. Even so, the failure rate is appalling."

"How does a machine failure affect the outcome?"

"Ha. What kind of machine? Do we even know the machine failed, that it didn't count all the votes? Is there a real voter marked ballot? Otherwise, we won't know because…*no voter-marked paper…no proof.*"

"Okay, Cady. You made your point. What's different this go 'round?"

"Two biggies, Neal. Trust."

"You said two, Cady."

"Yes. We learned the hard way, we can't trust Florida's Secretary of State and we can't trust our vendor." Cady looked to the floor, but not soon enough to hide the red splotching her cheeks. She'd gone too far.

"Cady," Neal covered her hand again with his own. "Just tell me, me and your big black book. No one else."

Cady silently surveyed her wobbly election strewn about the floor. *You're encroaching, Neal. You think you can just mosey in here with your Gulf Stream eyes and a smile and get anything you want. Well you can't. I don't care who you are. Look at this mess! It could implode any minute. And you're making nice…… You really want to see what we're dealing with here? Tallahassee, the governor, the Secretary of State, Stan, they didn't care. What about you, Neal? You're from State… My side? We'll see about that…… Watch out, Cady. Watch out.*

Neal studied Cady's face. Stoic, professional, but beneath the surface…he hoped he might learn to read her. Like a chameleon her expression changed. Not in her face. Her face remained frozen, controlled. Only her eyes flashed…warning, anger, fear, puzzlement, acceptance…cunning…caution…cunning.

"Okay, Cady, let me start. The Secretary of State approves the voting machines before you or any other Florida county can purchase them for your election."

"Yes, Neal. He certifies the machines work accurately for counting and recounting votes. One voter, one vote, every time."

"And?"

"And again and again he says the machines are sound and any problems we have with the machines, he blames on voter ineptitude."

"That's not right. Is it, Cady?"

"No. But as long as he tests the machines following ElecTron's guidelines, using ElecTron's ballots and ElecTron's test data…well, the machines test out okay."

"Cady? Even I know there's a big difference between reaffirming a machine will count votes on a couple of standard ballots and proving beyond a doubt the process will never break under any circumstances, no matter what the ballot looks like."

"Neal, you've been holding out on me."

"Not about the big things…" His eyes smiled to hers, but

then he looked away. "Cady, there are things you...I......Cady you do more real testing, don't you?"

"We do. But then again, we only test 2% of the machines before each election."

"What? That means ninety-eight percent of your machines just skate on through? No wonder we've got snags. Can't you test a bigger chunk? ...No, don't tell me. You don't have the staff, resources, time, budget?"

Maybe you're more than so much fluff, Nealspy. "Well, that and it's Florida's election law."

Neal shook his head. "And when you find a problem like this morning's crossed voter?"

"No mulligans in elections, Neal. There is no last minute fix."

Neal looked over at Cady's colored worksheets, "So what are you working on now?"

You spy! Charm me with your gentle whiskey-and-grit banter won't you, then whack! "Here," Cady scooped up her colored worksheets, pressing them into his outstretched hand, her own hand warm where it brushed against his. Miffed a careless graze of flesh on flesh should rush tremors through her arm. "You figure it out. I'm going to return the protocol binder to its post, check on things in the tabulation room. I'll be back in a few minutes. Leave my papers here on your way out," Cady directed, yanking the book off the table, shaking her wayward hand from the wrist as she passed through the tabulation room door.

27

Suits skittered across the room outside Cady's window. Inside, the relative calm of her tabulation room contrasted sharply with its secret of jumbled digits twisting in erratic trends of ricocheting results. And now there was Neal back at his post, watching it all come tumbling down. *You'll know soon enough best-buddy. Not all sunshine and flowers. When I locate Stan, I'll fill him in. Maybe he'll pass it on to you. Until then...until we can figure this out, I'm as much in the dark as you are...really.* She picked up a new report from the growing mound and nonchalantly checked a few numbers, hoping her casual look masked the clenching of her throat muscles squeezing tighter with each report.

Across the room, Izzy's mouse glided in sweeping geometric patterns, over and around an imaginary circle on her tabulation room desk, clicking here and there. Then with a final click-click she pushed back in her chair, stood up and ambled in Cady's direction. No quick movements to alert the auditors or excite the media hovering outside. An anxious look now...they'd fare better by throwing fresh chum at a school of hungry sharks. If the watchdogs smelled blood they'd beat down the door and still there would be nothing to tell. This moment Cady's hunches were just that, hunches, a gnawing deep in her gut, certainly based on a surplus of numeric trends past and present, but nothing concrete or provable. *How will you know it's right? ...How will you know it's WRONG!* If Cady ever found that evil man, she'd reconfigure his hardware.

Cady squinted toward the floodlights at the huddle of auditors milling around inside her glass wall. Fortunately for Cady's team, the quintet overseeing this triage weren't overly interested in the goings-on this early. As long as Cady's team followed protocol, didn't appear rattled, the auditors remained calm, the media ignored them.

Cady caught Izzy's eye then shot a look toward the stack of flash reports as Izzy brushed past on her way to the printer station. With that, Izzy stopped briefly, smiled, "How's it going?" Not waiting for an answer, Izzy offhandedly picked up the top report on the pile closest to Cady before continuing toward the printers. Cady watched Izzy glance casually toward the auditors and beyond to the bustle in the media room before picking up a sizable stack of papers from the printer. Then she passed Cady again before disappearing behind the line of computer cabinets that bisected the computer room.

***

Izzy's phone rang from somewhere under the pile of rubble on the break room table. Save these few brief stints at her newly installed notebook computer here and her too-public computer in the tabulation room, she'd zoomed around on her feet most of the day. No way was she about to stand up to answer the bleeping phone. She pushed herself back from her computer and seat-wheeled her chair backwards until it bumped into her worktable. Then she whirled herself around and flung a few computer listings aside searching for the phone underneath.

"So that's where you are," Izzy said to the phone. "I wondered how I'd explain losing another phone to Cady."

Izzy flipped the phone open with one hand while shuffling a small clearing on the table with the other in case she needed writing space. "Hello? Izzy Palacio here."

"How'd you like your little gift this morning?" the voice mewled, strained, anemic.

Izzy held the phone tighter to her ear, "Sorry? I can't hear you. Speak louder."

"I said how'd you like your gift?" The voice teased, louder this time, familiar.

"No. No gifts. No I didn't get one gift this morning. Did someone send me a gift?" Izzy asked gaily. A token from one of her friend-boys? Small, frilly little gifts, sometimes funny gifts, nothing serious, after all she wouldn't commit. Still they liked sending them. She liked receiving them. Maybe this was one of her friend-boys now disguising his voice, playing tricks on her. Shame on him for calling her today.

"I've got more for you. I've got so much more for you, little perfeccionista."

"*Qué?* Oh, there you're wrong. You must not know me after all. I'm the last girl in the world to be perfect," she laughed.

"I'm watching you…watching you, just you all day, all the way. I…I'll show you…you'll see…you and me."

Izzy yanked the phone away from her ear and glared at it for a few seconds, catching her breath. Then pulled it back again, "Who is this?"

"Oh, you know me. You'll figure it out, won't you? You know everything, tell everything, don't you?"

"I don't know what you're talking about."

"You will. You will, little perfeccionista. Didn't feel so nice, did it. But I'm gonna feel real nice, just watching…waiting and watching. Look up and I'll be there for you, sugar."

The line went dead as did Izzy's Election Day resolve. She buried her head on the stacks of papers on her worktable and sobbed.

***

Cady waited several minutes after Izzy left before plucking a page out of the forms section of the protocol binder and abandoning her post. All auditor eyes focused her way. She smiled pleasantly, her best nothing-amiss smile, then strolled over to Mario's console.

"So far so good here, Cady." Mario gave Cady a verbal snapshot of the upload progress. The two chatted, smiling now and then until the auditors lost interest. Mario, knowledgeable, calm, focused, perceptive. He'd felt her tension rise through several checkpoints as she reviewed the tallies. He kept on task, but more attentive to detail in those areas of primary vulnerability, if that was possible. "Precinct uploads are back on track. So far the actual number of votes remains comparable with numbers expected based on registered voters at each precinct."

"Thanks, Mario."

"Let me know if there's anything else you need, Cady."

Cady's hand rested briefly on the back of Mario's chair. "I will, Mario."

Mario looked up, his mouth drawn down at the corners. "You feel it too, don't you, Cady?"

"I don't just feel it, Mario. We've got some real live bleeps here." Cady set the vendor contact form on the console next to him. "As soon as you can break free, call ElecTron. Voting machines in three control precincts are rejecting votes."

"Wha...? Which ones? Some of those machines are interactive. They beep the voter when there's an error. The voter corrects it or the ballot won't go through."

"Tell the voting machines that, chico. Rejects are trickling through in small numbers now. Still, any number is significant."

"Doesn't make sense, Cady."

"No, it doesn't. Anyway, it's not a showstopper...yet." Cady paused for a moment scanning the media room and the auditors for hints of rising interest. "Not enough ruckus for them. They've lost interest. I'd like to keep it that way."

"Sure thing."

"You can use the phone in your own office. No need to shake the hive just yet. At least not 'til we get our facts sorted out."

"You can say that again. We'll be all tizzied up in a daylong bluster of hot air and black-suited talking-head blurs while they buzz back and forth churning out flurries of paper."

"Mario, you know you're the one I can always count on. So gentle, so steady, so genuine, so unstressed and then kabang." Cady teased, but her smile was heartfelt.

Mario chuckled softly. "Read you loud and clear, chica." Another chuckle before turning back to his console. "For you, I'll notify ElecTron of the rejections, document the contact person, recap our full conversation in detail and file my incident report," his voice low. "Then I'll update your Mr. Charles on all of it."

"Hmm-hmm. That's nice. Get him to sign-off on it too, okay? He can take over for both of us." They laughed softly together.

With that, Cady stifled an apparent yawn before announcing, "It's coffee time for me. I'll be back in a few minutes." But first she walked over to the chatting auditors. "We've gotten the latest flash report. I've filed it with the others."

"Thanks, Cady. We'll take a look at it." Cady knew they wouldn't. And they knew Cady knew. A little game they played, make nice, look good, look concerned, look busy, look...*important*. Don't ask, don't tell and you won't have to actually know anything. So long as her team followed protocol, it must be right, they all signed off on it. A good election. Prior debacles notwithstanding.

"I'm off for some coffee. You all need a break?"

"Thanks. No. Not time. Wouldn't look too good for us to disappear in the middle of all this."

"Right. Catch you later." Cady headed after Izzy, around the computer cabinets, out the back door into their break room.

28

Izzy lurched from her chair and tumbled into Cady's arms in a deluge of tissues and tears. And Cady knew. The viper hurt her again.

"Screw the election!"

"C-cady…you…you don't mean that. You…you know you don't. We've got so much to do with all this…to find out what…" Izzy waved her arms over random piles of computer reports littering the break room table. Then she choked before the tears surged again, huge rasping sobs.

"Well, I do mean it, Izzy. How about this, you're what's important here. Right here, now. You, your safety, your…peace. They're what count now."

Izzy leaned into Cady, her cheeks flushed, chest heaving in quick ragged breaths. Cady snuggled her close, consoling, murmuring, "Okay, Izzy. It'll be okay. Hush, now, Izzy. Shhh. Just words. Just horrible words. Horrible. But they can't hurt you. Words can't hurt you, Izzy. Hush, now, Izzy. It'll be okay. "

"C-cady, he said…he said he's in our computers and we can't get him out and we'll never find him."

"The virus? Did he say anything about the virus?"

"M-maybe. No. I think. But, he knows me, Cady. He knows about the election and I'm so tired, Cady."

"Isabel-l-l-a!" Cady reached for mother pitch.

"I…I'm afraid, Cady."

"Isabella, stop. Don't give in to it. Don't let it take control of you. Izzy. Isabella? Can you remember what else he said?" Cady's voice was stern, unsympathetic, willing Izzy to regain control.

"…It's just I'm scared. I'm so scared, Cady," Izzy whimpered.

"Of course you are, Izzy. Today's the last day. This is it. We'll change your phone numbers. We're done with him."

"But I...we've got..."

"Izzy, listen to me. Let's go to my office. You can lie down, take a time out. That brilliant brain of yours does us no good if it's stuck in frazzle mode. What if you pick the wrong keys...you know like Delete instead of Insert. We're all exhausted and this is just the idiocy to push us, anyone of us over the edge."

Fresh tears streaked down Izzy's cheeks.

"Look, Izzy. If he's on the other end of the phone line, we know he's not standing outside the door."

"But what if he is, Cady? If he set the virus he..."

"I thought about that, Izzy...I... Did he say anything else?"

"Said when he gets through with me, people will cross the street to let me pass just so they won't have to look at me." Izzy sobbed, long, retching sobs that left her winded and gasping for air.

"Oh, Isabella... Don't give in to it. It's not true. He's a phone creep."

"How do you know, Cady? How do you know he's not standing in the parking lot right now? How do you know he's not at my front door right now waiting for me to go home?"

"I don't. But freaks like that...he's using the phone for his weapon. Look, I'm calling Security. Let them know what's going on."

Izzy sniffled her response.

"Izzy. Please. I know it's hard, but try to push him out of your mind. We'll go to my office. Close the blinds tight to keep the sun out...one of us will sit with you, Izzy. You can rest."

"Cady, you know I can't do that. I've got those reports...you need the graphs...and Neal's dinner. It's almost time...for Neal...and I've still got stuff from this morning...and..."

"Izzy. We're fine. I'll track the upload reports. If I see a bigger jump in the numbers, I'll pull the machines offline. When you feel better..."

"What you're saying is that you don't need me."

"Isabella! Izzy, I'm saying we've got time. You don't want to risk slipping up because your brain's on overload. I need you sharp."

"Cady..."

"Oh, Izzy, I'm so sorry. I should have taken the bastard more seriously. This on top of everything else, the glitches…"

"Glitches? With elections? No-o-o!" Izzy stretched out her words.

"There's the Izzy we know," Cady laughed softly.

"I'm sorry, Cady. I know I'm being a big baby but…"

"No, Izzy. You're not. You're simply normal. No. You're stronger. Izzy, don't forget Mario's taking you home tonight. Or maybe you'll want to stay with your family. Or you can stay with me."

"That's silly. How do you think I'll feel when the guys find out I can't take care of myself? I'll be okay. Really."

"No. And, Izzy, when you're up to it…will you be okay to talk with Security?"

"Y-y-yes, Cady."

"Izzy. We can do this. Now please see if you can…"

"I'm staying right here, Cady. What are you going to do?"

"Call Security. Stan. Get back to these numbers."

"Hmph! You and the numbers? I feel better n-o-o-o-w," Izzy arced her eyes. "No, Cady, I do. We can do this, Cady," Izzy sniffed, wiping hot tears from her cheeks.

***

The security guard flipped through his notepad for a blank page then commenced snapping questions, all relevant, but not well-timed. "You recognize the caller? …Break up with your boyfriend? …Mouth off at anyone?"

"I…I…" Izzy sobbed again.

"Stop! Can't you see you're…" Cady paused then began again, more measured, more reasoned. "I know you're doing your job…but no. The answer to all your questions is no. If anything, this crackpot has to do with the stuff this morning. We find our virus-guy, we find this nutcase."

"What makes you think that?"

"Because this morning, the calls this morning were very pointed, election specific. And now I wonder if Izzy and I are the only ones. Has someone gotten hold of the precinct's on-call list?

...Well, even if they have, our addresses are unpublished. At least that's still sacred."

"How'd he know who I am, Cady? Where I am? How'd he know MY number, Cady? I'm so scared." Izzy's shoulders started heaving again. Cady's arm shot around her.

"I know, Izzy. I know." Cady patted Izzy's shoulder softly before giving it a gentle squeeze. "We'll figure it out."

"Okay. I've done all I can here," the guard snapped his notepad shut. "I'll call in a trace to her phone."

"Mine too. Did you get Izzy's cell phone number?" Cady asked. "Look, we're beyond Internal Security now. Let's get the police involved. See about tracing all calls to the personal cell phones, home phones. I don't even know if that's possible. And trace any outside calls to the phones in here and in the tabulation room."

"Yeah, Cady. You sure? About the police?"

"Yes," Cady turned her attention back to Izzy. "Izzy, don't answer your phone anymore. I'll ask one of the guys to screen your calls. At least that way..."

"I'll take it, Izzy. Don't you worry," Mario offered from the tabulation room door on his way into the break room.

"Thanks, Mario. Okay, Izzy. Do you want me to call your family? Want to go home?"

"She's better off staying here, Cady. Let her work. Get her mind off that psycho," Neal countered entering from the other door. No telling how long he stood outside the break room or how much he heard before opening the door.

"Izzy?" Cady asked softly.

"Yes, Cady. Neal's right," she smiled up at him. "Besides, it was only a phone call. Like you said, he can't hurt me through the telephone. It just.... Besides, Cady, I belong HERE. Who else can Mario blame for his runaway computer?" The old Izzy laughed, poking fun at her friend. "And I need to get your reports, Cady. Find out what's causing those rejections."

Cady shot a look over at Neal wondering if he picked up their latest election glitch. *Dammit. That's all we need...Oh, Izzy, hush now...no more.*

"Looks like I barged in on a real catastrophe. Anything I can do?" Neal looked from Cady to Izzy. "Izzy?"

"No, Neal," Izzy smiled wanly. Her brown eyes flashed up at him through thick wet lashes.

Swollen, red and...beautiful, Cady thought. *Of course. Well, Izzy, how many gilded arrows will it take to fell a Neal? And Neal what are you doing back here? You're supposed to be giving me space.*

"The guard downstairs called. Food's on its way up," Neal announced with aplomb. "Izzy do you think you can eat something? It will make you feel better."

"I...I'll try, Neal. I'll just go wash my face. And I'll try," she whispered softly, her eyes clung to his.

Oh, gak, Izzy! Reel him in!

"Good, Izzy. Cady? Everything okay?" Neal asked, noticing a flare to Cady's nostrils that appeared out of character if not outright unbecoming. "Mario?"

"Your timing's perfect, Neal." Mario offered, always the diplomat. "Cady?"

29

"Oh, Neal, paella! My favorite. And picadillo! All so... *delicioso*. Where to begin?" Izzy smiled up at Neal, her eyes sparkling through long dark lashes.

"Neal, it's a banquet." Cady breathed in the fragrance of commingling spices, garlic, onion, peppers, oregano, cumin, saffron, bay leaf.... Time itself took a break while they savored the Cuban fair. Arroz con pollo, puerco, ropa vieja, and at the heart of it all, Izzy's paella, the mammoth mound of yellow rice laden with a mariner's treasure trove of seafarer delights, rich hunks of crab, lobster, squid, shrimp, clams, mussels, and ham, capers... "Hmmm-hmmm."

"Then you accept my peace offering?" Neal glanced over at Cady.

"Oh yes, Neal," Izzy answered for her.

"Are you feeling better, Izzy?"

"I am now, Neal."

Give me a break. Down girl. Down spyboy.

"We can thank my friends at La Carreta."

"Hmm-hmm," Cady nodded. "They've several restaurants, haven't they? But I've never been."

"I...I'll take you sometime."

In a puerco-pigs eye!

"Oh, wouldn't that be fun? We could all go!" Izzy clapped her hands together.

"Count me in!" Mario heaped a spoonful of frijoles negros atop his rice. "Hmm. All this comfort out here bumping right up against the edge of Cadyclysm in there." Mario turned away from Cady's warning eyes, more to hide his slip of a smile than to disregard her warning.

But if Neal understood Mario's jab, he didn't let on.

"Nothing's too good for our county election crew. Besides, I wanted enough food for your whole team and the auditors. I'm not sure just how many bodies are buzzing in and out of there. And I called Stan…but…"

"He's AWOL," Mario looked over at Cady. "He likes to stay out of the way on big days. Doesn't want to answer the tough questions, make on-the-spot decisions."

"Mario."

"It's true, Cady, and you know it."

"We needn't hang our dirty laundry in front of our company here."

"Somebody needs to know. He's been hanging you out to dry for years."

"Mario!"

"Sorry, Cady."

"We're all tired. It's been a long day. Just…have a care, Mario."

"And last night was sure a long one." Izzy turned toward Neal. "Neal, this pork melts in my mouth it's so tender, so juicy." Izzy brought her fork up to her mouth rubbing the chunk of pork against her lips before nibbling a small piece and taking it into her mouth.

"So, Cady," Neal looked away from Izzy too quickly and focused his attention on Cady. "Back to our Cuban sampler here, you think I overdid it?"

Cady breathed in again. "Not from my perspective. Could be the first real food we've had in a week."

"Two, Cady. Two weeks isn't it, Izzy?"

"Yes, papi. A normal election," Izzy lowered her eyes. "Except for…"

"Izzy," Neal waited for Izzy to look him. "I don't want to push you, but…"

"It's all right, Neal." Izzy looked down at her plate while she swirled chunks of squid and lobster around in her rice.

"About your intruder…" Neal looked over to Cady.

"Shouldn't have happened. Should not have gotten in. We've had an outstanding work order for…I don't know how long, to install locks for that door. And every management meeting I harp on that issue, that and a few other soft areas."

"Why…"

"She's not mean enough. Not big enough," Mario puffed out his chest and muscled up his arms.

"Yeah. And her voice isn't deep enough, Mario. Don't forget that," Izzy added.

"Now, now boys and girls. Enough!" Cady scolded. "Security ordered a cardkey lock matching the ones in the tabulation room so it could be programmed with our existing cardkeys…. Guess it got complicated."

"Your No Admittance sign sure didn't work this morning."

"No. Of course not. A crook, a hacker intent on breaking in is going to get through somehow, someday." Cady replayed her lecture.

"Yes. This morning's breach proved that, didn't it?"

"But this was my fault, Neal. We've been so cautious. No other computers anywhere in or out of the building can access our election server. This is our command center, our brain. Without it we're…doomed." Cady lowered her voice an octave for effect.

"How'd he do it?"

"Here. Right here. We set up the computer in here for a little privacy away from our glasshouse. It's close, convenient, accessible by the auditors but not on display."

"The hacker slinked in through my backdoor," Mario snapped. "I left it hanging open for him, through the only computer outside the tabulation room with access to our central server."

"Notice the empty space?" Cady remarked, when Neal glanced over to Izzy's computer station against the wall.

"I keep a notebook computer in the tabulation room now when I'm not using it. And I don't leave it with jobs running. I don't even leave it alone to go to the…well I don't leave it alone. Period." Izzy offered before being asked.

"So, Izzy, does this mean you have another protocol to follow?" Neal taunted.

"Yes, Neal, it does."

"You have to check it in and out of the tabulation room? Sign your initials in blood?"

"You make sport, Neal," Cady teased.

"Well, yes, Cady, I do. But now I can see why the precautions."

"Doubtful. Look, protocols, procedures, firewalls, passwords they help…mind you…only help to keep the conscientious people conscientious, help the do-it-right-good-guys to do it right every time, even when they're physically and mentally exhausted."

"Don't they just wanna do it themselves without getting snarled up in a lot of nonsense checklists? Don't they ever balk?" Neal reasoned.

"Nonsense? No. Balk? Sure."

"Then what?"

Cady laughed softly, "Well, then I fire them, of course."

Neal's eyes shot up. "Damn."

"Truth is, Neal," Izzy smiled sweetly, waiting for Neal to turn away from Cady and back to her. "She let's us all slip up, you know, when we first gear up for election there's a lot of slack and she knows we all squeeze by a little without following *the* protocol to the letter."

"So she does, uh?"

"Yeah, she's an old softy," Izzy smiled at Neal.

"Sure. A softy. She just stands back and watches us fall on our butts," Mario chuckled.

"So tell me the truth, Cady never really fired anyone, did she?"

Mario looked at Izzy, Izzy looked at Cady and the room stopped. Even Neal paused fork midair, mouth open.

Mario was the first to break silence. "She sure did. You should've seen it. When Stan found out he tracked Cady down in the tab room. The whole crew stood there mouths gaping while Stan screamed at Cady how she couldn't just fire somebody he himself hired, shouted obscenities that…even the guys turned away. But Cady, she stood firm, looked Stan straight in his bulging eyes and answered calmly, 'Of course, Stan. Of course I would never fire one of your employees. Does Leonard report to you now? Because there's no slot for that misfit in my department.' Stan stormed out, pushing over my monitor on his way…. I tell you, Neal, the guy, Leonard he gave even me the creeps. Stan kept promising to put a muzzle on him but it never worked."

"Makes my skin crawl...psycho," Izzy rubbed her arms.

"Mine too, Izzy. He's gone now," Cady reassured gently.

"And that *bastardo,* he'll never be back, Izzy. Will he, Cady?"

"What did Stan see in the guy, Mario?" Neal asked.

"Rumor has it Stan got pressured from some high muckymuck." Mario looked over to Cady. Then cut his answer short, "Of course that's just rumor."

"A rumor with more details your not willing to share?" Neal paused for effect. "Quick, aren't I."

"Yes, Neal. But we knew that about you already," Izzy's dark eyes gazed up at Neal, her demure little smile hot enough to melt any frozen heart.

Mario and Cady exchanged glances before their laughter exploded about the room catching Neal by surprise, but not Izzy. And soon they all laughed, loud, raucous, contagious. Well-deserved, badly needed.

"Don't know what it was about. But I have to say it felt really good," Neal chuckled again.

"And I suspect you never will, Neal. Sometimes we Martians don't catch on until we're whacked up side the head with it."

"This is nice, Neal, very nice. But we've miles to go before..." Cady pushed back from the table.

"You don't really start ramping up for a while yet, do you?" Neal asked.

"Actually, that's generally the case. But we do have our little tasks to perform. And I'm looking though a couple of reports that..."

"Don't give us the warm cozies, Neal." Izzy smiled at him, all girly bunnies and flowers.

"Anything you care to share?" Neal smiled mischievously, then continued when no one responded. "Since you broke the spell, I've another question about this morning's episode. With this being the only viable entry point to your central server," Neal pointed to Izzy's empty computer station. "How'd your hacker know it was here?"

"We've been muddling over that question all day." Cady answered.

"So you mind telling me more about the man you fired, other than he gave everyone the creeps? What'd he look like?"

"Leonard…little, wiry, blond almost platinum, spiked hair…"

"Cady, think about the man you asked Security to track down. Your words describing him, 'little' and 'creep,' were there any physical similarities? Could the slimy little man be one in the same?"

"Ohmygosh! Mario. Izzy. You said you didn't see him. But think. Was there anyone in the media room…?" Cady grabbed her phone and speed dialed Security. "Pull Leonard's personnel file again. Make two copies of anything relevant and hand one copy over to the police. Get a copy of his employee photo. See if any of the guards on duty recognize him from this morning." Cady put her phone down and turned back to Neal. "Bluntly put, Leonard was the most frightening person I've ever known…met…bumped on the elevator. You know, not known in the daily news sense but actually come in contact with."

30

"This time it's for real, Neal." Cady stacked her dishes. She looked from Neal to Izzy watching Neal, and last to Mario watching Izzy.

"I'll let the other guys know the goodies are here…But first," Mario reached for the coffee pot. "Neal? Coffee?"

"I'm going to wash up, Cady. I'll see you back in the tabulation room," Izzy spoke to Cady, but her eyes beckoned Neal. She rolled her chair back and stretched her arms taut, pausing in motion, then folded her hands behind her neck. She pulled her head tight against her hands, sighing softly.

"Neal?" Mario repeated.

Cady looked over at Neal, riveted to the temptress maiden. Firm body, filmy blouse, ample cleavage, billowy hair. *Dammit.* Then she looked at Mario, observing her watching their secret dance. *Always with Izzy*…Mario smiled sadly to Cady, Cady donning her own feeble smile. They shrugged their shoulders, shoved back from the table and cleared their plates.

"Looks like he sailed off to Tahiti. Coffee, Cady?"

"So, Izzy," gray eyes beckoned brown, "Your pile of color tagged reports over there… Don't tell me about these reports or this election. But what is it you do in here? Say in years past?"

Mario nodded to Cady and left the room. Izzy glanced over her shoulder at the tabulation room door closing softly behind him.

"Well, Neal, I'm looking for information. You know should there be any weird stuff." Izzy leaned into Neal sitting so close.

Cady's eyes narrowed, but she rested her back against the kitchen counter and joined Izzy's game. No harm yet. "Yes, like when trends reverse."

"Like that, Neal. When vote counts go down instead of up,"

Izzy teased.

"That's absurd, Izzy. Vote counts can't go down. When a voter votes his vote gets *added* to a...counter somewhere. You just want to see how gullible I am."

"Not so, Neal," Izzy teased. "Dead serious. Truncation. Just lops the numbers clean off when they don't fit. So 120 votes magically transforms into 20 votes."

"Cady?"

"You're on your own, Neal." Cady twisted her ring back and forth.

"Okay, Izzy. Say I believe you. Then what trends are you looking for and why?"

"Why? Oh, Neal. If I could magically show you the votes from this election...this morning I could predict the winner. I could set up a clever little betting scam."

"In English, Izzy?" he laughed.

"Okay, Neal, let's say Homer Simpson is running for president," Neal and Izzy laughed. "Okay, and for several hours sixty percent of the voters cast their ballots for old Homer across all precincts. Well you don't need to wait for the 11 o'clock news to know who the next president is. You can actually predict winners in a precinct after a few hours worth of votes."

"I didn't know that."

"Yes, Neal." Izzy adjusted her neckline. "Now that's barring any huge news event that could turn voters' opinions. You know?"

"I see."

"Well, Neal, it's one reason the voting process is so guarded. You can see that sharing election results in the Eastern Time zone really can affect the outcome in the rest of the country. If people like the results, they may decide not to vote because their candidate is winning already. Or if the Western states don't like the results in the East, they may actually get out more votes and win when otherwise they would have lost."

"So, is that what you're doing there?" Neal pointed to Izzy's reports.

"Cady? What do I do now?"

"I think you dug your own hole, Izzy. But if you've the time and all you're doing is talking about some hypothetical election or even a previous election, you own it."

Izzy smiled up at Neal and Cady tugged on her ring. All the while Neal watched and waited for Cady's eyes to meet his. His eyes smiled knowingly into hers and then he looked away, to Izzy and Izzy's secrets.

"Well, Izzy. You and me," he smiled again with a sidelong glance to Cady. "I know you can't show me any of the last election's reports with actual data, but can you be more specific as to what you might find that would make you think there was a problem?"

"Actually, I could give you the reports. No way you could figure them out, Neal. They're scrambled, nonsensical. Only Cady. Cady and me and Mario……" Izzy's eyes on Cady now, "Cady…? …I'll run your reports right away."

"You up to it, Izzy? Sure you don't want to hang out on my couch for a while?"

"I am now. I'm sure."

"Couch?" Neal asked.

"Yes, Neal. As for you, don't forget. My offer stands. Use my office. You don't need to be watching us every second."

"I do need to make some phone calls…"

"I'll show you where it is," Izzy offered.

"Actually, Izzy, I think I know. I don't want to pull you away from your mission anymore than I have already."

"Okay. Well, catch you later. I'll be back in a minute, Cady. I'll set up your graphs." Izzy twirled on her heel and sashayed out of the break room, her hips swaying smoothly.

"Catch you later, Izzy," Neal called after her. "Cady, before your next group comes in for their break, can you explain one more thing about the voting machines?"

Cady glared at him.

"Don't they upload data to your network? Couldn't they infect your network just as the computer in here did?"

"They could. But it would be difficult." Cady hoped she sounded more confident than she felt.

"So how did the virus get in again?"

"A simple program was loaded into the machine here. But what I don't understand is why he didn't do more damage. He could have demolished our tabulation server. For sure we would have been plastered all over the eleven o'clock news again. "

"But he didn't."

"No."

"Could he have known? Was he playing with you?"

"Neal, I...I've gotta go, Neal. Use my office. Really."

***

Izzy sidled up to the long table and tentatively placed the solitary page in front of the mountain of flash reports Cady thumbed through for the past few minutes. She also placed her incident report documenting the anomaly of rejected votes on the table next to it. Cady ignored the incident report and picked up the solitary page.

"Exactly what I'm looking for," she shared the page with Izzy.

"There's more." Izzy handed her another page and the two friends leaned over the report forehead to forehead. "Look at this." Izzy pointed to one set of numbers on the report.

"Real simple formula, isn't it Izzy. Blue plus rejects is equal-to or greater-than red. It follows through with the machines in both precincts." She drew an imaginary line down the page mentally counting the serial numbers of every voting machine in the two precincts. "Whatever it is, they've all got it. It's too perfect to be coincidence."

31

The corridor to Cady's office was empty. Only the beep of Neal's cell phone competed with the swishing of the tabulation room door closing behind him.

"Hello. This isn't a good place for me to talk. I'll call you back in about three minutes, okay?"

Brice hung up.

Neal headed through the programming department and into Cady's office.

***

"Neal! What have you done?" Cady gasped. Neal stood there in an angry field of fawn carpet. He turned around slowly toward the sound of her voice, cautiously shuffling his feet as he pivoted in place. Her treasures scattered across the floor amidst toppled chairs and swollen gaping view binders with broken spines and crumpled wads of paper. Shards of gold and blue and red glittered fawn while her precious dogs lay face up, torn and ravaged but still smiling at her through slivers of smashed glass. Both her desk and credenza stood naked, empty, scarred. The words "BITCH" and "GOTCHA" greeted her in huge bold letters etched across the full width of each. The room reeked of lilacs from squiggles of hand lotion drying in opaque circles on her window and one wall. She'd remember to buy bottles instead of tubes next time, citrus... lemon.

"Cady, I..."

"What have you done?"

"Cady, I don't know. I just got here. I stopped for a minute on my way. I just got here. Cady..."

"I don't understand. Who would...?"

"I don't know, Cady." Neal bent over picking up a few larger items, her dogs, her calendar, the in-basket before rounding the desk where he stooped to retrieve her desk phone." He pushed the button for Security then righted a toppled chair. "Here Cady, sit. I'll take care of this."

"Why...?" Cady's eyes traveled over the walls, the scarred desk, cluttered floor. She wandered past him into her office bathroom.

Neal heard her retch, one gut wrenching dry heave before gasping, "Who?"

"Hello, this is Neal Charles. I'm with Cady Palmer in her office. There's been a break in here. Her office vandalized... She wasn't here... We don't know when it happened... No. We don't know who. Could be related to the incident this morning... No... You need to come up right away... Get the police involved ... Yes, I said, police. I said it's entirely possible, probable in fact this is related to this morning's break in."

Neal lowered his voice turning away from Cady's bathroom, "The man who did this could still be in the building. He means business. Come see... Yes, now." Neal leaned forward, using his pen to flick a piece of wadded paper over a couple of inches so it concealed a feminine thing-a-ma-gig before he realized a dozen or so were strewn about like pencils across the floor. "It's personal, very personal. He could be stalking her from the media room...."

Neal turned toward Cady leaning against her bathroom door mumbling words he couldn't understand. Some chant or incantation, he couldn't tell. "Look," his voice louder this time, "I need to take care of some things. Just come up here right away... No, she's okay, just fine in fact... No... I'm taking her out of the building for some air... Yes. My cell phone number is 850-555-0212... It's a Tallahassee area code... No, I live here... You'll get through to me on this number... No... We'll go back to the tabulation room in a little while." He hung up the phone.

"Not gonna ruin my perfect day. Not gonna ruin my perfect day. Not gonna ruin my perfect day..." She looked up at Neal, face rigid, eyes moist but no deluge of tears. Neal watched her, watched her rub her face in her hands, watched her mulling over the possibilities swirling around in her mind like so much broken debris. *How, when, who, why? Why? Why?*

Neal sprinted around the desk, banging his thigh on the corner, "Damn!" But didn't break stride until his arms encircled her and her head rested against his chest. His right hand rubbed her forehead gently, smoothing loose strands of hair back from her eyes. Gently, stroking front to back, front to back, resting for a moment on the bridge of her nose, kneading her forehead, her right temple, brushing her soft cheek.

"Not gonna ruin my perfect day. Not gonna ruin my perfect day. Not gonna ruin my perfect day...Not!"

"Oh, Cady, honey," front to back his hand caressed her forehead, the top of her head, her silky neck. "Cady..." And in that terrible moment, he felt his own thoughts collide. Hard...fast and hard like being walloped aside the head with one of those heavy three-inch view binders smashed on the floor. *Why? When? How? Why? Most women, hell most people could crush under this much pressure and she just shrugs it all off with, 'How do we fix it? Where do we go from here?' In fact the only thing he observed troubling her overmuch was he himself.* And that's the moment Cady chose to shake it off. She lifted her head, pulled away from him, composed her face, looked smack in his eyes and...smiled...at him. Sure it was a wan little smile, but she looked...radiant. *One tough lady...and she's ...beautiful...and...real.*

Neal smiled back, shrugging his shoulders, then picked up her phone again, pushing the button for Mario - Console. "Mario. This is Neal Charles.... Thank you, not well I'm afraid. Someone broke into Cady's office. I've called Security.... No, she wasn't here. Actually she's doing better than I would.... Yes, me too. I'd be pitching a fit.... I'm taking her outside for some air.... We'll be back in a few minutes. Okay? ...I don't know if anything's missing yet, but it's a mess and I don't say that lightly.... Not until after the police finish with it.... Yes, I've asked Security to call the police.... No. You've both got your hands full. I'll save what I can. Who should I call for clean up?" Neal printed a name and phone number on a small yellow square of paper he retrieved from his breast pocket. "Thanks, Mario."

"My jacket. I left it here. On the chair. Have you seen my jacket, Neal?"

"Cady…"

"Neal, have you seen my jacket?"

"No, Cady. Let's get out of here. We'll deal with this later."

"Neal, did you do…? Do you know why?"

"No, Cady. C'mon. Let's go." Neal rested his fingers on Cady's arm and tugged softly, gently. Cady knew because her blouse warmed where it touched her skin and she walked with him.

When they reached the hallway, Cady stopped. "Neal, thank you. Honestly, thank you. I was frazzled in there. Thank you for taking care of things. I…I might have been…unkind if I had to talk with Security again so soon. Neal, I don't have a clue about all this, but…"

"Don't think about it now, Cady. Let's just blow this pop stand."

Cady checked her watch, "That's what I'm telling you, Neal. I have to pass. Sounds nice, but remember? No mulligans? I'm waiting for a fresh series of flash reports in another few minutes and Stan…I was on my way to Stan…he's out of the loop. He can't be."

"No, Cady, you need a break."

"I'll tell you what. For the next few minutes or until I get my reports… I'm looking for a good spar and…well, I can't take it out on Izzy and Mario. They're working too hard."

"And I'm not?"

"No, Mr. Charles, knight-in-shining-armor stint excluded, seems your mission is to cast my shadow."

"I keep my distance every now and then. Shadow?"

"Yeah. Up for some shadow boxing? You never know, I might just deck you."

"I believe you might."

"You're on then." Cady started walking toward the break room.

"Wait, Cady. Trust me. You need a breather. Just for a minute." He caught up with her pace.

"No, Neal. Really, I need to focus on the big picture here. And diving into those numbers again will probably help me a lot more than wallowing. Besides," she smiled up at him, "you're not my only assignment today, shadow."

Neal laughed.

By the time they reached the break room, Cady laughed along with him. Her laughter too gay, too eager, too excessive she knew, but felt comfort wash over her.

"You know, Neal," Cady furrowed her brow, straightening her head to proper lecture demeanor. She held her hand up with her index finger nearly flicking his nose, 'One joy scatters a hundred griefs.'"

Neal paused before opening the door for her. His eyes narrowing as he puzzled over her words.

"I said, 'One joy…scatters…a hundred griefs.' I believe it's an ancient Chinese proverb or something…from my fortune cookie last night. And I believe it's true."

"Yes, I think so too. Is that what you were saying back there?"

"No. That was something else."

32

"Cady? What happened? You all right?" Mario scooted his chair back from the far side of the break-room table and hustled to Cady's side. But Izzy who shot out of her chair at the first sound of the door opening was already there, wrapping her arm around Cady's shoulder. Mario squeezed Cady's free arm.

"Cady! You okay, chica?"

"Of course I am. It's over now."

"Cady, what can I do?" Mario asked.

"It's not okay…and won't be. Not for a long time," Izzy blinked the sting from her eyes. "What can we do, Cady?" Izzy took her arm off Cady's shoulder and moved around to face her.

"Nothing. Nobody. Nowhere. Wait until…until next week I suppose…." Cady looked into Izzy's eyes, glistening now with her own pain. "Don't you start, Izzy. Don't you dare."

"Never, Cady," she sniffled, then shook it off. "Well, I wanna go see it. Mario? Wanna go?"

"Izzy, seriously. You don't."

"Actually, Security and the police need the run of the place for at least the next several hours. The police probably won't even get here for a while yet, since no one's in peril." Neal studied Izzy, so tender yet from her own ordeal.

"No peril here. Only my sanity." Cady added caustically.

"No real damage there, right?" Neal teased.

"Thanks, Neal. I'll remember that."

"You're most welcome, Cady."

"Woooo. Time for us to get back, Izzy. Cady, let me know." Mario touched Izzy's elbow and pointed to the clock.

"Me too, Cady," Izzy hugged her quickly before trailing Mario into the tabulation room.

"Cady…" Neal rested his hand on her back.

"Leave me alone, Neal."

"No, Cady. You need time, okay. But I'll stay close. I've things to take care of, but I'll be here for you, Cady." Neal leaned into her, tentatively, his lips inches from tasting her hair. Closer, he breathed in her scent. When she didn't object, he thought to move closer still, but held back. Instead he patted her back where his hand still clung hot and wanting and he left her to her jumble of numbers and colored papers, surprised by his own vulnerability.

***

Neal braced his back against the wall inside Cady's office. Better to get it over with Brice while he waited for Security. He dialed Brice with the new cell phone delivered this morning.

"What took so long?"

"Sorry, Brice. Someone ransacked the office I was calling you from. Security got involved.... It was Cady's office. They smashed up Cady's office."

"Friggin' circus. And Palmer?" his drawl firmly set for the day.

"She's okay. A little shaken up, but she's okay."

"I meant the election, Neal. Get your mind outta your...."

Neal curbed his response. "She's on top of it. They all are. Still trying to figure out some flaky stuff with the votes."

"Whaddya mean? They don't count votes until the polls close and then.... They tabulate the votes after the polls close. They can't do it now. They can't!"

"You're right, Brice."

"Then what...?"

"That's what I'm off to find out."

"You go stop it, Nealboy. Just tell 'em to count the f_____ numbers when it's time to count the f_____ numbers!"

"That's the point, Brice. Could be the numbers are wrong."

"Can't be. It's Palmer.... Think of her personal goals here, Nealboy. She's topped off. Gone as far as she can. Now she just wants you to know her pain, make the most of the time she's got left.... Least that's what Stan says."

"Stan may have his own agenda."

"Whaddya mean? You talked to him?"

"Barely. Not for lack of trying. Guy's a snake."

"You go talk to Stan. He'll set you straight about her."

"Brice, you've got it all wrong. She wants this thing to work just as much as you do. Her whole team, they're a dedicated…"

"Listen up, Neal. You tell her…don't go diggin' dirt where there is none."

"Didn't you send me here to make sure…?"

"I sent you there to control…to prevent those halfcocked renegades from setting off a media firestorm! Now that's three, three times. You need more? Or three make it clear enough?"

"Right."

"Listen, Neal, when the tallies come in, look at the numbers. If there's a snag here or there you can check it out. See if you really think somethin's goin' on. If there is, we'll deal with it then. In the mean time, tell Palmer not to go stoking any more fires, eh?"

***

"Seamless. Isn't that what you said? Your word, seamless?" air gushed out of Leonard's earpiece. His ear tingled with the volume of wet, hot breath. He shook his head, but couldn't shake the feeling.

"No problem. I'm in control."

"How? You tell me how. When I got calls comin' in from all directions tellin' me they've got stuff goin' down!" Air surged again. Leonard tugged the earphone off his ear.

"I'll fix it," Leonard spoke into his mouthpiece before pressing his off button. His sphincter muscle scrunched. Power, a regular joyride, hanging up on the man like that. *Cretin.*

The next number he dialed from memory. Funny how things like that worked.

"Yes, Mario, this is Marty from ElecTron," Leonard's voice lowered an octave, clear, crisp, concise. "I'm trying to isolate your problem……Yes, it is. But I need to verify some information with your programmer. Walk through the process with him…. Ah. Didn't know. Her name's Izzy you say? …Yes, I'll hold……… No. I'll be in and out of my office from now on. I'll call her back."

33

Cady stepped back from the whiteboard, grabbed her notepad and turned for the door, then realized her need to take action overrode common sense. No advantage to dashing in on Stan unawares. Just piss him off. Besides Juan hadn't called back, so definitely no gain in trudging to Stan's office if he remained absent or unavailable. Cady picked up the phone and speed-dialed the familiar number.

"Cady, I was just calling chou. Stan he's back." The cheerful lilt greeted her.

"Oh, good. I need a few minutes with him. It's important."

"Sure ting. You be here in de next half hour, Stan con see chou, Cady," Juan offered. So agreeable. So accommodating. "I'll keep him here for chou."

"Thanks, Juan." Cady cradled the phone and signaled Mario she was leaving. On her way through the break room, she stopped long enough to scoop up a fistful of gold-foiled bittersweet chocolates before picking up her pace on her way to Stan.

***

Cady reached Stan's office in record time, pausing briefly at Juan's reception desk. The smiling Juan continued talking into his headphone, motioning her by. Cady returned his smile, mouthing her thanks while gently piling the chocolates in a small neat heap on his desk. Then she pulled back her shoulders, and with a soft tap on Stan's door, let herself into his office.

Leaning back, his arms locked behind his neck, Stan glanced her way, then with a flick of his right eyebrow turned away to focus on the television in the corner cabinet. All the while Fox News talking heads chattered incessantly about opinion polls.

Cady noticed the day wore on Stan as well, his face puffed and pasty around his sagging eyes and moustache.

As she studied the man before her, Cady was reminded of her staff's off-handed sniggers when Stan's name entered into the conversation. And it clicked. Their more recent gibes of "Wally" and "Willy Wally Winkle" suddenly made perfect sense. All in all, the once handsome young dapper deputy director long since elevated to election power chief ironically conjured comedic images of a talking, waddling bull walrus.

Save those first ugly encounters, Cady hadn't seen him all day. For Stan, Election Day was a waiting game. So he filled his time with television and chatter. As the evening wore on, he'd breakaway from his television, pop in and out of the tabulation room, verify precinct counts against projections, parade in and out of the media room and basically act important.

After several moments more of Fox chatter, a commercial break. Stan turned her way, propped his elbows on the arms of his chair and leaned forward, "What's your problem NOW, Cady?" His belly heaved.

"Stan, it's the voting machines…" Cady watched Stan's eyes shift from her to the television. "We've been tracking a problem since late this morning. Here's the incident report." Cady leaned forward, her arm outstretched over his desk, holding the report for him. Stan turned slowly from the television, took the report and turned back again to Fox.

After several moments, "This morning you say? Why the hell didn't you tell me if you thought there was a problem?"

"Stan, I called your office, your cells and I left messages. I emailed you specifics."

"You've called ElecTron?" Stan's eyes jutted back and forth across the page, fingers fiddling his mustache.

"Yes," at last she had his attention.

"Well. Let's see what they have to say then," so nonchalant, he might have been yakking about a moldy boat shoe.

"They're working on it now, but it could take hours, days even before they find anything conclusive." Cady braced herself. "Stan this is serious."

"No. Serious is how paranoid you are, Cady."

"Stan, the phone calls, my office...you don't think there's a connection?"

"If there is, Cady, then you're the liability here."

"I could be. But the end results don't change."

"Okay, Cady. Let's have it then. Give me the short version. Forget the mumbo-jumbo. And, Cady, simple English."

"Right, Stan." She filled her lungs, then proceeded. "From the poll opening, trends favored Democrats by several points. That trend continued through the ten o'clock flash tally reports. During the first three hours, the flash upload reports detected no rejected ballots. That's as it should be."

Stan adjusted his tie and Cady paused until he turned her way again.

"Then, within one hour, between ten and eleven o'clock, the lead for Democrats took a decisive dive. With each successive flash upload, Democrat votes dropped while numbers of rejected ballots increased. Eventually, the Democrat lead slipped, in some cases flipped to a lead for Republicans."

Stan cleared his throat to speak. An impatient sneer quivered at the corners of his mouth, dragging his lips downward. His nostrils flared over the mountain peak jutting up from the rusty bristles of his moustache. Remnants of dimples, attractive in youth, now etched craggy lines down his fleshy cheeks. Fine red lines traced around his nostrils, spidering outward.

"You're saying Democrats still can't figure out a ballot?" Stan replied in his no-big-deal voice.

Glib. Patent. Arrant. Cady thought of several other words describing Stan's attitude, but resisted the temptation to get sucked in. Instead, she listened and waited while Stan ticked off his litany of likely rationale.

"Maybe the blue chips took off. Maybe another SwiftFarts for Crap launched a blitz. Anything could've turned the election." The aging walrus zinged.

"Yes, Stan. Any or all of those events could trigger changes in direction. But these precincts have consistently remained predictable in their voting patterns throughout past elections. That's why we rely on them for our control group. What remains problematic is the sudden appearance of rejected ballots. Stan, for some of these machines we have no source ballots. We've just got printouts of ballots, machine interpretations of what the voters said. No real documents to interpret voter intent. No paper trail of actual votes. There's nothing tangible for ElecTron to audit."

"Hell, Cady. You're right. Nothing tangible and you're wasting my time over a few ballots? Crap! I'm not about to be the laughing stock again." Appearances. So much of the brass didn't care a hoot about what was right anymore. All appearances. Well, she'd write her little blurb for the County Canvassing Board. If they didn't call it, there was no election-legal action or protocol she could follow for solving a problem the Board wouldn't recognize.

Cady presented her case. Words came out of her mouth. It seemed so damning. One plus one equals two. Coincidence? Possibly. Intriguing? For certain. Yet all the while she knew she tilted at windmills. She swore Stan's eyes visibly glazed over.

She had submitted the incident report to Stan. She presented the risks: the risks of doing nothing, the risks of overreacting, most significantly the risk of some media monger putting it together while the Elections Department and Cady's team palpably did naught, nada, zip. Cady reminded Stan of all the pre-election hype extolling benefits of their newest voting machines eliminating voting errors. Some post-election blogger was bound to sniff out the high reject count. It was public information, after all. Talk about exposure, it could be broadcast worldwide before the absentee ballots were tallied.

Stan stroked his chin. His alligator heal pushed up and down, rocking his chair back and forth.

"Cady, you know we can't hold up an election for a few votes," thumb and forefingers pulling at the corner of his mustache.

"We don't know how far-reaching this is. It could be that every voting machine in the county is running faulty software. It could be that anywhere from 2 to 6 percent or more votes in every precinct will not be counted. That's double the margin of error."

"So far, you've no proof. Nothing to back it up but speculation," once again twirling at a few miscreant longhairs.

"You know I'm not recommending holding up the election, Stan. But I am strongly advising pulling these machines offline, then immediately evaluating the others. Should it come down to the wire, I am recommending putting the brakes on our rush to certification. Give ElecTron time to come up with some answers."

"Can't do it Cady," Stan leaned back in his oversized chair, again wrapping his hands behind his head, elbows up.

She'd lost him. And there you have it. Stan's master of this, his domain. Cady stood there gaping, racking her mind for some scrap of information to tip the scales toward caution.

"Bring me something solid, Cady," Stan barked.

"Stan, it'll take a while. Izzy's printing graphs along with some more general comparisons. I'm on my way to work with her now. But the drill's the same as always. We can't access ElecTron's software, so we can't go digging for bugs. We can only present the errors to ElecTron and hope they're quick with the results."

"So let ElecTron do it then. Get Izzy back to her real job."

Cady wanted to shout for the world that she would diligently pursue all avenues of research open to her, at least those outlined by election protocol. Instead she held her breath for a moment and when she finally spoke her words were measured, her voice soft. "Stan, we have the votes, the actual data, real-time information for narrowing in on the voting patterns that caused the errors. The more data we look at, the more patterns we can give them, the faster they'll figure out the problems. We've only just begun looking at the scanner results."

"Forget it, Cady. Just get this wrapped up and locked up when we're done with the tallies tonight. All of it. All of it goes in the vault. Then we're done with it. Got it, Cady?" More command than request. Stan tapped his MontBlanc on the leather rim of his desk blotter, punctuating his last order with a firm quick tap-tap. "When are you scheduled to calibrate the machines?"

"Stan? We're in the middle of an election here. We can't even think about calibrating those machines yet." Calibrate. The phrase was a hold over from elections and equipment long past. Still somehow the genre fit and besides they all understood the intent. Calibrate the machines. Clear the slate, zero out the counters, set the machines for the next election. No paper ballot, no paper trail, no data, no proof, no problem. Stan's meaning was clear. This mess could get ugly.

"I'll check on scheduling, Stan." *Hell I will, Stan. Not until we figure this thing out.* Dammit, Stan. Stan had irked and bumbled and jerked his way through the system for more that fifteen years. And for several of those years, Cady stood beside him, stood her ground and got the damned job done. He'd ruffled her feathers more times than she could count. But this was blatantly irresponsible. Hadn't the razor thin margins of elections past taught them anything? But for Florida's ambiguous election laws, at least three previous elections would have been voided, scrapped, canned. Dammit. That was then. This is now. Focus dammit. Focus. Results must be accurate, stand on their own. Any whiff of error and we're meat.

"You know, Cady, you're too much about the picky stuff. You need to work on being a team player around here." Stan tugged the maroon handkerchief from the breast pocket of his camera-ready suit and dabbed at his face and forehead, then tossed it into the side drawer of his desk, pulled out another crisply folded one and tucked it into his breast pocket.

Cady nodded, her voice too knotted up in her throat to speak. She clutched her notepad and pen, hard, as though the act could muster up a veneer of strength. All the while Stan's eyes glazed over, her eyes burned and she felt an involuntary quiver slide along her lower lip before biting down on the errant thing, hard. *Oh, no! Damn it! Toughen up!* Her tongue jutted to the roof of her mouth. She breathed in a couple of quick whiffs of his cloying air. That alone, maddening enough to divert her attention from the sting she felt over another bad election.

"Yes, Stan." There were aspects of this job Cady hated. She knew it would be a while before he finished venting and was done with her.

"Suppositions. Shit. Speculations."

34

Neal stepped up to the wide reception desk in front of Stan's office. The receptionist, a slight young man with a flawless olive complexion chatted in soft measured tones into the mouthpiece of the headset clamped over his head and around the side of his face. He pushed and tugged at the headpiece, an inch forward, a millimeter back seeking the perfect comfort zone. Judging by the shaggy mounds of thick brown hair atop his otherwise well-groomed close-cropped square-back cut, the poor lad had been unable to attain a comfortable fit all day. There was none.

The receptionist looked up from his desk, acknowledging Neal immediately with a friendly smile and wave of his hand, before pushing a dwindling pile of candies in Neal's direction. A smaller pile of wrinkled gold wrappers shared the opposite corner of the desk alongside an oversized intercom office phone. The poor man's current phone call appeared to be only one of a series of pressing calls judging by the parade of flashing buttons on his phone base.

Neal mouthed, "Thank you," reaching down for one of the candies. He peeled away the delicate foil and the aroma of rich dark chocolate infused the air. Soon crumpled shreds of his own wrapper joined those in the pile on the desk and he wondered if these little treasures might have been a treat from Cady.

It took several moments more for the receptionist to wind down his current phone call, readjust his headset, jot down a few blurbs on the pink message pad, adjust his headset again and finally enter the caller's name and time of call on the pale green page of his dog-eared phone log. Affable fellow, Neal thought. The young man smiled intermittently at Neal, pointing his left index finger toward the ceiling, mouthing, "One moment, please.

Gracias. Thank you." After jotting several more lines on the message pad with his right hand, he pushed the remaining candies a few inches closer to Neal. Into the head phone, "Jes. Jes. I got it. Chure. Jes. I give him your message jesterday and I give him your message Friday. At this time he's just so busy with the election and everything."

All the while, rumblings flooded the doorway to Stan's office. The mahogany door ajar by several inches didn't offer the privacy the room's inhabitants must have assumed. A gruff male voice boomed, faster, louder, agitated. The woman's voice he knew, measured, concise, not yet grabbing the offending bait.

"Could be. Might be? Should be? What the hell, Cady! That's a lot of suppositions, Cady. Idle speculation, Cady!" the voice roared. "You wanna halt the f_____ election? Halt the whole damned county, hell the whole damned country on a supposition?" he screeched. "We're going with it, Cady. I'm not gonna let Florida be the country's laughing stock…not again." By now the histrionics conspicuous, "Can't believe you'd hold up this election for a couple o' lousy votes."

The young man behind the big reception desk smiled up at Neal, waiting expectantly after concluding his phone call, now his turn to be patient. "It's been a long year for them," he continued his smile evenly.

"Neal. Neal Charles. I…" Neal shrugged, laughing softly, admittedly caught eavesdropping. Rather unbecoming he concurred. *Though I am spook for a day,* still laughing.

The young man laughed too. "Meester Corbin he's expecting chou," the man assured, pushing the first button in line among the three columns of buttons on his phone, "Meester Charles here to see chou, Meester Corbin."

"I'll be done here in a few minutes," the gruff disembodied voice responded through the speaker on Juan's desk, echoing from behind the doorway.

"Right through that door, Meester Charles." Juan grinned, a quirky little grin. "Meester Corbin con see chou now," Juan stood up ushering Neal to the doorway behind him.

"Thank you, Juan."

"Maybe chou wait here a minute for…*tranqullidad.*"

***

Neal paused at the door. Could be a while then. From this side of the door Stan sounded primed and was punching hard.

"Yes, Stan. Got it."

"You wanna write a sentence or two for the Canvassing Board, fine. But keep it simple, short, sweet. No technical crap. No suppositions. No projections. Got it, Cady?"

"Yes, Stan."

"Meanwhile, don't waste anymore time on it, Cady. Wrap it up, Cady. My auditors signed off on all the protocol reports from this morning yet?"

"Not yet."

"Not a word of this to them, Cady. Got it? They find out for themselves, fine. But we're not gonna spell it out for them. Got it?"

"Yes, Stan."

"So when'd you say the calibration's scheduled? ...Accelerate the schedule. Get it out of the way. No sense in dragging this out."

"Yes, Stan."

"Can't believe you'd hold up this election for a couple o' lousy votes," Stan bellowed so loud he rose up in his chair.

Neal pressed the door open to see Stan leaning forward, hands braced on his desk, butt out of his chair, poised, ready to pounce on his Cady-prey. Cady, her back to the door sat in one of two burgundy leather occasional chairs facing Stan's desk, leaning forward, shoulders stooped, head bowed, staring at the floor.

"Stan. I'll dig deeper, look for more patterns. If we're lucky, ElecTron will get back to us later this evening."

"You lost your ears along with your sense, Cady? I said drop it. You really need to watch yourself, watch your...suppositions."

"Yes, Stan."

"Cady? We're all set here, aren't we?"

Cady nodded at Stan's wrap up. Though his dismissal dance could thrash about for a while yet.

"Besides, Cady, you're not gonna screw up my..."

Stan stopped midsentence, shifting his attention to the thick mahogany door swishing across the carpet as it arced open behind

Cady in the foyer. Then to Neal entering the room on hushed footfalls across plush burgundy carpet.

"Uh...er...Neal...uh, come on in. How are you? Neal, you can tell Brice we're coming off without a hitch, we are." Stan announced with enough panache to make Cady question the reality of their marathon meeting. Never overly subtle, Stan switched demeanor, picking right up from his my-way-or-the-highway attitude to his kissy-kiss-up public image.

"We're done here, aren't we, Cady?" Stan asked now jovial. "I said, aren't we, Cady?" Stan repeated.

"Yes, Stan," her defeat palpable. Then Cady turned to watch Neal walking tall and dignified and commanding through the dimly lighted foyer into the days-end golden sunshine filtering through Stan's sprawling windows and this rosy mahogany-and-burgundy room that didn't fit Stan, his character, his attitude, his slippery soul at all. Odd, she should consider it fit Neal. It didn't feel too plush, overdone... It didn't feel dirty with Neal in the room.

Dammit, Cady. Here she was on hell's fast track to doomsday having been kicked-down-ripped-open-split-apart-and-salted, all for doing her job. And the all-too-cheerful-for-the-day Florida sunshine swathed this stranger-spy in a gentle golden shower of light that bronzed his already perfect athlete's tan and flickered off the flecks of gray salting his temples and drew her attention to the eternal depths of dark aquamarine eyes. *Dammit. Dammit. Dammit!*

Cady stood up, glaring into the face of the man who'd hounded her since early morning, the man she knew to be on the other...at least not on her team. Yet he'd been so...easy to spill her guts to, easy to banter with...easy to...easy. And she resented the hell out of it. And here he was all calm and pleasant and smiling and breaking up her spat with Stan. And she resented the hell out of that too.

It wasn't that Neal hadn't suspected even detected more trouble. She knew he had. She watched him observe and poke and question and pry, attempting to flush out deviations in today's election. But nothing popped up on his radar, at least nothing Cady's team hadn't taken care of immediately and resolutely...at least not that Cady let him see anyway. In fact all indications were even the charged-up media remained totally bored with this election. But she wasn't. She was fired up and spitting mad. And she needed to stay that way to make it through the lunacy of it. Last thing she needed was this...this usurper nudging into her lane and being congenial at that. *Dammit.*

***

Neal watched Cady-interrupted turn toward him when he stopped by her side, close enough to touch. Green ice glared at him through dry shining eyes. The strain of confrontation, the chink in her armor betrayed only by the deepening hue of soft pink rimming her eyes.

"Well, er...Neal," Stan's butt thudded back into his chair. "Brice said you'd be hanging your hat here all day. You've met Susan Palmer?"

Cady cordially extended her hand, a formality catching Neal off guard since they'd basically rubbed shoulders and minds...and bodies...almost...on and off all day. Sharing chaos and war stories ...and almost each other, he hoped. Nonetheless, Neal responded in kind, taking her hand in his. Her palm so cool and dry and fresh this morning now burned hot enough to singe his own hand.

"Cady..." he started, wanting to know what had shaken her so, then thought better of grilling her in front of this Neanderthal. "Cady..." Neal started again before she cut him off.

"Neal," Cady croaked, her voice parched and jagged.

Neal noted Stan's eyes narrowing. In contrast, Cady's were propped open, too wide, too rigid, holding all expression at bay. But the pale line tracing lips pulled in tight between gnawing teeth belied a frustration aching to shriek free. Neal had studied Cady's demeanor all day, all venues, all variations. Even the episode in her office...she cracked briefly but didn't break. Throughout the entire troublesome day, Cady stood firm, measured, stoic in a flurry of circumstances that could make the strongest man crumble. So this particular look of pained unmitigated defeat was not among her repertoire. He wondered at what events transpired to shake her free of the professional cloak she wore so resolutely, so comfortably, so effortlessly until now.

Neal followed her here a few minutes ago. She'd been cool behind glass. No one in the media room seemed the wiser. But Neal knew. He watched her wither. Watched Izzy scramble, that is start to scramble, catch herself, then meander over to Cady. Watched their heads bowed together in a meeting of silent deductions. Neal recognized trouble in a ding-dong day of wretched mishaps. He needed to find out what was going on for Brice…and…. But he wanted to find out for Cady. A puzzlement.

Stan blundered into Neal's thoughts. "You getting the hang of how our little operation works, Neal?"

Cady imagined syrup dripping from the corners of Stan's mouth smearing his impeccably coiffed moustache.

"Yes, Stan, I have. Quite a team you've got here," Neal offered not letting go of Cady's hand.

Cady fumed. Beyond crimson. Her eyes stung with unsquelched anger. Anger at Neal for being here, for hanging onto her outstretched hand overlong. At Stan. This time, Stan crossed the line and she felt herself spiraling helter-skelter into the abyss. Cady tugged her hand. Her anger at Stan brushed up against her fury that Neal's whiskey-and-grit baritone had the effect of mellowing the edges off the frazzled tension crackling the air trapped within those four walls. *You're sick, Cady. Get back to work.*

"Yes," Stan responded. "Well, they may've worked enough elections to get the hang of it by now."

"I imagine one election's never quite like any other." Neal observed while Cady tugged three small tugs to free her hand still held firm in Neal's larger one.

Dammit, Neal. Don't you dare be condescending. Dammit don't you dare be…sympathetic! Don't you dare intercede. I don't know what I'll do now to make this right, legal, legitimate. Proof dammit. But dammit, don't you dare do something to weaken my defenses and get me all girly-girl. Dammit.

"Cady can always be…counted on to do an excellent job." Stan said in a voice so noble, Cady thought he might choke.

"Thanks, Stan," Cady answered graciously. Stan expected her to, though she thought she might literally heave all over his plush burgundy carpet.

"It's a wrap then, Cady. Thanks for the update. I'll be looking for your bullet points."

"Right, then." Cady yanked her hand free, free of the bogus security offered by Neal's large hand holding her own, toying with her. *Dammit what was I thinking?* She smiled at Stan. *Bastard.* She smiled at Neal. *Twit.*

"Stan," Neal started. "There are some issues…"

Cady didn't care what issues Neal might dredge up. She wanted outta there, and you bet she'd grab back a few of the golden wrapped chocolates from Juan's oversized desk.

"Catch you later, Neal. Stan," Cady murmured. Then she squared off her shoulders and turned away from them, pausing a moment before hightailing it out of there as fast as she could without tossing them another load of fodder.

"I'll be back at my post in the Observatory with the Fountain Pen or is it a Candlestick, Miss Scarlett." But Cady was already on her way out leaving Neal to his business with tyrant-ula.

Neal watched Cady's retreat until she disappeared behind the closing door. He turned back to the man in the too-showy suit still glaring at the void entryway. "Stan," he said firmly, at the same time hand motioning you-stay-put. "Hold on, Stan. I want to clear up a few points with you…" as he started after Cady. "Be right back," and he was out the door.

"Cady," Neal called as he left Stan's office. "Cady," he called again. He caught up with her at Juan's desk dipping into the dwindling pile of chocolates. "Cady…"

"Look, Neal, rescue me once, you can play at knight in shining armor, et al. Twice and it's unseemly."

"It's just…I want to talk with you, Cady." Neal brushed her arm. "Please, later?"

"Suit yourself." She turned and walked away before he could see her stinging eyes give up her weakness.

35

Neal claimed Cady's chair, the one closest to Stan's desk. From this angle, he grasped the visual of Cady's scrimmage with this man that was more telling than all the words he'd gleaned from eavesdropping behind Stan's door. Front and center of Stan's leather desk blotter, the wrinkled corner from one of Izzy's reports peaked out from a stack of papers crammed haphazardly into a maroon file folder. Two oily hand smudges on either side of the desk blotter left telltale reminders of Stan's final lurching affront. A pouncing Stan must present a menacing image to any woman…or man for that matter.

"Stan. I'm looking for substance here. You want to tell me what's going on?" Neal asked. Cady told him nothing and everything he needed to detect faults in the voting processes. But words, extent, probabilities he expected from Stan, at least to some rational degree. Enough to assess the magnitude of problems stewing in Cady's tightly capped cauldron. Was it time to pursue risk control? Did the governor and his spinmeisters need a heads up? How long should he wait? *Or is there more here? Do I plunge deeper? Look for clues, players? Proof of intent, collusion? Cady? No.*

"Stan?" Neal repeated.

"Why, yes… Sorry… Caught up in the headlines here, bein' the big day and all." Stan turned back to Neal. He smiled and asked in a soft genteel drawl, stretching his words in a cadence Neal decided must embody his best television persona, "Sooo, Neeeaalll, what ca-an I do-o for you?"

Neal was quick to temper his resentments toward the oaf. He moderated his approach to begin again. "Well, Stan, let me start again by first expressing my appreciation to you for inviting me to hang out here with you and your staff. As the governor probably shared with you this morning, he's concerned with this election and wants to ensure your success here."

Stan laughed, "And just how's he gonna do that? Just how're you gonna help?"

"And your answer, not and not. But, let me say that should things turn sour, I may be able to soften some of the bad publicity. That's all the governor expects. He likes to be on the crest of the wave, big or small."

"I suppose I'm just a little incensed he's chosen Miami-Dade County to be the brunt of his...I know we've had our problems in the past, but..."

"Stan, actually the governor hasn't singled out Miami-Dade. Reps are positioned in several strategic counties."

"You don't say. I wonder.... Uh, I didn't know," Stan sighed, his speech less affected.

"So, a good place to start is with the more visible issues here."

"Issues? No issues." Stan shrugged his shoulders, holding his hands out palms up.

"My mistake. Thought I heard there might be some problems with the voting machines. Wasn't there an incident on the news? Some error with one of the voters?"

"Oh, that. Nothing. All taken care of."

"Nothing else?"

"What? Problems? Hell no. The only problems I have are with that...that woman," Stan retorted in a well-practiced good-ol'-boy voice. "Every now and again she gets a little picky. Picky and pissy. You know all flustered with it being Election Day and all. She dreams up these harebrained ideas that, well, Neal, I'm afraid one day I might just lose my temper."

Neal waited, mute, his face remained devoid of expression. His pen flinched in his fingers, once, the only discernable movement on his side of Stan's desk.

"I just have to reel her in once in a while, is all. You know those technical types," Stan pushed up from his chair and walked over to the window. The waning sun shone bright around his ample frame. Neal readjusted his eyes to the glare. "You won't mind my saying, women are the worst. And she's a real ball buster, that one. Pushy bitch. Acts like she'd rather have a cast iron...

never mind." Stan caught himself before stepping on his own Stanley.

"So you're saying there's nothing else going on with the voting machines? No voting irregularities? Everything's as it should be?"

Stan fiddled with the blinds, absentmindedly scanning the parking lot. "Yep, she's a real ball bu…" he turned back to Neal and his words froze in the air as hooded cobalt steel glared back at him. This man of the governor's was hard to read, but maybe not in this. Stan didn't like the man's expression, not one bit. "I…uh," He cleared his throat. "All kidding aside. She's just tired, upset. You know all that computer mumbo-jumbo."

Contempt smoldered about the room like fire in the Everglades after a hard rain.

Neal smoothed out the disdain he felt creeping across his face. *Weasel.* "One voter, one vote. That's just what the governor wants to hear. Wants to know ahead of time if there's anything that might derail the process, stir up the media."

"I'm telling you, Neal, I don't know how plain I can be."

"Glad to hear it." Neal pushed up from his chair.

"You got everything you need, Neal? You just let me know if she doesn't get you what YOU need, eh?" Stan walked back to his desk. Still standing he picked up a stack of papers. "Well, we've got a lot to get our arms around today. Ya know, those damned computers, the more you have the more work they cause."

"Right, Stan."

***

"No, Brice, couldn't get anything out of him." Neal leaned his back against the wall outside the break room. "Something's muddled. They were going at it pretty strong. I'm just digging in. Not sure how big it is."

"That fool Stan. What'd he say? What makes you think…? What'd you hear exactly?"

"Exactly? The condensed version is Stan doesn't want to hold up the election for a couple of lousy votes."

"Well…makes sense on the face of it."

"Does it, Brice? From what I understand, these voting machines are supposed to get it right."

"This is true. But let's face it, some of those morons couldn't figure out a ballot if you held their hands and walked 'em through the whole f_____ thing."

"ElecTron's software is supposed to account for all possibilities. It's supposed to ensure a 100 percent one-ballot one-vote accuracy rate."

"Neal...Nealboy, your such an idealist. Keep your eye on it."

"Brice..." The line went dead. Neal flipped his phone shut. Damn. He was liking this less and less. Point of fact, he liked himself less and less as well. He was long overdue. Time to find another way...old friends...old habits...

***

"You take care of it boy?" Brice exhaled, whooshing over the phone line.

"I'm almost there." Leonard passed the media parking lot.

"Whaddya mean? Where? Whaddya doin'?"

"Meeting the little princess. We're talking numbers." *Cretin.* He pulled in beside the glistening building, nudged his rear bumper up to the loading bay. He jerked to a stop, shut off his engine and waited.

***

Stan leaned against the front of his mahogany desk, whining into his speaker phone. "I don't know why you had to send him down here anyway. The man's a freakin' nuisance. He's everywhere!"

"F____ you, Stan. For moments like this. Your girlie's in there now pokin' around. Get in there before she f____ things up more than she has already. She could ruin everything."

"You sure it's not just Neal Charles? You know he's got a real hard on for her. Hasn't figured it out yet...she won't play."

"That it, Stanley? Brains all wadded up in your pants when you should be cleaning up this election crap?"

36

Cady inched the door closed to soften the clank of the cardkey lock. She left Mario in the tabulation room monitoring his precinct uploads, isolating and accelerating her control precincts. Here in the break room, their worktable was again strewn with clusters of color-tagged, time-stamped reports. Squares and diamonds of powder-blue, gray and ecru sticky notes decorated the tan cabinets lining the north and west walls. Beside the tabulation room door on the south wall, Izzy leaned forward in her straight-back chair glaring into her computer screen. She turned away just long enough to make sure it was Cady who entered, then merely grunted an acknowledgment as Cady passed by.

Cady watched Izzy pushing and pulling at her mouse, fingers clicking the keyboard. "Seems to be working out okay in here again… Yes? Not too many interruptions? Auditors?"

"Neal hasn't been here."

"Izzy. I asked about the auditors."

"They haven't been here either… Cady, do you think Neal…" A wicked little smile played along the corners of Izzy's cherry pink mouth. "Cady, do you wonder about Neal as… in…*amoroso*?"

"Izzy. You're shameless!" Cady smiled, tugging at her ring.

"I just wanna play a while, I don't wanna take him home."

"And I believe you, Izzy, I…" Cady shook her head, smiling. "Izzy, looks like it could be a long night, for all of us… You know there's still flan in the fridge, if you…"

"No there's not," Izzy laughed.

"Always with Izzy," Cady laughed. "Okay, Izzy. Anything so far?"

"Spoilsport," Izzy moaned. "Oh, you mean with the *election*… I'm not sure. I isolated three of your precincts, fire station-ecru, church-blue, and school-gray along with their time-stamped upload reports. Interesting."

"I was afraid of that. Let's have it."

"Well, as I said, I'm not quite sure. The numbers, well I wanted to make sure the numbers weren't tripping over my brain fuzz, so like you said I ran graphs for a visual."

"Yes, yes."

"You know how sometimes the numbers start swirling around until they all look alike or they never look alike or they all fall into buckets they're not supposed to?"

"Gets a little scary, uh? Look. There. Same trend." Cady leaned over Izzy's shoulder, studying the juxtaposing colors on Izzy's graph.

"Yes. And basically all the machines follow the same pattern," Izzy's hand swept across the screen. "If you only look at the first few hours, blue wins by a well not huge, not a landslide exactly, but…"

"What's the margin?"

"57 percent to 42 percent."

"A 15 percent margin? That's wide, Izzy."

"Yes. Less than one percent goes to the insignificant others."

"Like you said, not a landslide, but definitive." Cady studied the colorfully striped graph lines representing each of the four machines. Blue pairs climbed up, up, up, higher and higher while red trailed by ever increasing margins. Then boom, blue hovered and sputtered and went flat like week-old foil balloons.

"Now look at this." Izzy glided the mouse shifting the screen to the right, panning in on the last two hours. She traced her finger over blue striped lines as they plunged downward again before flattening out.

"So my mind wasn't playing tricks on me…" Cady grimaced.

"Not at all. You had it pegged. Wish congratulations were in order," remorse dragged on her words. "Here this'll make you feel lots better," she said sarcastically.

Cady bent closer to the screen. Same striped lines, but this time the numbers they represented were much lower and the trends were the reverse of those on the previous graph.

"These are your rejections, Cady." Izzy glided her mouse,

panning the screen from left to right.

"And this column? What are these numbers?"

"Undervotes, Cady."

"Tell me again, who goes to an election and doesn't vote for the main event. These are big numbers, Izzy. I think they're bigger than the routine rejections we got with the old machines, bigger than punch-cards even." Cady rubbed at the right side of her forehead. "And we're sure these are the new voting machines?"

"Sorry, Cady. This year's newest play station."

"Izzy, we can't stop here. We need more information. See if you can figure out why the ballots were rejected. Look for voting patterns, say a certain combination of candidates or issues or even one issue throws a kink in the process and kicks the ballot out?"

"You mean for example, any vote for the last item on the ballot causes a reject? Or the first? Or something like that?" Izzy jotted notes on her legal pad.

"Yes. Exactly. Or maybe voters vote for every office and every issue on the ballot and it's too much for the computer to keep track of……but we tested that. "

Izzy scrawled a few more lines on the page before twisting her mechanical pencil to wheel out more lead.

"Izzy, look into how the number of rejects on these machines compares with other types of voting machines. Go back to the ballot scanners in the last election. You might even dredge up punch-card ballots for the same precincts."

"You don't want much, do you?" Izzy rolled her eyes. "Seriously, Cady, this really is taking a lot of time away from my must-do stuff and even with these shifting numbers…it's not a whole lot of votes. You sure this is where you want my time?"

"Et tu, Izzy? Just a few votes? It matters, Izzy. We don't know when it started and more importantly we don't know where it ends."

"Izzy, I like your colors," Neal walked over to Izzy's side of her computer as the break room door closed behind him. "So is this it top secret too or can you share?"

Cady's eyes narrowed at Neal. Then she turned to Izzy with a warning look.

"Oh, Neal, of course not. We were just going to take a look at some previous elections."

Cady's left eyebrow shot up, then she laughed at the truth of it in Izzy's next assignment.

"Now? Whatever for?"

"Well, Neal, sometimes looking to the past…it helps us to understand things, that's all." Izzy craned her neck to look up at him standing so close.

"I get it, I think. So tell me one of the problems you had before, you know with your Homer Simpson," Neal laughed and Izzy joined him. Neal pulled up a chair and sat beside her.

Cady left them to their laughter and settled in at the break room table, spreading out Izzy's reports and printed graphs the full length of the table.

"Well, before…the most serious is…say early on in one election, say around ten in the morning, Homer Simpson was in the lead, then boom he took a nosedive and the other candidate took the lead. And, oh, by the way, we had a minor flurry of rejected ballots… Now, get this. When we, Cady and I, when we added the number of rejected ballots to Homer Simpson's now trailing votes, Homer Simpson wins or ties."

"Scary, but I think I understand. Not a good thing. And if you believe the opinion polls, this election could be extremely close."

"Funny. Stan didn't seem to understand." Cady said absently.

"Cady, it's his job to understand."

"Be that as it may, he doesn't want us to waste time on it. All he wants is brief generic bullet points for the Canvassing Board."

"Cady!"

Neal turned from Cady to Izzy, "Izzy, that election when you found out about Homer, how far off were the vote counts?"

"Oh, Neal, well, when we found the numbers…. Not by bazillions, but enough to make the whole process suspect."

"Devils advocate here. Say that happened this election. If numbers aren't substantial, they don't change the ultimate winner, right? Democrats would still be winning."

"How can you know that?" Izzy's eyes opened wide.

"Exit polls…inside information."

Cady looked up from her reports, "Say that's true. But the margins are shrinking."

"Is that really a problem? I mean, your guy, my guy's climbing up in the numbers."

"What is it with everybody today?" Cady stood up from the table.

"Don't you want your guy to win?"

"Win? You mean in a fair and square match? Look, Neal. Red team, blue team, Independents. What good is it, if it's not right? What about Team USA? Doesn't that trump everything else? Do I want the red team to win? Yes. Do I want the blue team to lose? Yes."

"Well…"

"Neal. Do I want Team USA to lose in the process? No I don't."

"Cady, I didn't mean it that way."

"No? Sounds like you're advocating a flawed election."

"Hold on everybody. Remember, we're talking hypothetical here." Izzy stood up, tugging at the hem of her skirt and brushing the creases from her tummy. Then she stretched her arms taut to the naughty popping of her wayward top button. Cady watched Neal admiring the show.

"So, Cady, if you won't be needing this computer, I'll haul it back to the tabulation room." Not waiting for an answer, Izzy turned her back on Cady and Neal. She bent over her workstation with her temptress-maiden bottom poised perfectly for Cady to smack and she almost did.

With but a glance at Izzy, Neal studied Cady, her eyes, her scowl, her hand dragging her ring back and forth and he smiled.

Izzy closed the machine and lugged it under her arm as she backed her way through the tabulation room door. Within seconds, the door popped open and Izzy poked her head inside. "Cady, when you get a break you need to catch the opinion poll chatter." A brief shake of her head and Izzy headed back into the hallowed walls of the tabulation room. The door clanked shut to the sounds of Cady's shuffling through Izzy's reports and Neal looking on.

37

"Cady, I thought we were making progress here. You know mutual admiration, respect. Perhaps even a modicum of trust." Neal picked up Izzy's half-nibbled cookie and tossed it into the basket.

"Just how big is a modicum anyway, Neal?" she smiled a moment before narrowing her eyes. "Come on, Neal, I'm tired. You're always after my secrets and you share nothing. Tell me, what's your real purpose here?" Cady fiddled with her ring, pulling it side-to-side on its chain.

"Real or imagined, Cady?" Neal watched Cady tuck her ring into the warmth beneath her silky blouse. "Devised or invented?"

Cady shook her head and glared.

"Cady, you know already. I'm here to observe, lookout for snags in this election. Maybe I can control spin by preventing bad information from blasting across the networks. Definitely I need to keep some people informed."

"And?" she queried.

"And nothing. Nothing except that I'm bored playing babysitter out there. Maybe I'm getting the hang of this stuff. Maybe it's rubbing off on me, you're 'sanctity of the election' pre-recorded messages."

Cady laughed.

"And maybe, Cady, I'm not feeling so good about some things right now. Maybe I feel like I need to atone for...and maybe I don't know. But I do want to help.... Look. It's no secret you had a hefty row with your boss. No secret I heard all I could without mashing my ear against his door."

"Now we're getting somewhere." Cady laughed at the image of Neal smashed into Stan's pricey door.

"Cady, again, no secret my mission *is* information. It is a secret however that I'm not comfortable with some intangibles. Don't ask specifics. I can't give them to you."

Cady waited for him to continue.

"Look, Stan's a buffoon. He said you were riled up, imagining things. Too picky for your own good. I…well, Cady, I wonder how anyone can be too picky when the numbers don't jibe."

"Don't mind him, Neal," Cady shrugged, pasting on her business face. Defending the man to the 'public,' when privately she'd like to staple his black tongue to his worn-out zipper. "It's just classic Stan. Numbers make him nervous. I think maybe Stan doesn't get it, that we're in a new technological age."

"Maybe. But when you see the buzzards circling, something's foul, Cady. You're out on a limb here. I don't understand all the details. But I do want to help. Maybe I feel a little like I'm out here with you. Can I help you, Cady?"

"Neal, I've dangled on this limb before, Stan's personal scapegoat. I know it. He knows it. Flows down. No wallowing, just is. But for all the chronic angst, I care about this stuff, this job. But maybe not enough to go through another one. It just gets nuttier and nuttier and I'm not ready to be chopped up and mixed in with their fruitcake."

"Cady…Can I help?"

Neal studied Cady's changing expressions. Whatever was going on behind those eyes, that flicker of a smile could be very interesting. For it was evident to him at that moment, Cady directed a full inner chorus, reciting her own private litany of rationale, advantages, disadvantages, pros, cons that just might let him into her tight circle of confidantes and…champions. And Neal, he wanted admission. Funny, he didn't feel like a spook.

"Well? Cady? How about it? Or are you content to tell yourself your own private little jokes over there?"

"Can't believe I keep opening up doors around here for you to slink in," Cady shook her head, then breathed in deep. "But…well, Mr. Charles, must be your lucky day. Seems I need someone who…isn't technical, a sounding board to bounce this stuff around with. And Stan, well you see, he didn't exactly work out. Looks like tag-you're-it."

"Bring it on, Cady. I'm your man. For sure I'm not technical."

"Let's say I agree. Then I need to lay the ground rules for this sham. And I'm not sure…"

"Ground rules?"

"Yes. For one thing, you don't belong here. You don't work in this department. You aren't part of my team. You're an intruder."

"A little harsh, Cady."

"Just the facts, Neal. Now, there's *INFORMATION* and there's *information*."

"Right. Makes perfect sense," Neal laughed.

"Yes it does," Cady laughed with him. "They can drag my techie tush off to jail for passing out voting data prior to poll closing. Even to you."

"A moot point, isn't it? Okay, some of your numbers are wrong. I got that. But just what real…relevant voting information can you give me before the polls close?"

"Plenty and that's the tangle you broke up with Stan and me."

"I knew it. I watched you and I knew something was wrong. That's why I…followed you…"

"Hah. And I knew you didn't just show up by accident. There are names for people like you. Bad names…"

"Yeah, but you won't use them, because at the heart of it, you know I'm one of the good guys."

"How would I know that? Besides, you're still just a…spy."

Neal smiled. *If you only knew, Cady. If only…forget it, Neal.* "Cady, please." Neal thought for a moment. "Okay. I'll share something with you, Cady, something very private, something if…well later when you put it all together you'll understand."

"Ah," Cady smiled, a lopsided smirk that reminded Neal of a little tomboy playing pranks on one of her toad-trapping friend-boys. "Quid pro quo, is it? We gonna trade secrets, Neal?"

"No, Cady. This one's on me. You can do with it what you will. No strings. No reciprocity. Understand?"

"No."

"Maybe you're not the only one who needs to offload and play it back, Cady. What would you say if I told you something doesn't feel right to me. Don't ask for specifics because I don't have them. And if I did, I wouldn't share them with anyone. Not anyone, not yet, Cady. I just know that...look, I've been with... I've basically worked for the same...team since college."

"That's quite a record, a *really* long time in one job."

"Not *that* long, Cady. Alright, it is a long time. But more recently, there's been a strain. I've seen gradual changes in Bri... things...that are sucking me into a place I don't want to be. I've doubts, misgivings and quite frankly I'm ready for this stretch to be over so I can walk away. Maybe if letting it ride wasn't so much easier than the alternative, I'd have been gone long before now."

"I might understand, Neal," Cady nodded.

"Well, if you're fisticuffs with Stan earlier was any indication of your norm here, you probably do. I think my...unease goes more to my own personal sense of transgressions or perhaps encounters with them. Sometimes we do things in life out of necessity that can make us feel...unclean."

"Make you feel like a prostitute? Like doing things you know aren't quite right or fair, maybe not illegal, but not right and having to do them anyway because your boss said so and you like your paycheck? It makes you feel dirty?"

"Ahhh...something like that...I think. No. Exactly like that."

Cady studied the man, searching his stormy eyes for answers to questions she did not yet know. Did he?

"Okay, Neal. You're on. Welcome to my world. How's this for a start?" Cady stopped for a moment, took in a deep breath and began, "It appears we have some...voting irregularities."

"Yes." He looked into her eyes, eyes that trusted him. "Cady, I need to tell you something......Can you forget for just a second that I'm not on your...team? Can I tell you...look, you need to document everything that's happened here. Document everything in detail. Document your meetings with Stan and his requests...in detail. Gather as much hard information as you can. Document it and file it...off site."

"I planned to put this all down on paper. But you...Neal, what should I know?"

"How can I tell you when I don't even know myself? But, Cady, if it doesn't feel right...might not be. And if it's not right...."

38

"Where's Izzy? She's working on some new information for me," Cady asked without breaking stride as she rounded the corner on her way to Mario at his console.

"She got a call from the guy at ElecTron." Mario glanced over his shoulder at the auditors, then lowered his voice. "Said he reproduced our rejections on the voting machines at his office. Wants to show her his results."

"Excellent." Cady scanned the tabulation room and the media room again. "So where is she?"

"She went out back to meet him. Thought it best to avoid the lobby, you know the reporters and all."

"Odd. Who would know some guy from ElecTron? Well, let's hope he's really on to something this time. We can use a breakthrough here."

"Yeah. Let me tell you, she's excited alright. She almost flew out of here."

"Bet she is. Mario, I'm sure she'll track me down right away. But in case she doesn't, will you let me know as soon as she gets back? I'm in the break room with Neal showing him how the ballots work."

"Really…" he chuckled softly. "Sure thing, I'll let you know."

***

Neal studied studied Cady's colored pages of jumbled numbers spread out across the break room table, not pretending they made any sense at all. But he gained a fair understanding of the process, the concepts and pressed her for more.

Strumming the pale-blue pages with his fingers, Neal turned in his chair and leaned in close to Cady. "Let's say you trap the problem and you know what's wrong. Why can't you fix it?"

Cady scooted back from the table to face him. "You know why, Neal. It's ElecTron's software. But at this point, it's mostly about prevention and containment. If we know what causes the problem, we might be able to work around it by telling the voters, do this a different way or don't do that."

"So you correct the process without fixing the problem."

"Right. Then we trust ElecTron can fix the problem before the next election."

Neal picked up a paper ballot off the table. "But this ballot changes every election, doesn't it? Does that mean ElecTron dings you for reprogramming their voting machines every election too?" Their knees grazed.

"No. Actually, ballots are set up right here. We tell our voting machines who the candidates are and where everything goes on the ballot."

"What if you set it up wrong?"

"Oh and we have, Neal. It's not hard to do. One tiny mistake and you turn an election upside down." Cady leaned back to the table and ripped a page from her legal pad. "Let's say this is your ballot." She scribbled a few lines across the page. "Your entire election." Her finger traced around the outside edges of the ballot.

"So, how you do it?" Neal reached over to tilt the ballot toward him, brushing Cady's hand in the process. Cady jerked back rubbing the tingles out of her errant fingers.

"I…" Cady stared down at the paper. She gawked at Neal's hand, still rubbing her own. "Not important."

He nodded his head, his expression serious. But his eyes flashed mischief. "So tell me something that could go wrong, that you might not catch right away."

"Big stuff. Say you don't allow for enough votes for a candidate or you don't set up enough room on reports or in some of the vote tallying processes. If your computers think 99 is the maximum number of votes for a candidate, you'll overflow. In other words, after 99 votes have been counted, any vote past that goes into the big bucket in the sky. You'll never count any number of votes past 99 on any of your voting machines. Here, may I?" Cady took the ballot from him. Their hands met again. She smacked the ballot on the table and drew a line down the page illustrating the lost votes. Then she rubbed her fingers again.

"That is big stuff."

"Yes. But there's more. You could flip blue and red candidates on the ballot or anywhere down the line in the tallying process or on your reports. Now that would cause an upset."

"I think I understand why so much protocol, Cady."

"Yes and why we work with ElecTron beyond protocol, beyond expectations to help them achieve a more stable product. But again, since we can't see, smell, touch ElecTron's programs ..."

"You can't fix it."

"Exactly." Cady exclaimed, scooting forward in her chair, bumping Neal's leg with her toe. Her own leg jerked back, but not before the burning flashed through her body and her words lost their way in her addled brain.

Neal held on to his smile, but his eyes couldn't hide his pleasure. "Cady, I…you can't fix it?"

"I…uh…No," she shook her head, then started again. "We're completely locked out of ElecTron's program code…and when we run into a glut of…bugs and boondoggles and they can't seem to get it right. Well, it's frustrating. Especially since we're all programmers here. We know how it should work. Sometimes I wonder if they do."

"Did this happen in the last election, the glitches?"

"You know it did. Every election. Not that we don't try to stop it."

"How's that?"

"Well as soon as we know the candidates and issues, and the ballot design jells, we set up our own private mini-election. We process hundreds of ballots, checking each ballot variation. When we run into unpredictable results, we document the error for ElecTron and they're supposed to fix it."

"Like they fixed your crossed voter error?"

"Right. What you don't know is that in the months before this election, ElecTron rolled out fix after bungled fix. You know, Neal, this level of ineptitude…in the private sector, incompetence on this scale would have resulted in ElecTron being fired long ago, if not sued. Yet somehow, Stan lets them hang on. This time they told Stan they'd make it right by sending in their techs to upgrade their defective software in our chronically faulty machines."

"And the crossed voters prove they didn't get the job done? How does all this bungling happen?"

"Well, part of the problem is that ElecTron farms out work, some offshore, while we ultimately wind up doing their quality assurance job for them. We're really the ones who test ElecTron's faulty software. We test from beginning to end, over and over until they supposedly get it right."

"But they didn't, did they?"

"Sadly, no and we pay for it…The public pays for it."

39

Artificial lighting in the tabulation room masked the passage of real time and the darkened sky outside. The only notable difference between sunrise and sunset here was the intensity of the crowds in the media room...and the absence of Izzy. Mario waved Cady over to his console.

"Hey, Cady," Mario whispered. "You hear about the exit polls...? Doesn't look good. Some pollsters predict a landslide."

Cady pulled a chair up next to his console. "Not what our control precincts are registering, Mario. But then, this whole thing is a barrel of hog feathers. Damn I wish we'd hear from Izzy."

"Me too. I'm worried. She wouldn't just take off like that without telling me, without telling someone, especially today."

"That's what I told the police. But technically, she's not missing."

"Did you tell them about your phone calls?"

"Yes. But that doesn't seem to account for much. Neal said…"

"What can he do?"

"Well, he's trying to pull some strings. Trigger a real investigation. At least get some detectives out here to collect whatever evidence or witnesses there might be here, now as opposed to tomorrow or next week or whenever they decide she's really missing."

"Cady, I've been wondering if I should start calling people, you know her friends or something?"

"Her parents are already taking care of it. Besides, Mario, we're kicking into high gear here. Thirty minutes before the polls close."

"I know. I know. I just want to do something, chica."

"I feel the same. Look at them." Cady nodded toward the media room. "They're all so fresh faced and eager and I'm...I'm ready to vomit. Does it show?" Cady's eyes were squinted, her lips pursed. She shook her head to blot out terrifying images of some psycho hurting their nascent flower.

Cady looked over at Neal, caught his eye, shrugged her shoulders. He answered her, shaking his head. No smiles for each other now. She nodded her head toward the break room. Instantly, he pushed back from his table to meet her there.

***

"Neal. Anything?"

"Nothing."

"I...I don't know what to do. I don't think I can..."

"Cady, listen to me. There's nothing you can do about Izzy. Detectives interviewed your Security and all your employees who've had access to the area. They've been in the media room checking things out. They questioned every group of reporters there. They've hung out in both restrooms. So far, nothing. But..."

"So where is she? What can they do now?"

"Security's given them your creep's employee file. They're pursuing him. And they're tracing the phones."

"But I thought they already did that."

"No, not yet. And they're posting a crew here, just in case there's another lead, another call."

"I don't think I can..."

"Cady," Neal held his arms open for her. When she moved toward him, he stepped into her and hugged her close. "Oh, Cady. I'm so sorry. I wish..." He continued pulling her to him, holding her tight until he feared he might squeeze her breath away. He loosened his grip. But then it was she who pulled, her arms circling strong enough to never let him go. "Cady, Cady."

"I don't think I can do this anymore. I'm so afraid for her...so tired. The madness..."

"I know, Cady. I know. You're taking hits from all angles, first that lunatic, the election, Stan, and now this. But here's what you're going to do. You're going to snuggle up here for a while.

You're going to cry a little. Then in a few minutes, you'll blow your nose, wash your face, maybe comb your hair," he brushed his hand over her forehead, smoothing back her hair. "Then you're going to march back into that jungle of yours and take charge. You're going to get this tabulation stuff going and, Cady…"

She pulled her head back and looked up at him, "Y-y-e-e-s, Neal?"

"Then I'm taking you home."

***

Neal walked Cady to the tabulation room door, his hand resting on the small of her back. He held the door for her and continued holding it open, watching her walk away from him until she disappeared behind the computer cabinets. She didn't turn around. He wanted to follow. He let the door clank shut when his phone buzzed.

"Not enough they've been takin' potshots at this election all day…but you, you get us all tangled up with the police. You tryin' ta take me down, Neal?"

"Brice, no. Come on. What's got you so riled?"

"You layin' it on the police, that's what. Gettin' 'em all stirred up. And for what?"

"For a woman who's gone missing, Brice."

"Nealboy! I'm surprised at you! Fact is, you've takin' on a few of those yourself, women I mean. Known you to hole up for days with one of your beauties."

"Different, Brice. Not the same at all. This woman…well she's barely a woman yet."

"Hot, uh? Fresh meat?"

"She's very attractive, Brice. What does that have to do with it?"

"Probably took off with some other hot blooded young…"

"Brice, she's in the middle of an election."

"Ah, right. How 'bout the auditors. Any of them missing? Maybe one of 'em lured her off to balance his books, if you catch my drift."

"Hardly. Though I wish it was that. I do."

"How d'you know it's not?"

"Too many related incidents. You know, the threats, the vandal, and of course you know the voting problems pestering them all day."

"Told you to stop that crap, Neal."

"Yes, Brice, and I told you I'll track it and make sure that if and when it's outed it's done so quickly, with such an abundance of factual information and confidence and diplomacy that it's old news before it becomes news."

"Yeah? When's that gonna be, Neal. You're the one stirring the pot down there?"

"Hold on, Brice. I'm advising you…take a breath. This has nothing to do with your part in the election. You've done all the politicking you can. You can't lure anymore voters to the polls. You can't control their votes. It's done. They're gone. It's all over but for the counting. Now…"

"See, Nealboy. Just why I keep you around. But why do ya' keep stickin' your face in where it doesn't belong?"

"Brice, listen. He wrecked Cady's office. A building full of reporters and security guards, and this pervert marches right in, sets off a virus and ransacks her office. But you know that."

"Balls. If he was so creepy, Security woulda nabbed him before he set his scrawny toe inside the building."

"Right……scrawny…… One would think… Actually, 'creepy man' is their description of a software engineer who worked here briefly, before Cady fired him."

"So, what's that got to do with it?"

"Well, creepy man is their main suspect right now. He has knowledge of their operation here, enough knowledge in fact to pull off the other incidents. And it seems he had motive."

"You really suspect foul play then?"

"Brice, been foul play off and on all day. Threatening phone calls for weeks actually. By the way, when I asked why Cady hired creepy man in the first place, she said Stan hired him. The word is Stan got pressured from higher up."

"She said…uh…? Doesn't wanna own up to her own mistakes?"

"Correction, 'they' said. You have any idea what it's about?"

"Why…'spose it coulda been one of his Board members. Most likely Stan blowin' wind out his tailpipe."

"Right. Good."

"Why good?"

"Police are checking him out. Security here handed over his personnel file this morning…Brice?"

***

Leonard ignored his vibrating hip for as long as he could stand it, longer. Then he finally yanked his cell phone off his belt and flipped it open.

"You sick bastard. Look what you've done!"

His phone went dead.

40

"It's more hurry up and wait now, Neal, at least for my part. Of course Mario's kicked into high gear. As soon as the precincts close, Mario starts uploading voting data from the voting machines...for real this time. Then our worry shifts from voting errors to failures that might prevent us from counting all the votes the machines give us."

"So it's a wrap then, Cady?"

"Hardly. The tallies, the reports, Board review, certification... and perhaps more reports or even a rerun of the tallies...as if that could somehow change the numbers. But it's happened. Then there's my friend Murphy. He might intercede at anytime with anything from minor hiccups to a raging catastrophe."

"I thought..."

"We've got it covered with contingency operations? We do. That is every preventable failure known to man. Though sometimes Murphy zings us a curveball. But, Neal, your part's done here. I mean we can still run into snags and delays, but with the polls closed the risk of public humiliation diminishes."

"And if it's another close election?"

"There is that. And we can always miss the eleven o'clock news."

"But essentially you're trying to dump me...already? No, Cady. I'm taking you home, remember? Besides if there's news of Izzy...."

"I worry so. For all her flash, Neal, she's such an innocent. And whoever took her, whatever they've done..." Neal's arm tightened around her shoulder, pulling her close to his chest. Cady rested her forehead in the curve of his neck. His skin felt like warm velvet and she felt safe...until the soft brrrr of his phone broke silence and Cady left him alone closing the tabulation room door softly behind her.

***

"What's happenin' down there?" Brice grated, his voice hoarse.

"Nothing new, Brice. No news. They haven't found her yet." Neal checked his watch, feeling Izzy's time tick-tick away. With Cady gone he let his guard down, "I'm afraid for her, Brice."

"Found who? What?"

"Sorry. Misunderstood." Should have known.

"I'll say, Nealboy. They're countin' the votes now, aren't they?"

"The polls only closed ten minutes ago, Brice."

"Right. When then?"

"Soon. Poll workers at the smaller precincts should be wrapping up their closeout tasks soon."

"And the others?"

"Some of the larger precincts clog up toward the end of the day. People voting after work. Those precincts stay open, taking in the last of the stragglers who made it to the lines before seven."

"Let me know the second it starts."

***

Leonard took another swig. Feet up, eyes forward staring at his television, he glared at the talking heads, the commercial breaks, previews of return-to-your-regular program, red-state-blue-state analysts, and what-shall-we-do-if Florida screws up again. Finally, the cameras panned the tabulation room. Finally, the fisheye lens swept over the computer cabinets, the holy table, and... *Shit. Mr. Omnipresent still at the console. Where's your piece-a-fluff now, you suck-up. Counting your votes yet? Idiot. Bet not. Moron. First you gotta grab all those pesky little vote tallies from every one of my voting machines and suck 'em into your f_____ tabulation computer. Suppose by now you've cleaned out the residue from my nasty little prank this morning. Shit. That felt good. Cady looked catatonic. Sure she put on her happy face, but inside I bet she crumbled. Bitch. Where is she?*

"THERE YOU HAVE IT. POLLS HAVE ALL CLOSED IN MIAMI-DADE COUNTY, FLORIDA. ELECTION SUPERVISOR STAN CORBIN IS FEELING A

DEEP SENSE OF RELIEF NOW. THE ONLY THING LEFT FOR HIM IS TO COUNT THE VOTES. BACK TO YOU, MIGUEL." The Miami reporter signed off and the talking heads popped back on screen. *Shit.*

Leonard clicked DVD, rewind, then play. His own lens zoomed in on Cady. Perfect Cady. Leonard bent forward. His feet jerked off the coffee table and smacked on the floor. Oblivious to the beer drizzling over his jeans.

The camera swerved to pan Izzy approach Cady at the whiteboard, then followed the two women to the communications table where they huddled. Leonard's hand squeezed the beer can. Small dents formed under his thumb and middle finger. Beer sloshed on the carpet. *You black-haired witch! Couldn't just leave me alone, could you? You snitch! Couldn't mind your own business. No. You stupid little snitch. Ran to Cady-bitch every chance you got for every stupid little thing. Earn a few more points…points at my f_____ expense. If it hadn't a been for your sorry ass, I'd have done fine, you bitch.*

Leonard slammed the beer on the table and ripped his glasses off flinging them onto the table where they skipped to the edge before flipping to the floor. Then, covering his face with his two grimy hands, Leonard sobbed.

"Bitch. Bitch. Bitch. You and your little fan club can just rot in hell."

41

Cady stood beside Mario's chair and watched the numbers flashing around-and-around on his console as precincts closed down for the night. She waited while Mario answered his phone.

"ElecTron for you Cady. Eight-thirty...'bout time, isn't it?" Mario shrugged his shoulders, holding the phone out for Cady.

Cady nodded taking the phone, "Hello. This is Cady Palmer."

"Miss Palmer? Susan Ca-a-dy Pa-a-al-mer?" the man asked.

"Yes. And you are...?"

"Having...fun?" he sniggered.

"Sorry. I didn't catch your name." Cady put her hand over the mouth piece and mouthed to Mario, "ElecTron? You sure?"

Mario nodded, whispering, "What's going on? They find something?"

"I see you," the man taunted.

Cady squinted into the floodlights looking for her caller. Network cameras panned her tabulation room.

"I see you. You lose something? You don't look so happy now, do you? You thought you had it all figured out, you and your little pet. Where's your pretty now, missy? ...Where's your little pretty now?"

"Wha...?"

"You look so baffled, Cady. You know your little raven haired chickie, the one who keeps no secrets."

Cady looked frantically about the tabulation room, the media room. The phone slipped from her fingers. By the time Mario stooped to pick it up Cady had fled out the break room door.

"This is Mario. Can I help you?" The line was dead. Mario scrolled the phone for incoming calls. Pressed *69. Blocked number. "Hey, can one of you take over here?" He called to his backup teammates. "Hey!" Three heads turned from their workstations against the back wall, their hectic phone and research support still active. Mario motioned to his console and darted after Cady, not waiting for their answer.

***

Neal pushed back from his small table the instant Cady dropped her phone, quickly scanning the room to see if others noticed. Puzzled, no one had. Pausing on his way out the No Admittance door he scanned the room again, this time looking for Cady's creepy little man.

***

"Yes. I made a mistake. I know it…I know I should have kept him talking…I know it's impossible to trace…Did you trace it? …I will. If he calls again, I will." Cady swiped at the wisps of hair taunting her eyes. "Yes. Damage done. But Izzy…he has her. He as much as told me he has her…. Yes, I'll wait to hear from you." Cady hung up the phone.

"Cady…you okay? Was that your guy?" Neal pulled out a chair and motioned for her to sit down. He grabbed the chair next to her and sat down facing her, knees grazing. He took her hands in his own.

"Yes. I lost it, Neal. The psycho's got Izzy and I lost it and I forgot to keep him talking and I…"

"Cady," Mario joined them. "How do we return calls with these office phones? He's got a locked number so I couldn't get it back… And I never use these phones except for elections."

Cady took the phone from Mario, "Like this…"

"Wait, Cady," Neal rested his hand on top of Cady's. "Let Security do it. They might get a lead, a trace if it goes through, if they know when the call starts."

"Good point. I'll take it downstairs." Mario looked from Cady to Neal and then to their hands reluctant to move. He retrieved his phone from Cady's free hand. "Anything else? Cady?"

"No. No. Thanks, Mario. Everything under control in there?" Cady nodded toward the tabulation room.

"Yeah. We're plodding along. It'll be a while," Mario warned, then left them to each other, closing the door softly behind him.

Neal rested his hand on Cady's shoulder. "What can I do? You look frazzled."

"Oh...that helps, Neal. Security, the police, they said we don't have a victim yet. Will this call make a difference? ...They've roped off our offices." She patted her hair. "Can't get to my comb."

"I...here." Neal reached into his breast pocket for his comb.

Cady took it and combed at her willful locks with limited success.

"Here," Neal took back his comb and gently tidied her hair.

"Hmm. You've found my weakness, Mr. Charles. And I'm shameless. A time like this to be..." eyes still closed.

"Not. Here keep this, Cady. I'm going down to talk with Security. See what they're about. Then I'll follow up with the police again. Okay?"

Cady offered Neal a feeble smile, tucking his comb into her skirt pocket.

***

"Easy, Brice." Neal answered, rounding the landing in Izzy's back stairwell as he retraced the steps Izzy climbed down to meet with her ElecTron phantom. Neal didn't break pace. Brice's frequent gotta-have-gotta-know volleys left little time in between. "It kicked into high gear a few minutes ago, Brice. But don't expect anything tangible for a while yet." Neal reined in his own annoyance. *Yes, Brice, I know. Cady's not my job. Getting down to Security's not my job. You are. I know who writes my paycheck...not for long, Briceboy. Obligation trumps money. You never understood. This election muddle...my obligation. Sadly you're the other side. You crossed over or you'd understand why this trumps even loyalty to you.*

"What's that mean to me?" Brice gushed.

"Phones are busy in the tabulation room. Lots of bustle. Even the auditors perked up. They're finally toddling back and forth to the communications table. But Cady said this is just the beginning. There's lots to do yet before..."

"What's Palmer doing?"

Neal decided against mentioning Cady's latest phone call or Izzy or the police. "She's verifying reports. Looks like the printers are spitting them out faster than the programmers can pick them up and log them in. They've got a couple of programmers now wearing grooves in the floor between the print stations and the communications table."

"F____. What's she brewin' up now? She's lookin' for more trouble, isn't she? I know it. I'll tell ya, Neal, Stan's dumber than fly speck. Said that chit's on our side. She's not, you know. She's f_____ dangerous. You keep on her. Hear? Don't let that little bitch outta your sight. I mean it. What's taking so long? Whadda those reports do anyway?"

"It's their preprocessing, Brice. Before they add up all the votes they pull in the vote tallies from each voting machine. They scan every precinct for the obvious irregularities, more votes than registered voters, things like that. They don't want to contaminate the tabulation mix with bad data."

"Nealboy, you missed your calling. You up for Stan's job?"

Neal didn't answer.

"You seen the exit polls, Nealboy?"

"No. It's been hectic. The only time I take a breather is when the programmers do and trust me, that's not often."

"Looks bad, real bad. I'm flippin' through the channels. Talking heads, they're giddy with it. All of 'em. Exit polls are damning. Half the voters think the country's on the wrong track. What do you think, Neal?"

"You know what I think, Brice."

"Promised I'd bring Florida home again. Maybe I can't. Florida's trending Democrat."

42

When Neal joined Cady in the break room, he found her slouched in Izzy's chair shooting rubber bands at the light switch next to the doorway. Her look pensive, determined. Clusters of bands dotted the shiny floor. She swerved her aim shooting him in the chest as he approached.

"Ouch! What'd I do?"

"You're here, fair game."

"Well, I suppose that's reasonable."

"It's not the rejects, Neal."

"I wondered…before…looked like things might not be going so well in there with your tabulations."

"No. I was having trouble with my happy face so I came back here to sort it out. The tallies, the reports, our conjecture…we're wrong. It's not the rejects."

"But your numbers matched. Slam dunk. One plus one is two. What happened?"

Cady poured fresh coffee, handing Neal his mug. "Careful, it's hot."

"Thank you, Cady. Is it privileged or can you share?"

"Both. It's privileged and I can share. They vanished. Rejected ballots…they vanished."

"But they're here on these reports." Neal pointed to the ragged pages scattered across the table. "Are all the reports wrong?"

"No, Neal. The reports were dead on. But now the rejected ballots are simply poof, zip, gone. Except from the scanners."

"How about the numbers?"

"Still off. And there's another bump in red."

"Look, Cady. I'm not election literate here, but if something was there before, it can't just not be there now." He thought for a moment. "It can't disappear."

"No? All we have is numbers printed on a page. Think about a bank transfer. It's funny money. No money actually changes hands. But you know you got it and the amount checks out and you spend it. Then it's gone. The only proof you have is a number printed on your bank statement at the end of the month."

"Okay... How does that relate?"

"The rejections were there. We printed snapshots of the voting machines' internal vote counters. The snapshots told us the number of votes rejected for error. But once the machines were closed out, signed off and the vote data was uploaded for the final time, rejects were gone. They.... Oh, no!" Cady gasped. She sprinted to the tabulation room door, jammed her cardkey into the door, opened it a crack and whispered loudly, "Mario...Mario!"

"Cady, what is it?" Mario hustled up to Cady at the open door.

"Are the church voting machines all closed out yet?"

"No, Cady. They're only halfway through. It'll be a while."

"Okay. Good. Do another upload so we have the final vote counts. Send one of the guys over to pick up my control machines. Okay? Before they're closed out. This is important."

"Yes, Cady. I'm on it."

"How about scanners. Are there any scanners anywhere that aren't closed out?"

"I'll find them, Cady. I'll upload their data too."

"They don't need to unpack the machines tonight. Just pick them up. Understand? Leave them in the van."

"Yes, Cady." Mario disappeared behind the closing tabulation room door.

Neal waited a moment, "Cady? What are you thinking?"

"Neal, I'm thinking... Neal. You see that door over there?" Cady pointed to the tabulation room door. "The other side of that door is a room full of people and all of them, every last one of them wants to run the perfect election. And I'm thinking...Neal... electrons and bits and bytes to figure out why it's not the perfect election. And you don't fit. Now you see that door over there?" Cady pointed to the hallway door. "That's your way out. I've got enough to do here without chatting it up with you, Neal."

"No, Cady. Listen. You've no one. I was there remember? With Stan. And I heard you...soft and clear and beaten. And I heard that weasel you call a boss stonewalling you."

"I can't go there, Neal. I've got to find some reason to this, work it out so that it makes sense. If it's wrong and the votes are skewed, I've got to parse it down for my reports so the Board can understand. They can't certify it."

"Look, what I'm trying to say is you need someone on your side, Cady. Let it be me."

"Thanks, Neal. I appreciate it. I do. But you're so...not technical and I need a number cruncher to hypothesize and...and cogitate with me. I need...Izzy."

"I know, Cady. And we'll find her. We will. But for now, hear me out. Maybe my being untech isn't such a bad thing. Talk to me. Work through it with me. If it turns out that I'm more bumble than help, I'll leave. I promise."

Neal scooted his chair up to the table, picked up a pencil and propped his arms against the table's edge. He looked over the bundles of reports, "Okay, you said rejects are gone, but the red numbers got bigger right?"

"Yes."

"Did red increase by the same amount that was in your reject column?"

"No."

"What about the other candidates? What happened to their numbers?"

"We weren't tracking them. But..."

"Where could the rejects go?"

"I see where you're headed, Neal. They could fall off the edge of the earth. But then our final results would show that more people voted than we counted votes. Actually my latest reports showed a high number of undervotes. And the scanners recorded the opposite, a high number of overvotes."

"How do you know how many people voted...? What about blue?"

"Flat. So red climbs. Blue's flat. We've got undervotes, overvotes, and possibly a push to other candidates. And we expected..."

"Right. What results did you expect in these precincts?"

"Well, overall we expected a higher turn out. So far, our reports show a 73 percent turnout, ballots cast as compared with registered voters. That's more than the 72 percent that showed up in the last election."

"Yes. But this year it's more contentious."

"Plus there are over 150 thousand new voters."

"New voters are more motivated to vote aren't they?"

"Yes, but look at this report. Here's another control group that fell from a 70 percent turnout in the last election to a 30 percent turnout this time. That's a 40 percent drop. And look here. It's exactly the opposite. Here's 75 percent red vote. Apparently, red get-out-the-vote campaigns worked."

"Voter turnout aside, what else did you expect, Cady."

"Well, based on our earlier reports," Cady reached across the table for a report tagged with an orange sticky note. Holding the report open for Neal, "When we compare the blue votes with total votes cast within each precinct, these individual precincts show blue pulling ahead with 58 percent, 55 percent, 57 percent of the ballots cast. Given it should level off some because there are pockets of red strongholds within precincts. But not by huge numbers."

"How do your later results compare with the exit polls?"

"The exit polls give blue the win claiming 59 percent of the vote. Everything we've seen falls short. Maybe 51 or 52 percent for blue. Blue's still on top. It's squirrelly. Why mess with an election at all if you're not targeting a win?"

"Cady, you're graphs and your numbers and your percents... even your overvotes and undervotes and rejects and...the rest of your tech-speak...okay, so you're right. I'm not technical enough to help pinpoint your...algorithms."

Cady said nothing and she didn't smirk...exactly.

But Neal did. "Still, Cady, I do wonder. When I look for reason or constancy here, two points stand out."

"Oh? And just what are they, Neal?"

"First is Neal's corollary to 'if it feels too good to be true'...Actually I stole it from someone else but the effect's the same. Ready? ...If the fish smells bad, it's probably spoiled."

Cady laughed spite of herself. "Neal, my election's gone bonkers and I'm spiraling headlong into the abyss. How can you?"

"Okay. Okay. It's a bad election. You know it. I know it. Izzy knew it. By the way, Stan knows it too."

"And? So? What's your second point?"

"Maybe they just skimmed off the top. Cady, maybe the intent is not for red to carry Miami. Maybe the intent is to shave off just enough blue votes so that red realistically carries the state."

Cady's eyes narrowed. "Go on."

"Cady, Miami-Dade is only one county voting with ElecTron machines. How many other Florida counties own ElecTrons? Twenty? Thirty? Big ones? Chip away at enough blue votes spread across the state and you carry the day. Red gets the win statewide but there's no damning big bang to cause suspicion."

"Neal, it fits. Think about it. I keep going back to the rejects. Why? You know the voting machine could easily display a confirmation for blue but tally a vote for red inside the machine. That would definitely push the win to red. But if someone wanted a more believable win they wouldn't just indiscriminately flip votes, would they? They'd wait to see how many votes they needed to flip and still keep up appearances."

"Geek-speak. What does that have to do with rejects?"

"They used the reject counter to keep track of stolen blue votes. Then when the machines closed out, they took those votes and spread them across acceptable scenarios. You know, to other candidates, undervotes, red and some back to blue. Neal, it proves intent. Not just some freakish glitch."

"And no one's the wiser. That is no one except Cady who's monitoring the machines throughout the day. Next step?"

"Next step? Ohmygosh. No. Rejects. Think. So the guy's hacking along, stealing votes from the blue team. One for me, reject for you, two for me, reject for you. All's well and good until he realizes these voting machines don't allow rejects, so he dumps his rejected votes somewhere else…for these machines. But his code still works on the ballot scanners. Understand? He's got the same rigged tabulation code on the scanners. Okay, next step, I write up my report for the Board, for Stan."

43

Leonard scrunched his can and tossed it to the coffee table in the general direction of the other empties. It skipped over the edge, toppling another can with it onto the dampening carpet. Leonard sniggered. "I did it. Me, Cady. Me... Leonard."

"Do you have a status for me, Leonard?" he jeered, mimicking Cady's voice.

"Done. Over. Polls closed. Ballots uploaded," he answered. "No more calls, least not from ElecTron. They're all tucked in for the night. Pointless little waiting game, isn't it? I'm used to waiting now, aren't I, Cady?" Leonard sniggered. Who woulda guessed a piss-grunt job in defense could jack him up to the porker-belly's call list. No doubt Brice's getting his blow-by-blows of the ballot tabulation from his suck-up over there at Elections.

"But we're on target, aren't we, Cady?" Leonard looked up to Cady's image paused, hovering on his 102 inch widescreen high-definition-plasma television. "On target, on plan, on budget uh, Cady." Leonard yanked another beer from his six-pack and popped it open. Beer fizzled onto his lap. He didn't flinch. Must be poking along as planned...or he woulda heard from Brice by now. Lucky thing too...guzzled enough beer and whiskey and shit to short circuit his synapses...shit...what with *puta* in the next room. He looked over at Izzy's door then to Cady and to Cady's light flickering off her scissors on the table in front of him. He downed the beer.

Leonard stretched back on the couch. Remote in hand, legs up, fly open, he clicked the TV button and glared up at the talking heads replacing Cady's image. *Damn. Did they ever listen to themselves yap? Same shit over and over nonstop election coverage.*

"*Assholes*. What do you know anyway?" he asked the talking heads. "You were all so ladeda happy earlier with your friggin' exit poll chatter. Now what? Caught with your pants down again, uh? Heh-heh me too. Well I did that. Me. Leonard. I skewed your friggin' results. Me, Leonard, Lennyboy!

"And my part so smooth, not a ripple…haha…ha! And the votes? Knocked down a few pegs, I'd say." Leonard flicked channels, another set of talking heads. "I hate you f_____ assholes." But then his screen panned into the Elections Department and he got sucked in, waiting, waiting for the shots he hoped would come. He pressed record.

"Hel-l-l-o-o!" Cady walked toward the fisheye lens. Her silky blouse and skirt still fresh after the long day. "F___ you, Cady!" He studied the lines of her blouse, the V of her neckline pointing toward cleavage hidden from his view.

"Now that you lost your stupid scarf," Leonard reached into his pocket pulling the silky thing onto his lap, rubbing the fabric between his thumb and fingers. "The better to see you with, eh." He studied her neckline, touched his own chest in the spot where Cady's mole peeked above her blouse. Smoothed his fingers up and down his chest where faint shadows dusted the soft curve between Cady's breasts before dipping below her top button.

Leonard looped Cady's scarf around his neck with one hand, the other latched onto his clicker. "You feelin' my heat? All my special…joy today. Shit. You bitch, even with all that extra peek-a-boo skin you still look like the f_____ prude you are… Oops. I can see your dots. Lost your jacket too, did ya?" Leonard rubbed at his breast pocket. "Too bad about your jacket."

Leonard fooled with the buttons on his remote. The pictures flickered backwards until he found the frame he wanted, Cady early this morning before the day started popping. The two middle buttons of her suit jacket fastened, the filmy crimson scarf draped loosely around her jacket collar. He fumbled with the scarf around his neck in a clumsy attempt to mimic Cady. He flattened the front of her jacket against his chest, buttoned the middle two buttons. He brushed his hands back over his hair, smoothing it straight back from his forehead.

"You're lookin' a little haggard, bitch hag. How long's it gonna take you and your trusty bookends to wrap up for the night? ...Oh, sorry... One of your little bookends is...occupied, isn't she? Oops... What are your thoughts on that Miss Palmer? F___ you!"

Leonard groped around the coffee table in front of him for another beer. He split the last two cans apart from the plastic harness and slammed one can down with a firm thud, beer sloshing inside the can. Then he snapped the tab off his Bud. Cold, sticky foam spewed and hissed from the can. "Shit." Leonard wiped his wet hand on the front thigh of his jeans. "Shit." He slurped at the sudsy brew, wiped his mouth with the back of his sticky hand. The fresh tang of chilled hops roiled with the stench of stale beer and warm yeast permeating the room. Leonard swooped up several capsules in front of him and guzzled them down with his beer, swiping the back of his hand over his mouth again.

When the whimpering from behind his bedroom door interrupted his conversation with Cady, he glared at the open can in his hand and flung it at the door. The can banged once before bouncing on the floor, fizz spewing in a puddle of white and yellow. The *puta* racket crap stopped and he glared up at Cady. "Your fault, bitch, all of it."

Leonard sneered up at Cady, "So what's up with your votes? Sniffed out any...irregularities lately?" Leonard asked the freeze-framed Cady. "You think Merry Mario can help you? Shit. Never. What does he know? ...Even with Izzy there...shit she was so far off target. Rejects...Imagine...Where have all the rejects gone, Cady? ...*Morons*. I'm the only real brains you got and you... dumped all over me."

"You just couldn't see it could you? Couldn't see me. Had to make you see. And rigging the votes, what's that prove if you don't know it? And now what do you know, Cady? Zilch. Too bad the Cretin got so pissy. I coulda really had some fun today. But seein' as how he's got the bucks, well I've gotta stroke his backside a bit, don't I? Besides he owns the power...power and plans. Bigger than this stinkin' election. Huge, Cady, really huge. Got your attention now, Miss Palmer?" Leonard yanked a fifth of whiskey off the coffee table.

"I blitzed you good didn't I? Had to. Not enough to raid your votes, when you don't know it. I get to feel it too. And I did too when I zapped your network. Every line of code...I did for you. I set it up, right here on my own computer...so I could watch it grow, test it, touch it, feel it ram it into your f_____ brain center. I even stuck my f_____ virus where you'd find it. I deserve some thrills out of this! Why should Cretin be the only winner here? Surprised me though you caught on so fast. Shit too close today!"

Leonard grabbed his crotch. He rubbed his hand up and down and clenched tight before letting go to slide his hand into Cady's jacket pocket and pull out her lipstick, jerking the cap off and flicking it onto the coffee table where it rolled across the table and onto the floor. "Shit. Stay there." He grabbed the lipstick with both hands twisting the base of the stick until an inch of red protruded over the top. This he traced around and around his lips before sticking the red into his mouth. He twirled it, mouthed it, sucked it softly enough to keep from breaking it, hard enough to feel it gooey on his tongue. All the while he stared at supersized Cady. His free hand moved to his crotch again.

Leonard placed the lipstick gently on the coffee table straight up before slouching back down on the couch with his feet stretched out spread-eagled on the table. "There, bitch," he said holding himself exposed for Cady, when the whimpering from behind bedroom door started up again.

"F___! I'll show you, *puta!*" Leonard fumed. He squeezed his crotch then sprang up from the couch, tugging up on his jeans still slung low around his hips, his fly unzipped. He flung the bedroom door open so hard it banged against the wall and bounced back whacking his arm. "Shit!" He paused for a moment rubbing his arm. "Shit!" Then as his eyes adjusted to the darkness he moved toward the bed and Izzy. She lay curled up in a tight ball in the middle of his bed exactly as he left her, duct tape sealing her lips, leashing her wrists. No need. She was still out of it from the drugs he'd blended in with her Starbucks.

Fool. She's so used to people, men giving her things, she didn't even question his greeting her at the loading bay with mug in hand, sweet and syrupy and spiked. She figured she deserved it. "Here," he said. "Thought you might need this, all the problems you've run into with our software. Inexcusable. But I think we've figured it out. The listings are in my car. I'll just go get them." And the ditzy-Izzy little *puta* just tagged right along after him. Could it have been any easier?

"C'mon, Princess Puta," he rasped. "Miss Palmer's waiting. She wants to see you…and me. Lenny's sacrificial offering to the goddess bitch. She wants us, *puta,* wants us bad…together. She's out there now waiting for me." Leonard pushed on her arm. Nothing. Then he bent over her, wrapped her hair around his one hand and grabbed her arm with his other. He pulled himself backwards off the bed dragging her along with him. And he kept dragging until they reached Cady in the living room.

44

"ABC and CBS called Florida. CNN, Fox, NBC, they're not saying anything yet. You heard there's a group mounting a challenge already? F___ that technocrat of yours…"

"Brice?"

"You just handle her. That's all. She goes public with any of this crap and… F___! What's she got?"

"Nothing," Neal lied. "Fluke. The tides changed. Another wave of voters got to the polls. You should know, your volunteers called people all day asking if they needed rides, anything to get out the vote. Proved damned effective, that's all."

"That's what she's sayin' now?"

"Yes. She's written up her incident report. She has to. But it's bland, nondescript." Neal lied again, but he could change that. "She's as weary of this as everyone else. Just wants it over."

Neal left for the break room to wait for Cady.

***

"Cady, let me see your incident report."

"In a flying pig's eye!"

"Come here." Neal tugged her arm and pulled her out the door. He led her to Izzy's stairwell where he put his arm around her shoulders, rotating her half a turn so they both faced the wall in the corner. "Who do you have, Cady?"

"I…"

"Tell me, Cady. Who can you trust?"

"I…"

"No. Who can you give this bombshell to? Who will believe you? And if they do, who's ready to stick his neck on the block for you? Who, Cady? Stan?"

"No! Dammit, no!" Cady shook her head angrily. "Neal, I...my Mario, Izzy."

"Izzy's gone, Cady. Who's next? Mario? You?"

"I've got to get back. Too much to do."

"No, Cady. Listen to me. Now. You need to dummy down your report."

"You're asking me to file a false report?"

"No, Cady. I know better. I'm not asking you to lie or misrepresent the truth. I'm not even asking you to suppress it. I'm telling you to be...to...speak softly, Cady. Listen to me. Tell what happened. Period. Don't speculate on why or where or how. Just tell what happened. Understand?"

"No."

"Don't look at the floor! Look at me, damn it!" Neal held on to her eyes with his own. "What do you see?"

"I..."

"Do you see a thief? A liar? Have I pressured you this whole cockamamie day? No. Please, Cady. Trust me now. I'll explain it all later and I promise...I'll help you get to the truth of this."

"How can you?"

"Later. I'll tell you later. I promise. But for now, you can't alter the results of this election. It will be whatever the numbers say tonight. But if it's as dirty as we think, I'll get the information to the right people. I know people, Cady. I may not have a lot of clout, but I've brushed shoulders with enough people who do."

"Dammit. Just 'cause you're from Tallahassee, you think you can sashay on up to the governor? You think he'd..."

"Hell no, Cady. Come on." Neal stopped her before she drilled to the truth of it. "In no way would any governor favor another upset in Florida. More importantly, Cady, under the circumstances, I believe there are people who would quash any unfavorable information you find. Do you understand? And ruin you in the process."

"And Izzy? ...If Izzy...she wouldn't have a chance." Cady bowed her head. "Neal...? It is too big for me, too big for me alone. If it's real they'll snuff me out too, won't they?"

"Cady, stop."

"What about you, Neal? ...Why are you doing this?"

"It's the buzzards, Cady, and today the sky's thick with them."
"What about…?"
"My job? Something's going down here. It's too dark to let it ride. Cady, I'm nicely compensated for what I do. And I've wiggled people out of more scrapes than you can imagine. I can spin the truth in a dozen ways. But no one pays me to lie and no one owns my soul. No one does that, Cady."

Cady swiped at the wet on her cheek.

"One more thing. When you redo it, I want you to make two copies. And can you scan it?" Cady nodded. "Scan it in and email it to…damn. E-mail it to my personal account." Neal scribbled his email address on a business card. "Do you have a home account?"

"Why?"

"Just do it. Next I want you to put the original in Stan's pudgy mitt…in front of me."

"Why? He won't file it with the election reports. You know he won't. He'll just toss it in his circular file."

Neal didn't answer. He just looked down at her with a wry smile lingering on the corners of his mouth. "Cady? Trust me? Please?"

***

"Here pussy, pussy. Look, Mi-i-a-ss P-a-al-l-mer! I found your pet *puta*." Leonard glared up at Cady, "How do you want it?" He lifted his leg, kicking at the clutter on the coffee table. Cady's scissors spun around on the table and thudded to the floor in a shower of sprinkled crystals.

Clutching Izzy by the waist he unfolded her face-down over the table, her hair swirling in puddles of beer and ashes. Her arms and hands hung over the table in front of her waist. Her knees scraped the carpet on the floor. "Slut." He kicked her leg.

"Who's got your pretty now?" Leonard squatted beside Izzy, tugging at her tight skirt, inching it upwards toward her waist in a battle of will over chastity. Finally the side-slit above her knee, so stylish in the morning split open in a zzzt of frayed fabric. "Ahhh, Cady…" Leonard yanked Izzy's panties down to her knees exposing her perfect plump heart-shaped flesh, firm and creamy white. "Cady..." He rubbed his hand over warm flesh, iridescent in Cady's light and she wet herself. "Shit. You damned *puta*."

"You did this, didn't you, bitch?" Leonard said glaring up at Cady. "You think this'll make a difference?" He stood up and faced Cady pulling his own pants down exposing himself for her once more. Holding himself with one hand he reached down for the beer at the opposite end of the table. "Here's to yah, Mi-i-a-ss P-a-al-l-mer!" He held the can up toasting to Cady before gulping a mouthful of the warm fizzle. Then he stepped behind Izzy and sank to his knees, knees wet with beer and whiskey and urine.

Leonard lifted the can to his lips again, glanced up at Cady and down at Izzy's bare bottom and back up to Cady and kneaded Izzy's warm flesh with his sticky free hand all the while staring at Cady. Slowly he tipped his can drizzling beer over Izzy's bare bottom and up and down his penis and back to Izzy's bottom trickling it between her legs. "Here, Cady, this bud's for you... This bud's for you, Lennie." And he gripped himself and wiggled in closer nudging up to Izzy's heat, feeling for the right spot and he rammed against her and rammed...and...rammed again and pulled back to take better aim and...he exploded all over himself. "You f_____ whore!" he screamed at Cady, grabbed for the whisky, unscrewed the cap and swilled from the bottle. Then still looking at Cady he held the mouth of the bottle to Izzy and pushed. "Shit! Shit!" It wouldn't slide in.

Too drunk to find her spot, he tipped the bottle up to his own lips and guzzled the contents again before shoving Izzy off the table. He stood up and kicked her away from the table. And he kicked her spine and head and chest until he could no longer stand. Then he climbed on top of her, punching her face and chest and pulling and squeezing at her breasts. All the while Cady watched from the widescreen high-definition-plasma television. He looked for the mole on her breast in his hands. And he sobbed, sobbed and vomited. He reached for Cady's scissors before falling off beside her passing out in a puddle of vomit and pee. He didn't hear the door when it opened.

45

"Hmm." Neal reached for the bottle and turned it in his hands, examining the label. "Nice. Never pegged you for a scotch drinker."

Cady laughed softly. It sounded good, felt better—to both of them. "It's my father-in-law's."

"I didn't…"

"So's this house…well technically it isn't….my name's on the deed…but," Cady paused looking out somewhere beyond her screened patio.

Neal listened, silently plucking ice cubes from the ice bucket one at a time and gently setting each on the bottom of their tumblers. The hush broken only by ice cracking as it saluted the warm amber liquid.

"I moved in with them when my husband deployed for Desert Storm. We were so…young. I was in college. He didn't… he didn't want me to wait alone. Then when he didn't come back…." she whispered and the only sound in the world at that moment was the rush of warm air escaping Neal's lips. "Well his mother passed shortly after he…cancer…quick…a shock. And well my father-in-law stuck around just long enough to…make sure I was okay. He stops by every now and then."

Neal leaned against the counter, holding one drink in each hand but waiting for her to finish her thoughts before approaching. He suspected she still held many secrets too dear or too painful to share and she honored him with her candor…and he hated himself for the relief he felt deep in his chest.

"The room you're in," Cady nodded her head back toward his room at the far tip of the L of rooms bordering the patio. "That was his room growing up, mine too, I guess. It's the room I lived in when he went away…and part of me died there too."

Neal's mouth fell open to no sound. Just anguish for this woman who suffered too much sorrow and today survived another kind of hell. Yet she trooped on with dignity and kindness and empathy for her associates, her friends and for her lost Izzy.

"There now. All done." Cady pivoted her bottom around on the pool's edge so she faced away from Neal. She dipped a toe in the water, "Perfect." Then stood up on the steps and plowed in, her head and body skimming just inches under the surface.

Neal poured himself another scotch.

***

"More stamina than I, Cady," Neal savored her ascent, statuesque, illusive in her delicacy. Her shimmering china persona veiled solid titanium beneath. Stan and Brice missed their mark on this one. If indeed they conspired in some devious coup d'état…and as sure as he stood there gaping like a drooling adolescent, he hoped beyond logic and evidence they did not. They misjudged. No doubt in a fair fight she'd bring them down. She brought him to his knees…with her smile. But to tackle them would require more fortitude, a more covert approach atypical for her, and a level playing field. These things he could give her. Suddenly, he felt clean, free.

"Used to it. We don't get much opportunity for exercise…get up in the dark, come home in the dark. This works for me. My time to reflect on the day ahead or chill out in the evening."

"You've got that right."

"Funny, I took you for a swimmer."

"There such a thing as a fair-weather swimmer? Indoor pool, you know?"

"I see."

"Here. Let me." He held out his hand for her towel. Cady surrendered it to him accompanied by a keen sidelong glance and a playful smirk.

He dabbed at her back and arms then draped the towel around her shoulders.

She reached for her drink and sat down poolside, her feet dangling in the water where Neal joined her. He rested his hand gently on her neck, rubbing lightly at first then more assertively.

"Neal…"

"Cady. Me first. Pact. I promise not to…take advantage of you…tonight."

"Better not. Izzy wants you first. Oh, Neal what can I do for Izzy?"

"I don't know, Cady. The police are on it. They're looking for Leonard. If there's anyone else you can think of who might have reason to…hate to sound like your Security officer this afternoon, but boyfriends? Man scorned? Women adversaries?"

Cady leaned away from him to study his face. "Look at her Neal. Can you imagine a female in the world who wouldn't flinch just a little when standing up against such…splendor?"

"I…"

"Don't answer that. The point is she's such an innocent. She plays. She has fun. But that's what it is with her, a fun game. She'd back off in a second if she thought one of her dalliances caused hurt. And truthfully, I don't believe any of her…hovering honey bees ever sampled her nectar."

Neal couldn't help himself. He laughed aloud at her passion, notwithstanding her conviction, her loyalty.

"Tomorrow we'll go over it all again. While you're doing your election thing, I'll see what I can dig up, get back with the police. That is, Cady, if you promise not to stir up anymore trouble on your own. No more pleas for ration or time from Stan. He won't listen anyway. Promise?"

"I promise."

"And I promise, Cady. I promise to help you find your truth."

Cady looked squarely at him, her eyes searching his. "I trust you, Neal."

"Finally. One thing, Cady…"

"Here it comes, the almighty caveat."

"Yes, Cady. Here it comes. I can't stay with you. In a few days, maybe less I'll need to back off until this thing simmers down. Understand?"

"Of course you do."

"Yes. But probably not for the reasons you've conjured up."

Neal reached across her and took her small right hand in his own large ones. She didn't object, not even when he rested it palm up on his thigh. He held her wrist with his own right hand and with his other hand gently rubbed and tugged and kneaded at each of her fingers one by one. He took her hand in his, smoothing her palm up and down with his thumbs.

"Carpal tunnel?" he asked about the faint white line at the base of her wrist.

"Hmmm."

He rubbed her forearm concentrating on the tight muscles midway to her elbow. When her hand fell limp in his he rested it on her own thigh with a soft pat and lifted her left hand. The same soothing ritual. Then he stood up.

"Oh..." she sighed.

"Just a minute," he smiled at her fading defenses and walked away to retrieve a long cushion from the chaise lounge closest to them. This he flattened out on the river rock beside her. Then patting it firmly, "Here, Cady. On your belly."

"I knew it," she drolled. Then smiling impishly, "Or you really are a rogue, aren't you?" But she scooted onto the pillow without hesitation, not waiting for his answer, not caring.

"I'm a man, Cady. You know I'm a scoundrel." But she was already stretched out and waiting for him.

Neal raised her legs long enough to sit at the base of her cushion and rest her feet on his lap. Soon his hands smothered her feet and she melted. As he had with her hands, he tugged gently on each toe, rubbed the balls of her feet, her arches, heels, ankles. She moaned. He kneaded the muscles up and down along her calves, rubbed her shins then returned to her ankles, her feet. She moaned again. His hands wandered up and down along her spine, her neck, shoulders, pushing, rubbing, pressing, squeezing. His fingers spread out at the base of her head and tangled with her wet hair. He pulled and pushed gently massaging her scalp. She groaned.

"Turn over, Cady." And she did.

He brushed her hair away from her face, stroked her forehead, her temples, neck. Outlined her ears, her eyebrows, eyes. When he brushed his hand along her cheek, she turned her head and nuzzled against his hand and kissed it gently, sweetly. She sighed and he caved.

Scoundrel. Definitely a scoundrel, he thought. She slept and he smiled as he listened to her breathing. Here amidst the lush tropical palms and ferns clustered about her patio, the stone fountain nestled deep within her Japanese rock garden babbled to the geishas and laughing Buddha. Cady's enchanted refuge.

Cady lay quiet beside him. And he wanted her more than anything he had ever wanted in his life. More than any other woman or car or money or prize or childhood toy, he wanted this woman. Paradoxically, he wanted her friendship more. Go figure.

Neal vacated his post and made the rounds, shutting off the outdoor heaters, the pool light, pinching out candles. He closed and locked all the sliding glass doors they opened earlier, his bedroom, the kitchen, the living room, save one. This he carried her through and glided it closed behind them with her still in his arms. He was certain she slept until she sighed softly and turned her head to his chest and kissed him again, another gentle, love kiss, not passionate, just warm and caring and…pure. And he pulled back the covers on her bed and set her down tenderly. And when he tugged at her swimsuit she let him, even lifted her bottom to help him wiggle the suit off her body, no easy feat. He pulled the covers up to her shoulders, tucking them beneath her chin. And then he climbed into bed beside her on top of the covers and put his arm around her. She sighed and snuggled in next to him before her breathing deepened in quiet life-healing sleep.

As he lay there beside her, in pain and in joy, he wondered about Cady and about tomorrow and about Izzy. Was it already too late for Izzy? He wondered who had done such terrible things today and why? And he wondered about Brice and Stan. He would never condemn Brice until convincing evidence mounted irrefutably against him. Even so Brice harbored guilt for suppressing the pursuit of truth if nothing else. Would Brice have been so adamant had the voting favored the other party? Think not. And he wondered about his old friend and about friendship-killed, collateral damage. And he wondered about Cady and knew that leaving her would be the hardest of all.

Sometime before dawn Cady squirmed and fidgeted and twisted beneath her covers. He stroked her forehead as before, "Hush now, Cady. It's alright now. I'm here."

At last he slept.

46

"I wake you up ol' boy?" Brice's hot air gushed over the phone.

"Ah, no. Just, uh, going over the results," Stan stifled his yawn.

"Worked out okay, didn't it?"

"Yes. Just another regular election far as I'm concerned."

"Make sure it stays that way."

"You bet. All pretty much standard from here on."

"Anything more from Palmer?"

"No. Went out like a lamb."

"Good. Keep it that way," Brice stubbed out his cigar. "Your boy Lenny's a real psycho, you know?"

Stan played along with Brice's wisecrack, anything to end another one of his wee-hour dialogues. "Oh yeah? Guys a regular pencil head. Ha-ha. They're all of them off plumb. It's in the lead…you know from all those pencils, eh, Brice?"

"Rise and shine, boy. You've a mess to clean up." Ice clinked in crystal. "Your boy's spinning outta control. We might all of us get smashed up if you can't slow him down."

"What are you talking about? Who?"

"Your boy. I'm tellin' you, he's psycho. Blood, guts all over."

"You're serious."

"You bet. Get over there, now. Clean things up."

"Clean up? What? Who? Tell me who."

"Did I stutter? Leonard."

"He killed himself? Who found him?"

"Not yet. You just need to get over there."

"What am I supposed to do about it? Call the police?"

"Hell, no. Don't need them sickin' their dogs in on it yet. But your little Mexicali, she's there."

"Mexi…"

"Your little spitfire got in the way. He picked her up."

"Who? Izzy? Who picked her up? Leonard?"

"Yeah."

"Oh, shit. She okay?"

"You go to the apartment. Get her out of there. Get rid of her, Stan. You do it before the police start sniffin' around."

"I…I…don't understand."

"Yeah? Well I do. You bungled it. Didn't rein 'em in with that vote monitor crap. Then Leonard. Shit. He goes off and grabs her. Now whaddya s'pose she knows?"

"I…she's…not much. She's just a kid and I…"

"Your mess, you and your half-cocked staff. Get rid of her!"

"What do you want me to do?"

"F___ it. Here. I'll f_____ lay it out for you. Go pee. Drive around to the back of the apartment. Park. March yourself right on in there and take care of it."

"Can't one of your…"

"No. Don't have anybody to clean up after the likes of you. If you'd a been f_____ on top of this, it wouldn't of happened. You're in too far, Stan. Too deep to leave a whole lot a loose ends trailing outta your behind. Now get over there…before the police…could be on there way now. Ya hear?"

***

Stan nudged the door open with his elbow and peered into Leonard's apartment before stepping inside. He carried a flashlight but didn't need it, not really. The doorway of the apartment opened into a small hallway, the kitchen on the right and living area straight ahead. And there was Cady staring out at him, big and bright and framed by the entryway. Her face looked down on the carnage below from the wall-size plasma television screen that overpowered the room.

Stan jerked back as though Cady reached out from the magic screen and struck him. And though his eyes adjusted to the muted light without difficulty, he couldn't move his feet forward. He froze. He gagged. And he wanted to run. Instead he just stood there and stared. Cady stared back. On the couch Leonard slouched low and gazed forward.

Before this started, Brice put the screws on Stan to hire Leonard. So of course, Stan pressured Cady to take him on. But within months Leonard was out of there. Stan balked, but the guy proved too menacing even for Stan, though he'd taken a pounding from Brice. So now, here he was freeze framed in a macabre diorama that proved too bizarre to believe even if he did see it with his own eyes. Leonard. Sick bastard, spiked hair dyed jet-black, face skewed, glazed eyes glaring at Cady…and ultra bright glossy red lipstick swirled around his lips in a smudgy swollen inch-thick outline, drawn up to his nose and around and down to his chin and back up to his nose. And then his jacket. A women's suit jacket. Cady's jacket that she wore all the while she stared down at them.

Finally, Stan took a deep breath and stepped into the room. He wanted to run. Instead he stepped closer. Blood and vomit soaked the front of Leonard's shirt and jacket, his mouth gaped open. Stan wondered how Brice knew, but the thought passed. Stan crushed it. Leonard's eyes rolled off Cady and onto Stan. Stan jumped back.

"Leonard? Leonard. Can you hear me?" Stan fanned his hand in front of Leonard's smeared face. "Brice's right, you sick f___."

Leonard's eyes rolled back to Cady. He grasped something dark and fuzzy to his chest, but Stan couldn't edge himself any closer to see what it was. Clearly, the man was stoned. No threat. But the sudden flutter on the floor below the bay window was and Stan turned on his heel and bolted for the door. He would have made his escape too, but for the gentle moan beneath the window reminding him of his mission. He turned back.

There was Isabella, curled up in a diminutive ball facing the window, her bare bottom exposed and shining softly in the reflection of Cady's light. And her head, her head was bare as well, with big clumps of jagged hair butchered off. Stan ran to the bathroom and heaved, dry gut grinding heaves.

At least she's alive. Alive. Now what do I do. F___ you, Brice! I let you bait me and bully and bribe me into this. Now what? I'm screwed! And you f_____ waggle your lily white ass on to the f_____ White House.

Stan located the master bedroom. Its door a clear shot from the living room sofa displayed scars from an apparent battering.

The carpet sopped with beer. He turned the doorknob with his shirttail and pushed the door open. So far he'd touched nothing. Aside from dank beer, it smelled of a family of rats nesting in a pile of discarded gym shoes simmering in the summer sun at high noon. He stepped cautiously across the carpet cluttered with piles of presumably soiled clothes by the stench. After rejecting the bedspread as too bulky for his purpose, he yanked the top sheet off the bed in the dark, went back to Izzy, covered her head first then wrapped the rest of the sheet around her.

"You poor baby." Stan grimaced, his thoughts at odds with his own plan. Stan scooped the frail sheet-thing into his arms and walked out the apartment the way he had come in, without so much as a glance back at Cady or Leonard. He pulled the front door partway closed as much as he could with the corner of the sheet he peeled away from Izzy's body. He touched nothing. Keep it that way. F____ you, Brice. F_____ you, Izzy. Then he smelled her. Izzy...floral Izzy exposed and unwrapped...Izzy and sex and filth and stale booze...a lethal blend exhuming the essence of his own primal hell as stoked by a lifetime of insecurities and pain...wholesale rage, frustration, fear.

Stan faltered. He turned back, back to the outrage and Cady and her election on the wall and bloodied, stupored Leonard worshiping at her feet. F____ you, Brice. F____ me. F____ my bloodsucker-wife. F___ Brice and Cady and...and my whole f_____ life. F___ you, pa.

"It's your own fault, Isabella. Flouncing around in your skimpy little skirts and skinny blouses. Why should Leonard and who knows how many driveling whelps......who else? Brice...? Why should they be the only ones?"

Drugged up...never know...dead by morning. Stan glanced toward catatonic Leonard before wedging Izzy through the bedroom door, swinging the door closed with his foot. He tossed Izzy down at the end of Leonard's rancid bed, rolled her over...mean... rough, her hands still bound behind her back, her mouth taped, and his hate spilled over onto her. He squeezed her hips, waist, breasts. He tugged at her shredded blouse, clutched her breasts again and stopped there. Then he buried his face into her softness, into the warmth of her bruised breasts and he sobbed.

"Isabella. Izzy…"

As he lay beside Izzy half on the bed, knees on the floor, he began again, stroking softly with the tips of his fingers, round and round. He stroked her soft, lithe yielding flesh, everything his pinched face wife was not. His strokes gentled to caresses. Izzy moaned. And he lost himself to the world inside his own trance where her warmth was real. When he pushed toward Izzy, he was young again and viral and his thrust a lover's thrust, not hard…except at first. He had to just at first.

Done, he shimmied up his blood smeared briefs, his pants…the brisk zipper sound punctuated his shame. Then he folded Izzy again in Leonard's soiled bed sheet, dragging her down the back stairwell. His baggage light at first grew heavier the farther he lugged it down the stairwell, until finally, he half carried half dragged the load, its feet dangling along the floor, thumping down from one stair to the one below it. F___ you, Brice. He leaned against the wall for a moment catching his breath, but then pushed himself away from the wall with one elbow gaining momentum, and moving much more quickly than before when the blare of sirens broke through the silent dark, police sirens gaining volume.

At the bottom of the stairwell, Stan pushed against the door bar with his back, shoving the door open and backing out. His BMW 530i waited there, trunk open. And he heaved her into the trunk, tugging on the bundle here and there, scrunching her up and pushing her legs down so she'd fit. Her head bared in the dim light exposed crusted patches of shorn scalp. He gagged…ripped the tape off her mouth, jimmied her in some more and slammed the trunk closed. Then he rushed around to the driver side, slid into his seat and started the engine before his door closed. He squealed out of the parking lot heading west toward Tamiami Trail. He'd figure out something, a plan. Cady was good at plans. F___ you, Cady. His gas gauge read full.

He tugged a bottle out of his console and gulped at the thick pink slime. Through his rearview mirror he watched a flurry of flashing lights close in on him then disappear as they turned into the complex he'd just vacated. F___ you, Brice. F___ you and your sleazy friends and your devious plans. F___ you, Cady, for teaching her all this f_____ election guru shit. F____ you all, all of you! Stan thought of the ravaged bundle in his trunk, thought of his mission and for the second time in his adult life he wept.

***

Behind him, the lights of the great city invoked surreal images of Dorothy's vision of her domed city of Oz. Here on the Trail it was black. Ink black. But too soon, at least by the time he headed back toward the city, dawn would peak over the eastern sky and he would be expected in for the absentee ballots and certification brouhaha shit. Cady'd take care of it. She always did.

For now if he could just carry on a while longer, get this over with...then what. He'd passed the last remnants of civilization several miles back, a mountain of a Miccosukee casino rising high above the flat glade, looking rich, substantial and very much out of place, as was he. At least now he had a plan and it irked him to keep steady within the speed limit. He wanted to get it over with, still he couldn't risk some maverick cop pulling him over and checking his trunk for drugs. Not many cars out this time of the morning, a good thing. Those early risers clipped past him at NASCAR speeds. On the way back he'd slam the pedal to the metal, depending.

***

The leathered Indian woke immediately, alert with the changing night sounds. The insect chatter shut down when the car slowed, creeping along the road before stopping, the engine cutting off just shy of the abandoned village where he made his bed. More sounds, the trunk opening, the scraping and snagging of material against metal. *No fishing here, mister. Canals along this strip too shallow this time of year. Now get.*

But the intruder didn't get. The ancient waited to the sounds of dragging...gravel alongside the road, across the weeds, the grass and then the heavy splash of water. Slow lingering steps back to the car. The engine purred, then whirred, spinning wheels churned up the dry earth before grabbing and racing off. The Indian waited. Soon the car would come back this way and slow down again before speeding off to the city.

47

Neal sat softly beside Cady on her bed, watching her peaceful slumber for a few moments more instead of waking her to responsibility. Already her radio alarm broadcast election news throughout the house on her intercom. He smiled. Hadn't she enough reality in doing her job without inviting the rest of the world into her morning?

"Miss me?" he whispered to blinking eyes.

She gasped. Shrinking to the far side of the bed, she yanked the covers over her head. "Dammit! Dammit! Dammit!" And when Neal laughed, she began again, "Dammit! Dammit! Dammit!"

Neal leaned across the bed and rested his hand on her shoulder, "Come on bright eyes, time to start our day."

With another muffled, "Dammit," she rolled toward his voice, tugging the duvet along with her, pulling it over her shoulders and tight up under her chin.

"I fetched breakfast for us."

"Oh, my. What have I wrought?"

"Might be we've embarked on a beautiful friendship."

"Ah, Bogie. How nice. Now, if you'll excuse me. I'll get a wiggle on. Duty calls and all."

"Cady. Wait. No. I didn't mean it like that. I mean…" He brushed the hair back from her eyes, tucking it down behind her ear. He smoothed the line creasing her forehead. His fingertips stroked softly, her cheek, her temple, her jaw line, her neck. "This is…big for me. Really. I've never…I'm not married. Divorced. Two years. Not engaged. Lovers? A few. But, Cady, I've never been blessed with a…friend. Lovers, yes. They're easy to come by."

Cady raised her eyebrows.

"Yes, Cady. You know that. Adjust your standards a notch or so one way or the other and yes, easy to come by. But friends? Not so easy. And friends who are lovers?" Neal reached beneath her covers and tugged her hands free from the sheet clutched under her chin. Holding her hands in his own, "Look, Cady, I don't know what we'll be to each other next week, next year, or even what we are to each other this moment. But I do know that I want more of the same, more of you."

Cady grunted.

"And, Cady, I believe you do too."

She reached out, her covers falling away and she pulled him to her. "Dammit."

***

"Now you're sounding paranoid." Cady snuggled up to him under the sheets.

"Cady this isn't about me. It's you." Neal tightened his arm around her, pulling her closer still.

"Why? Ah, I get it. Now's the time you tell me you're married after all or engaged or have some incurable disease. Right?" Cady tilted her head a trace higher. "It's okay. No need to go that far. There's no investment on this end."

"Cady, that's not true and you know it. I can feel it. All yesterday, a veritable electrical storm with more lightning strikes arcing between we two than is seemly."

"Not!"

"Right, Cady. And last night?"

"Pressure. Pain. Fear. Release."

"And just now? I won't let you off so easy, Cady. You know we can't go back after this. We can only go sideways or forward. I choose forward.... But for now, Cady, we need to talk shop."

"Not yet.... Just how old are you, Neal?"

"Old enough to appreciate you, my dear. Young enough to enjoy you," he grinned. "I've got a bit more tread on my tires than you have, five, maybe six years. Can we get back to business here?"

"Yes, Neal." She stroked her fingers across his chest.

"Wait, Cady. This is serious. I want you to leave the election crap alone. No. That's wrong. Don't leave it alone. Just don't pursue it with Stan or anyone else for that matter."

"What do you mean?"

"I want you to keep working on it, but don't discuss it with anyone. Understand? No one. Not even Mario."

"Why?"

"Let's just say I believe you. No. I do believe you. I believe you've got a botched election. Period."

"Finally. A voice of reason. When did you come to that conclusion?"

"I suppose I always believed you, that is believed you read the numbers correctly and interpreted them accordingly. But I didn't want to believe…conspiracy, collusion, intent."

"And?"

"And you found a…problem."

"So then why…"

"Because your problem could have been the result of an unintended circumstance, a mishap, a mistake, a computer programming error."

"And now?"

"Now I believe that you interpreted the numbers correctly but the cause is more diabolical."

"So why don't you want me to pursue it with Stan or Mario?"

"Because sweet geek that you are, you're thinking numbers and logic. But you're not thinking people. If…then, who, and why?"

"If, then, else, do-loop. Sounds like program code to me," she smiled.

"Not intended for humor, Cady. Beyond the act is the purpose. And it could get nasty. Understand?"

"You think that's what happened to Izzy, don't you?"

"Could be, Cady. I hope not. But it could be just that."

"And whoever did this…?"

"Whoever did this went through a lot of hoops to keep Izzy from ferreting out the truth." Neal searched her eyes while choosing his words. "And either they're too obtuse to know Izzy followed your lead or they were stalling for the win, knowing you couldn't run the election and bust their code at the same time."

"So what do you mean, exactly?"

"You continue poking around and they'll be after you too. If they're not already. Do you understand, Cady? Most likely you're in danger too."

"I…"

"What we don't know yet is the who."

"But we do, Neal. I'm certain it's Leonard."

"No doubt, Cady. But Leonard's only the drone. He's nothing. This is big, Cady, very, very big. I could be closer to the source than either of us can imagine. And I…I don't want to lose you now. Do you understand that, geek-girl?"

Cady paused on his last words first. Her expression warm with tender possibilities fell short when the gravity of his suspicions tarnished her soft mood. "You? Close? …The governor?"

Neal's phone whirred on the nightstand. He picked it up, checked the number. "Cady…I'm sorry, Cady. I have to take this." He rubbed Cady's thigh before turning his back to her and talking into his phone. "Yes…Yes, I'll make sure…No. Like I said last night, just a blip…Turns out their reports, the ones monitoring the voting machines, they picked up some bad information… Must've been a fluke because it went away. Their final numbers…… No. She turned her incident report over to Stan. I was there…They're running absentee ballots this morning… Sure… Yes… If you think it's necessary. Will do."

Neal clicked his phone off and turned back to Cady. "Tsk-tsk, Cady. I'm to keep tabs on you for a few days," he grinned. "Not to let you out of my sight. Day or…night."

Cady opened her arms, "You're going to need a lot more stamina to carry out your mission, Neal. Do I get to file your performance reports?"

48

"Voting machines performed. Not a hitch. Votes tallied and done. Timely." Stan smirked, "But you see Ohio? Ohio's on the griddle again. We beat Ohio, that's for sure. The governor's got to be damned pleased with the results."

"The end results aren't his concern, Stan. Florida's process is his concern. As governor he takes his responsibilities for this election process very seriously. Wants no repeat of…"

"Absolutely not, Neal."

"Don't want to get our heads up from the news channels."

"Absolutely not."

"That also means a purity of the process. No niggling loose ends, Stan. No surprises. Don't want to find out there's a problem from CNN."

"Absolutely."

***

Neal entered the media room through the No Admittance door to reclaim his table close to Cady. Brice's call beeped him before he had time to look for her.

"Hey, Nealboy, what's happening?"

"Just finished with Stan. Says everything's on track."

"Course he'd say that! Jeez he's pathetic. Forget him. What about the rest of it. What d'you see there?"

"A lot of detail and scurrying around."

"Your gal down there behaving herself?" Again Brice building the framework for mounting charges of Cady's incompetence.

"What do you mean, Brice?" Neal baited him, just to hear it again from Brice's own mouth. More affirmation of Brice's role in yesterday's election snags. Cady's truth must out. But where and how it led them…that was Brice's show. For certain, Neal would be there to steady Cady's ride. Whether or not he attempted to channel Brice's resolve, as if that was even possible these days, depended on the depth of Brice's culpability.

Half their lifetimes, Neal and Brice had been friends and allies. Together they'd embarked on their crusade. Get Brice in office, do good, help the needy, educate. Move on to the White House. But then…and Neal pinned it on Brice's first stunning failure, his one political loss…their high-minded aspirations splintered and Brice's personal crusade degenerated into a vendetta of political war games where the win, the kill trumped all else.

Their friendship shifted as well to a relationship more singly weighted to business, politics and damage control. Neal still watched Brice's back, alert for the chinks most likely to harm him. But warnings went unheeded as Brice's knotty course dislodged reason. Neal shut his eyes to the erosion of good and soldiered on.

But it rested heavily on Neal's soul. Never one to seek the spotlight, Neal looked forward to the fair fight, the endgame result. Over time, fairness eroded and the endgame? Brice lost sight of the endgame. Win at all costs. Not his idea, not good. His way or no way. Power, pure and simple. Power and covert rewards. So when Cady cautiously shared her first suspicions of fraud, Neal seemed duly surprised and incredulous. Ironically, the systematic convergence of Brice and Stan berating Cady, fueled by their staunch refusal to consider even the remote possibility of faulty results only confirmed Neal's heretofore shaky conclusions.

"You know what I mean, Nealboy. She's just…well you know my boy. She still stirring up trouble or you put that fire out for me…?" Brice chuckled, "By kindling another?"

Neal ignored the innuendo. "They wrapped it up last night. Tied it into a neat little package and delivered it to the Board. You got the results."

"Yeah. Just thought as fussy as Stan says she is, she might press on with those nitpicking schemes."

"I believe she's as thrilled as anyone for this election to be over," Neal stayed on track. "You've checked with Stan?"

"That f___. Poor pee brain. Hell, in one day you've learned more about elections than he has in his whole twenty years."

"I've learned a lot, Brice. But I sure wouldn't go that far."

"Your AWOL piece turn up?"

"My...Izzy?"

"Yeah."

"No word of her. Nothing from the police."

"I keep telling ya she probly got a better offer, Nealboy. She probly even told Stan where she was off to. Never know with him."

Neal took the bait. "Any other team, any other time and I might agree with you. But you should see these people, Brice. They're dedicated, sharp, loyal..."

"Okay. Okay. Got it. So, she a good lay, Nealboy?"

Neal's stomach lurched. Rage lodged in his throat like a fire sword and if he could reach over the phone line and wrap his hands around Brice's pudgy neck, he would. "Who? You got someone in mind, Brice?"

"You just keep your eyes open. Like I said, stick to her day...and night if you can. Stink on shit. See what she's about. No need to cloud up this victory 'cause she gets a burr under her saddle. Enjoy your ride ol' boy."

Neal pulled the phone away from his ear, and spoke back to the steady hum of the dial tone, "You crass SOB..." You don't get it. You always took to the steady string of one-nighters, before and after your advantageous more permanent liaisons.

Loyalty has its price on both sides of the equation. And mine's not for sale. Never has been. I gave it to you freely for our vision. But it's a rusted vision now, Brice. For you it's all about winning. Winning in poker, the tracks, sex and conquest. Always the one-up. There's more to this than winning...there's more.

My loyalty to you? You tossed it out with last night's stogie...Now you buy my time, nothing else. I would have taken off before, but my loyalties step to higher ground. So I stick to the plan, hang around, do your bidding...for a while. There are answers to be found and I'll find them. And if it turns out you're duplicitous in any way, this time, you've crossed the line, old boy. My path rests easier on my soul now.

Politics is a blood sport...ol' man and it's stolen your soul. Saddened by the resolute admission of his...their loss, Neal knew he indeed mourned the passing of his friend long ago. As for me,

I've chosen another path. My heart's careening off the tracks, speeding home and it feels…magnificent. Neal looked at the reporters stationed around him. Could they see his metamorphosis? He looked at Cady…tired…sad…concerned…beautiful…….radiant.

***

Neal surveyed the crowd scattered around the tables in the media room. Not much had changed, except the media crowd thinned considerably. No big names. Only the underlings hoping for a worthy scoop, but expecting the anticipated anticlimactic results of the certified totals and computer reports.

Today's crowd appeared noticeably worn, no spit-polished shines as they'd been yesterday. Late night, one-for-the-road with their comrades, early morning. That would do it. Neal wondered how he in turn must look to them, if they were even remotely aware of his existence. Did he look saddened by his loss of faith, friendship, rusted visions? Did he look worried by Izzy's continued absence? Concerned that Cady's stalker might return? Or did he wear the glow from their morning's splendor and the anticipation of what tonight would bring. Smitten. Been bedded, been wedded, been…never been so…what was the song, "easy like Sunday morning." He'd ask Cady tonight. Yesterday, their minds and souls tussled all day. This morning their bodies enjoined. Tonight…? Now who's waxing poetic?

Okay, c'mon back, Neal. You're still on the payroll…even if that has nothing to do with your motivation or your mission. In the tabulation room, Cady and her team still dashed back and forth from computers to printers. Mario hovered vigilant at his console. And Cady's team at the back wall tapped away on their computers stopping only occasionally to answer phones and check in with Cady. The auditors languished at their post in front of the media window. A paradox, individual snapshots of yesterday and today would be indistinguishable to even the most scrupulous observer, save one tragic omission. Izzy.

Certain he could stake claim inside the venerable tabulation room today if he pressed, Neal chose to maintain his distance, respect the privacy of their inner sanctum. Though he wanted nothing so much at this moment than to brush shoulders with Cady, just once, just a brief touch that's all. *Knock it off. Things to do.*

Neal checked his general cell for messages. Nothing from the police yet. Nothing on Izzy. Nothing on yesterday's break in. Nothing on one missing former employee, Leonard Martin. Of course Brice would hold the inside track to any investigation. No telling how many goons aside from himself sallied on Brice's payroll. No. Not fun anymore.

Neal unzipped his inside jacket pocket and pulled out a new prepaid cell phone. He pressed the number. "You said I'd know when.... You were right.... Early next week."

Now for Izzy. What to do with Brice's tidbit. Could Stan know about Izzy if Cady did not? Doubtful. But you never knew with Brice. Neal would start with another visit to Stan, ferret out any loose ends. Then he'd check with the police before quizzing Cady again...reminding her of yesterday's terrors. As if she needed reminding of Izzy. They must all be missing her like crazy in there.

***

Neal walked past Juan with a nod, a flick of a wave and a courtesy smile. Juan held up a hand to dissuade him from walking in on Stan unannounced, but noting the resolve in Neal's steeled eyes, waved him on. Poor Juan, this stranger sure had a way of tripping Stan's wires. And this election topped all others in the angst and the absurd.

"Neal, I.... What happened to Juan? Didn't Juan greet you?"

"Oh, he's out there, Stan. Doing a fine job...."

"What can I do for you?"

"Well, Stan, I'm on a fact gathering mission."

"What? We fall short on your election goals?"

"Actually, no. My concern is more in line with the periphery."

"Ah...the...what is it you want then?"

"Stan, you heard from Izzy?"

"They found her? You sure? I...thought...how..." sweat blistered the puffy flesh below Stan's hollow eyes.

Neal just stood there studying the man. As a rule, Stan was adept at being inept, but this time... "Now I'm puzzled. Brice thought..."

49

Leonard clenched the remote while the TV flickered to his incessant click-click-click as he jabbed buttons, wandering through local channels, searching for a replay of last night's election highlights. Click. "...BACK IN A MOMENT WITH YOUR UP-TO-DATE REPORT ON THE WEATHER..." Click. Click. "BALMY THROUGH FRIDAY..." Click.

Her fault. This whole week her fault. She did this to him. *Bitch.*

Click. Must be something...Soon now. There! This is it! Leonard jammed the RECORD button. There she is! Rheumy eyes squinted through oblong lenses as he dissected the late night report. Again. Sure she's way off in the background, but *he* knew *her*. Hair pulled back, business suit, not-to-tight skirt appropriately draped demurely to her knees, silky tailored blouse, sensible pumps and all. Her uniform. He'd pick her out anywhere.

In the foreground, Stan talked into the camera, "A few voters failed to follow directions, otherwise, a near perfect election."

Leonard's chest heaved. Had to put up with it, after all Cady wasn't the focus of the newscast. So what if he couldn't hear her talk. He could see her behind glass in her tabulation room. Even without sound he knew the exact words she mouthed. Knew what she was doing. Barking orders. TV cameras panned the room. The reporter droned on, "THERE YOU HAVE IT FROM SUPERVISOR OF ELECTIONS STAN CORBIN......NO EXPLANATION WHY ELECTION EXIT POLL RESULTS MISSED THE MARK..." Good. Keep going.

Once again Leonard watched her grip the final election night tally in one hand as she pointed to some obscure results on the report with the other. And Leonard knew...that moment he knew she requested a rerun of the final numbers she received from the county's precincts, along with substantiating reports. Leonard knew those stupid reports well. She'd ordered him to program them. "…Liars figure and figures lie," he could hear her still. Hell, she'd repeated the phase often enough. And hell he'd gone through to program her picky-detailed specifications and get his final work accepted by her quality assurance team.

Leonard liked that she used his reports to analyze election results. His heart lunged. For months he'd envisioned this very moment over and over. And then lived through it again and again since last night.

For months he'd visualized her examining the precinct tallies one-by-one as the returns came in. Imagined her predicting the final outcome with only a small number of her key precincts reporting. And these she'd have figured out with only a fraction of votes counted. This time though, she'd be so wrong.

Leonard was confident that before anyone else even thought of questioning the returns, bitch'd have them ripped apart, analyzed to death. She'd know they were flawed.

He smirked. She'd know. So…prove it, *bitch*. So do something about it. What could she do? Nothing! She was just a bent-up spoke in a rusty old wheel, churning numbers. No, a worn-out bead on an old abacus. Abracadabra abacus. Leonard flicked his middle finger at the television.

Leonard wondered if she'd gotten all her reports by now. Wondered how late she stayed up last night working through the numbers. How many pots of coffee they drained. Did she think of him while she studied his reports? Did she miss puta?

Leonard pushed himself off the couch and stumbled his way into his bedroom after Izzy. "Shit!" He looked under the bed, in the closet, bathroom. "Shit." Kitchen. Pantry. "No-o-o-o….!" Cady glared down at him from the living room. He leaned out over the balcony, searching the grounds, the bushes, the pool for Izzy.

***

Hot. Muggy. The afternoon sun glared off Stan's sterling hood, burning his eyes through the hot windshield, searing through designer sunglasses. His car's air conditioner couldn't catch up enough to cool him down with all his stop and goes. Driving up and down, start and stop all along this two-lane strip since early this morning, dragging himself out of bed before his alarm sounded, creeping across thick white carpet and into his closet for clothes. He pulled on his trousers and shirt in the dark. Everything else he needed, shoes, wallet, keys, glasses, flashlight, towels, briefcase he stashed in his car last night. He needn't have fretted waking his wife. Habitual avoidance. Hell her snoring blared on without so much as a snort when he passed by her bed, holding his pee for her downstairs powder room on his way out.

Stan eased off the gas for his last approach. Past the curve, past the casino, past the break in trees across the canal, miles of canal. This gotta be it! He squealed his car stopped, got out, smelled smoke before seeing it from behind the tree hedge on the other side of the canal. Ragged thatched chikees peaked out from behind the trees. *No this can't be it. Screw you, Izzy!* Shit he was so late. Boss or no boss, appearances and protocol and reporters and Brice all being what they are. *Where are you, damn you? Maybe the gators snagged you after all. What have I done, mama?*

Stan pulled his shirt away from his wet chest to puff in some air before climbing back in his car for another run. He reached forward for his key, put his head on the steering wheel and wept.

"What have I done? What have I done, mama?" he sobbed. "How did I come to this?"

***

"I took care of your diversion, sport."

Leonard sucked on the end of his crimson scarf.

"You snivelly faced punk! I said I took care of it. Now you see to it you drag yourself outta that cesspool. We got stuff to do. Big plans boy."

"Whoa, dude? ......You got Izzy?"

"What's your risk?...You deaf? What's your risk here?"

"Shit. I don't think she knew who the f___ I was. She's one of those I'm-too-good-for-you *princesas*. You know the kind that looks right through you. She did it when I worked for Cady. She did it Election Day."

"See to it that it doesn't happen again, Lenboy. Can't afford officers of my corporation gettin' in hot with the law."

50

Cady poured two mugs of coffee knowing Neal would follow her as soon as she picked up her papers and turned away from him on her way to the break room.

"Here," she placed the mugs on the table while Neal closed the door behind him.

"Thanks. Making progress in there?" Neal nodded toward the tabulation room.

"Oh, yeah," she handed him her papers. "Official results. You should be thrilled. We both should. Red took the state." Cady's voice raised an octave, sounding shrill to her own ears.

"But we're not. Not either of us, are we?" Neal's voice mellowed. "Are we, Cady?"

"No. Look. Stop. I am. I'm done here. It's over. It's certified. There's no going back. Understand?"

"And if it's wrong? If it's another quote-quote stolen election, only this time for real?"

"Whose side are you on anyway?" Her voice cracked.

"Yours, Cady, always yours…from the beginning. Just neither of us knew it. But we do now, don't we, Cady?"

"No. You'd put the country through another Florida debacle? Court battles? Raging tempers? Months of uncertainty?"

"Cady, other states had trouble with their machines too. And Sarasota's backed up with statistically improbable results…again."

"Sarasota. Yeah, look what happened to them last time they went to the mat. The Government Accountability Office tested *two*, Neal *two* PROPERLY functioning touch screens before it announced that malfunctioning screens were not a factor in Sarasota's cockamamie results. They didn't even look at the 95,000 missing votes in the statewide Attorney General's race. Same machines, same vendor, Neal. The courts, the rancor, the government. All that and what? In the end, nothing. They pinched off the investigation before it got interesting. Whitewashed it after only a few tests on a few paltry machines."

"Their investigation was obstructed from the get go, Cady. Somebody drew a broad line in the sand and they couldn't cross it. Plus Sarasota's Election Supervisor and our Secretary of State balked every step of the way."

"So? What's different? You think Stan won't balk?"

"You're the difference, Cady. You and your real-time data. Sarasota didn't have the live votes to back up their claim."

"And this time? Let them plug their own holes."

"I don't think they can, Cady."

"How do you know that, Mr. You-can't-stop-now? Doesn't matter. I don't care."

"I think it caught them by surprise. None of them were on the lookout. You were."

"A lot of good it did us. Besides, half the state cranks up ElecTron's voting machines. Let's just see what the rest of Florida dredges up. Or Ohio. Or Pennsylvania or…or…California."

"That's what I'm telling you, Cady, I don't think they can. They don't have enough marbles to play the game."

Cady laughed and it felt good. "And I've lost all mine. Marbles that is."

"I'm right there with you, Cady. We'll find other games to play, later," he smiled.

"Maybe later's not soon enough," Cady taunted.

"Now you stop. I know what you're doing," he rubbed her forearm. "But we're on ElecTron here…. I don't think any other county or state took it as far as you did with all your techie protocol and processes. Let's face it, you were ready for a voting machine insurgence. You knew what to look for because you've been there before and because you didn't want to go there again."

"So?"

"That gives you the advantage. You saw it. You trapped it. You tracked the votes going down. It'll be at least another two years for other counties to break through to where you are now. You think we should wait?"

"Yes. And you know why?"

"Because you're sizzled up to the top of your pointy head?"

"No. Because I was wrong. No harm, no foul. Or hadn't you noticed, Neal?"

"What's that supposed to mean?"

"Miami-Dade ran blue. All within the margin of error."

"But the win...they weren't real numbers, Cady."

"Does it matter? They won, Neal. It makes no difference to the outcome here."

"No, Cady. It does make a difference. Yes, for all the warm-fuzzy intangible reasons you've prattled on about all along. One voter, one vote, heritage, values, rights and all that."

"But at the end of the day, it's no BFD. It doesn't change a thing. Miami's only a measly fraction of the voters."

"And you're convinced that's where it ends?"

"Well it sure ends for me." Cady nodded with a silent hmph.

"Okay, Cady. We both hope this is some crazy fluke. But what if it isn't? Is it worth the risk not to find out?"

"In the first place, if it's not just a blip in Miami then one of the other counties will see it. Let them deal with it. Let someone else with fewer battles scars carry the flag."

"Will they see it, Cady? Didn't you tell me you think you're the only one to monitor the voting machines in Florida? Forget Florida, the country? How would the others know?"

"Well, the exit polls..."

"No, Cady. Exit polls reflect what people say, not what they do. It's the votes, Cady, and you're the one."

"No. It's over, Neal. Just let it go."

"Then what? What about the next election? And the one after that? What if it's not a fluke? What if...someone can actually spot-control the wins? What if it goes undetected? What if it spreads? First Florida, then Ohio, Pennsylvania, and yes, California. Or Texas. Is it such a reach?"

"Another conspiracy, Neal? The silent coup? I raised that banner. No one listened and all I wanted was to stop a bad vote count."

"Silent coup. Yes. Here we are the most powerful nation ever and democracy as we know it stops here, in Florida. Cady, our vote, it's the heart of our democracy, the soul of America. Think about it. People thought Orson Wells radical too, but by the time 1984 arrived…"

"Yeah. Yeah."

"Please, Cady, you ripped the blinders off my eyes. I want back in the race."

"You've lost me, Neal."

"Let's just say I'm in a position to see things, to know things and yes, to ignore things. Cady, I…"

"So we two swapped places? What changed your mind?"

"You, Cady. Your diligence. You, the opinion polls. Everyday news, scandals to scoundrels…medical extortion, war, big oil extortion, insurance extortion, electronic surveillance to wiretaps, to this administration's unchecked aggression. Heck, I'm even skittish of wireless networks. We've come a long way. But when I put it all together with insider information from my…job…"

"Aggression?"

"Yes, Cady. Politics. Power. Aggression. The belief that, 'We know better than you, better than the rest of the world.' It's all related."

"Wooo, Neal."

"Heady stuff, Cady. No way is it just a job. At first maybe you want to do good, make the world better, make a difference…all the clichés. And maybe you walk the party line and work the party line because it seems the straightest path. But, Cady, you've got to lie with a lot of dogs to get there. And if you're not careful, you sell your soul."

"Is that lie-down or lie-to, Neal?"

"Yes."

"And your soul, Neal?"

"Bruised."

"Neal…I…I'm not going to ruin a nation to bring down an election, bad or good, duplicitous or no. Besides, the word I'm hearing is voters didn't vote the full ballot because of all the negative campaigning, too contentious. Not a machine problem."

"That's ludicrous and you know it. Besides, the absentee votes and the audits of paper ballots don't support that. And why did the problems occur mostly in predominantly Democratic precincts?"

"They have explanations for that, too."

"Cady, you're not actually buying that, are you?"

"It's what they're all saying."

"Cady...look, you say anything long enough and loud enough and strong enough and somebody's gonna believe you. The longer you keep it up, the more people believe you. Standard echo chamber...propaganda machine. Damn."

"And you'd know wouldn't you, you...spinmonger."

"Cady, I...not like that anyway. But think about all the rhetoric to get us to the polls. Guns, guts, glory. Really. Abortion's down in this county. And gay people? No one chooses to be gay. They just want to end legal discrimination. And immigration? Come on.... Cady, you really can't give up. If you don't do it, who will? Who, Cady?"

Tears stung Cady's eyes as she lashed out at him, "Now you throw my mother's words back at me?"

"Cady, I didn't mean...I'm sorry." His arms encircled her, shutting out the world, if only for a moment. "Cady, I'll drop it. Okay?"

"Yes." She let him hold her a minute longer before pulling away and squaring off her shoulders. "No. It's me..." She shook her head. "Wow. Where did that come from?"

"You alright?"

"Yes, of course." She smiled up at him and flicked his arm for good measure.

"Oh, Cady. Okay, I will drop it. Just one more point? And if you don't agree, I'm forever silent...at least where you're concerned."

"You'll pursue this without me?"

"I'll try, admittedly without the faintest hope of success."

"Go on."

"Okay. First how many ElecTron speak-and-spell toys are out there, all types of voting machines and scanners?"

"In Florida?"

"No. Nationwide. Say eight thousand?"

"Neal, at times we've had nearly that many in Miami-Dade alone. More like ten times that, Neal. Half the counties in

Florida…and then countrywide? …But just so we can get to your point, let's pick a conservative number, say fifty thousand. "

"I didn't realize. It makes my argument so much easier. Okay, let me start with the improbable, then work back from there."

"That would be?"

"If, IF and we know this is not the case, Cady. But IF all ElecTron elections in the country were run on machines with your spiked software, then…"

"You're back to the chipping away theme. Okay, I'm with you. Then, for grins only, take fifty thousand machines. And let's just say we grab around 10 votes on each machine…"

"Go on."

"I get it, Neal. Even tried the same logic on Stan. Funny, he didn't understand. But okay, let's go with it. Ten votes on each machine and poof you've hedged your bets by five hundred thousand votes going for the wrong guy. Take those votes, disperse them among the other candidates according to the trending ratio for those candidates…throw in a few undervotes… drop some ballots off the edge of cyberspace for good measure…"

"Add the electoral college factor. Apply you're gizmo to targeted zones. We don't even need to stick with fixed percentage points. Adjust up or down for the win."

"And, Neal, you've got your cyber win, not a total wipeout just plus or minus the margin of error."

"We agree then?"

"On what?"

"On moving forward, finding proof that your voting machines actually are infected…controlled."

"Or that they're not, Neal."

"Right. Either way, Cady, you need to keep on, keepin' on."

Cady shook her head. "Not good enough. This opera's over." But as she watched Neal his demeanor didn't waiver. Only the level of disappointment registering in his eyes surprised her. "I'll…let me think about it a while. A few days won't change anything."

"Cady, wait." He rested his hand on hers. "One more thing…please."

She turned her hand over in his and smiled patiently. "This had better be good, Neal."

"Yesterday you said some things about Stan and your voting machines and about who rules everything election and...Cady, there's more you didn't tell me about your...governor connection. Will you tell me now?"

"You don't give up, do you? Look, forget what I believe or what you think I believe. Okay? If I tell you what I know to be true.... If I give you the main events, then you'll leave me alone and go off somewhere to draw your own conclusions?"

"Yes, Cady."

"Can't believe you're suckering me in again...." Cady looked at the clock over Izzy's computer desk, then down to Izzy's empty chair.

"Cady, I..."

"No, Neal," she met his eyes with her own then took a deep breath. "Okay, I need to get back so this is the abridged version. You already know ElecTron wasn't the best."

"Yes, Cady."

"Then forget the innuendoes and suppositions. These are the facts. Understand? All honest-to-goodness facts. Ready?"

"Yes, Cady."

"Fact: ElecTron's chief lobbyist just happened to be the governor's running mate his first go 'round. She's also a former Secretary of State. That may or may not be relevant. But she should have known better, should have felt her keen responsibility to this state and its people to present only the best.

Fact: The governor convinced the Florida Representatives of County Government organization to endorse ElecTron. In return for their endorsement, the organization received a fee for every county signing a contract with ElecTron." Cady paused for breath.

"Is that payola, Cady?"

"No. I don't think so. You're off topic.... Fact: I already told you, the governor's top dog on Florida's Elections Canvassing Commission. He oversees the election. Fact: Worse, the governor hand picks his two members of Cabinet to serve on the Commission with him. He's so in charge, Neal."

"Is that all?"

"No, Neal… Fact: We got dinged around two hundred dollars more per machine in our purchasing price than one of the other counties that went with another vendor and we bought lots more machines than they did. Oh, by the way that doesn't include all the consulting fees and hocus-pocus dollars."

"Cady, you sure you have that right? Your price, ElecTron's price should have gone down on volume."

"One would think, Neal. But it didn't," she said slowly. "And, oh, did I tell you the other county's elections run like clockwork."

"And we know about yours, don't we, Cady?"

51

The two waded in the shallows at the pools edge, thighs touching, water lapping at Cady's breasts. The heated water warmed them in the cool night air. Neal took his hand from Cady's thigh and reached his arm around her shoulder, hugging her tight against his chest. She felt silky and hot to his touch and he was glad they hadn't turned the pool light on tonight and he knew within moments he would share her warmth. But first he must tell her....

"Cady?"

"Hmm?" Her fingers tightened around his inner thigh.

"No, Cady. We need to talk."

"Okay." She stroked up and down along his thigh.

"Ahhh-hem...No, Cady. This is serious."

Cady let go, but only to reach behind him pulling her body taught against his left side, pressing her breast on his arm as she wiggled and stretched to retrieve the near-spent bottle of shiraz behind him.

"Cady," he sighed. "You know, if you don't let me have my say, you'll be very angry with me in the morning."

Still snugged firmly against his side, she refilled their glasses before setting the bottle back down farther away from her reach than before so she pushed harder against him. Neal's hand reached under her belly and around to her bottom where he squeezed firmly.

"Oo. I don't know if I like your wicked reprimand. Don't know if it feels good or really bad."

"You let me talk and I'll do better." He too nuzzled his head under her outstretched arm and snuggled his face between her breasts. "Cady...you feel so good."

Cady flopped back into the water, 'accidentally' splashing him a few times before finally settling down beside him, this time leaving a few inches of space between their bodies. "You've got the floor, Neal."

"Swell. Now you say." He watched her, waiting for her eyes to raise to his.

"Well, I must say, Mr. Charles, first you complain when I'm not interested. Now you complain when you have me and I'm very interested indeed. Name your poison."

"The way you are, now, tonight and for these last nights we've stayed together. That's exactly how I want you."

"Then what's you're problem?"

"I'm leaving in the morning, Cady."

"Okay," she said matter-of-factly in the manner of accepting a refill of stale wine. She would not let him see her heart crack.

"Brice awakens, Cady. He figures you've lost interest. You're no longer a threat."

"Brice? Who…doesn't matter…. You said before you'd be leaving. So now's the time." She shrugged her shoulders, slipping her ring back and forth along its chain.

"Cady, I…"

"Look, Neal, we've had a nice little diversion. It was good. But we both know what it was. Now it's time to let the world back in. So if you're looking for hearts-and-flowers from me, you'll have a very long wait."

"Cady, please…"

Cady held up her glass for him to clink with his own, but what she really wanted to do was smash it against the rock fountain. "Prost!" she said too cheerfully.

"Cheers," he returned, but he was anything but cheerful. His gut wrenched at leaving her…and like this.

Cady gulped at her wine.

"Cady, we both know how serious this is. You're in danger from whoever sabotaged the election and abducted Izzy. We can't find Izzy. And we still don't know the who of it. Creepy man targeted you. That was personal. But he's not our…not your only threat. There's a higher power here and I intend to find it."

"You mean someone, like he said Election Day, 'someone big wants this?' You still think he wasn't acting alone?"

"You know that, Cady. It's precisely why I asked you to dumb down your election reports and keep a low profile."

"What does this have to do with your leaving tomorrow?"

"I can't tell you. Not yet. Oh, Cady, I feel so dirty."

"From me? From us?"

"Hell no. You're the freshest breeze that's unfurled my sails in a…well, ever."

"Then what?"

"I can't say now. But I will tell you. One day soon. Cady, understand there is real danger in the knowledge we share. And I wouldn't leave you now if I didn't believe we need…must follow this through."

"But I haven't even had anymore of those calls."

"No. That doesn't mean it's over. Cady, there's something I… you must know. It's about Tallahassee, my job."

"You're a real spy, aren't you?"

"Not the way you think. It's Brice…Brice Daniels. He's my job."

"Brice…Bud Daniels? Governor Bud Daniels? I didn't… Why didn't you…? He's your boss?"

"I…yes, Cady."

"And when were you going to tell me?"

"I don't…I was…maybe tomorrow before I leave…maybe over the phone…I don't know."

"Don't you think that's something you might have shared? I mean here I've hurled accusations at him since you first broke into my election, accusing him of all manner of…"

"But, Cady, I…"

"And you let me do it. And you…you're the enemy here… talking about saving democracy and…" But when Cady looked into his eyes again, her anger turned to sorrow. She expected guilt. She expected a chagrined look that said, "Okay I'm a bad boy, now give me my licks and let's move on." Instead Neal wore the face of grief, deep pained hurt, compassion…fear. And she responded. "Neal, tell me. You let me rant not just because you wanted to know what I know. You think he could have a part in this, don't you?"

"I can't afford to think anything for your sake. Do you understand, Cady?"

"I…I…when will you be back? Will you come back?"

"The trip should only take a couple of days. But with Brice on his game, I need to keep my distance."

"You mean from me?"

"I mean from you and anything associated with you or this election."

"Oh."

"Cady, you will unravel this thing. And when you do, we…I will take it to the next level. I promise."

"The next level?"

"Don't you squander your sweet brainpower on the particulars. Just trust. Please. And when I do, I promise, Cady, I promise we'll have our time. We'll begin here, with this." He circled his arms around her and hugged her close and they slipped deeper into the pool, the water lapping, lapping along the pool's edge.

***

Neal stood beside Cady's bed and waited for her to fluff up her pillows and scoot back against the headboard. Steam swirled up from her morning coffee on the bedside table where he placed it.

"Here, Cady, take this," he held out a thin prepaid cell phone.

"What's this? I already have a business phone, a personal phone, a pager and I'm on overload as it is."

"No, Cady, hear me out, okay?"

"Yeah. Yeah. Whatever," she smiled.

"Hmm-hmm. One of those eh?" he leaned over and kissed her forehead. "Okay, Cady, what we have here is two, count them two," Neal held both arms up, a small phone lodged in each hand. "Two new prepaid, number blocked, ambiguous, anonymous, non-traceable cell phones."

"And the function thereof?"

"Remember, Cady, even paranoids have real enemies. And this I learned from Brice."

"What? About paranoids?"

"No about cell phones. But these are for us. You take one, I take one. You take my number…"

"And you've already got my number, Neal."

"I hope so, Cady. I hope so. This is what I want you to do. Our…protocol for phone use." They laughed together.

"You do catch on, Neal."

"Yes. Perfectly trainable. So for our protocol, each of us checks our phones morning and night for messages…non-emergency stuff."

"How sweet."

"Not really. Any messages we leave must be short. Understand? Even though the phones are generic…no telling whose tiptoeing around in our shadows. So far I think we're pretty much off the radar, but no sense in being careless."

"You're serious about this aren't you?"

"Damn straight, Cady. Now, if there's an emergency, call me on every number you've got and keep calling. Time doesn't matter." He set the phones on her table. "One more thing, leave your phone on for a while at night before you go to sleep. I'll call you then."

Neal sat down beside her on the bed and reached for her coffee, holding it out for her. "Here. You don't like it after it cools down."

52

Cady waited in the dark for his call. Her restless dogs finally bedded down for the night, she leaned back in her bedroom chaise overlooking the patio. The glass doors were closed, blocking out her night sounds and she hated it. When her phone finally buzzed, it jolted her.

"Cady?"

"Yes."

"Anything?"

"No, Neal."

"Cady…How was your day?"

"Choppy, Neal. It was a choppy sort of a day, couldn't stay on task. You know, do this, no do that."

"Me too. You're being careful? Doors, windows locked? Alarm on?"

"Yes, Neal."

"Take care."

"Yes."

***

Leonard glared at the numbers flashing on his phone, feeling it pulse, hoping he'd just go away. Cretin. But he wouldn't. Leonard knew he wouldn't.

"Yeah," Leonard chafed.

"Before…before ya…did she tell ya what she knew? What she found in your voting machines? Do ya think…could she tell 'em?"

"Doesn't matter now. All the hard evidence was in the numbers Election Day. Gone as soon as the precincts closed down."

"What about the machines? They've got a parcel o' those alright. Can they find out anything from the machines?"

***

"Cady?"

"Yes."

"Anything?"

"No."

"You're being safe?"

"Yes. But Neal. Nothing's happening…at all. Except the police. The police drive by now at odd hours, more than they did before…before it happened."

"Did you give the police your names of Izzy's friends?"

"Yes."

"And?"

"And nothing. I think they dropped it. Not interested. Trail's cold."

"No."

"Then what?"

"They're doing what they do, following leads."

"I'm wondering…my phone calls…still nothing since election night."

"You mean from creepy guy?"

"Yes. Nothing."

"Good."

"Not good. I'm worried. Do you suppose Izzy's…?"

"No. I don't want you to think about it."

"But I do. I can't help but think about it. What does it mean? Izzy disappears. The election's done. And the phone calls stop."

"It probably means the freak's crawled back into his cave until the next time he smells blood. Or maybe he got the results he wanted or…."

"Or maybe he's occupied."

"Occupied?"

"With Izzy."

"Cady, don't. Please don't. We'll go mad playing what-ifs. And, Cady, you need to do everything you can to stay strong."

"I know."

"Do you? Really?"

"Yes."

"Anything from ElecTron?"

"No. I'm trying to be blasé about it, like I don't care, like I'm just trying to close out our incident reports. And they're holding tight to their proprietary rights clause. Saying they complied with our contract. They insist on a court order for anything else."

"Cady, I…"

"I know. Too public. Besides I'd have to bring Stan in on it. And even if we thought that wasn't such a bad idea, he was so adamant about my not pursuing this on Election Day. Imagine his reaction to a courtroom duel. Picture us punching our chads out in the courts again. Never happen on his watch."

"What then?"

"I pursue it from the programming angle. If I could offer ElecTron more substantial proof, maybe some test cases, well they might grow friendly. Of course then they'd know I'm still working on it for real."

"Not good."

"No, but I don't hear you offering to help."

"Arm's length, Cady."

"Yes."

"Take care."

"Yes."

***

Leonard didn't sign-up for this, the pushy picky nagging calls near drivin' him nuts. He motioned to toss his cell in the john… How many times could he go over the same crap?

"What about the votin' machines? Can they break into them?"

"Like I told you. Doesn't matter. The software's encrypted. ElecTron's hardcopies don't list my programs. We're clean."

"Suppose they start dickin' around with those machines?"

"I've got some surprises in their calibration procedures that'll wipe out all the evidence, fix them up good."

"But then…how…" Brice dragged on his stogie over the phone line.

"That's what you've got me for, dude. Besides you don't want it to work the same way every election. You might want other stuff done. I'm here for you, dude."

"F____. When do they calibrate the f_____ machines? Do ya know?"

"Should be calibrating them soon, maybe next month."

"F___."

"Hey, dude, we're in the clear. The algorithms I conjured up in those babies are complex-slick mothers. Take anyone years to figure it out and that's if they get the source programs to work with."

"How they do that?"

"Can't. I encrypted it. All they'll get is gibberish. There is no source code, no translatable copy anywhere, at least not where they can get at it."

***

Cady's project spilled over from her home office into her dining room. Columns of papers lined the table, each marked up with colored scribbles and lines and arrows and sticky notes. Cady leaned over her papers, lost in work and time when her phone buzzed.

"Cady?"

"Yes."

"Anything?"

"No. Yes. Sort of."

"O—k-a-y."

"I set up test ballots to mimic the voting trends we saw election morning…before the jell-o."

"Jell-o?"

"Yes. You know before the counts started quivering."

"Okay…and?"

"And the test ballots tell me precisely how to vote on my voting machines. I follow each test ballot exactly. And every finger poke, every completed ballot I enter into the voting machine is documented. It's my control group."

"O—k-a-y…and?"

"And my results on the computer after entering my ballot control group must match my ballot results on paper. Ten votes for red, ten votes for blue, one for you, two for me, and so on."

"I see…I think…and the jell-o?"

"Yes and the jell-o. But it wasn't consistent on every voting machine I tested, at least not with my first control groups."

"Uh, doesn't sound good."

"Oh, yes, Neal. It does!"

"What am I missing here?"

"The technical."

"Okay, English?"

"Three voting machines. Same hardware setup. Same software. Same data. Get it?"

"No. But you're enjoying this too much, Cady."

"Perhaps. I do have a captive audience here. You think I'm not going to play it for all it's worth?"

"I see your point. And…"

"And take a computer, any computer. Its only job is to do exactly what you tell it to do. Tell your computer to add two numbers together. And it does it, same way, every time. No deviations. Your computer is going to do exactly the same thing every time…every single time…given identical data with the same set of circumstances. Now, take a second computer with exactly the same hardware and software. It will behave exactly like your first computer, every time. That is unless one of them breaks. Or unless they're not exactly alike after all."

"But if I understand, yours didn't…behave."

"Precisely my point."

"And you're positively giddy that your tests failed. I don't understand."

"Same hardware. Same software. Same data. And same ballots. No hardware-software-light-flickering failures. Should have given me the same results."

"Yet it didn't. So…and…"

"So…something was different."

"And what was that, Cady?"

"Two things for certain. One I should have fessed up right away. I entered my data identical to the test ballots. And my first few tests produced results consistent with my paper results."

"So ElecTron's software works and there was no vote rigging after all."

"One would think."

"Everyone except my Cady?"

"Yes."

"Go on…"

"So I did it again. And again. And again. But I didn't clear out the machine."

"Why."

"Because. I believed my test ballots represent an accurate snapshot of election morning. Percentage of blue votes, red votes, other votes."

"If you believe it, Cady, I believe it."

"Thank you. Sometimes when we're absolutely adamant about things, that's the time we trip up. And when a computer's involved, the trip up is so much more grand. I don't mean that in a good way either."

"Cady, I'm still waiting for your two things that were different."

"Yes, Neal. Obviously, the number of votes made a difference. Nothing went amiss until I entered a lot…a lot of votes."

"Hmm. So in a normal testing cycle…"

"Wouldn't show up unless you're really into pain. But there was another trigger."

"That caused the first or in combination?"

"Enabled the first trigger. Same program. Same computer. Same everything. Should have worked the same, but it didn't."

"What was different, Cady?"

"The date, Neal."

"So our phantom…is the date?"

"Yes. Well, one of our phantoms. The system date…not just a date parameter entered by an operator or poll worker…but the inside-the-guts-of-the-computer system date must be equal to the first Tuesday in November, after the first Monday, that is. It triggers the coup."

"And the year?"

"Any year, Neal."

53

The next evening as Cady made her rounds closing windows and blinds to the encroaching dusk, she caught sight of Neal's car driving past and she waited by the window while he circled the block before pulling into her driveway. And she waited, so eager for him she could almost feel his arms around her. Instead their phone rang and she sprinted back to her bedroom, out of breath when she answered.

"Cady?"

"Oh…Neal," the disappointment in her voice carried across the phone line.

"You were expecting someone else?"

"Yes…no…I mean, I just saw your Beemer drive by. I hoped…"

"No, Cady, I've got to stay away. You know that. It's for you."

"Yes, Neal."

"Anything?"

"ElecTron handed over the election certified source code."

"Just like that?"

"Yes."

"Too soon to tell anything?"

"No. It's not the same code installed on our machines."

"How do you know?"

"I took two of the voting machines we used Election Day. On one I left the programs intact. I didn't touch it. On the other I installed ElecTron's certified software they just sent me. By the way it wasn't encrypted, so I could visually follow line-by-line everything the computer was doing…real time, in slow motion."

"Okay, Cady. You lost me after the part where you loaded their software."

"Sorry. It just means I didn't need a Rosetta Stone to figure out what the computer was doing."

"Good. So then?"

"Then I parallel tested the two machines. Performed identical tests, identical ballots, identical data, identical November system date, identical time of day and everything. And ba-da-bing! Different results."

"Different as in…"

"As in the voting machines with the certified software. It correctly produced completely Democratic ballots when I selected Democratic candidates."

"And the other voting machines resulted in Republican ballots when you selected Democratic candidates?"

"No."

"I don't understand. That sort of blows our theory, doesn't it?"

"I…I don't think so. Not exactly. My theory hasn't jelled, at least not completely. But hear me out."

"Go on."

"The Election Day machines produced un-Democrat, un-Blue votes. And not for every vote either. And not right away. It wasn't until after I entered a bunch of votes. That's when things got interesting…started taking shape actually"

"So what did you see?"

"The un-Blue votes sprinkled around various OTHER options. Some were rejects, some for lesser candidates, some as no-votes, and yes some for Red."

"Uh…Cady?"

"Don't you see? They need to keep the margin of victory in line with the margin of error.…No that's not right. They need to keep it believable, realistic. If every un-Blue vote went for Red it would be too obvious."

"But as it is, in all practicality, any un-Blue vote IS a vote for Red."

"And any un-Blue vote converted directly into a Red vote is actually two votes for the Red candidate."

"Uh?"

"Take one vote away from Blue. That's one. Add that one vote from Blue to a vote for Red. That's two. Two votes."

***

Stan clipped his nails. He couldn't seem to get the grime out from under them. He felt so dirty. His wife found Izzy's blood on his underwear. "As a matter of fact, Brice, I told her Election Day to push up the calibration date."

"I don't want it pushed up. Do it now."

"Law says we've gotta keep the voting-machines around awhile as is. Could be challenges."

"F___. Who's gonna challenge? Democrats? They won your county."

"Could be any number of challenges, if…"

"If what?"

"If they can't find some logic behind the exit polls. Those are damning, Brice."

"So what if they can't. What if they challenge the results?"

"The numbers on the machines will be the same as they were when the polls closed. Nothing's going to change that…unless we calibrate."

"Don' cha love it? Calibrate the f____ers!"

***

Neatly typed envelope. When Cady tore it open, it didn't register that the letter was addressed formally to Deputy Supervisor of Elections Susan Cady Palmer or that it was sent to her home or that it was squashy to handle. Midnight tresses spilled onto her terracotta kitchen floor. Cady fell to the floor after them, scooping up the shiny black strands off the cold tile and to her chest. No scream came.

"Neal?"

"Cady. What's wrong?"

"I got a letter today…a letter. It said, 'LEAVE IT ALONE OR SHE GETS IT.'"

"Cady…It's Izzy, isn't it? This means she's alive."

"Her hair. Her beautiful hair all bloody, Neal. They sent me her hair."

"Cady...you...I want to be there with you. You know that don't you?"

"Yes."

"Call the police."

"I did, Neal. They said it doesn't mean anything. They took everything for testing. But..."

"Right."

"Neal, the next time it could be a finger...or.... What should I do?"

"Cady, you just keep on keepin' on. Don't get online. Don't talk to anyone. They don't know what you're doing behind closed doors, Cady."

***

"Stanboy, whaddya know? Ya wanna tell me about it?"

"What's that, Brice?"

"You're little spitfire. Said you took care of it?"

"Who, Cady?"

"Idiot. Your Mexicali. Somebody sent a wad of her hair to Palmer."

"No, Brice, you're wrong. I took care of it for you. It's Leonard. It's gotta be Leonard. The bastard's got a trove of relics. That night...Leonard...he scalped her, Brice. Sliced her hair clean off her head...passed out clutching a wad of Izzy's hair to his belly."

***

"Cady?"

"Yes."

"Anything?"

"No. Still tracking cause and effect. Slow going."

"Can I help?"

"You're already helping, Neal, just by..."

"I mean anything tangible, though it's good to hear you think so."

"I've got to figure out a way to unencrypt the program code on my Election Day voting machines so that I can actually get my mitts on the source code. That way I'll be able to provide a visual A-B-C, 1-2-3 hardcopy proof of the discrepancies."

"Right. Well…I…ah…"

"Uh-uh. My fair-weather friend."

"Cady, I'm setting up a couple of meetings in the next few weeks. If you can't get your hardcopy, can you jot down a few notes for me? I want to make sure I get it right."

"Sure."

***

"Cady?"

"Yes."

"Anything?"

"Nothing new."

"No new phone calls?"

"No…just the letter."

"Hmm. Of course that's good news, but…"

"Me too. I wonder what it means."

***

"Cady?"

"Yes."

"Meet me."

"Yes." Cady pulled out her schlep bag. And before Neal completed his directions she'd finished stuffing it with essentials, swimsuit, shorts, tee-shirts, one pair of black slacks and a windbreaker.

Cady stood in front of her vanity table, studying the woman staring back at her, wiser, older, not the child she left behind just weeks ago. She reached behind her neck and unfastened the delicate chain. As she cupped the ring in her palm, the bright stone glistened in the light, winking at her. "It's time, Cady," it whispered. "It's time." She kissed the ring softly, opened the bottom drawer of her jewelry box and gently set the ring to rest on soft black velvet. "It is time. Time for me to go. Time to let go." Cady swiped at the tears trickling down her cheeks. She opened the patio door and dove into the pool.

54

Cady and Neal flanked their kayak and dragged it up onto dry sand, ruts furrowing behind them. A trio of iguanas watched curiously from the seawall. Fruit-for-us their eyes asserted imperially as they inspected the ice chest, towels, tote.

"Come on," Neal took Cady's hand and led her over to the jetty where they ambled along the pitted seawall.

"Look," Cady pointed to a stretch of shallow sea bottom swaying to and fro with the placid tide as a silent orchestra of sea anemone waved in time to the gentle current. "They're herbs, you know, related to the butter cup."

Neal chuckled softly, hugging her close, "I…I love you, Cady. I really love you."

"I know, Neal. I love you too."

They stood at the tip of the jetty with only nature around them, breathing in the salty afternoon.

"God, I love this place," Neal whispered, more of a prayer than to Cady. Then he said to her, "It's one of the few spots left on this island that faintly resembles the real Florida Keys…only a few acres left. You can't imagine the storms that ripped across these islands. But it wasn't nature that did them in. And look at those old bungalows, no frills, just concrete boxes. They weather everything nature pummels at them. And probably one day…soon…somebody will name the right price and they'll be ripped down, replaced with a gargantuan luxury something-or-other that'll wash out with the first wave." Neal tweaked Cady's nose. "Looks like we should have smeared on some more goo. You're glowing pink."

"My freckles showing?" she smiled up at him.

"Your freckles always show," he kissed her nose. "Very alluring."

"You toad! You're allured by…by…"

"By everything about you, Cady," he finished for her. "Want to bask out here under the shade of the banyans or go back to the bungalow?"

"Let's stay here for a while. It's so lush and tropical and…romantic and…sexy."

"You talk about me. Well seems we have something in common after all, Miss Palmer."

"Perhaps. Though I don't know really," she teased before changing the subject. "How old do you think these banyans are anyway?"

"I don't know, big, how old is a big banyan? You know if things get rough in the city, we could hang out in one of these colossal canopies for weeks, years. They'd never find us."

"And dine on flamingo eggs and fish and…IGUANA!"

"Don't! You wicked woman. You'll frighten them."

"Hardly. Nothing discourages those beasties. Just look at them. First they'll cart off our ice chest. Next they'll swim away with our kayak. Brazen."

"They do look rather…militant." Neal's smile turned serious, "Cady, we've got to talk."

"I know. What's for dinner? Want to grill those steaks?"

"Cady."

"Do you know those ferns over there? They were around before the dinosaurs. Before iguanas. Well not those specific ferns, but ferns in general."

"Cady."

"You're such a spoilsport, Neal. You know that?"

"Yes, Cady, I do. But sooner or later, more likely sooner, life's going to march in on us. And we need to be ready."

"I understand, Neal. But can't it wait 'til after dinner?"

"And then you'll want to wait until morning and we don't have much time left. Besides, me, myself and I, that's three to your one. We don't want to spoil the mood tonight, do we? Better to do it now and get it over with."

Cady glanced over at him through tender, hungry eyes, "And you're certain you'd like to spoil the mood now?" she smiled. "Neal?"

Neal rubbed her forearm, then rested his hand on hers. "Cady, I know I've been more closed-mouth than you'd like about this…"

"I know the drill, Neal. You have your reasons. And there's the matter of trust."

"Well, yes, exactly. I do have reasons, but nothing to do with trust. You survived Elections without losing your tongue. That's figuratively and literally."

"Hmm. Times I suspected you'd as soon yank it out of my head as hear me speak."

"Could be. But, Cady, listen. I kept my own counsel for two, no for several reasons. Sure, I wanted to tell you in person, wanted to find Izzy. But primarily, your safety. Yours, Cady. The stakes here, they're incredibly high and not just because some psycho's running loose. And, Cady, I didn't want to give you false hopes. But now…well, here goes. It all starts with me, but it radiates broadly. No, Cady. Hell it doesn't start with me. I'm just a conduit. That's what I am or a…a spoke on Brice's wheel and Brice is the hub. So much you don't know, can't know. My…affiliation with Brice, his plodding corrosion, and my own failures."

"Your failures, Neal?"

"Yes, Cady. I hung in too long, called it loyalty, friendship. When in fact it was me. I faltered, be it laziness or fear…fear of the unknown. And I couldn't or wouldn't move forward."

"You're anything but lazy, Neal. And the world knows you're no coward."

"Thank you for that, Cady. There's so much you don't know."

"So, fill me in. I'll respect you in the morning," she smiled coyly.

"That's a guy line, Cady…. Okay, you promise. From the beginning. You know I've worked for Brice since graduation. You know we roomed in college."

"Yes. And you nurtured high hopes."

"Yes, Cady, hopes and dreams and desires. I think…I believe when Brice ran for governor the first time and lost…I believe he ran a clean campaign. But Brice…he hates to lose…anything. And I think after the sting of that very public defeat he decided never to lose again, no matter what the cost, perhaps even his soul, definitely his integrity.

"I haven't told you this before, Cady, but you already know as well as anyone, there've been a few elections now that alarmed a number of people. Some played out in court, but none was ever resolved and put to rest."

"You're telling me."

"When Florida outlawed punch cards and acquired those first touch screens, well the collective relief in Washington was palpable, like releasing pressure from a hot air balloon."

Neal shifted in his chair and Cady waited.

"Then came another few skittish elections, the questions, the niggling suspicions. That was my turning point, Cady, when I first felt…tarnished. I started checking my options in a world without Brice, surreptitiously of course, but fishing around nonetheless."

"But you stayed."

"Yes, Cady, I stayed."

"Why?"

"Ah, yes. And the reason for all my dark secrets."

"And you're dragging out the telling, Neal. Come on."

"Before I had the chance to make headway with my job queries, I was summoned to Washington, again surreptitiously of course. Everything in Washington's a secret. And sometimes as in this case, the secrets actually remain secret."

"So what's your secret, Neal?"

"My secret is the senators."

"Oh? The senators? And which senators would they be?"

"Ah. Still secret, Cady. But I can tell you there are two of them, two powerful, long-term, awe inspiring icons, and believe it or not, one from each side of the aisle. Imagine my amazement there."

"What did they want from you?"

"Actually, they asked me to stay with Brice."

"So, they wanted you to spy on him?"

"Not really. At least not in the usual sense. They didn't want me to follow Brice's moves and then report back to them."

"What then?"

"The way they put it was that Brice is a good man but may be embroiled in circumstances that could influence his...his better judgment. They believed he and ironically the country could be better served if I stayed with him and continued to remind him, even pressure him to walk the line."

"Wow."

"Guess their reasoning was either Brice would straighten up or I'd do it until I couldn't do it anymore."

"But what's left? This was his last big party. He goes away, done. It's over. He's even told the press he's out of it."

"Must be true then…. Even if it were true, let's just say his term ends but his power doesn't."

"Okay…."

"Then when the climate's right he beelines to the White House."

"Is that his intention?"

"No doubt. Why stop now? This election was just one more stepping stone. Stack and cement the political powerhouse to his advantage and who looks more presidential?"

"So he simply calls in his favors and steps up to the podium?"

"Yes, Cady. And it was just providence that Brice wanted me at your election. I'm sure the senators were sitting in their balcony seats applauding. They didn't have to show their hands."

Cady thought for a moment. "Let's see if I understand what you've told me. You started with Brice. You wanted to leave Brice. The senators asked you not to leave. And you decided to stay until you couldn't stay. Is that right?" Cady laughed softly, shaking her head.

"That's it exactly, Cady."

"So…."

"So, let's say it wasn't unexpected that something might tarnish your election. And Brice had it from Stan that you were quote-quote one of us. To Brice that means you can be had for your…fervent political persuasions. Then election morning you walked in all tall and beautiful and sure of yourself with your red scarf and your little yellow victory pin and well…"

"Beautiful? Neal, you thought I was beautiful?"

"Oh good grief. Of course I thought you were beautiful, Cady."

"And you thought I was on the take?"

"I thought everything, Cady. Everything and nothing."

"And so here we are, we two and your senators and the rest of the world. If you can stay with Brice until you can't stay with Brice, how will you know you can't stay with him?" Cady smiled.

"You're having too much fun with this, Cady."

"Perhaps."

"Cady, I knew by the end of Election Day. I was done. Maybe before that, when I watched you in action and decided I wanted to know you and couldn't since I might have to…take you down."

Cady glared at him and repeated in a hoarse whisper, "Take me down, Neal?"

It was Neal's turn to laugh, "No. Not like that." Then his smile faded and he was serious again. "But if the election turned out differently, say all systems crashed due to your incompetence, well, I would have had you fired. Stan too. And your staff."

"My, that's comforting."

"It should be…well maybe not. But, Cady, you're the one who wants most for these voting machines to work. And I didn't know you then. It was just business, Cady."

"So you've stayed until you can't stay any longer?"

"Yes, Cady."

"And now?"

"And now there's you."

"Hmm." Cady reached for him, but pulled back. "I thought for a moment you were being personal. But you're not. You're back to the senators, aren't you?"

"Yes, Cady. I've been talking with them since first you convinced me your votes were muddled, when I felt Brice's complicity, and when I knew he'd slipped beyond…redemption. It must be stopped, Cady. And, Cady, it's been rough."

"I know, Neal."

"Yes, but not for the reasons you might think. My own self-image vacillates from that of a traitorous hypocrite to champion of the free world. Not a day goes by that I don't feel like I've let Brice down. When I talk with him, I hate myself."

"No, Neal. You tried to save him. He turned. He chose. He's a spoiled brat born into privilege with…you know, the arrogance of entitlement. Probably always got everything he wanted. When confronted with losing, he changed the rules."

"Yes, but…"

"Neal, think. Should he pursue his ambitions unleashed…we can't even comprehend a future in which the voting process is owned by one or a few self-serving men. You wouldn't let me quit when I wanted to. Now it's my turn. If not you, Neal, who?"

"But…"

"No! Listen! God trumps country. Country trumps party. Party trumps friendship."

"And family? You and me?"

"You trump me, Neal. Just fine."

"You're incorrigible. Doesn't family trump party?"

"You're right, Neal. Family trumps party. So does friendship. And your senators? Where do your senators fit into this?"

"More likely where do you fit in with my senators?"

"Me?"

"Yes. They want hard proof, Cady. They want solid evidence."

"I…and then?"

"Then you'll trek off to Washington."

"Whatever for?"

"To present your case of course."

"And if they don't believe me?"

"They will."

"Then what?"

"Two things. They will immediately launch an investigation to flush out all the players, top secret. No one is to know."

"And the second?"

"They want you involved in establishing guidelines, standards, protocol for voting machines."

"What?"

"Forget that for now. Let's just get to step one. Okay?"

"Will you go with me?"

"Step one. Get your hard proof. We'll talk about the rest later."

"What if I can't get hard proof? What if they can't catch Leonard or if it's not him? What if I fail?"

"You won't fail, Cady. You may not be able to get everything you want, you know, to point out specific lines of program code that fixed the election. But if you can't do that, you can repeat your test cases and prove beyond doubt that votes were skewed."

"Will that be enough?"

"It has to be. And I believe it will be. But we need to freeze a few more voting machines and lock them up. They're ultimately the real proof. We lose them and we have nothing."

55

"Hello....Hello..." Cady braced to hang up as soon as the phone creep took another breath. But only muffled sobs greeted her.

"Izzy. Izzy. Where are you?"

Ragged whimpers answered.

"Izzy?"

"Hello? Miss? Miss...ah..."

"Cady Palmer. What's wrong? Is it Isabella? Is she there?"

"Well, hold on, Miss Palmer. Don't know 'xactly where you fit in ta this. But there's a young woman here. She's hurt bad..."

"Isabella? Is it Isabella? What happened? Where are you?"

"Hold on there. Don't rightly know her name, ma'am. She doesn't have an ID on her...beat up bad. Wearin' a blanket is all."

"I'm looking for Esmeralda Isabella Palacio. She's slender. Cuban. Long dark wavy hair. Very beautiful. About 5'4."

"Miss...ah...This lady's hair's most gone, chopped off to 'er scalp. She's in a bad way...Can't tell about her looks. Took a helluva beating. Face all puffed, bruised and she's chewed up by the damned mosquitoes. She does look to be about 5'4 though. Probly left for dead."

"Oh Izzy, my poor Izzy."

"I was just calling an ambulance when she reached up and grabbed my phone and she dialed your number somehow. She can't talk. Think her jaw's broken."

Cady gagged. Her hand flew to her mouth.

"Pale. Like she's lost lots of blood. Gotta get her to a hospital. She's in and out conscious, you know?"

"What can I do?"

"Well, ma'am. You can get off the phone so I can call an ambulance. We're way out here in the middle of the Glades and I need to get to that ambulance so they can…"

"Ambulance. To the Everglades? That'll take hours. What about a MediVac?"

"Look, I don't rightly know…"

Cady pulled the phone away from her ear long enough to read the phone number. She grabbed her pencil and scribbled the number on her notepad, checked it against the phone again.

"Okay. Okay. Listen. Hold off on the ambulance. Just two minutes. Let me see if I can get someone to fly out there. Okay?"

"Yeah. You'll call right back?"

"Yes. I'll call right back. And…and can you, can you not tell anyone? I mean she's…I don't know if…who's after her."

"You're tellin' me. One peek at the poor tyke…'bout gives me the heebies. You'll call right back though."

"Yes. Right away. And oh, thank you. Thank you."

Cady hung up and dialed Neal's number. Neal, he'll do something…Neal…he'll know what to do.

***

Cady stood outside in the parking lot waiting for them when the helicopter landed. The pilot and doctor up front, Neal at the rear. Neal extended his hand and pulled her in. The craft was airborne before Neal closed the door.

"Neal…I'm so scared."

"Let's hold off on that now, Cady. We've found her. Let's get there and bring her home."

Cady nodded. "But what if she's dead when we get there? What if it's not her? What…"

"Cady, it's her. Too much coincidence not to be. And, Cady, she's hung on this long, she'll make it. Tell me what happened."

"I don't know, Neal. You know everything. The man from the station called. Said an old Miccosukee from one of the abandoned villages found her…middle of the night, lying half-in half-out a canal along Tamiami Trail, some miles west of the casino. Said she was lucky the gators hadn't carried her off yet."

"Damn. Hadn't thought about that."

"Me either. He said the old man didn't know what to do… No phone of course. Couldn't leave her long enough to go off and get help. So he just dragged her into his chikee. Force fed her herbal brews and doused her with healing potions. Tried as best he could to make her comfortable, mopping her with damp cloths to get her fever down, and smoking and fanning the bugs away."

"When did the old man find her?"

"Don't know…a while…. He said if anyone else found her she'd surely be dead by now. Said she was probably better off with the old man than she would have been in a hospital. Seems the old timer shows up now and again. Folks around there seek him out… customs…cures…"

"And so the legend of Isabella weaves its way into the rich tapestry of Miccosukee folklore?"

"I…she's such a…a little girly-girl, Neal."

"I know, Cady. But you yourself told me she's tough as nails. It's hard, Cady, and it may get worse. But we'll get through this, all of us."

***

"Boys said you took the big chopper again."

"Yes, Brice. With you up in Tallahassee it's not logging enough flight time. Thanks by the way…emergency at the Elections Department."

"Oh?"

"Cady's programmer turned up in the Everglades. She needed medical attention. Fast. No quick way to get to her."

"That so?"

"Yes. She's still critical."

"What'd she have to say for herself? Choke up under pressure? Out for a moonlight sonata?"

"Doubt it. She's beaten up pretty bad. Doesn't know what happened. It's a miracle she made this far."

"That so?"

"What's her excuse for dodgin' out on Election Day?"

"Damn, Brice, you sound like it's her fault."

"Well, she did abandon her post, right?"

"Police believe she was abducted. Maybe the same psychopath who was phone stalking them. Maybe the hacker who infected their tabulation equipment. Maybe they're the same guy."

"Well, you keep your nose out of it, hear? No need for you to be pokin' around, gettin' all caught up in the news. Didn't I call you off?"

"Yes, Brice. I am off it. Haven't been to the Elections Department since they wrapped up the official returns."

"You still hangin' out with that gal over there?"

"I picked up my things the day you pulled me off the job, Brice. You did pull me off surveillance, yes? So there's no reason.... But they needed help with getting Izzy out from the Glades and into the hospital."

"Where would that be?"

"South Miami."

"Go check her out. See what you can wheedle outta her."

"Anything specific?"

"Anything she's got about the election, about her abduction."

"Right. I'll stop in this evening."

***

"Well, Stanley. Asked you to do one thing...one simple thing and you screw it up like everythin' else."

"What, Brice, I... What?"

"Take care of that little baggage, that's what!"

"Baggage?"

"Your little Mexicali."

"I did, Brice, and it was awful."

"How come she turned up alive and well and maybe squawking!"

"I...can't be. She couldn't survive all that..." Stan sputtered, choking on his jumbled emotions. Relief at Izzy alive. Terror she might remember. Glee his wife's weapon wielded diminishing power over him. "Brice, I went looking for her. I made sure...the next day."

"How're you gonna fix this?"

56

Izzy slept. Her once glorious tresses cropped short, very short, but now at least an even length and stylish. She often spiked it into a pert, punky-smart I-am-woman-watch-me-soar 'do. The style actually accentuated her femininity and the delicate features of her face, all healed and healthy. Only one pale line beneath her eye and another tiny diagonal swoosh on the bridge of her nose lingered, reminding her friends of her terrible ordeal. Neal knew the right doctors and surgeons and pulled enough strings to get them on her team. Judging from her looks now, they served her extremely well.

Once again magnolia-rose lovely, but a deeper, richer, more vibrant hue. Once again glorious Izzy. The stuff young men's dreams are made of.

Stitches removed, bruises faded, skin silky smooth with or without makeup. Only her swelling tummy shouted out, "Rape! I am the spawn of Satan. Rip my head off and yank me out and flush me away!"

No one can know of this. Wait until I'm better, stronger.

***

"No. I've no memory whatsoever. None." Izzy lounged on her parent's sofa, her mother's hand-knit teal and fawn lap shawl snugged around her legs.

"On the one hand, it's a good thing, Izzy, because you're spared…"

"I know, Neal. But I do have these fuzzy dreams and they're horrible, horrible dreams. But they make no sense to me."

"Can you tell us about them, Izzy?" Cady asked softly.

"Yes. The police weren't interested in my dreams. But if you think it could help."

"We can't know until you tell us."

"Even then we'll probably need time to digest them."

"Well, okay. Here goes. Cady, you were there. You were always there, big and strong and watching over me."

"But, Izzy, I.."

"Cady, this is Izzy's dream."

"Yes, of course, Neal. Izzy, I'm sorry. Please…"

"Okay. Anyway, Cady, you were wearing your Election Day suit. Not the way you were in the afternoon, with just your blouse and skirt, but like you were first thing in the morning, in your full regalia."

"How do you mean, Izzy?" Neal asked.

"Well, her jacket properly buttoned and her scarf draped just so around her neckline. And she wore her little yellow ribbon pin."

"Yes. I remember. That's how she looked when I first met her that morning. What else?"

"Well she stood so regally and still and huge. I knew I'd be okay because she was there watching, still and pretty as a picture."

"Oh, Izzy, you sweet, sweet baby." Cady chewed on her bottom lip to stay on focus and keep from tearing up.

"Izzy, what can you remember of your dream besides Cady?"

"I felt so groggy. I was lying on a bed and the sheets smelled of unwashed hair and sweat and I wanted to leave but I…too weak to lift my head or my arms or my legs. And I tried calling for help and…Cady wasn't there…and each time I tried I just groaned and then there'd be banging on the wall and then beer. I smelled so much beer and…I hate beer. I'll never drink beer again. Ever! And then…that's weird…"

"What, Izzy?"

"Well, it can't be."

"That's okay. Tell us anyway. It doesn't matter if it makes sense. Remember, it's just a dream."

"Yes. A dream. Well, Cady came in and carried me into the another room. But it wasn't Cady. Because Cady was standing against the wall all big and gazing down at us. But…it was… Cady…Cady's jacket and scarf carried me into the room where Cady was. But it was all wrong. The person carrying me…he…

he…it was a he and his hair was black and stiff and jagged and he smelled of beer. More beer. And he threw me on the altar in front of Cady. And that's it. That's all I remember…. Some dream, eh?"

"Yes, Izzy, it is. And after all that, how can you even stand to look at me?"

"Oh no, Cady, you've got it all wrong. The whole time I knew you watched over me, keeping me safe."

"Woo," Cady's sighed, more the moan of a wounded animal.

"Oh, yes, there's more. I forgot."

"Go on, Izzy," Neal encouraged gently.

"Stan. I smelled Stan. You know his cologne. You know how a little smells good but then he keeps putting more on all day long and by the end of the day it just makes you gag?"

"Yes, Izzy. I do know. He…he was so concerned about you, Izzy. When I told him we found you he went on and on asking how you were…he…"

"Cady," Neal cautioned.

"…Well that's the smell, that cloying smell that stays in your nostrils even after you leave his office, you know that please-spray-me-with-a-fire-hose smell."

"And what then?"

"He stood over me and kicked me and kicked me and I don't remember. I guess I fell asleep or something."

"And did you wake up in your dream?"

"Yes. Stan was standing over me and that smell and he had a sheet and I thought he was going to wrap it around me to make me warm but he put it over my head and it smelled of pee and he wrapped it so tight I couldn't breath and he lifted me up and he carried me and then he dragged me and my feet thumped on the ground and then he put me in a box. And I couldn't breathe and then I was wet and then an old Indian blew smoke in my face and hummed chants over me and held his arms over my chest and blew more smoke but it wasn't cigarettes or cigars it was fire smoke and it smelled good and sweet and then he poured this awful tasting broth stuff down my throat and caked me with mud and all the while he hummed and he chanted."

"Izzy," Neal rested his hand on her arm. "One day…a long time from now understand…when you feel better, we might talk about this again. Okay?"

"Sure, Neal. But you know later, later there really was an Indian, Cady, and he was good and kind and he fanned me to keep the bugs away and he rubbed me with stinkybalm and he stroked my hair." Izzy brushed her hand over her short-cropped hair. "My head was black and swirling and spinning and…like black water whirling, churning down a drain and I just wanted it to end but he wouldn't let me end it and he kept calling me, calling me back. He wouldn't let me go. And then there was another man and he had a phone and I called you, Cady."

"Yes, Izzy, you did. I'm so glad you did, Izzy."

57

"Cady, I'll be out of town for a few days. Victory gala in Tallahassee. Brice's last hurrah. He wants to remind everyone that he's the one who held Florida for them. I have to go, Cady. Brice likes to keep his goons close. Same protocol as always. I'll call when I get back."

"Okay."

"Cady?"

"Yes."

"You alright?"

"Yes."

"I'm with you, Cady. I'm with you all the way."

"Yes."

"She'll be okay, Cady. She will."

"Yes. Neal, have you been driving around my neighborhood?"

"No, Cady. Why?"

"Someone…Beemer like yours…I thought maybe you were out on patrol or something."

"No, Cady……Cady?"

"Yes, Neal."

"The Beemer…Brice…It's a lease car, Cady…a perk. Brice gets these deals going. I know he's leased a small fleet of Beemers, but what I don't know is who he's got driving them."

"You think Brice…?"

"No, but……I…. Be careful, Cady. Please be careful."

***

Neal detested the frenzy of it. He liked being away from Cady even less. Any pleasure he garnered from this night was in the knowing it to be his last, and his loathing of the tinsel-pomp made all that he must do so much easier. Still, the smile he wore was not the patient-soon-to-be-over smile he usually donned for these events. His heart found Cady at last. Soon his soul would find peace.

The caterwauling prickled his ears with its incessant, "Four more years! Four more years!" Couldn't one in the crowd be more original? Neal popped a couple ibuprofen...neat. Ach. The acrid pills raked their way down his throat, snagging at every bump. Ah, he hated this, the mob, the pushing, the shoving, the nuttiness...the noise, the relentless noise. And the closed in stink of too many hysterical perfumed bodies packed into excessively close quarters. Damn, the hoopla was outrageous.

But for Brice, Neal'd be home catching his twenty winks...with Cady. Whipped. Spent. The words never felt so fitting. He'd busted his butt with the rest of them, reaching for the unattainable. The irony of it all is he and Brice's team-Daniels actually caught the brass ring, the chance to achieve their dreams, something good. There was some of that, but how harshly dreams withered.

Then came E-day...and Cady...and the turnaround. Polls closed, vote tabulation drudged on, then poof! What seemed an inevitable loss early on, morphed to a strategic win for team-Daniels, not for Brice but for his move-on strategy. So here they were, all of them bleary-eyed, frazzled zombies being crushed for crowd bait. Waiting for the big moment...Brice's victorious farewell...out with the old, in with the new. Except Brice wasn't going. He was growing. He was glowing, wasn't he?

Neal assessed the gathering of loyal makers and takers, by now a roaring, cheering pandemonium of confetti, balloons, tears, wolf-howls, laughter, hand-pumping and jump-up-and-down hugs. From his immediate right to his left, Brice's entourage peppered the horde closest to the dais. Neal recognized the edgy swarm of undercover agents braced for the occasional nuttier-than-the-rest electorate slipping through the ubiquitous security checkpoints.

Neal watched the victory parade at long last march onto the podium, Florida royals surrounded by the sea of scarlet revelers hooting and chanting, "Four more years! Four more years! Four more years!" The royals milled about while being arranged in picture-pecking order. Brice stood left-center, positioned to pass his torch, pumped up but contained. Exhausted, like the rest of them, dark hollow circles smudged his eyes, his attention strayed off the dais.

Subtle undercurrents swirled between Brice and the movement below the dais. Neal followed Brice's gaze down to the small polished clique of Washington power brokers. Neal recognized them at once, the elite group chattering and fawning over the pudgy little kingmaker at the front and center of their cluster. But Pudge's attention wavered as he snatched a peek at Brice. Brice glanced his way. In a flash, their eyes locked. Ever so slightly, a rise and dip of Pudge's head, a raised eyebrow followed by a brief sidelong curl of his upper lip. Brice responded, tilting his head slightly forward and slowly shutting his eyes for a moment.

Certain his battle-fatigued brain tripped up on him Neal watched for an instant replay. It came. Though Pudge stood straight as a bayonet, he watched Brice's every move. Once again Pudge met and held Brice's gaze. Pudge inhaled deeply, jutting his jaw forward and lifting his left eyebrow. Then they were strangers again.

In all the years Neal worked with Brice, never had he known Brice to chum with those guys. Except for a couple of brief dashes to home plate, they played in altogether different ballparks. And here Brice was sharing intimate eye-speak with them. Odd. Still, with Brice one could only imagine.

Funny thing about integrity, once you give it away, you can never buy it back. Neal studied his culprits-by-association. Tight with shared secrets. Who knew why? ...Now Cady had him doing it, sniffing intent at every encounter. Why? Who? Well, Neal smirked, the why of it was fairly obvious. The who was vexing. Cady, the analyst searched and chewed, sought layer upon layer of information then searched and chewed some more. Neal never got caught up in the conundrum. That is, until now. Now, the stench of espionage permeated every juncture.

Cady challenged him with motive. Irrefutable proof of fraud wasn't enough for her. It surely didn't appease his senators. Now she compelled him to rack his brain for villains. And here the villains clung together like velcro.

There could be no question as to what happened with this election. Cady just had to unlock the code for Neal's senators. But just how far reaching the rot? Perhaps the last two presidential elections as well, if not rigged, definitely tainted, manipulated. Brice's fingerprints walked all over them. Neal just needed to catch Brice ratcheted up and babbling on his victory high. After a relaxing tipple-fest Brice was certain to flaunt his successes. He might fess it all up. Early on, before Brice sent Neal to spy on Cady's election, Brice bragged at pushing the outcome. Neal just needed to hold on, hang in a while longer. Then Neal would dump the whole trash heap of it at the senators' feet and be done with it.

Motive? Why? Who? Who else? When does a man turn corrupt? Defeat? Failure? Both Brice and his new chum had suffered losses of momentous magnitude. Pudge's undoubtedly a lonely personal failure. Pure and simple. He'd flunked out of college. Never quite able to squelch the bilious taste of failure. Forever tainted by the fear of a repeat. What would such a man do to succeed?

The second man, Brice of patrician heritage, posh, upper-crust, never wanting for anything, that is anything money can buy. Perhaps his mother's favorite. Surely the splendid symbol of success against his family's black sheep mantra. Always the shining example with which to counter his sister's perpetual disgrace. How it must have anguished him when his sister who literally failed at everything whizzed past him in their unspoken race to glory. How it must have pained him to lose his first bid for the governorship.

Confetti flecked heads and shoulders in a flurry of incandescent snowflakes. Pudge flicked pointlessly at his lapel, before smoothing a chunky hand over his forehead, dabbing at the few paltry sprigs. Brice stood firm, looking presidential. Pudge scanned the podium again before landing on Brice. Their eyes connected once more. Neal imagined Pudge's thoughts, "Maybe we can wedge him in next after all. Lay off a while. Give it a rest. Then comes the dark horse brightly. I can pull it off. He could be the one…next. I could do a lot for that one…must get Brice out in the public eye more. Must get him more involved in world affairs. More involved in the war so the herd will trust him when his time comes."

Neal looked away, looked around the audience, the cameras, the flag, his flag. His shoulders fell. *Gotta get done with this. How much do the senators know? Suspect?* Neal felt Brice's eyes peruse him. He didn't look up.

***

After the attaboys and hand-pumping brouhaha, Brice excused himself from the revelers long enough to make two calls in quick succession.

"Lennyboy, what do you hear over at ElecTron? I…don't have a good feelin' about this. Not at all…. You'd know if they're still working on your…project, wouldn't you? …Get on it."

Brice's second call just annoyed him. "Stanley, remind me again what is it you do to collect that fat paycheck of yours? Don't answer your phone. Not showin' up at your office? Snap back, you idiot……Somethin's up. Can't put my finger on it……Your girl still flushin' though the election crap?"

***

"Got your pretty back?"

"Who is this?"

"Why, Cady, forget me so soon. How 'bout your pretty? Not so pretty now, is she?"

"Leonard?" Cady tested his name on her lips. "Leonard, is that you?"

"I'm not through with her you know….a shame. Then it's your turn, Cady. I'll come for you next."

"What do you want?"

"It's you. It's always you. Where's boyfriend now? Ditch you now he got what he wanted?"

58

"Neal? Thank God...Neal, he's back. He's back! ...He...he called. He said, I don't know. He said he's coming for me next."

"Did you phone the police?"

"No. I called you."

"Okay then. Good. Are you okay to talk about it some more?"

"I...yes. Neal, I called him by his name, Neal. If he is Leonard, I called him by his name."

"Did he answer you, Cady? Any indication..."

"Nothing. He passed over it like I hadn't said anything at all."

"...Cady, did he sound...the same? Same voice? No...I mean more aggressive? Sure of himself?"

"Yes. He did. Before it took days for him to talk. He just breathed. This time he started right in, said, Neal he said he's not through with Izzy. What can I do?"

"I...how can that be? It makes no sense."

"What? Why?"

"Because he dumped her."

"Unless she...maybe she escaped on her own, Neal."

"And wound up in the Everglades?"

"I guess not, unh?"

"Not likely. And he said he's coming after you? Anything else?"

"I don't know. I lost it. I slammed the phone down on him."

"That's probably best. Okay, let's see if we can piece this thing together. Figure out what it means."

"It means he's back."

"Right. And for certain now we know it's all connected. Hell, the creep's call election night, I kept telling myself it could have been anyone calling you, anyone who'd been watching the action on television or from the media room and noticed her missing. I kept telling myself that maybe, just maybe the calls weren't related to Izzy's disappearance."

"Believe me, Neal, so did I."

"And then we got Izzy back. By then I'd convinced myself the incidents were unrelated, not the same person…."

"And if they were, maybe Izzy'd castrated the S.O.B. Or the pervert went back to sleep until the next election."

"Right. So what have we got? We've got Izzy…Izzy who was hot on the trail of vote tallies gone bonkers…Izzy who talks to some lunatic who says he's from ElecTron and then she gets carted off in the middle of the election."

"Yes. Except ElecTron knows nothing about it. They claim knowledge of only one call and that was from Mario early in the day. Anything else and they know nothing. No record of any other calls. Nothing."

"So they got the initial call from Mario. Then the next thing we know is someone claiming to be from ElecTron contacts Izzy. Izzy tells Mario the ElecTron rep wants to meet with her to go over important information."

"Yes. And that's the last we saw of her."

"But later in the evening, that other phone call asking you where your Izzy was."

"Yes."

"And that's the last phone call you had from him."

"Yes. Until tonight."

"Call the police. Don't tell them you talked with me. Tell them everything you've told me. Tell them about Izzy, everything. Are you okay to do that, Cady?"

"Yes, Neal."

"Are you okay to call her parents too? Tell them there's been another threat?"

"Yes. I can do that. In fact, I was packing up some things to take over to her, now that she's feeling human again. You know frou-frou stuff and a couple of books."

"Cady…"

"Yes, Neal."

"Stay home. Don't go. I'm on my way back. I'll be there in a few hours, maybe less."

"You can't. You said…"

"I know what I said, Cady. But that was before."

"Don't come. I just wanted… I wanted to hear your voice."

"Hold on for a little while and you'll hear it in person."

"No, Neal. You can't come here. You said so yourself. What if they see you?"

"What then? I can't just leave you there alone, Cady."

"I'll call the police like you said. They'll know what to do."

"Cady. Listen, the senators…with this sicko waking up again, I don't think we can afford to wait for more proof."

"You're talking in riddles, Neal."

"Yes. I suppose I am. Look, just…I want you to button down the hatches. Everything. No swimming. Stay put."

"I got that loud and clear already, Neal. And I have been, all hunkered down like a hurricane's tearing through."

"Don't go out. Don't. Not until you hear back from me. Don't answer your phone. Especially don't answer the door either. If the police show up to talk with you in person, call headquarters and verify. Have them show you their badges."

"Neal, I will, but I…I can't hideaway forever. And if I do, he wins."

"Not forever, Cady. Just until I figure something out. Cady, it won't be long. Give me a few hours."

***

"Cady?"

"Yes."

"Cady. This is what I want you to do. Are you listening?"

"Yes, Neal."

"You've been working with several voting machines. Do you need them all?"

"No. Not now. I proved the one with ElecTron's certified software works differently than the ones from Election Day. That's really what I needed. Now I'm just concentrating on one machine."

"Good. Pack-up your computers, papers, whatever you need. But, Cady, pack as light and as tight as you can. You'll need to carry it yourself and it can't be conspicuous. Can you do that?"

"Yes."

"Take everything you need to keep working, understand? Load it in your trunk. But don't open your garage door until everything's packed and you're ready to drive out. Okay?"

"Yes, but where am I going? What about my dogs?"

"Right. Your dogs. Just go ahead and feed them. Unlock your doggy doors. Don't tell your neighbor you're going to be away, at least not yet. Don't even talk to him. You said he has a key, right?"

"Yes. Always. He always takes care of everything anytime I'm tied up."

"Poor choice of words, Cady." Neal chuckled gently, trying to make light of it. "You have his number with you?"

"Yes. It's in my cell phone."

"No. Write it down. I want all your cell phones, all your gadgets off, except for the one. I'll call him from a payphone."

"Neal, all this cloak and dagger…"

"Stakes are high for somebody, Cady. Look what they did to Izzy."

"Yeah, but she…"

"We don't know that. We don't know if it was the psycho or if that first call to ElecTron tipped someone off. Then whoever she talked to later knew she was getting close. We can bet it's all related to what you're working on now. Better to be safe, Cady."

"I know you're right. And that call, his voice. I'm still shaky."

"I know, Cady. But you've got several more hours to go and you have to go it alone for my plan to work."

"Yes."

"You understand, if they see us together, they'll know."

"Yes."

"Okay. Car loaded. Leave some lights on in your house. Go to…our place in Key Largo. Park behind the main house under the banyans. See if anyone…"

"See if anyone's following me? …Oh, Neal."

"Yes. How are you doing so far?"

"I…I'm fine with it, really."

"Right. Well, hang in there. There's more."

"Yes."

"Your gear...what kind of volume?"

"My gosh. Lots..."

"Too much to fit into a shopping cart so you can leave your car at the bungalow?"

"Maybe lots too much. Maybe not. How big's the cart? Why?"

"Can you meet me at the *African Queen*?"

"Just like Bogie and Bacall?"

"No, Cady...Hepburn. Bogie and Hepburn. You remember, it's ocean-side there at the hotel marina. It'll be easier on Izzy...a quicker ride."

"You're bringing Izzy? In your boat?"

"No choice, Cady. We can't leave her."

"You're taking us...in your boat? Where?"

"Later."

"Can she even travel? Why don't I fetch her?"

"You think she's not being watched? The two of you together, you might as well send out a public broadcast that you're up to something... I can work around it."

"You...you...womanizer."

"Right. No. Well, if I was, I'm not now. Cady, if for one second you get a hunch you're being followed, head to the Miami airport and hop on a flight for Washington. I'll meet you there."

"Neal?"

"I'm serious."

"Seattle or D.C."

"D.C."

"Good. It's a shorter flight.... Neal?"

"Yes, Cady."

"It's all too bizarre. I don't know whether to laugh or cry."

"We'll get through it, Cady. We all will. And, Cady, make sure to charge our phone."

59

"It feels like we've dropped off the edge of the earth, doesn't it, Izzy? They'll never find us here." Morning mist cloaked the island. The channel beyond was lost to them in the fog. Cady held Izzy's arm steadying her as they followed Neal down the stone walkway, actually enjoying the adventure of it all. Last night, Neal made it sound like they'd be trapped in a primitive bug-infested moldy old tent. Instead he treated them to this enchanted island and his getaway cottage, a Florida cracker house replete with modern conveniences, for the most part anyway.

Meanwhile, Neal recited his litany of rules as they strolled to the edge of the scrub trees where he'd set up rows of cans for Cady's lessons. "Now remember, cooking daylight only. It'll give the cooking odors time to dissipate before dark. Lights out, generator off before sunset…"

"In other words any work, any food, any fun done and over before dusk," Cady grumped, albeit good naturedly.

"Right. But you can go ahead and work your computers…it'll just be mostly in the dark. Once your batteries run down…"

"Swell. Some of my most productive, creative hours are past sundown."

"You'll do just fine, I'm sure. Besides, the sea air out here has a way of lulling even the most hardy into repose. You know, early to bed, early to rise, etc."

"We'll see."

"Remember, light travels far out here in the dark. Candles, lanterns inside rooms only. And, oh yes, there's a box of batteries for the radio and whatever in the pantry."

Cady nodded.

"I brought another cell phone for you. But I don't want you to use it unless you absolutely have to. Besides, reception out here is iffy. Use the VHF like we talked about."

"You're really paranoid about phones, aren't you?" Izzy asked.

"Habit I picked up from Bri...on the job. Always issuing me a new phone, new number. No telling how many he...those people cart around with them. One for every purpose. Don't know how he keeps things straight."

"Excessive isn't it, Izzy?"

Neal stopped and turned to face them. "I used to think so too, Cady. But...well, for us, for here it's not. All these precautions...I can't stay with you and I just need you and Izzy safe, and for me I want to rest easier."

"I understand, Neal."

"And make sure you conserve water. Drink and cook with the bottled water. Use the cistern water for everything else."

"Are we done yet?"

***

Cady took aim like Neal showed her. She steadied her arm and squeezed the trigger. Bang. And she hit a tree several yards to the right of her target.

"Cady, what are you shooting at? ...Did you look through the site? ...Line up your target? ...Don't just go pulling the trigger before taking aim."

"Dammit, Neal. Look, presumably anything out to get us will be bigger than a tin can! Why are we doing this anyway?"

"I just want you to know how, Cady. That's all. You won't need it of course, but..."

"Okay then. Just show me how to load and unload the things again."

"You do it."

Izzy watched from her perch in the hammock. Neal patient and Cady fuming as the sparks ricocheted between them. Cady lowered the heavy rifle, pointing the long barrel to the ground. Cartridges jettisoned onto the stone walkway. She had an easier time of it with the Glock, snapping the clip out with her hand and into her pocket.

"Okay, Cady, reload." And she did.

***

The mist lifted, unveiling the island to a brilliant crystal blue morning. Cady walked Neal down to his boat and she manned the lines while he started his engines and prepared to push off.

"Cady, promise, you will lock the windows and doors." He looked over at Izzy lazing on her hammock. "Izzy, you'll watch to make sure she does it, yes?"

"Yes, Neal."

Cady scoffed, "But we're the only ones on the island. Who'm I locking out, the skunk ape? Or the boogey man? You think skunk ape's swim?"

"No road signs on the bay, Cady. People troll their boats around here thinking they're in Biscayne National Park or Pennekamp Coral Reef Park. We're so close. And some of the locals know the island's past."

"Ooo. What's that?"

"Well, there's the Pirates Lair. Nothing to do with pirates, but it was the CIA's safe house. And then the Bay of Pigs connection. Every once in a while some misguided locals poke around looking for the ruins, adventure…. So you see, just precautions, Cady. Just precautions."

"CIA? Pirates? Ruins? Can we go there?" Izzy asked cheerfully.

"No! Remember, lights out, no cooking, lock the doors. Know where the guns are…guns with you at all times."

Cady tossed the lines onto the boat and pushed her foot at the bow. He tapped his throttles and the boat blub-blub-blubbed forward and away up the channel.

Cady and Izzy waved until he rounded the mangrove bend. Then Cady marched back along the stone walkway, back to the cottage, up the steps and into the kitchen where she promptly ejected the bullets from both guns. She tucked the guns upstairs under her bed. The rifle cartridges, the clip for the Glock she stored on the top shelf in the kitchen pantry. Izzy watched.

60

Stan glared at the phone in his hand, angry, hurt, impatient, used. Why wouldn't Brice answer him? Brice had the power. He'd snap his fingers and Stan's problems, at least his immediate problem would be over. Done. *He wants me to beg. Damn bastard. But I won't. I won't beg the bastard for all I've done for him.* Stan pulled the phone back to his ear.

"Brice, I said I need a place to stay." Stan whined into his phone.

"What's happening with that tech-bitch of yours? Something's goin' on. I can feel it. Don't want this blowin' up in our faces, now do we, sport?"

"Nothing. Haven't heard a peep from her. Fact is, she's out of the office, been working from home for a time. A little off-season perk."

"F___. Now, boy, whaddya s'pose she's doin' there, uh?"

"I…well, I…"

"F___. You get on it, you hear!"

"Yeah. Sure. But, Brice, what about your apartment?"

"My what? Why? What's goin' on down there?" Brice puffed out intermittent plumes of smoke. Stan heard him over the line. He thought of Alice's Cheshire cat lounged atop the mushroom, crafting bigger and better smoke rings.

"My wife, Brice, she kicked me out." *Off with his head the queen shouted.*

"She what? Prissy mousey-milk-toast kick you out? Shit! I'd 've liked to see that one. What happened?" Brice didn't care, but what the hell. Good spirits bred…what, post election tolerance for the old goat?

"Don't know exactly, Brice. She just goes through these little stints every now and again." Yeah, like finding blood on his briefs,

Izzy's blood, the little harlot. The whole thing, Izzy's fault sashaying herself around in those flouncy little skirts and silky blouses that hugged her breasts so close and round. She egged men on, drove them out of their wits. Did it on purpose. Shook her ass at him every time she walked by. Out of his mind with it on a normal day. And then that night, that f_____ night. Shit. And before the night, the day, the worst ever Election Day all day long with Brice and his phobia and Cady and afraid of being caught and terrified of Cady catching him and Brice and he hated Brice and he hated Cady and he hated them all and there was that freak on the couch and Izzy on the floor and Cady glaring down at him all-knowing, and Izzy smelling like sex and…he knew how easy she was…….but she wasn't….

"So what am I s'pose to do, Stanboy?"

"You have that apartment on South Beach. I thought I could…"

"Sorry, my man. It's taken. Folks stayin' there already."

"What about…"

"Nope. All tapped out."

"Brice, you owe me! I need help!"

"Quit your sniveling, Stanley. Check yourself into a hotel until you can figure out what you can do."

"But, Brice, I don't even have a change of underwear." Stan grimaced. Too late to take back this grotty reminder of his wife's power. *Off with his head.*

"That's a problem then. Never figured her for that kind of backbone. You can't go home? Pack up? Need to keep your nose clean and outta the news. But I can send some men in to help you with it."

"She's got something on me, Brice. She's got something of Izzy's?"

"What's she got? The poor girl worked Elections. You crossed paths all the time. Easy to see where you might wind up with a little something of hers."

"Not this."

"You're not gonna queer this deal for me! Hear? You f____ this up, you're on your own!"

"Brice? I don't get it. All this…it was all for you, all of it. I let you take over, everything."

"You let me? I don't think I heard you right, boy. You let me?" Brice snorted. "I've got plans for us, big plans. You just get your stuff cleaned up and we'll get on with them."

"Yes, Brice."

"I'll be in Boca Grande for a few days. Planning meeting. When I get back we'll…we'll…You're in those plans, ol' boy."

"How, Brice? How am I in your plans?"

"Can't talk about it now. Later."

"What, Brice? What will we do? Where can I go?" But Brice was already gone. When will we talk, Brice?

***

"What about you, Lennyboy?" Brice grilled Leonard.

"What about me?"

"Ya know where those election geeks hang out these days?"

"I…she doesn't answer her phones. Lights on, but nothing going on."

"Scoop on ElecTron? Anyone else pursuin' vote issues?"

"No, Brice. Nothing."

"I tell you, I don't have a good feelin' 'bout this. Stan's whole department's out. Don't know what the f___ goin' down. He's clueless."

"What do you want from me, dude?"

"Nothing. Just concerned is all. Concerned they've got a napalm ticking time somewhere. Can't just let it run on autopilot, ya know? Wonder if they're holed up at Neal's."

"Ocean Reef?"

"No. He's got this little island north of there…. Doesn't matter. Not a problem. Stan's not worried. Sure he's got things well in hand."

"Right or left?" Leonard sniggered.

61

The soft evening smelled of sea breeze and oranges. And garlic and onion and tender palomilla steaks marinated in sour orange and garlic. And apple and orange fruited sangria. It was even Neal's idea to linger past sunset.

For one night only they ignored Neal's no cooking after dark rule. After all it was a special occasion. Real food, good wine and Mario pilfered the ballot scanners and other computers Cady needed from Elections. Though with Cady absent and Stan no where to be found, Mario was de facto in charge. Another cause for celebration.

The foursome done with their feast lingered around the table on the front porch breathing in the essence of Florida. Wavelets lapped at the dock. Mullet smacked the water. A dolphin whooshed close by, followed by another and another.

"You know our offshore sonar testing is killing whales. Destroys their natural sonar systems so they beach themselves." Cady arrived carrying her tray of coconut flan. She set it down on the table then headed back to the kitchen for more treats.

"Ouch. You've some talent for messing with my mood, chica."

"I was about to spoil the moment anyway, Mario. You suppose it's the same with dolphins?" Neal called after her.

"Not sure. Every so often we hear of whole pods beaching, but I don't know if it's related."

"Would make sense though, wouldn't it?" Neal didn't wait for an answer before dousing the crew with his own splash of reality. "Okay, let's get this over with…safety. Mario, I understand they needed you to procure their equipment and… you…"

"Yes and the poor girls were so hungry. For real food."

"Yes, yes, of course."

"Si. You understand then. What could I do?" Mario smiled with a shrug.

"You had to do," Neal swept his hands over the remains of their feast, "exactly this. You told no one, Mario?"

"No. On my honor, sir."

"And no one must know, ever, Mario."

"No. I understand, Neal. No one."

"Mario…just be careful on your way back," Neal warned softly. Then, loud enough for Cady to hear from the kitchen, "And all three of you, for your own safety, only use your phone, Cady's phone for emergencies only, that is if you can get a tower. No e-mails. No wireless network."

"Okay, two espressos and two café con leche coming up," Cady called out, interrupting Neal's lecture.

"You spoil us so, Cady. Sure I can't help in there?" Izzy asked not moving, her head resting lazily against the cushion propped on the back of her chair, her hand resting on her puffed little tummy.

"She can't accept, Izzy," Neal groaned as he scraped and stacked their dinner plates. "She already rejected my help."

"Maybe she likes me better," Izzy teased.

"Ha, chica! She'll never like you better. You were too ready to toss them all in jail, Izzy."

"You two still harping on that madam affair?" Cady chimed in on her way back from the kitchen. "Long standing debate, Neal. All those fine upstanding men, role models…hit below the belt. It transcends the transfer of power, don't you think?"

"And how's that, Cady?"

"Sense of the times. Symptomatic of the whole problem. Look, in many things I'm conservative to the core. But maybe I've grown up or grown more tolerant. So I accept politicians as human. I believe there is a stem cell compromise. I don't want babies to die. But nothing is absolute black or white and I can't be on a team that doesn't aim for the fair win. And the madam fiasco merely illustrates the chronic rot in Washington."

"Does this mean Pogo's right? 'We've met the enemy and he is us?'"

"Yes, Neal. Cheat. Cheat on everything from truth to taxes. Cheat to win. I say no. Look to the win for the good of the country and the people will follow. Do the best job you can to get the job, to keep the job."

"But, chica, I think about that a lot. Don't you think it's always been that way? Everyone does it?"

"No, Mario, I don't. But let's say there's truth in that. Doesn't make it right and it's not an excuse to continue. Raise the bar…"

"Isn't it what Abraham Lincoln predicted? He said, 'The way to destroy this great nation is from within.'" Izzy sighed.

"Yes, Izzy…Again you with your history. But it doesn't have to be that way. I say we should stop it…and maybe we should end this chatter for tonight or we'll muck up our evening as well. But, Mario, you started this, so to your point. You don't hold any get-out-of-jail-free passes either. Izzy's never razzed me about not having the proper peepee equipment."

"Oh, chica, I don't think so. You've not got the…"

"Hold on there cowboy! I'm right here and I can hear you loud and clear. How it is you're always the perfect gentleman at work, but here, in my home…well Neal's home of all places…"

"Cady, it's not my fault. Since Natalia passed, well I'm skidding hard on the downhill run."

"Mario…it's been nearly three years. Don't you think it's time? If not for you, for your babies," Cady said as she scooped up an armload of dishes and headed for the kitchen.

"Not babies anymore, Cady. Besides mama's so good with them."

"Mario, perhaps I can give you some advice here," Neal started, but was cut off soundly.

"Thanks, Neal, but the only flower I've ever wanted in my garden…that is since Natalia…well this flower, she calls me 'papi.' How close do you think I'll get to her, bro?"

Neal's mouth opened to speak, but knew better and his face masked his thoughts. Cady ceased her tinkering in the kitchen while Mario tippled the last of his sangria.

The only audible sound at that moment was the serene night air rushing into Izzy's pouty mouth, that is before she recovered. "Oh, papi, me? How sweet," she smiled demurely. "But I'm sorry. You understand, it has nothing to do with you. You see," she looked down at her diminutive belly.

"Izzy, I know I'm older, but…"

"I'm pregnant."

The earth shuddered. In the kitchen, Cady's spoon clanked to the tile floor. Mario's mouth hardened and his eyes shot away from Izzy and to the table. He grabbed the carafe of sangria, filling his goblet to the brim. Only Neal grasped Izzy's news for its tortured sorrow when his eyes met hers. He reached his arm over and took her hand in his own, rubbing it gently.

"Izzy! I didn't…" Cady called on her way out from the kitchen, but words ceased as she rushed over to hug her friend.

Mario studied the fussing trio. "I don't get it. She's…mi madre, Izzy. Mi madre. What do we do?"

Izzy looked up at him dry eyed, "Stop everyone. I'm fine. Really. Thank you, but…thank you. I don't know, Mario. I don't know how… I don't even know…" Her eyes dry no longer. "I just don't know."

"Izzy, have you talked with anyone?" Cady asked.

"Only my priest, no one else."

"And?"

"He…I…I can't talk about it. And I can't think forgiveness and…sanctity of life…and I…when I just want to die myself. Sometimes it's so hard, I just want to die."

"Izzy. We need to get you someone who can…understand," Cady rubbed Izzy's back. "Someone to help you work through this and help you with your future. You have so many people who love you, Izzy. But a counselor will know what and how you feel before you do yourself and she will help you with that."

Mario placed both hands firmly on the table and leaned into Izzy across from him. The two might have been alone for the intimacy of his words. "Izzy, you know how I feel about you…and…"

"Yes, papi, and don't you think I'm not grateful," her smile tender.

"That's not what I mean, Isabella. The world, it's tough out there. You grew up in your family cocoon, all safe and warm and carefree. You've got no clue to what it will take."

"And you do?"

"You know I do. I've got three beautiful children as proof, don't I?"

"Yes, papi. But your wife and your mama raised them." Izzy crossed herself.

"My point, Izzy. You think you can do this alone?"

"Maybe not. I've been thinking…but my time's running out. Maybe I shouldn't keep it at all."

"We need to get you to a counselor, Izzy." Cady suggested, more urgently than before.

"Why if I just want to make it go away?"

"Izzy, I'm not saying that's wrong…"

"No. Not you. Especially since your mother campaigned for abortions."

"No, Izzy. That's not it. My mother was profoundly opposed to abortions."

"But I thought…"

"And you're right there. But she was against abortion."

"I don't understand, Cady."

"Izzy, she championed women's rights, for your right to decide what is best for you and your body and the baby cells forming inside you. But my mother envisioned a world in which informed women are free to decide whether or not to terminate pregnancy, but choose…choose…not to. Do you see the difference, Izzy?"

"I…I think so. But what would you do, Cady?"

"Woo! Oh, Izzy, it doesn't matter what I would do. The only thing that matters here is what's best for you."

"You're wrong, Cady. Tell me!"

"Izzy, I used to believe there was never any way in this world I could abort a baby growing inside me. I don't feel that way anymore."

"Why not, Cady?"

"After you? When I saw you and when I thought of what they did to you? And what we didn't know. And I thought then what if…? Any hard convictions I ever had flew out the window of that helicopter that brought you home."

"What do you mean, Cady?"

"What I mean is, how can I presume to know what's best for you or for anyone?"

"You're hedging. Do you, Susan Cady Palmer believe abortion is a moral issue?"

"A moral issue? Like going to confession or attending church or not eating fish on Friday? Or how about birth control? Maybe the fish-on-Friday thing isn't a good example."

"Right. Even good Catholics eat fish now."

"Yes. But it used to be a sin, didn't it?" Cady continued without waiting for Izzy's answer. "So your question, regarding moral issues, whose morals are we asking about? Mine? Yours? Or the church's? My church or your church or somebody else's synagogue or mosque or temple? You see, Izzy, my belief and my interpretation of scriptures can be different from everyone else's on the planet. So, Izzy, how could I presume to know what God wants for you? I have a hard enough time trying to figure out what He wants for me. And I think I get it wrong most of the time."

"Cady, you skipped over my question."

"Oh, Izzy. So the world's in deep trouble. One reason is we have too many people on the planet, starvation, pestilence. Did the church let up on birth control? Still they refute the morning after pill. And no abortion. Don't misunderstand me. I'm not tossing them all in the same bag. But isn't it ironic that women are firmly wedged between taboos...against reliable birth control and if we get pregnant as a result, we can't do anything about that, either?"

"Are you really so bitter, Cady?" Neal asked.

"No. Yes. Puzzled. It's time for universal birth control. And it's time for everybody to stop fighting about abortion and do something constructive about it. Like reduce pregnancies. Abortions are already down in this country. Oh, Izzy, I'm so sorry. This is about you...and here I am.... You really asked a fair question and I blunder into hurtful dissertations."

"And I forgive you, Cady. So what's the answer to my question?"

"Won't give up, will you? When I hold a new baby or when I look at baby sonograms and see their little heads and arms and legs...and tiny hands doing a little high-five...and I know their minds aren't yet developed...Oh, Izzy! There's a huge difference. If I simply goofed and got pregnant, no, I couldn't do it.."

"And?" Neal prompted her to continue.

"And...but, but if I were raped, all bets are off. You had no part in this, Izzy. I mean that's why I think you need, must talk with a professional. This baby's father's a sick animal. You know that. It hurts. He raped you. He stole your innocence and now you carry a child against your will. The anguish you feel in knowing this must be a driving force behind your decisions. Then there's the big nature-versus-nurture debate. Can a mother overcome a bad seed?"

"Is there really such a thing, Cady?"

"Izzy, there is genetics. But we can't any of us know about any conception until a baby is actually born and grown into a free-willed adult."

"If I may, Izzy," Neal asked. "I think what Cady's saying is that it's a crap shoot no matter if the baby's conceived in love or planned or...or...not. It's not just the baby though. It's you and how you adjust to growing a baby inside you that will always be a reminder of the violence committed against you. Then watching that baby grow up. I don't know that I could do it. And then there's the adoption alternative to consider. Is that an option?"

"Can't they do a prenatal paternity test nowadays?" Mario asked.

"I think so. But it may be risky and who do you check the results against? We don't even know for sure who took Izzy in the first place."

"Basically, I'm out of time here. I didn't know, didn't expect... didn't think..."

"What does your mother say?"

"She doesn't know."

"Izzy..."

Izzy looked at each of her friends huddled around her, "I thought, I've been thinking I just want to get rid of it. Why would I want to birth a monster?"

"Izzy, look at me," Mario pleaded with the woman-child. "I am here. Do you understand that, Izzy? I am here with you, for you, whatever you choose, if you will have me, Izzy."

62

Stan's BMW gleamed like polished sterling under the bright lights of the guard house entrance to the posh yachting community. Stan concluded the car's value exceeded the young security guard's gross annual income.

"Sorry, Mr. ...err," the guard leaned out from his air conditioned hut again.

"Corbin. Mr. Stanley Corbin."

"Sorry, Mr. Corbin, but if I let you in they'd have my job."

"Sorry doesn't get it done, now does it, boy?"

"No, sir, but..."

"Look. Do you know who I am?"

"No, su...sir, I don't."

"Well then, I'm Supervisor of Elections, that's who, and I need to talk with my deputy, Miss Susan Cady Palmer. Now then, kindly open that gate!"

"You could be the governor of Florida, sir, and I still can't let you in."

"You don't understand. I must see her!" Stan stuck his fist at the guard, fanning a wad of fifties. "Here."

The guard's gaze never wavered, not once straying from Stan's face to peek at Stan's impotent prize. "No, Mr. Corbin, sorry, we can't take tips. You know how it is. But I'll try his phone again if you'll just wait there for a minute, sir." The guard dialed Neal's number again.

"Well..."

"No, Mr. Corbin, he doesn't answer.... We're not at liberty to say who's home and who's out. That's their own private business. I could lose my job. All I can say, Mr. Corbin, is he doesn't answer his phone.... No, Mr. Corbin, I tried the only phone number I have for Mr. Charles. He should answer his home phone if he's there, sir. Either that or he doesn't want to be disturbed, sir. Or, this is a boating community. Mr. Charles could be out night fishing. Same difference, isn't it, Mr. Corbin? …Would you like to leave a message for Mr. Charles, sir? …In that case, is there anything else I can do for you? …No? Please pull around, sir. Goodnight, Mr. Corbin."

Stan tried to reach Cady all day, ever since his human resources director left his office after dropping the big bomb. Izzy needed more paid leave. Izzy was kidnapped from the Election Department. Izzy needed counseling. Izzy could sue. If Izzy did sue, she'd win. Do you know if Izzy was raped? If Izzy's pregnant…she'll keep the baby…won't terminate the pregnancy, you know. More tests. Maternity leave. She'd win a lawsuit big time. Could Elections be held accountable for her baby?

Who the hell does Neal think he is, some piss-ant big shot? All cloistered up in that locked gate yacht club. I want Cady and he's got her. He's Brice's f_____ gopher, a f_____ grunt.

***

The moon full and bright on the water cast a misty glow over the island, the channel, and the two snuggled against the chill in Neal's cockpit. The boat bumped gently against the dock pads with each rise and fall of the waves lapping at the freeboard, brushing up against the shore. Receding water crackled softly against the barnacles that flourished on the dock's pilings.

"In spite of it all, you lead a charmed life, Neal."

"Of course I do, and I feel it anytime I'm with you, Cady," he teased, not intending to mask the truth he felt in his words. They both laughed.

"No, seriously, look around you. All this? How did you manage to snag an island a puddle jump away from Miami, from Pennekamp?"

"Ah, my paradise? Given to me…an old-timer. I used to tag-along with him on fishing jaunts. That is when he couldn't stir up another crew. Then he'd take me. But that was a long time ago, Cady. Before college, before Brice. Before now."

"Given to you? See what I mean? Charmed."

"With you beside me, Cady." Neal topped off her Shiraz. "Cady, in spite of my third degree earlier, it's probably a good thing you got Mario out here. Can he stay?"

"No, why?"

"I've got to go away again for a couple of days, maybe three or four."

"When?"

"Tomorrow, first thing. Boca Grande. Brice wants me there. Early. I found out this afternoon. Afterwards I've got a flight to… I'm meeting up with the senators under the radar. It's important."

"Oh. Why are we wasting time then?" Cady reached for Neal's glass, setting their two glasses down on the cockpit table. Then she snuggled in tighter to him, pulling him closer, closer until he covered the full length of her, his face buried in the soft curve of her neck. Goodbye's took longer these evenings. Always one more thing to say, to do…to feel. The moon crested over the horizon and the rise and fall of Neal's boat bumped less gently now against the dock, to a rhythm all their own.

***

Stan earnestly contemplated murder. He couldn't with Izzy, so lovely, frail and battered…and used in the moonlight. But then, Izzy was a stranger. She worked for him, through Cady of course, nonetheless she was a stranger. But his wife, with her pinched-up anemic prune-face, well now together they'd crusted up twenty-seven years of resentment. Stan surmised that if their never-ending barbs were flecks of marble dust, they might well have razed the world's mightiest temples, chip by chip. And his damned stupid pissy wife mounted on her high horse with her, "Stanley, I've had enough. Get out. Get out of my house now. I'll pack up your things and ship them to you."

"What's gotten in to you?" Stan just stood there with his mouth dropped, baffled. After all she laid him just the night before…on her own initiative, black nightie and all. But he was quick enough to chomp at the opportunity. "If you've had enough, you get out. You sat on your ass all the while I paid for this and every other f_____ house we ever lived in. You get out."

"No, Stanley. You seem to forget, it was me, I pulled you out of your lean-to, mannered you up and dragged you through school. Besides, my attorneys told me, they said I've got rights here, to the house, stocks, bank accounts and yes, my BMW of course." Boiled sugar dribbled from her mouth, sugar crystallizing on thin rust-colored lips when she said, "Oh, and by the way, Stanley, he has your shorts."

"My what?"

"You know, the ones all smeared inside…you know with…blood?"

And he thought of his wife in her musty black negligee putting out for him, lights on, touching him, licking him when all the time she inspected for scratches, a rash, a latent source of his own blood. How delighted she was…delighted he was clean. And next morning she pranced giddily along to her attorneys, blood prize in her greedy lumpy-veined fist.

63

Cady and Izzy lingered on the front porch long after the men said their goodbyes. They were pensive mostly, quiet, listening to night sounds. Neither broached Izzy's worry. Off in the distance the muffled hum of an outboard gave up a fisherman trolling the bay.

"Do you believe in God, Cady?"

"I...I..." Cady poured Izzy another water.

"I don't. Not anymore, Cady."

"I can't even imagine your hurt, Izzy. You deserve absolute yes or no answers, but there are none. I can tell you only what I believe. And I can offer only the metaphorical..."

"What's that, Cady?"

"Oh, Izzy...you're lost in the forest and must choose between one of two paths. One path leads to a searing hot lava pit, no food, no water, no refuge. You're going to die. The other path surely leads to safety, comfort, shelter, food, water, home. A storm hovers over the forest. Rain pricks at your face like a thousand needles. Lightening strikes at trees close by. You're frightened. You don't know which way to go. But wait, in the middle of the forest where the paths divide you spot a map. What to do? Pick up the map and plot your journey? Or do you step over the map and blunder along hoping the path you've chosen is the right path?"

"How do you know the map isn't a trick, Cady?"

"You don't. Except, consider that same map's been studied by scholars for thousands of years. And no one's ever proven it false. Think about it."

"No, Cady. If God did exist, He wouldn't let this happen to me."

"Maybe, Izzy. For my part, I've never experienced anything that comes close to what you lived through. Still, I don't believe I myself could have made it though some of the punches life's thrown at me without God…… Izzy, evil exists, unimaginable evil. We're not puppets. Bad people do very bad things. Good people get horribly hurt. But suppose…could it also be that God took your hand and guided you through this? He gave you strength to survive, Izzy?"

64

Ah. Gotta be the one. Leonard smelled girl. He scouted these islands for days, starting at Key Largo and working his way north, in and around the channels, in and out the mangrove canals. Didn't know exactly what to look for, just that Neal's little getaway was on the east side of Linderman, a little key north of Largo. Not even on his map. If that's all they tell you, how can you know how to find it? For days he navigated up and down the east side of the north Keys. Logical to focus on the east, right? Up and down he scouted in the friggin' water-spray of a boat. Choppy, wet, windy, freakin' cold on the ocean. Key Largo north to Card Sound Bridge, north past Ocean Reef, north beyond all the islands, speed up, slow down, veer in, veer out until he got to Elliott Key. There the rangers directed him south again. Nothing. Crap.

Hell, like a fool he rented this crappy boat in Key Largo. Florida Keys, you'd think? Key Largo? Then he bucked the waves and the currents and the weather all the way north. Shit. What'd he know about friggin' boats anyway? He was from west Texas. Shit. And the friggin' boat, he had to turn it in every night before dark or they'd send an armed posse after him. Not that he wanted to be out on that black ocean after dark anyway, some freakin' big fish out there! But what they should've said was west of friggin' Homestead. South of Miami. That's what they should've said.

One more time. That's what he gave himself today. One last run and this was it. He whipped around to the west side of the stinkin' little islands for a calmer ride back…and boom he spotted Mario's Donzi skimming across the wave tops. Could've been anyone, a shitload of Donzis in Miami. But Leonard knew it was Mario standing proud at the console, darting across the bay toward Cady, leaning with the boat when he slowed his engines and curved into a channel behind the mangroves.

Leonard held off, just bobbed around on the bay swells, waiting until he felt freakin' green, until Mario's engines trailed off. Then he putt-putted after Mario's course. And there it was, the island with a house sticking up on a knoll. He scoped it out, fishing on the flats along the west side. He turned into the channel on the south side and there was another friggin' house. He just kept fishing, trolling east and there tucked way back in the trees he saw another rooftop. No one said anything about three, count them three houses. Which one? When?

Leonard trolled to the next channel south and hung out along the mangroves until after dark. The mosquitoes and sand fleas chewed on him like friggin' vampires, far worse than behind Cady's friggin' wall. But by nightfall the dark water and night-sea noises on the open bay didn't rest easy with him. He stuck it out in the channel. He radioed in to Key Largo that his engine failed north of Elliott. Give them something to do while he hung out here.

Crap he couldn't exactly hike across the island, even in daylight. So he motored as close as he could then rowed to shore. He checked out the house on the knoll first. It looked like a Brice getaway, not the old part, but pecky cypress walls, high on a hill, well the highest hillet around anyway.

Three houses on this mosquito infested rat hole of an island. Leonard worked his way though the first two. No one there. It had to be this one. And he was sure it was. He smelled girl.

Primitive. Friggin' cistern atop the house to collect rainwater, probably little water to spare for washing. And he still smelled girl. All lemon and spice, the two of them a freakin' bouquet. Crap. The smell clung to his nostrils long after Izzy'd gone. How'd she do it anyway? How'd she get away from him? And she probably even told Cady how he couldn't get it. Probably had a good laugh too. Well, princess, I'm a comin' now. Look out. On my way right now. Come on baby.

65

"Shhh! Izzy, Quiet. Listen. Izzy, I'm going to tell you something. You can't cry. You can't scream. You can't make a sound. Okay, Izzy?"

Cady couldn't see her clock on the nightstand. Fog settled in on the bay and the thick billowy cloud cover loomed low and heavy across the late night sky blocking natural light from the stars. The island was dark, island dark. Dark and still and very quiet save the occasional flip-flap of the filmy curtains snapping the window screen. But not enough breeze to rustle the trees.

Must be really late or very early, the wee hours. Not even occasional life sounds from the mangroves or the neighboring keys or from nearby Ocean Reef wafted across the water on the wake of the bay breezes.

Even the tides stilled and island night creatures hunkered down, perhaps for a storm. *Except one*, thought Cady as the dull thud of terracotta on wood reminded her of the wild orchids she potted yesterday to cozy up the downstairs deck. The moment she set the plants on the wooden railing, she wondered how long before a careless seabird or raccoon knocked them off. Oh, well, question answered. Not long.

Raccoons. Pesky critters looking for an early breakfast, so at ease here on Neal's Florida cracker porch, they evidently grew careless, probably didn't even look, didn't expect things out of place. That is except for a piece of stray fruit or sandwich or other munchy.

Another thud. Cady bolted upright in bed…she stared out the window and listened. Only the curtains flapped back at her. But then other sounds. Footfalls, too heavy for the small wild life on this island, too quiet for Neal. Besides, she would have heard the hum of Neal's boat engines.

More footfalls. Another foot press. Another. A pause. Another foot press and the deck plank below the kitchen window creaked briefly under weight then ceased quickly as the weight lifted. The kitchen doorknob jiggled.

Cady forced herself to breathe, to calm before leaning over close to Izzy. She felt Izzy's breath on her own face, but it was too dark to see her.

"What is it, Cady?" Izzy asked, her sleep-voice hoarse, slow, groggy.

"Shh! Izzy, listen! Don't say a word!" Cady rested her hand on Izzy's cheek as she would that of a child. "I want you to take your blanket and go into the closet," she said to Izzy's silhouette.

No sound, but Izzy's shoulders heaved with quick ragged breaths. Soon she would hyperventilate or rant or scream or cry and Cady must stop her.

"Hush, Izzy. Hush. You must trust me. Do you? Do you trust me, Izzy?" Cady whispered.

Izzy nodded.

"Izzy. Listen. I want you to tip-toe. Understand? Go slowly. Don't make a sound. Watch that floorboard in front of the closet. Step around it. Okay, Izzy?"

"Y-y-yes, Cady," Izzy quivered.

"Now, Izzy, we've got to hurry, now. You must stay in the closet until I come for you. Do you understand? ...Do you understand, Izzy?"

"Yes, Cady."

"It will be dark. But you must stay there."

"I...I..."

"You can do this, Izzy. I hear something. I think there's somebody downstairs...outside. Just in case, Izzy, I'm going to make it look like we're still in the bed. And then I'll wait. I'll be behind the bedroom door, right outside your closet door there." Cady pointed to the door before realizing Izzy couldn't see her in the dark. "You must not make a sound, Izzy. Even if you hear me moving around. Even if you hear something...bad. You must stay there and say nothing. Do you understand? ...Izzy!"

"I understand, Cady," Izzy whispered softly.

"Izzy, don't come out, no matter what, not until I come for you. Okay?"

"Okay, Cady." Izzy rolled over onto her tummy and back-crawled feet first off the closet-side of the bed. She wrapped her light cotton blanket around her shoulders and slowly stepped flat footed toward the closet, balancing her weight evenly along the full length of each foot.

Cady walked softly behind her resting her hand on the small of Izzy's back. She squeezed Izzy tightly before opening the closet door. "It'll be okay, Izzy. I'll come for you as soon as I can."

"Cady, be careful," Izzy whispered.

"Of course, Izzy..."

"I love you, Cady."

"I love you too, Izzy. Hush now."

Cady closed the door gently, not letting the latch click. She held her breath and waited...no sounds. Nothing. She stepped softly, quietly over to the bed and stood in place while grabbing each pillow, fluffing it and setting the pillows end-to-end in the middle of the bed. Then she pulled up the bedspread almost to the headboard, tucking it around the back of the top pillow where her head would be. She hoped the worn-out pillow trick looked like a sleeping person here in the dark. Next she crouched down and felt around the floor underneath the bed, up by the headboard until her hand bumped against the cold barrel of Neal's rifle. She swept her hand along the metal and grabbed at the wooden butt, carefully lifting the heavy weapon evenly, completely off the floor so it wouldn't scrape as she pulled it out. *Damn it's heavy.* Then she stood up, cautiously, rifle in hand and hugged it close to her and patted it on the butt at her hip.

Dammit, she mouthed, realizing the utter impotence of the weapon cradled in her arms. *Dammit*, she recognized her folly, storing the bullets safely in the kitchen pantry. *Dammit*. She was as helpless as the injured woman-child hiding in their closet.

No help for it now, Cady thought, stepping softly once again toward the closet and to the open bedroom door beside it. *Dammit*, she mouthed again, this time at her creaking floorboard, jerking her foot back as by electric shock. It took precious seconds for her to realize the affronting noise was not the result of her own floorboards, but those on the stairway at the end of the hall. She tucked in behind the open bedroom door, gripping the barrel of the rifle in her sweaty hands, its smooth wooden butt bumping against her chin, its scope scraping her leg. *Dammit.* Cady heard Izzy shuffling around behind her, behind the closed closet door. *Oh, Izzy, quiet. Please, please be quiet.*

Cady listened silently, breathing in quick shallow breaths. Their intruder entered Neal's room down the hall, feeling his way around the room, the bed, under the bed, the closet. He scraped a hand along the bureau top. *What do you want?* But she knew. In her heart, in her mind she knew. And it wouldn't be pretty.

Can't see. Lights out. Generator's not running. *You and me, bucko. You're the one.* Cady clutched the rifle barrel, her hands wet, squeezing the warming metal midway up from the trigger.

***

Nothing here. Shit. Go on, go on, next room, last room. There ahead. Miss Pa-a-l-m-e-r, I'm coming now, Cady. No way out this time. Here Izzy, Izzy.

66

Elections Supervisor, Mr. Stanley Corbin stared down at the black current ripping around the bridge pilings below. Black foam of his wife's negligee...black satin pleats of his mother's funeral garb... raven swirls of Izzy's hair.

Pops dragged him fishing here before this bridge was built. Stan hated fishing. Of course he could never do anything right and he hated reaching down into his father's stinky bucket to pull out the squirming pricking shrimp he impaled on his hook, a hook so huge most fish in these waters couldn't get their mouths around it. Instead smaller fish and crabs deftly nibbled away his tattered shrimp. Predictable results, always. By night's end, Stan could count on his father whacking him up 'side the head with a garbled, "freakin' no-count...dumb-dumb wimp." Stan hated shrimp... any seafood for that matter.

At long last cigarettes and booze finally killed the bastard but not soon enough, not before he barked one last order at Stan. "Son, take my ashes out to Card Sound where we two buddies... we had so much fun together. Son, sprinkle my ashes right there on the outgoing tide."

The dutiful son, Stan complied, with the sprinkling part anyway. He drove to the rattiest, XXX motel he could find, rented a room and sprinkled pop's ashes right there in the pee encrusted toilet and he flushed and he watched the swirling remnants of his father recoil down the rust-stained toilet. And he laughed and he laughed at the swirling mush. But he could never, never be free.

Stan looked down into the black for the reflection that would not be there and he saw his father's face. "Mama, you wanted better for me. But, mama, I am pop's son after all. I am father. Mama!" Stan wept, clenching the rail with both hands. But not for long.

His sobbing broke with the purr of an approaching car, its bright headlights beaming in on him. Closer and brighter they flooded his bridge, veering alongside the rail before lurching to a stop. Stan knew his intruder as soon as the car door shut with the familiar tight hushed-thunk sound of his own car. He recognized the confident shadow striding decisively up the catwalk even as the flashlight glared in his face.

Stan swiped at the soot and wet on his cheeks before stepping toward the light. "What are you doing down here?"

67

Izzy cowered on the floor in the dark, shivering. She gripped her blanket, tugging it tighter, tighter, afraid to move, afraid to breathe in the hot suffocating black of her closet.

Cady was so smart, so savvy, so quick and so very, very stupid. The first day after they came to Neal's island, Izzy watched Neal wrap his long arms all around Cady and show her how to shoot a dead tin can. Mi madre. The pair didn't want to disturb poor Izzy. Treated her like such a delicate little flower. Thought she wasn't paying attention. Sure she was tender. But she survived the crazy once, didn't she. And she'd do it again and again and again if she had to, that is if she didn't get the chance to kill him first.

Izzy watched savvy, fearless Cady listen attentively to Neal's instructions about keeping the guns loaded and ready. And she watched Cady wait until she heard the hum of Neal's engines fading in the distance before brazenly grabbing each gun, ejecting the bullets and "hiding" them safely in the ammo box deep in the dark kitchen pantry…away from poor Izzy. Had to be for Izzy's protection, no one else came out to this lonely island paradise. Their first day here, Izzy'd wandered down the old stone pathway to the dock. She basked in the sun with her feet dangling gaily in the sparkly saltwater for at least three minutes before Cady dragged her back to the house. Said she needed Izzy's help with the voting machine programs. Right. Like Cady ever really needed her help. Everything Izzy knew was from Cady. And it was Cady…she was so close to figuring out those voting machines. What Cady really needed was an extra 18 hours in each day and another four arms. Oh, and a bottomless jug of java.

Coraje. Coraje, Izzy. Courage. The dinky closet smelled of cedar and it was hot and steamy and Izzy couldn't breathe and she hated it here and she wanted to tell Cady, "No! I will not!" But she was in truth frightened of what might come. Terrified! Okay, so she was a teensy delicate of late. Who wouldn't be? Still they didn't need to pretend she wasn't in the room when they talked about the serious stuff, the guns and such.

Cady stuck Izzy in this closet for her own good. Cady read people well and she directed them and she orchestrated. And she knew Leonard was bad, within a week of his hire she knew he was bad. She didn't need Izzy to tell her about Leonard tampering with restricted programs, about his digging into voter tabulation code. Cady knew. And for all Cady's kowtowing to Stan, the only time Izzy ever saw Cady really angry, ballistic was when after calmly sifting through Leonard's affronts, Cady seethed, "Leonard... goes...Stan." Izzy knew Cady's calm masked unbelievable rage. Evidently so did Stan. Within thirty minutes of Cady's mandate, Security walked Leonard out of the building.

Izzy knew Cady's crisp orders to get Izzy into the closet and away from harm masked Cady's rage...and fear. Cady presented calm to Izzy, but they both knew terror could be climbing up the stairs to get them...right now. And if not now, tomorrow or the day after and they could not be safe until the terror was dead. And Izzy thought of Cady and the guns and the bullets and the fear and the bullets and the gun and...she smiled in the black of the closet. She smiled at the shelf above her head and the plastic shoebox crammed with yet unused makeup high on the shelf above her head. And she loosened her grip on the cotton blanket shawled about her neck.

***

Izzy knew the second Cady tucked into place behind the bedroom door, not from the sounds outside her closet. The only sound she heard from Cady at all was the brief shift of Cady's cotton pajamas. But she felt Cady's presence. And that made her feel safe. Even though here in her closet, the creaks and groans echoing through the skeleton of the house played themselves back in her hiding place.

Odd, Izzy felt calm wash over now her like a summer wave. Weeks of terror and trepidation, fearing she...they'd be found again. And she felt exhilarated that it would end here in the dark.

With Cady tucked into place, Izzy loosened the blanket from her shoulders and stood up from her crouching position, feet in place, arms raised but not touching the wall. *Not a sound, Cady, not a sound.* She pivoted in place, no squeaking floor boards. No sound, Cady. She reached out at head level, slowly, lightly and when her fingers touched the clothes bar, she slid her hand left and lifted both hands above the bar to the plastic box on the shelf. She lifted the box, slowly, noiselessly and knelt back down on the floor on top of the cotton blanket and set the box on top of the blanket in front of her. *Could you hear that, Cady? I hope not. No sound, Cady, no sound.*

Izzy hurried, her nimble fingers shaking as she pealed away the plastic lid. The house groaned louder now and he was coming. She jolted when she heard one finger rub softly against the outside of her closet door. *Sorry, Cady.* Izzy couldn't help it. She'd buried her treasure so well within the diminutive bottles and pencils and tubes in her box, there would be noise. There would be noise if she pulled it out. *Okay, Cady. Okay. I hear you.* And she waited.

Izzy waited, hovering over her box, hands cupped on its sides. The monster's steps grew steady, faster now, predatory. Secure in the knowing he'd found them and trapped them in this room.

The bedroom door creaked on its hinges. He must have pushed it open wider. But Cady not yet discovered stood still. Izzy swallowed her scream. If Cady could be silent outside with the monster in her room, Izzy could be brave huddled in here with her treasure.

Suddenly, it started. The house erupted inside Izzy's closet. Thud-thud-groan-scrape-thud-smash. Izzy dug her hands into her box. Pencils and bottles and tubes spilled out over the sides until she felt metal and grabbed for the handle, jabbing her index finger onto the trigger guard and rising to her feet in one fluid motion. She listened at the door for the direction of the commotion outside before flinging the door open and jumping into the bedroom. But it was dark, too dark. Surely two phantoms were fighting, but Izzy couldn't tell them apart. What she could see was the one figure standing above the other, wielding a long...hatchet or hammer and beating and pounding and bludgeoning and the other phantom cowering and hugging the floor.

Quick, Izzy, do something. Izzy hoisted the Glock with both hands, pointed it toward the open bedroom door and fired down the hallway. The Glock kicked back, Izzy jumped, but the pounding stopped.

"Izzy, it's me," Cady's voice shouted at her from the standing phantom.

"*Mi madre*! Chica!" Izzy wanted to laugh. She wanted to scream. Loud. Instead she pointed her gun at the floor phantom and waited for Cady's direction.

"We need some light here. Can you aim the gun and light the lantern? Or...."

"You do it, Cady. My gun's pointed at the soft spot between the S.O.B.'s eyes!" Of course she couldn't see the bastard's eyes in the dark, but it felt good to say it and Cady knew she had him covered.

Cady cautiously lifted her foot from the floor phantom's chest, still poised to commence bludgeoning should he flinch one muscle. But he just wheezed in short raspy gulps and Cady backed away carefully. She felt around on the night table for the lighter and lamp.

Leonard's rheumy eyes glared up at them from his bashed and bloodied face.

"Cady, you didn't tell me you were a sumo wrestler."

"And you didn't tell me you were a wild gunslinger, Izzy."

"We all have our secrets, don't we, Cady?"

"You bet. Now what do we do? I don't know where there's rope, but we've got the power strips and I saw extension cords in the pantry. Let's tie the asshole up before we do anything else."

"Here, Cady, you take this." Izzy's gun stayed fixed on Leonard as she shifted her arm elbow first toward Cady. "I'd better fetch the cords or I might just shoot the bastard for the fun of it. I think I saw some duct tape in Neal's junk drawer."

"Good. Don't take too long, Izzy, or I might shoot him myself. He looks about ready to move to me. Does he to you, Izzy?"

"Sure does. Remember, Cady, I only fired one shot. You've got lots left."

"Come on, Leonard. Let me use 'em!" Cady warned. "Izzy. Call Neal on the VHS. Tell him to come on. Fish are biting in the Gulf Stream."

"Yes, boss."

"You and me Leonard." Cady wiped her free hand on her pajama leg, smearing Leonard's blood on baby-blue cotton. "Come on."

68

"Cady, he doesn't answer. What do we do?"

"I don't know, Izzy…We can't call the police…not yet."

"Why not?"

"Because he'd be out on bail before Neal gets back. Then what?"

"After what he…he…did to me…? But the election…won't they hold him for…"

"Exactly. What do we tell them? He stole the election? They'd never believe it. Besides, he'd lawyer up so fast or even hightail it out of the country. Then we've lost him."

"Mario…what about Mario?"

"What can he do but come out here and babysit along with us?" Cady shook her head. She turned to the man who wreaked such pain on Izzy, on herself…the psycho insurgent who ruled the future…if only for a night. And it would be only one night. His control over elections stopped here. "No, Izzy. It would draw too much attention for Mario to disappear along with the two of us. What a flaky damned year."

"What a kerfuffley day."

"Can you even stand to look at him?"

"He's nothing to me, Cady. Nothing. A chunk of foul rubbish. Always was. I still can't figure out what Stan saw in him."

"You can't, Izzy? I think I can. And I think it has to do with a much broader scope than the elections department."

"Stan knew, Cady? He let that pervert take me…let him…"

"Oh, Izzy. I think so."

"Cady? Will they…arrest us…for kidnapping?"

"How can they? We've no boat, no way off the island at all. We don't even have a phone for goodness sake."

"But, Cady, we've got…"

"Right. We can try Leonard's cell…I hope his batteries aren't dead."

69

The falling sun outside mirrored Neal's mood as he navigated his way through Brice's entourage in the backroom of Casa Hermano. Jabbing his cardkey in the brass slot beside the elevator, he tempered the irksome lurch in his gut, his own disobedient response to the brigade of well-trained eyes surreptitiously roving his person for unexpected bulges.

No matter that Neal was Brice's most trusted ally...except now he wasn't. Besides neither friends in high places nor top clearance ever secured a free pass with these suits. A prime reason Neal routinely left his briefcase behind, rather than permitting their loutish rummage through his personal business. Security wasn't tight these days, it was pure paranoia. And no matter how many times he parried Brice's gauntlet, Neal breathed easier once clearing the first tier. Yet more often than not, upon crossing the elevator's threshold he couldn't resist speculating the likelihood of something gone awry. Especially now. Neal considered the odds of Brice summoning him here to have it out over Cady.

The elevator doors swished shut. Neal checked his reflection in the polished brass wall, smoothing his pockets and straightening the collar of his hand printed Key West shirt. There. Ready. The elevator doors opened on cue.

More suits at the tables left and right of the elevator. Behind the bar, Santos retrieved a bottle from his mahogany and mirror panels and poured Neal's drink.

"Mr. Charles," Santos greeted softly. Neal followed him to a table overlooking the balcony and the gray-blue Gulf of Mexico beyond. Outside, terrace palms ruffled with the freshening sea breeze. Santos placed napkin and drink on the marble topped table between two ample chairs. Smoke, thick and heavy swirled from the chair on the right. Neal eased himself into the other chair to the soft scrunching of thick brown leather.

"Thank you, Santos," Neal said to Santos's back as he retreated to his station behind the bar. This part he'd miss.

More scrunching as Neal propped both feet on the footstool, leaning back in his chair. "Ah," he lifted his glass before glancing toward Brice.

Brice, cigar in one hand, cognac in the other, face forward. He sucked on his Cuban, artfully puffing out billows of smoke in tidy opaque clouds. Eyes focused beyond this room and the man beside him, perhaps a sail on the faraway horizon, more likely his own future. Another puff. Exhale slow, deliberate. "I want you to get rid of Cruella...ah...Patricia...I want her gone, Neal. Out."

Neal swirled his Dewar's, studying amber ripples on crystal, reflecting on the absence of the customary "Nealboy" or "Sport." Brice's omission could mean Brice felt the depth of Neal's mutiny or Brice wanted this bad. Could be both.

"Cruella." Neal recalled vividly the moment of christening. Brice 'carelessly' tossed out the moniker to a couple reporters several years ago, after using her badly...for one of his more devious schemes. Of course he apologized immediately and profusely, begging them never, never to be so disrespectful as he at that moment of his unforgivable blunder. He beseeched them never, ever to repeat such a slanderous defamation. Of course the slur stuck, she was forever relegated to the ranks of cartoon characters. Brice, clever Brice could be cruel. But Patsy, whose run for office Brice vigorously supported, would never be a threat. And Brice walked away with clean hands. Brice never made mistakes.

Assuming for the moment Brice wanted to skirt the rift between them, Neal played along. He mulled over Brice's order before plunging headlong into waters a skosh deep for all but a select few in Brice's inner circle. "Not the sharpest tool in the shed, Brice. But, hell you knew that when you supported her bid. You were key to her win. So what am I missing?"

Another swig of Cognac. Another plume wafted, hovering briefly before swirling efficiently up and around and out by the band of paddle fans high overhead. "Not negotiable, Nealboy.

She's a big girl. Knew what she was gettin' into playin' with the big boys. Or should have."

"Hey, Brice. You know I was never in her court. Just a minor curiosity."

"Outlived her usefulness, Nealboy. She's a friggin' liability now and I don't want her hangin' 'round. Get rid of her before she turns, before she writes a f_____ book about me. Too controversial. Leaves a bad taste. I've got bigger fish to fry. Don't want the sight of her continually dredging up reminders." Brice at last turned to face his old roomy, putting his official stamp on the directive.

"Settled then. How'd you envision her ouster? She's still visible." Neal knew Brice always worked out his schemes before he summoned.

Brice set his empty glass on the marble table with a decisive clink. Neal looked toward the bar, waving his hand with a brief flick of his wrist. A hollow gesture since Santos already headed their way with Brice's refill in one hand and a tray of fruit, cheese, and canapés in the other. These he placed on the table with quiet efficiency.

Brice reached for his glass without taking his eyes off Neal. "Tell her she's gotta go. Tell her the Party loves her in spite of how things played out. Tell her the Party still has great things in store for her. Bygones be bygones. Hell, hint at a VP or some other big slot. Just waiting for the right time." Brice laughed.

Neal's drink caught in his throat. "You'd actually consider her? Think she'll go for it?"

"Like you said, Nealboy...." Brice's tilted his head back, rolling his eyes in feigned intolerance. For a moment they were old friends again. He enjoyed toying with Neal. For all their shared muck, Neal remained a lamb shouldered in by a field of wolves.

"Why'd the Party want her in the first place?" Neal reached for a smoked-mullet canapé.

"No. Why'd I want her, Nealboy? Why'd I want her?"

"Okay, Brice. Why'd *you* want her?"

"Hah! See, still got some things you can learn from me."

Neal chuckled before draining his Dewar's. Santos instantly replaced it with a tumbler of Perrier garnished with Key lime. Neal smiled his thanks. He turned back to Brice.

"Think, boy. Remember one of the primary axioms for successful business? Hire the best and brightest. Even if you don't have a spot, create one. Hire the best of the best."

"Huh. Don't remind me…. We're talking Patsy, right?" Ice pinged against portly crystal.

"Right. Now think the opposite. Corporate America we're not. We're talking politics, baby. Those rules are o-u-t. In politics you need skillful strategists, brilliant behind the scenes guys to get you there and keep you there, like you, Nealboy. Movers and shakers, Nealboy. Movers and shakers. But that's it. We're not grooming successors here. Don't want anybody close enough to knock us off our ladder."

Neal's eyes narrowed perceptibly.

"Here I thought I'd taught you everything there was to know about winning and losing and playing. Weren't you ever curious?"

"Hell yes, Brice. It's just that I chalked it up to political favors, rich coffers, with a fair share of hoodwinking and blind luck."

"No such thing as luck, Nealboy. I learned that early on. In politics you wanna surround yourself with enough incompetence and enough yahoos to bend the rules, leaves us out as the heavies. Get somebody high on ambition and low on competence and when the time comes they'll serve your own ambitions without being the wiser. Devious little strategy, uh?"

"I'll say."

"Hah! Take Patsy. She wasn't even a spit in the Gulf. Tough to work with, no savvy, not terribly bright on issues of import, no background in state law. But she had ambition. Stampeded up and over the backs of her colleagues. Way too ambitious for her own good."

"You knew that about her. So why'd you want a case like that in your administration?"

"Here's why, boy," Brice sniggered softly. "Tell those people what they wanna believe. Paint 'em a pretty picture of a rainbow complete with the pot of shiny gold at the end and they'll leap for it every time. Coddle 'em, praise 'em, use 'em, then sweep 'em out with last night's confetti." Brice grabbed the fresh Cognac from Santos' waiting hand.

"Your fingerprints were stamped all over the last few elections, especially the ones that wound up in the courts. But I didn't ask. And you didn't confide. I figured you had it taken care of and it was just safer all around if I didn't know, in case the pandemonium evolved into a more…dappled legal juncture. For certain, I wouldn't have to lie about something of which I had no knowledge."

"Precisely. You were there if I needed you. But I didn't need you, did I."

"No. And I don't even know how or what you pulled off."

"That's the genius, the purity of it all. I didn't. At least not the first one. Opportunity knocked is all. Pure magic. Magic and synergy. Like a fine game of chess. All players on board, I simply directed some devious strategic moves."

Neal nodded knowingly. If anything, Brice was shrewd.

"Florida law's ambiguous on so many key points. We could basically pick and choose each step of the way."

"And you, you're a walkin' civics book, Brice."

"Evidently the only one. Ironic. No one. NO ONE stopped to consider that voting machines did fail. And by law…."

Neal listened to Cady's explanations repeated through Brice's own admissions. Same theme, different words. Cady's election seemed so long ago.

"Ludicrous. I jus' lay low." Brice slurred his words now. "Stayed in the background, lettin' my pawns make their moves. Take Cruella. Forced her hand. Encouraged her to act presidential, stand for the good of the State, for the good of the Country, for the good of the Party. Let her suck up the heat and held my breath. Above the fray, that's me……Well, I may've inadvertently provided some direction for her interpretin' Florida law, through some well-placed legals, that is. Strongly advised the lawyers, albeit behind the scenes. Hell, no one in the damned state knew Florida election law. And you'd think no one knew how to read."

Classic Brice, Neal thought.

"Never for a moment did I believe we wouldn't...she wouldn't get called on that one. But no one caught on. No one said a peep."

"But, why was there no controversy over the machine aspect? Surely some Election Supervisors...the good ones pour over the books. They merrily tick off points of Florida law for a multitude of incidents less consequential. Hell they'll tell you there's to be a recount even before the candidates call it."

"No one wanted to be first to stick his neck under the blade. Easier to oops...misinterpret the law, avoid the turmoil. Ironic there was no friggin' ambiguity on that point. By law we must rerun the whole friggin' election. But by the time it worked its way to the Supreme Court – and we knew if we could push it up that far, we'd win. Safer for the Court to err on the side of status quo, get it over with, don't keep the country waiting."

"True. The delays, the ridicule…. What if the Court overturned it? The country, the world would have lost confidence."

"And to think, it was all made possible by one inept ambition junky with a lust for attention and power." Brice searched his breast pocket for another Cuban. Santos appeared box in hand. His gold lighter flashed at the ready. Brice sucked his Cuban to an avalanche of smoke churning, roiling. "Devious," he grinned. "Devious, but not illegal."

Neal watched his old roomy. Brice's soft baby face belied the harshness within. He could be callous, cruel...ruthless.

***

Can't scalp 'em, boy. Can only shave 'em off the top… Gotta get the pollsters right." Brice paused, sipped his Cognac. His eyes narrowed.

Neal felt Brice's trust waiver, felt him wondering, questioning, uncertain Neal's loyalties hadn't slipped along the way. They had. The old Brice would have come out with it, some cynical remark drawing the two into a cleansing row. But the chasm between them gaped too wide. And Neal's gut churned with it. For as certain as Izzy disappeared election night, as sure as Brice's sights took aim on Cady, he Neal could be coffined off. But more easily, more resolutely, and certainly more permanently. One more floater in the Gulf of Mexico, more likely still, the Gulf Stream.

For so long Neal skillfully donned his stoic persona as armor against a legion of Brice's enemies. But he never perfected it against Brice. Brice was shrewd in reading his mood, sometimes his thoughts. Can he read me now? My betrayal? No. Not betrayal, loyalty to the higher cause. Neal felt his persona withering.

He stood up, walked over to the window. His back to Brice, he studied the Gulf. He breathed in the calm outside his window, the afterglow of the sun falling over the horizon splashing orange and yellow ripples across darkening waters. *Yes, I could be out there tomorrow, bobbing face down, shark bait.*

Neal laughed aloud, walking back to Brice. He reached for another canapé. He looked toward the bar, but Santos already walked his way, drink in hand. It wasn't Perrier. "Brice, you old fox," Neal laughed again, swirling his drink.

"You surprised? I just broadened my skill base is all. You know you can always buy a crowd. Done it...plenty. Buy a protest or a whacko banging down doors. You think I didn't pull a lot a strings to set things up for my next run? Not my game board anymore. Not this time. But I can still nudge the players around, uh? Cruise control...never trust it, Nealboy. You give them too much credit. Mayhap I give you too much credit."

"You do, Brice, because I've no idea what you're talking about."

"You don't think my last win fell on the good graces of the voters, do you. Hah. I'll tell you. Just need to ratchet it up a few notches from here...."

"No, Brice, no. Don't tell me anymore. You'll have to kill me." Neal laughed, reaching his tumbler over to clink Brice's. Brice laughed too.

"Might at that, Nealboy. That or send you off to a monastery. Too many skirts for ya here. Don't know how to pace yourself, boy."

Cady hung between them like barbed wire. As soon as Brice could prove it he would move in for retribution, but he wouldn't ask outright, not now. And it was a problem for Brice, because he couldn't know for certain since he wouldn't let himself ask honestly.

"You might have something there, Brice," Neal laughed. "Either that or...you think I could...well, Brice, I've done so poorly...how about I take a stint as your understudy. Can you use an understudy, Brice?"

"Smoothie aren't ya? I can see right through ya, Nealboy."

"Oh?" Neal's face felt hot, his hands cold against his glass.

"Yeah. You want my drippin's after all and..." Brice looked up to see Santos and grimaced at the interruption. But he accepted the fresh Cognac without comment.

"Busted," Neal grimaced. "There you have it......So I figure out about Patsy. Anything else? I can't help but wonder why Patsy now?"

"Think presidential, Nealboy. Don't need that kind of baggage."

"Of course, but now? I thought you'd give it some air, you know wait until the climate turns more receptive," Neal baited him.

"Yeah, well it's gettin' more receptive all the time, isn't it? Take this election. Close wasn't it? But I worked it out. I learned from before alright. Risky to push too hard for the win if it's not close. Before when the pollsters predicted the Democrat win for president and we took it anyway, the techsters and the pencil heads...too many picksters cried foul...bad publicity...learned from that...could ruin everything. Keep it real, boy, keep it real."

"How do you do that, Brice?"

"Margin of error. Gotta stick in the margins...gotta get control of a pollster group...before my presidential...too much ridin' on it to let all the opinion polls predict a win for them... more to my point, a loss for me."

Neal waited while Brice swigged his cognac.

"Look at this election. We coulda blocked the enemy sweep. But the exit polls...margin's too wide. They all stood against us. We control the exit polls, we control the spin. My plan works...win-win. Hah! Control-spin, win-win, I'm in! Get it?"

"Brice...I..."

"Pushed 'em over the top. Now think big, real big. Yeah. And you don't think it worked. But it did! Don't just think the really big wins either. Takes a lot of small fish to serve up a fish fry. Played it safe, conservative this time. Think really big sweep. Wonder why not? Look at the close races. Could be they're mine…maybe all of them, almost. Gotta get more machines in place, marketing Nealboy, marketing. Deploy more machines across the country."

"Another diabolical little plan, Brice?"

"You bet. Wait 'til you see what goes on with the U.S. Attorneys. All of 'em not loyal? Enough…outta here. Whaddya think about the pollsters? Gotta hurry up and get me a pollster. Next election…well you're lookin' at the president of these here fine United States. You look into that for me, Neal. Find a national polling group we can take over."

"Sure, Brice. I'll look into it."

"By the way, go ahead and set up another Delaware corporation, nothing serious, just a small company. You can follow the same basic structure as the others, but do what you have to with the wording. I'm gonna dabble in the manufacture and programming of voting machines."

"Sure. At the end of the day you'll hold all the pieces on the game board, won't you, Brice?" Neal's congratulatory laugh masked the pain knifing through his gut…he hoped.

"And by the way, I want you to meet someone, a young man who works for ElecTron, Incorporated. Yeah, ElecTron, I'm toying with the idea of purchasing the company and this boy's got a few intriguing…insights."

70

The steady hum of the generator in the pitch black of early morning outside Neal's cottage alluded to the chatty hubbub within. Inside bright lights exposed the ordered disarray of progress. Voting machines and notebook computers and printers commandeered the great room. Stacks of papers, some organized, others discarded, cluttered the floor, and wads of paper overflowed the wastebasket, piling high in one corner. A more orderly assortment of papers lined up atop the kitchen counter along with several white view binders and a hole puncher. Paper dots littered the floor.

In the far corner of the great room, Leonard whimpered wanly from his makeshift powder room prison, cut off from the light and the election clutter.

Neal looked from Cady to Izzy. "And he's been here four days? Lashed to the damned latrine?"

"We didn't know what else to do. Look at him. You think Izzy and I wanted to parade that monster back and forth to the potty? This way he's secure. We're safe. And we knew you'd come for us."

"Cady...I never should have left you. If I even suspected.... But I should have, Cady. I should have known." Neal glanced at Leonard doubled over on his throne.

"None of us expected this, Neal. Besides, that's not what's important now. Tell us about your meeting with Brice...and what happened with your senators."

Neal put his arms around the women and led them away from Leonard's cell. "The Brice thing sickened me, Cady. I mean, I shouldn't be surprised, but I don't know who he is anymore."

"Neal, I...we caught his press conference. He sounded mulish, especially when he pushed for oil rigs offshore. But isn't that normal for him?"

"Normal? He can't see, think, feel anything beyond the presidency...his presidency." Neal felt the pang of icy claws reach in and rip at his insides. "Whatever it takes, Cady. But right now the climate's too negative for him. So instead of running, he's out there working his devious little schemes to shuffle a few more players into office. That's what this election was about, improving his odds. You saw who he got elected. And no doubt his courtship with big oil is one more aspect of cementing his coalition. Next election he steps up, plugs in Leonard's voting machines across the country, and he wins."

Neal picked up a wad of paper and tossed it onto the pile in the corner. It bounced back to the floor again. "Hard proof or no, we've got to end this thing...for all of us. Get you back to the mainland. You're ready. I'm ready. You're prisoners out here too, not certain when or who intends to do you harm. Leonard found you here. I don't want to consider what it means that he found you here."

"But you know what it means, Neal. Don't you? Someone who knows about you and your island dangled the bait for Leonard. Or...someone's following us."

"Or both. Someone close to me, Cady. And if he didn't send Leonard here, he at least knew Leonard would come once he was prodded and told where to find you. For certain, it's no longer safe."

"You believe it's Brice, don't you?" Cady sought his eyes and knew the sorrow she found there.

Neal nodded. "Or anyone of Brice's lackeys that Leonard pushed into office. I mean look at this election. It could be any number of people with vested interests in winning elections and what's more keeping them won. That means shutting you up, both of you...and me."

"You...you...think...there's...some...someone else?" Izzy looked around the room, her eyes pausing on every window, every lock.

"I do, Izzy. But when we get the facts out there, make it known that your voting machines skewed the election and we publish the details of how they did it…."

"I see. Their secret's out. Is that it, Neal? No point to coming after us then. Is that right?" The relief in Izzy's voice was palpable.

"Oh, Izzy…" Cady rubbed her arm gently. "Neal, don't you see? We're still in their way because we hold the truth. We've got the machines and we know how they rigged the election."

"But my senators…."

"What about them? Without us, it's status quo. Maybe you've got more of the right people willing to go to the mat. But it's still a perpetual stalemate with the party in power holding on to the win. I mean look at the last few elections. Everyone knew they were bad. But without the laws to right them, and the courts to enforce the laws, and politicals willing to sacrifice their victories for truth, we just swirl around in the same failed cycle, election after bad election."

"You mean no matter what, they'll still come after us? Cady and me?" Izzy whisked her hair back, glorious tresses that were no longer there.

"I'm sorry, Izzy. Forget what I said. Maybe with Neal's senators it really will be different this time. Maybe it depends on how much clout the senators have and how vocal they are and how much they can do."

"You're right about that, Cady, and that's why I went to see them. To find out how much they can do, are willing to do without more solid evidence and be taken seriously."

"You don't think it's enough that we can demonstrate how to alter any election on every single model of ElecTron's voting machines? We know exactly what ballots to enter and how many are needed to start siphoning off votes."

"It's enough for me, Cady. But, your demonstration shows how to flip votes, it doesn't prove intent. It's not as convincing as pointing to actual premeditated black and white instructions in the hardcopy computer program code and saying, 'Here it is. This did it.' Besides, the whole thing is so convoluted, not to mention time consuming. Unless people understand computers and elections in the first place, it's just more smoke and mirrors. One more whacky conspiracy theory. And that's if you can hold them still long enough to talk them through it."

"He's right, Cady. You know how people shut down just when things get interesting…uh, complicated. Especially anything to do with computers or elections. But, Neal," Izzy pointed to the binders lined up along his kitchen counter. "I don't know what you two are spatting about. Cady's got your proof. She polished it off yesterday at sunrise, after all this." Izzy swept her hand around the room toward Leonard and then back over the fat white binders again.

"Cady…? Why didn't you tell me?"

"No phone. No email. No Neal." Cady shrugged.

"We wrapped it up by lantern light. We took turns…you know…on watch." Izzy casually inspected her jagged fingernails.

"Yes. Vote Theft for Dummies…especially for you, Neal." Cady's smile was impish, but brief and did little to mask the concern in her eyes. "Nothing left to speculation or confusion or…rejection."

"I get the dummies part, Cady. But you found it? His code?"

"Cady broke the encryption, Neal."

"Yes. And we found where Leonard sandwiched his vote-rigging gimmicks into ElecTron's standard programs. He was clever enough to blend it in with their regular code."

"Clever or not, why didn't ElecTron catch it? How'd he finagle his souped up programs through their quality control?"

"Incompetence!" Izzy's eyes arced to the ceiling.

"There is some of that. I suspect they didn't test with enough votes or the right ballot mix to trigger his vote-snatching switches. Most likely they didn't consider dates when testing either…never changed the computer's internal system date to match the real election date."

"I remember. The first Tuesday in November, any year. That's when his program kicks in, right?" Neal looked from Cady to Izzy.

"I'm impressed, Neal," Izzy smiled up at him. "But do you understand that if it's any other day of the year, say April 1, then all the votes tally up. It's a perfect election."

"Uh-uh…" Neal nodded vaguely.

"Wait, Neal, do you also understand the implications? Say you suspect something's wrong election day. So you redo a stack of ballots the next day. Only this time all the votes tally up the way they should. Well, then, blame it on the voters. After all they must have botched it election day. It's clear because everything works just fine for you."

"That's what 'they've' been saying right along, isn't it?"

"Yes. It's the voters' fault. And something else. Leonard was smart enough to scramble the results, which made it harder to detect."

"Uh?"

"Well, his scheme siphoned votes away from blue, then scattered those votes here and there among other candidate and rejected ballots and undervotes. He knew his pilfered votes couldn't all be dumped into red. Too obvious, we'd catch on."

"So he put some thought into this. He wasn't just looking for a hacker's high, he was in for the long haul. What else did you find?"

"I think that about covers it, doesn't it, Izzy?"

"The big stuff, anyway."

"Good…We're back to human-speak then?"

Cady and Izzy exchanged smiles. Then Izzy flashed her eyes at Neal, her smile enchanting. The old Izzy was back and they knew it. They all laughed as the wire-tight tension in the room slackened.

"Neal, when will you tell Brice you're going to Washington?"

Neal's smile waned. "I won't, Cady. You're flying solo." Neal looked from Izzy to Cady. "I've got to stay arms length, at least for a while."

"Right. You buckle me into the hot seat and what do you do, sail off to Tahiti?"

"Cady, you know I'll do whatever I can…from a distance." He put his arm around her.

"Sure," she pulled away.

"Cady…please…I…Cady, if not you, who? Who will do it?"

"Right," she said more caustically than intended, then nudged back under his arm. "Later," she smiled up at him.

"Come on…enough already." Izzy's heart-pursed lips couldn't hold back her smile. "What's going on anyway?"

"Cady's off to Washington. She's meeting up with the senators to show them what happened with your election."

"Ooooo, Cady. I can help. And Mario. And…."

"Thanks, Izzy. I need you. I do…. Neal, what will they do with Brice and Stan and…?" Cady nodded at their kingmaker, bound and pantless on his throne.

"Clearly, he's going to prison. But for kidnapping, assault, rape, attempted murder. Nothing to do with his part in the election."

"Why not?" Izzy asked.

"Too big. Think of the ramifications. Where would it end? First, half the country won't believe it. And if they do, then what? Imagine the chaos. Announcing the president isn't the president. The governor isn't the governor. When did they pick the locks to your system? How many elections did he tweak across the country? It has worldwide implications. The senators are convinced it would be more harmful to the country to shake people's faith in our democracy than to maintain the status quo."

"That means Brice and Stan…"

"Walk. Stan will be forced out of course and Brice…Brice remains rich and successful…and free. Just out of politics when this is over."

"But why?"

"Same reasons, plus reasonable doubt, Cady. Indisputable proof of his involvement with Leonard or your election. Brice is crafty. There will be no trail. He gets other people to do his dirty work. You'll never find his fingerprints anywhere near this. Even if Leonard squawks, he'll be taken for the raving lunatic he is. But, if things work out according to the senators' plan, Brice is done in Washington."

"And the president?"

"Ironically, the president is probably oblivious to any of this. Even if he's guilty as hell, what do you do, ask him to step down? And if he doesn't? Who enforces it? What then? The senators believe his term will be wasted without any momentous accomplishments, left or right."

"When does she go?" Izzy asked.

"Tomorrow." Neal looked at Cady, his eyes half pleading, half trusting her consent.

"And you?"

Neal shook his head and looked away, but not before Cady read the pain in his eyes and noticed the firm set to his jaw. He reached over the row of Cady's secret binders and flipped on the kitchen radio. Soon the definitive chords of Antonín Dvořák's *American Suite* dusted the foul air with normalcy as invisible fingers danced across their magical instruments.

At last Neal's eyes sought hers. He smiled. But his smile was hard and straight and his eyes were dark and stormy. "Cady, I want you to get online now. Email these documents." He pointed to the binders before scribbling an address on a crumpled piece of paper he retrieved from the floor. "Here. Send a copy to Mario too, and the three of us. Can you do that, Cady? Now?" Neal tousled her hair gently and left her to her computer and the cyber lights flickering across her face.

He walked to the front of the cottage, opening the windows to first faint fringes of sunrise peaking over the horizon. He stood at the window for a moment, breathing in the salty air and listening to the muted sounds of island dawn. Soon the island would waken. Already slivers of sorbet tipped wavelets sparkled in the dark channel, pointing the way to the Gulf Stream.

When at last he turned back to Cady, pain etched his face. He took his paper from her, lit a match to it and watched it burn in the kitchen sink. Then he washed the ashes down the drain.

"Cady, with Brice it's all about power. It's never been the politics, not really. I know that now. Politics is only the means, power's his endgame. Control the win, you win the power."

"If he's on to me, Neal, doesn't it stand to reason you're a close second?"

"Brice already suspects me, Cady. I feel it. But of what misdeeds? Consorting with you? Protecting you? Helping you even? You see, I don't believe he grasps how much we know…of the election…of his culpability. For certain he's prepared to lay it all at Stan's feet. And he's cocky enough to believe I'll follow him like always. Cady, he still looks to me for certain things and he's asked me to do a couple jobs. I need to follow through...want to. It starts with him. But where does it end? ...Sure, I have suspicions. But if I can hang on a while longer maybe I'll find out for certain."

"I...I...understand, Neal. We've got to stop him."

"And you, Cady? You'll go? ...Cady?"

Pop......Pop...Pop...Ratta-tat-tat-tat...pop...pop.

"What's that...?" Cady asked before bullets from an unseen Uzi ripped through the cottage, and the great room swirled in a flurry of papers and splintered wood. Glass shards clinked across the blood spattered floor.

"GOOD MORNING. THIS IS NPR NEWS......ALL EYES ARE ON FLORIDA THIS MORNING ...... MIAMI-DADE COUNTY ELECTIONS SUPERVISOR **STAN CORBIN**...BODY RECOVERED FROM CARD SOUND YESTERDAY...IN WATER SEVERAL DAYS...NO EVIDENCE OF FOUL PLAY...DUBIOUS SUCCESS WITH VOTING MACHINES ...... **GOVERNOR BUD DANIELS** EXPRESSES SORROW AT FLORIDA'S TRAGIC LOSS... 'SUPERVISOR CORBIN WAS A LOYAL AND RESPECTED OFFICER OF ELECTIONS......TURNED DADE COUNTY AROUND' ...MORE ON OUR WEBSITE ....

"**ONE MOMENT PLEASE** .... JUST IN FROM OUR NEWSDESK IN WASHINGTON...... **SIMULTANEOUS EXPLOSIONS** ...... INBOUND CARGO SHIPS DISABLE THREE FLORIDA PORTS....... PORT OF MIAMI, PORT EVERGLADES, PORT OF TAMPA...... NOW WORD YET ON CASUALTIES......"

Pop pop. Ratta-tat-tat-ratta-tat-tat. Pop......pop...pop.

"Cady...Izzy..."

Ratta-tat-ratta-tat...

"NEAL!"

"GOOD MORNING. FROM NPR NEWS IN..." Ratta-tat-tat-ratta-tat-tat. Pop. Pop.

The island hushed to the palms quivering noiselessly in the tangy sea air. The silence broken only once by a mocking seagull cawing its hysterical laughing, haw-haw-haw-haw-haw. The island stilled once more.

Made in the USA